Play ho

MW01059082

EDEN'S VOICE

Sass and Steam
Book 1

CATHERINE STEIN

To all girls and women who love sports:
play hard and let your fan colors fly.

And to all loyal Wolverines: Go Blue!

· · · ✿ · · ·

Special thank you to my friends Linda Hill and Dorte Birch
for their invaluable help with the details of Eden's hearing
loss and character quirks. You really helped bring her to life.

PROLOGUE

St. Louis, Missouri
August 30, 1904

BRUCE MISSED THE DRAGON by about three inches. His tires skidded and the bicycle toppled, sending him sprawling across the dust-covered road. An hour in and already the Olympic marathon had turned into a disaster. He swore, righted himself, and adjusted the cloth that covered his mouth and nose. One of the athletes had inhaled so much dust he'd needed medical attention. Bruce wasn't about to let the same thing happen to him.

A yelp of fright made him whirl around. The dragon, which resembled a large dog with unnecessarily long teeth and a rat-like tail, had homed in on one of the runners. The unfortunate man cried out and scampered away from the mechanical beast, veering wildly off course. Bruce scanned the area for anyone who might be the owner of the dragon—not that he expected anyone to admit to it, even if they were nearby. Nothing. The runaway creature would go until it ran out of fuel or someone was brave enough to get near it and find the off switch.

"Damn," he muttered. He'd been rooting for the South African runner. What better than a shocking article about how US athletes had lost on home soil? At least now he could write about strange dragon mishaps.

A delivery truck flew by, honking incessantly and kicking up yet more dust. Bruce wiped his goggles clear. They were, he concluded, one of the wisest purchases of his life. He jotted notes and hopped back on the bicycle.

Conditions worsened as the marathon dragged on. The dust grew thicker and the heat was oppressive. Bruce could find no water stations along the route. Several runners dropped out, suffering cramps. An affable Cuban running in street clothes ate a bad apple and lay down for a nap to sleep off the effects. Bruce jotted more notes.

By the halfway point, his right knee was throbbing, despite its brass and iron supports. He would never claim as much suffering as the runners, but every time a vehicle rattled by with coaches, trainers, or even other members of the press aboard, he felt a surge of indignation.

Dodging belching steam cars and carriages pulled by equine dragons with ridiculous false wings, he pedaled up and down hills, keeping track of the top runners. With miles left to go yet, he'd begun to fear no one might finish the race. The leader, one Mr. Hicks, was in such poor shape that trainers had left their cars to assist him. Bruce jumped from his bike and jogged alongside. A burst of pain shot through his knee, but he ignored it.

"Are you giving him water? There isn't enough water along this course." The lack of concern for the health of the athletes was appalling, and Bruce was going to make certain everyone knew it.

"No, no," the trainer answered. "A good stimulant. Keep his legs going. Strychnine and egg whites."

"What?" Bruce gasped. "Strychnine is poisonous!"

"Only in large quantities. Joe, is he ready for another dose?"

"Not sure. Should we try the brandy?"

"Good God." Bruce scribbled furiously. If Hicks collapsed, he was riding ahead and fetching a doctor, journalistic integrity be damned.

A carriage barreled toward them, men leaning out the windows to shout.

"A winner! We have a winner! Lorz has done it!"

What? Impossible. Bruce sank to the ground, cursing. How had this happened? He'd sworn he'd seen no one pass Hicks. Lorz must have slipped past while Bruce was checking on another contestant. That damned dragon incident, probably.

He'd missed it. No water. No story. Today crept ever closer to the title of worst day of his life. At least now he could fetch a doctor and not worry that he was interfering with the race.

He'd gone no more than half a mile when another news-flash came along, courtesy of a steam-belching motorcar. The so-called winner had admitted to dropping out and hitching a ride to the finish line. Bruce cursed more and stopped to make additional notes. He would need to do interviews with people who had been at the finish line, but the article could proceed.

Some three and a half hours after this fiasco had begun, Hicks crossed the finish line, pulled along by his trainers. The crowd cheered the real victor, but he had fallen too ill to celebrate. He looked half dead. A team of doctors rushed to assist.

Bruce stood on wobbly legs, asking questions of anyone who walked by and waiting for the remaining racers to finish. He limped toward a race official, wincing.

"Could I get some water? Are the athletes being given water?"

"What's that? Water? I suppose there must be some about somewhere."

"Why wasn't there more to drink along the racecourse?"

Bruce demanded. His voice was hoarse, his throat parched. He didn't sound as authoritative as he'd intended.

"Ah! Scientific research, my boy! It's all the rage, you know. We are studying prolonged and intentional dehydration."

Prolonged. Intentional. His head swam. He couldn't tell how much was from exhaustion and overheating, and how much from the rush of anger.

"Would you like to make a statement for our notes?" the official inquired. "You are the only cyclist I've seen today. I understand you traveled back and forth keeping an eye on all the racers? You must have gone quite fifty miles. Is there anything you'd like to say?"

"Yeah. Go to hell."

Bruce whirled away before he could punch the man, and staggered off, leaning on his bicycle to stay upright. Three steps later, his knee buckled. He collapsed, the audible snap of breaking metal ringing in his ears.

No. Not again.

The pain hardly registered through his despair. Repairs to his biomechanics would cost hundreds. All his savings, gone. His hopes, crushed.

He was trapped in this dead-end job. Underpaid, underappreciated, and never knowing where the hell they would send him next.

1

Ann Arbor, Michigan
October 1, 1904

A two-month assignment in a Midwest hick town. What grave sin had Bruce committed to deserve this? He paced the sideline, notebook in hand, writing nothing.

Promotion. Focus on the promotion.

His boss had loved his coverage of the World's Fair and the Olympic Games. Fulton had tossed about words like "gritty" and "authentic" and raved about how people wanted the scoop from the inside. He'd implied that something better might be coming if Bruce could do the same on this assignment.

Such implications had been made before, with nothing coming of them. Bruce figured he was being played for a fool. It wasn't as if everyone at the paper didn't know his ambitions: higher pay, a say in which stories to pursue, perhaps an editorial position someday. A pipe dream. And yet he'd taken the bait. Again.

Was it optimism, or simply desperation? He was fed up

with taking orders and going wherever others wanted him to go. He was tired of low pay, no perks, and long, unpleasant assignments. This would be the last. If Fulton didn't make good on his promises, he'd go somewhere else. He'd find a way to be his own boss.

Right.

Idiot.

And it had to be football. Bruce had spent years trying not to pay attention to football, pretending he didn't care. Futile years. As a sports reporter, the topic was unavoidable. Worst was fielding the questions from friends and family every season: *Who will be our toughest match? How is Harvard v. Yale shaping up this year? What's all this talk about someone called Yost and a point-a-minute machine at Michigan? Where the hell is Michigan, anyway? Is that one of the ones in the middle? No, it's the one with all the lakes that looks like a mitten. They're making motorcars there now, I hear.*

Bruce had yet to see a motorcar in Michigan. Not that he'd been here long. He'd taken the train up from Toledo direct to Ann Arbor yesterday. Transportation in the little five-square-mile town looked to consist primarily of horse-drawn carriages and bicycles. He hadn't even seen any of the dragon-pulled vehicles that were a mark of status out East. A nice trolley ringed downtown, however, and train transport in and out of town was plentiful. They had to get people here to watch football, after all.

Bruce had to admit a certain curiosity about the long-undefeated Wolverines. The athlete inside him hadn't fully died with his sporting career, and Coach Yost sounded like a true innovator. Writing about the games might actually be fun, if he stopped dwelling on the past and let himself enjoy it.

A large crowd had turned out today, waving "M" banners and in good cheer, expecting their team to crush the poor men from Case Academy. Bruce didn't doubt they would get their wish. Michigan had a band to entertain the masses, and students with megaphones to lead the cheers. The atmosphere struck him as typical for a football crowd. None of it would have been out of the ordinary for a game back home.

A single oddity drew his attention. Directly across the field, a girl paced the sidelines, several steps behind what looked to be a mechanical wolverine. She appeared perfectly at ease, though everyone else nearby shied away from the dragon-mascot. Intrigued, Bruce set off to investigate.

Upon closer inspection, he discovered the dragon's keeper wasn't a girl, but a fully-grown woman. She was tiny, only reaching to his shoulder, and she wore her hair pulled back into two tails with bits of ribbon, but there was nothing girlish in her face or figure. She wore a short-sleeved white blouse beneath a blue and gold brocade corset-top with a high, stiff collar and long tails that hung to her knees like a half-skirt. Tight, black trousers and sturdy boots completed the unconventional ensemble. Bruce had seen women dressed in similar style back home in Boston—artists, inventors, and other creative types, for the most part. It wasn't what he expected from a young lady in Michigan. Certainly no one else he had seen in town dressed as she did.

Her jewelry was similarly unique. A gold cuff wrapped around and over her left ear, with a penny-sized blue crystal fitted into the center of her ear. The bottom of the piece connected to a dangle earring, also in gold, with smaller blue crystals. A matching dangle adorned her otherwise plain right ear.

The wolverine snarled, and Bruce sprang back, startled. The metal beast gnashed long, shiny teeth. Glowing eyes fixated on him. Unlike most untethered automata, it had no discernible dials or switches along its back for controlling it. With no clear indication of how to stop it, he didn't wonder people kept their distance. He tensed up, prepared to run if the creature sprang at him.

"Don't worry, he hasn't bitten anyone yet," the woman

informed him. Her voice had something of the Midwest accent common to others here, but her pronunciation was unusually precise, her words crisp. The dragon snarled again. "But he does strike fear into the hearts of our enemies."

Bruce laughed, his stance relaxing. "I was under the impression the team doesn't need help doing that."

The woman stared boldly at his face. "We don't," she answered, with noticeable pride.

Bruce gestured at the wolverine. "How do you control him?"

"He responds to vocal commands. I rarely use them, though, because all he does is walk, snap, and snarl. This is his second year. The officials don't like him, I think, but as long as I keep the correct distance from the field of play, they can't stop me."

Bruce jotted a note. "May I quote you?"

Her blue eyes, still fixed on him, lit up. "Certainly! You're a reporter?"

"Yes, with the Boston Herald." He tucked the notebook into his pocket and offered his hand. "Bruce Caldwell. A pleasure to meet you."

She frowned as she shook his hand. The expression made a little crinkle between her dark blond eyebrows. "Caldwell. That sounds familiar. Boston, you said? Oh! Are you the A. B. Caldwell who wrote about the Olympic Games?"

"I am."

"I read all your articles!" she exclaimed. "Were there truly female archers? Did you watch them compete? Was the marathon as awful as you made it sound, with no water and dust and dragons and poison?"

"Er…" Bruce was uncertain which question to answer first. He'd never had a fan. This was the last place he would have thought to find one. "Yes, to everything," he answered at last. "Whatever you read in those articles was one-hundred percent truthful."

"It must have been so exciting. I wish I could have been there."

Another dragon, a small, winged creature, landed on the woman's shoulder. A bit smaller than a football, but with a similar oblong shape, the dragon had four legs, a chain-like tail, and long, thin antennae. Like the wolverine, it was unadorned brass, save for the blue crystals of its eyes that matched the jewel in the woman's ear. The dragon's wings folded in against its body as it settled in place. The woman wasn't perturbed in the slightest, and carried on as if nothing had happened.

"You're here to write about football?" She still hadn't stopped staring at him. He didn't think she was flirting, but it was difficult to be certain. He was accustomed to Boston socialites who weren't so... inquisitive.

"Yes. I'm to follow the team for the entire season. People back East are wildly curious about the way things are done out here."

"We are to play Columbia on Thanksgiving."

"So I understand."

"That will settle it. You'll all have to own how good we are when we kick their... um, rears."

He chuckled. "I will write all about it. Could I get your name, Miss?"

"Oh, sorry. I forget that sort of thing. I'm Eden. Eden Randall." She thrust out her hand and he shook it once again.

"A pleasure, Miss Randall. Thank you for reading my articles. I like your style and your festive blue and gold colors."

"Maize and blue," she corrected.

"Right." He jotted that down. "Perhaps we could talk again sometime? I'll be in town the entire season."

She regarded him with suspicion for a moment, then asked, "Will you tell me more about the Olympic Games?"

"If you'd like."

A sparkle of excitement replaced the mistrust in her

eyes. "Okay. I'll be around." She snapped her fingers at the wolverine. "Turn."

The dragon obeyed her command and stalked off in the opposite direction, still baring its teeth and growling. Eden followed it, but then glanced over her shoulder and gave a little wave.

"Bye." The flying dragon fluttered down to walk beside her. "Until next time."

Bruce turned his attention to the field. The game was set to begin. He needed to get on with the work of investigating the football team. He had a promotion to earn, and—regrettably— no one was going to pay him to investigate Miss Eden Randall.

2

Eden entered the party at the president's house bubbling with a mix of excitement and apprehension. She had little experience of parties in her twenty-three years of life. She was, in fact, considered antisocial and peculiar by most who knew her. It was only to be expected. Her parents were introverted people, and quite unusual themselves. Their little family didn't often join bustling social gatherings.

Eden scanned the house and its occupants, taking in the decor, the outfits, and the refreshments. In her head, she reviewed all the data she had gathered from descriptions of parties in novels. She thought she knew how to behave, more or less. Her one concern was that most of those books had been written a half-century ago or more. And they usually mentioned dinners or balls. Pity this party would have speeches and awards rather than dancing.

Not that she knew any formal dances. She didn't even know the difference between a gavotte and a quadrille. Or whatever people danced these days. Still, she would've liked to try.

A man bearing a tray of champagne passed by, and Eden's eyes lit up. He disappeared into the throng before she could take a glass, but she determined to track him down. She wouldn't miss her chance to try a new drink.

She wormed her way through the crowd, trying not to bump anyone in her voluminous skirts. Her party dress was magical. The long-sleeved, fitted bodice was of supple brown leather, buckled at the waist, with an asymmetrical hem. Layers of black and gray skirts puffed out over a fluffy petticoat. They draped fully to the floor, so she could wear her favorite boots instead of silly little slippers and none would be the wiser. Perfection. A cross between a warrior's armor and a princess' ball gown.

Her mother, who wore a white blouse and slim, neutral-colored skirt every day, hadn't altered this habit for the party. She'd eyed Eden's dress with quiet suspicion, as she did all of Eden's clothes. Penelope Randall was a mechanical genius, but she had no understanding of fashion—at least, not of Eden's edgy, bohemian fashions.

Eden had to admit she didn't look at all like the other ladies. Gauzy and filmy were the fashion words of the night. Most ladies sported high necklines and lace trimmings, and their skirts had a much slimmer silhouette. Unsurprisingly, she was the only woman with her hair down. Two narrow braids ran from her temples to meet at the back, holding it out of her face. Like most of her hairstyles, it was considered childish. Eden did as she liked. Since she rarely expected anyone to do much more than politely nod to acknowledge her presence, she didn't see any point in catering to their whims.

The house tonight was packed with professors, their families, and important visitors. Everyone was talking at once. Eden twisted the earring that dangled from her left ear. This was the part of parties and other gatherings that made her anxious. The confusion of so many sounds one atop of the other unsettled her. She had a difficult time sorting out words in the din. It made her feel out of control.

She kept Vox tucked tightly under her arm. She could have let the dragon fly up to perch on a chandelier, or sit on a nearby table, but having hold of her eased Eden's nerves. Her oblong, metal body was comfortingly familiar. Eden stroked her on the head between her antennae and continued her search for the champagne.

She spied her father across the room, talking with the president of the university and a man she didn't recognize. Father was difficult to miss, to be honest, in his blue and black velvet coat, and a towering top hat decorated with gears that spun and clacked for no purpose other than that he found it funny. He looked splendid, in her opinion. Even strangers would know him for an automechanologist, and he stood out from the crowd, as a guest of honor ought.

Still, he was almost shabby compared to the unknown man at his side. Ever curious, Eden moved in for a better look.

The mysterious stranger was shorter than average, but devastatingly handsome, with dark, tousled hair and a neatly trimmed moustache and goatee. He was rich, that was certain. His tailcoat and trousers were cut and styled to fit him with a perfection Eden had only seen in fashion magazines. The red and black vest looked to be silk, and his buttons and watch fob gleamed. He turned his head in her direction, glanced her over, then turned away. His indifference didn't dampen her curiosity. She had inherited from her parents a deep desire to know everything, and she was accustomed to men underestimating her.

Before she could approach her father and demand an introduction to the attractive but haughty stranger, the official business of the party began. The man with the champagne came around again at last, and Eden snagged a glass just in time to toast the first guest of honor. While several English Department professors read excerpts from his award-winning writing, she lounged against the wall, enjoying the tingle of the bubbles against her nose and the dryness of the alcohol. By the time she had drained her glass, she felt relaxed enough to let Vox fly up to the rafters. She accepted another glass for the toast of her father, positioning herself for a good look at the speaker.

"This summer, our own Emerick Randall was named to the prestigious Brass Cog Inventors Society for his fine work in the field of Automechanology and Teletics," President Angell announced. "His research on the topic of voice-controlled automata received their highest award and has cemented our status as one of the top AM&T schools in all the country."

Eden joined in with the enthusiastic applause. She was proud his achievements had been recognized, though she wished someone would recognize her mother as well. Her father's ideas and plans were brilliant, but he was a hopeless mechanic. His prototypes fell apart if you breathed on them. Penelope Randall stood at her husband's side, beaming. She didn't seem to mind that her part in the inventions was glossed over. Eden took it upon herself to be offended on her mother's behalf. Newspapers liked sensation. Could she find one to print a letter entitled *In Praise of Women Mechanics*?

The memory of Mr. Bruce Caldwell the reporter flashed through her mind. Perhaps she could ask him about it. If he truly did wish to talk to her after all the babbling she'd done during the game that afternoon. She'd messed up the introduction, of course. But he'd been so interesting. Young. And handsome. She'd not expected that. Reading his articles, she'd always imagined A. B. Caldwell to be a scholar of sport, gray-haired and bespectacled. Not an athlete, himself.

"To demonstrate this wonderful new technology for all of you," Angell continued, "Professor Randall and his wife have brought a recently constructed dragon from their impressive collection."

Eden put her attention back where it belonged. This

dragon wasn't one of the most impressive specimens, in her opinion, but it was small and portable, and one of her mother's favorites. Shaped like a parrot, it had delicate brass wings and a colorful, enameled body. Her parents wowed the onlookers by instructing it to talk, fly, play dead, and various other tricks. Everyone looked suitably impressed, but Eden could only shake her head. The parrot was no more than a toy when compared to Vox.

She called for the dragon, who obediently fluttered down into her arms.

"I don't believe we have been introduced yet, Miss...?" a sultry voice murmured.

She spun around, looking for the speaker, certain she must have misheard. The smartly-dressed stranger stood behind her, an expectant look on his handsome face. Apparently he *had* been addressing her. Baffled as to why he had taken an interest, she thrust out her hand awkwardly and introduced herself, pleased she'd remembered not to simply blurt out a question.

"Randall. Eden Randall."

His brows twitched. A satisfied smile played across his mouth. "Eden, is it?" He took her hand, but rather than shaking it, he raised it to his lips. His eyes smoldered, and she found herself blushing for no good reason. "Like the Garden of Paradise."

"Indeed. I'm full of evil serpents and bad apples."

He seemed taken aback, but only momentarily. "I can't believe that of so lovely a woman as yourself."

Eden pulled her hand away, perhaps a bit more roughly than necessary. She didn't trust this man. People didn't compliment the strange girl unless they wanted something. "And you are?"

"Evan Tagget." He made a brief bow.

It was Eden's turn to look aghast. "Evan Tagget. As in Tagget Industries?"

"The very same."

"You recently acquired Dynalux," she informed him, which seemed a stupid thing to say after the fact.

"I did. I expect it to be most profitable. I'm always on the lookout for... interesting ventures." He looked her up and down. Was he implying that *she* was interesting? She tried not to feel flattered, but she was unaccustomed to such attentions. He probably knew that.

She met his gaze coolly. "Such as?"

"Your dragon, for instance."

Eden instinctively clutched Vox tighter, then realized she was making things worse. Letting him see the dragon was special would only arouse his curiosity.

"One of your father's creations?"

"Yes. She runs on luxene—the simple stuff, no fancy additives needed." It was a deliberate dig at Dynalux and their attempts to lure people into the purchase of a branded, more expensive product. Eden's mother said their fuel wasn't worth the price, and she would know.

Tagget only chuckled. "What does it do? Squawk like the parrot?"

"She flies. Vox, up." The dragon fluttered her metal wings and flew back to the ceiling, perching among the glowing bulbs of the electric chandelier. She was safe there, where no one could grab her. "She also bites anyone who isn't me."

It was the wrong thing to say. He looked, if anything, even more intrigued. "How does it recognize you?"

His persistence in calling her dragon "it" irked her. "I have no idea," she lied. "I'm not an automechanologist. I have somewhere else to be, now. Please excuse me, Mr. Tagget. It was *interesting* meeting you."

Eden turned and walked toward the nearest door. Vox flittered from one high perch to the next, following along. She always kept in range.

It was time to find some food. All parties had food, right?

Eden was certain she had read about people nibbling on little appetizers.

With luck, the remainder of this party would have more champagne and sweets and fewer suspicious millionaires. If not, she would claim overstimulation and walk home. She caught Vox out of the air and twisted at her earring again. She didn't need to hear what these people were saying, anyhow.

3

October 3

"Do I look different to you?" Eden asked her friend as they strolled across campus.

Lilah's dark eyebrows drew together. "Different than what?"

"Than usual."

Lilah looked her up and down. "Not that I can see. You're as scandalous as you always are when the sun's out."

Eden had to grin at that. Today her outfit consisted of a short, white dress, with a leather underbust corset and mid-calf brown boots. It left a good portion of bare leg exposed below the knee. These warm autumn days were precious and few, and she wasn't about to let other people's hatred of uncovered flesh prevent her from reveling in the fine weather.

"And odd, right?"

"Odd for Ann Arbor," Lilah agreed. "But not entirely odd. You read fashion magazines. You know your style isn't so far removed from that of many young ladies in the bigger cities."

"Maybe that's it."

"That's what?"

"I was complimented by two different gentlemen this weekend."

"So?"

Eden sighed. Of course Lilah wouldn't understand. With her flawless brown skin and sparkling dark eyes she could grace any stage in the world. Men seldom failed to notice her. Her trouble was that none of them could match her for wits.

"That never happens. But one of the men was from Boston and the other from New York, so perhaps I don't look peculiar to them. Also, according to the papers, personal dragons are all the rage out East, so Vox doesn't put them off. Although, really, she might be the only reason that Mr. Tagget actually spoke with me."

"Mr. Tagget the industrialist? The one who is recruiting here on campus?"

"Yes. I met him at my father's award party and he called me a 'garden of paradise' and kissed my hand. I think he was trying to fluster me into telling him secrets about Vox."

"You haven't even told *me* all her secrets. I can't imagine you telling a stranger, no matter how he tries to charm you."

"Yes, but Mr. Tagget doesn't know that."

"Well, you take care. He is notorious for getting what he wants." The two women paused on the library steps. "What of the other gentleman?"

"Oh, he was just a reporter."

Eden must have betrayed something with her tone of voice, because Lilah cocked her head and peered down at her in disbelief.

"Just a reporter."

"From Boston."

"And?"

Surely it was only the sun making her cheeks warm. "He's the man who wrote all those articles on the Olympic Games.

He complimented my gameday outfit, but in truth we hardly spoke. He wanted to mention the wolverine in his article."

"The Olympics writer? And you didn't bombard him with questions?"

"No. Well, maybe a little."

A lot. Darn her flushing cheeks. It was silly to like someone she didn't know simply for writing exciting stories about sports. "I may have agreed to talk with him again. If we happen to meet."

Which they would. He would be at every football game.

"Eden, you stalked the delivery man waiting for each new paper to arrive. You will meet this reporter again." Lilah waved a hand toward the door. "Are you coming into the library?"

"Not today. There's a mechanical engineering class I wanted to drop in on. I'm still honing my skills so I can do Vox's maintenance myself."

"You never stop learning, do you?"

"Of course not! I may not be a student any longer, but I'll never have time enough to study everything I want to learn. Which is why I intend to remain here forever."

"It's a good place for that, I suppose. Enjoy your class."

"Thank you. Will you come by for dinner tonight? I'm making a squash soup and a baby greens salad with walnuts and dried fruit."

"Sounds delicious. I'll be there."

Eden waved goodbye and left Lilah to her studies. She sat through the class, picked up a few useful tips, and spent the rest of the morning reading in the sun. This was a day best spent outdoors. With no urgent errands for the afternoon, she took a leisurely lunch before wandering down to the athletic grounds to watch the football team practice.

To her surprise, Bruce Caldwell stood beside the field, observing the proceedings and making notes. He was dressed in the same informal style as she had noticed at the game the other day, with no jacket and the cuffs of his shirtsleeves rolled up to expose most of his forearms. Bright red suspenders stood out against his black vest, and a newsboy cap sat slightly askew atop his unruly brown hair. His bowtie, also red, wasn't tight against his neck. It didn't even look as if his top button was done up underneath it. Eden could see more of his throat than most gentlemen revealed.

And why was she even looking at that? It wasn't as if she'd never seen a man's bare neck before. The athletes stripped down much more than that on warm days like this. It was only sensible. Still, there was something tantalizing about that little gap at the top of his shirt.

Eden strode towards him, rehearsing in her head what she would say when she reached his side. She wanted to know how he had talked his way into the practice. It wasn't like Coach to let an outsider snoop around. Too much chance for Stagg or another rival to steal secrets.

Bruce would write good and fair articles, Eden was certain of that. She regularly read more than half-a-dozen newspapers, and his Olympics coverage had been unrivaled.

He spied her approaching and paused in his writing to wave. She returned the gesture as she walked up to him.

"Miss Randall, how nice to see you again."

"Hello, Br.... Mr. Caldwell." She scolded herself for even considering calling him by his first name. They had only just met.

Formality didn't come naturally to her. She'd learned many rules of etiquette from her books, but applying them to real life wasn't as easy as one might hope. A result, she suspected, of rarely attending social events.

"I realized I didn't ask you before, what does the 'A' in 'A. B.' stand for?"

And... that was *not* how she had meant to begin this conversation.

He grimaced. "Archibald. I'm Archibald Bruce Caldwell

IV. Thankfully, I'm an even number. My father is an Archie. My grandfather and I are Bruce."

"Is your grandfather still living?" She had no memory of her own grandparents and had often wondered what it might be like to have another generation of family.

"Yes, but he's elderly and hard of hearing. He uses an ear trumpet and even so he can't always make out what I say."

"Ear trumpet," Eden snorted. "Worthless. It can only pick up sounds from a single direction and its amplification is weak. He needs a proper mechanical apparatus to collect all ambient sounds and transmit them directly into the ear canal. A biomechanical device would provide the greatest benefit, though depending on the type of hearing loss it could require not merely an amplifier but surgical implantation and an external sound gathering…" She trailed off, as Bruce had lost all interest in the practice and was staring at her, mouth agape.

"Please, continue," he said. "You sound quite knowledgeable on the subject."

"Uh, I only meant to add that our present technology can't undo all damage, as the ear is small and delicate."

"Very interesting. May I ask how you came by this knowledge?"

He had gotten nosy again. Was this a result of his job, or had he become a reporter because he couldn't help prying into other people's business?

"My father is a professor of automechanology and teletics. He studies this sort of thing. Mechanical recognition of sounds is important for voice control."

"Naturally. Is your dragon an example of his work?"

Eden glanced down at Vox, who sat obediently at her feet. "Her inner workings are his design. My mother shaped and built her, and invented the working wings. Most dragons can't fly, you know. Most of those that can have enormous wings relative to their bodies or else they just flap about and glide a bit."

"Do you always carry her with you?"

So many questions.

"Yes."

She could tell he was unsatisfied with her answer by the way he raised his eyebrows. He had deep, brown eyes that lent him an air of innocence when he widened them. She suspected he got answers to many questions by looking at people that way. She was surprised, then, when he changed the subject.

"Tell me about this contraption the fellows are using. Is it also of your father's making?"

Eden eyed the padded metal projections jutting out from the five-foot-tall metal monstrosity. A group of players barreled into it, trying to shove the arms aside or knock the hefty machine down.

She chuckled. "No, my father has no interest in football. That was designed by Professor Hart. It's for blocking practice. Each section can be adjusted for height, speed, and power to simulate different schemes and opponents. My friend Joey says it builds excellent endurance. Once you've practiced against a machine, another man feels like nothing. He's a reserve, though, so he's only ever played in a few games."

"Better than none," Bruce replied. His face contorted into a look of pain. Had he once warmed the bench for a football team, longing to play? He was tall and strong and moved with the controlled energy she recognized in top athletes. It was difficult to imagine him failing at his chosen sport. Unless the problem was related to the bit of a limp he had when he walked.

Eden was considering how to respond, when an unfamiliar roaring sound caught her attention. She looked all around, trying to determine what might be making the noise. Where was it coming from? For several seconds it grew louder, then faded at about the same rate.

Bruce had turned to look toward State Street. Eden wracked her brain, but couldn't think of anything in that direction that might have made such a sound.

"What was that?" she asked.

"Someone is racing a motorcar."

She frowned. "But we have no motorcars in town."

"It seems you do now. Shall we investigate?" He offered his arm to escort her.

Eden couldn't remember the last time a man other than her father had walked her about in such a fashion. Paul, perhaps? How peculiar. Was Bruce after Vox, too?

She called the dragon up and tucked her under an arm. The lure of a mysterious motorcar was irresistible. Her fingers curled around Bruce's arm.

"Yes. Let's."

4

SKY BLUE EYES PEERED UP AT HIM. "Really, though, shouldn't you be staying to watch more of practice? Isn't that your job?"

She certainly was curious, this woman. Their conversations made Bruce feel as if *she* was the journalist, eager for a story.

"What about you?" he countered. "Shouldn't you be in class or studying?"

They passed through the Ferry Field gates and turned south down State at a casual stroll. Eden carried her dragon tucked in the crook of her arm like a football. She frowned up at him.

"I have a degree already. I just turned twenty-three, you know."

He hadn't known, of course, but he nodded.

"I enrolled when I was seventeen, so I finished two years ago," she continued. "It was a standard four-year program."

"What in?"

"Classics. I read and write both Latin and Greek and am well versed in history and antiquities, particularly the Roman conquest and occupation of Britain."

Odd, the way she so freely offered up information one moment, then became withdrawn the next.

"I studied English Literature," Bruce replied. "My father thought it a precursor to law school until I took the job at the paper."

"Where did you study?"

"Harvard."

"Oh." There was a note of distaste in her tone that amused him.

"You don't approve of my alma mater?" he chuckled. He'd never possessed a great deal of school pride. He'd gone to Harvard because all Caldwells went to Harvard and had done so since before the Revolutionary War.

"I imagine I think of your school what you think of mine."

"That we are all backwater hicks who think overly well of themselves?"

"Precisely."

He laughed, but didn't have a chance to reply. Eden froze beside him and released his arm, holding up her hand to silence him.

"Shh..." She twisted the earring in her left ear in what appeared to be a nervous gesture. The same gold cuff she had worn on Saturday covered her lobe today. "I hear the motorcar again."

Bruce could hear it, too, ahead of them, the sound increasing as the car drove back toward town. Eden stared out across the street, her mouth turned in a frown of concentration. He found it odd that she seemed to be listening intently, yet wasn't facing in the direction of the sound. She twiddled the earring again, her eyes turning to him, then following his gaze. He nudged her when he spied the car.

"Here it comes."

The vehicle tore down the road, flying past them at a velocity Bruce had never seen from an automobile. Some twenty yards further on it slowed, then made a wide u-turn. It trundled up to them and stopped. The driver hopped out and pushed up his goggles.

Bruce nearly flinched. He recognized the man: Evan Tagget, owner of Tagget Industries and self-made millionaire. The Dynalux deal that summer had gotten his face plastered on magazines. Tagget looked more smug in person.

"Why, if it isn't the enchanting Miss Randall," Tagget simpered in an irritating New York accent. He bowed to Eden. "And I see you've brought your pet."

"No, he's just a reporter," she quipped, waving a hand at Bruce. Tagget looked bewildered, and Bruce coughed to hide his laugh.

"Very witty, Miss Randall," Tagget chuckled, recovering. "You know, of course, I meant your dragon. Do you carry it often? Miniature dragons are the height of fashion in Europe these days, though yours doesn't resemble those I've seen in Paris or Vienna. Have you been to Europe, Miss Randall?"

"Only to the British Isles. When I was fifteen, my father spent a summer at Cambridge working in collaboration with a professor there. We toured quite a bit, but never went to the continent."

"Ah. That is unfortunate. I think Paris would suit you. The City of Light always welcomes an extra sparkle."

Eden's cheeks were pink. How did Tagget manage to sound so smooth? If Bruce had said that to a woman she would have laughed in his face. Eden wasn't laughing. She was, however, clutching her dragon.

"What brings you to this part of the country, Tagget?" Bruce asked, attempting to draw the conversation away from her.

Tagget looked at Bruce properly for the first time. "I don't recall having met."

"Bruce Caldwell, Boston Herald." He held out a hand and Tagget shook it for the sake of appearances. Bruce doubted he would have done so had Eden not been there. "I'm working on a story on the rise of engineering and technological studies at

Midwestern universities. I would love to have the thoughts of a leader in the industry."

"I'm afraid I don't have time to give interviews." Tagget sounded sincere, though Bruce suspected he wasn't. "We are here to search out students who possess the ambition and expertise to seek a position at Tagget Industries. We also work with the faculty at any institution we visit, reviewing their research and inventions. Often there are creations of great commercial and societal value that come out of university studies. One of the goals of my business is to see that these technologies do not become lost in the mires of academia."

"How noble." Damn. That had come out more sarcastic than Bruce had intended.

Tagget narrowed his perfectly trimmed eyebrows. "It is important and demanding work."

"Demanding enough that you must relax by driving your motorcar at breakneck speed?"

"Research," Tagget answered, still sounding disgustingly unperturbed. "I can't neglect my own work, naturally." He looked back at Eden and waved a hand at the car. "Have you seen the new design from Mercedes, Miss Randall? Stylish and sleek. They have been so good as to make some modifications for me. She has no heavy boilers or smoky steam engines. Instead, she runs on luxene."

"Luxene?" Eden gasped. "No. That's crazy!"

Bruce agreed with her, but Tagget continued to smile.

"It must take gallons of fuel to power something so large," Eden continued. "Even the few teaspoons that power Vox are dear. You'll waste your entire fortune on your motorcar!"

Tagget chuckled. "My fortune is sufficiently vast, Miss Randall, but I thank you for the concern on my behalf. This is where my research comes into play, you see. Dynalux continues to study modifications to the formula and fuel additives to increase the efficiency of the luxene they sell. I test them in my automobile, and evaluate which work and which do not.

The hope is someday the fuel will be suitable for the average man's use."

"I think you're living in a fantasy world, Mr. Tagget," Eden said.

"Naturally, my flower. How do you think I became the man I am today? One can't be an inventor or entrepreneur without dreaming of the impossible." He bowed to her. "Please excuse me, I must get back to my work. I hope to see you again soon."

"If you're on campus recruiting employees I doubt it can be avoided."

"I'm delighted to hear it. Until then." Tagget pulled down his goggles and hopped into the car. He turned the vehicle in a leisurely circle and drove into town with a degree more moderation than he had exhibited before.

"Well, he's an ass," Bruce muttered.

"I want to ride in that car," Eden sighed.

"Oh, I'm certain he'd love to take you for a ride." Bruce immediately regretted the words. Why could he never think before he spoke? No wonder he couldn't charm women. He hoped Eden was too innocent to understand the double entendre.

She shook her head, looking neither disgusted nor puzzled. He'd dodged that particular bullet. "Impossible. I couldn't take Vox."

"Your dragon?" His eyes fell to the creature, which she held tight to her side. "Why not?"

"Please excuse me, Mr. Caldwell, I should be getting home."

Yet again she refused to talk about the dragon. Bruce was dying to know why.

"May I walk you there?"

She looked startled, then her cheeks flushed. "No, thank you. I have disrupted your work enough already. Also, it's a good mile and a half from here, and I wouldn't want to tax you."

"You don't think I'm capable of walking so short a distance?" he sputtered.

"Oh, I didn't mean that. It's only that you walk with a slight hitch to your step, and I assumed you must have suffered some injury. I would feel bad if I caused a setback in the healing process."

She'd noticed. His limp was minor enough that few people did. He'd thought the recent repairs had all but eliminated it.

"It's a very old injury, and it's as healed as it will ever be."

"Oh." She put her fist to her chest and made an odd circular gesture. "Sorry. I thought it must have been recent. Some sporting mishap. You strike me as an athlete."

Her statement caused an odd burst of happiness and he thought it best not to attempt to sort out why that might be.

"Thank you, Miss Randall. I regret I haven't yet had a chance to regale you with tales of the Olympic Games. When you have time to hear my stories, look me up. I'm staying at Cook's Hotel."

"The Temperance hotel? Don't you drink?"

"My boss selects and pays for the room. I take what I get. I'll have to go out when I feel like a beer."

"We have many saloons in town. I can show you the best ones."

He grinned. "I'd like that. Do the saloons here have women's entrances?"

She stared at him blankly. "What?"

"You know, separate rooms with special entrances so women don't need to enter the main room with all the rowdy men."

"Oh." Her brow crinkled in a look of puzzlement. "Oh! I didn't realize there were such things. Maybe that's why so many places threw me out when I tried to visit. I thought they just didn't allow women at all."

"Some saloons don't. Most that do have separate entrances. I'm surprised you've never heard of it."

"I, um, sometimes don't know things about..." She waved a hand. "You know, society. Or I don't pay attention if they don't seem interesting."

Peculiar. Fascinating. Bruce liked this woman more all the time. "So, the good saloons?"

"I walk right in the front door and no one minds. Not that I would even consider using a special separate entrance if one existed. I'm just as much a person as you are, and I should have just as much right to enter a place as you do."

"I absolutely agree."

Eden's smile was radiant. "Good. I'll take you to my favorite saloon after the game on Wednesday."

Bruce felt his own mouth curving to match hers. "I can't wait."

5

October 4

$\mathcal{A}$ PLAGUE OF TAGGET INDUSTRIES MEN swarmed the area in and around the engineering building and the AM&T labs. Some moved about in silence, notebooks in hand. Others struck up conversations with students. To a man they appeared well-dressed and serious. Tagget brooked no nonsense in his recruiting.

Eden paused by an information table and picked up one of several pamphlets that had been spread out in neat arcs. A photograph on the front showed a designer at a drafting table, while the inside contained concise lists detailing current projects and job openings.

"And what sort of salary could a new employee expect to make?" she asked.

"Looking to marry an engineer?" The man at the table chuckled.

Eden fixed him with an icy stare. "No."

"Well, miss, we may be primarily a teletics business, but if you're looking for a job as a telephone operator, you will have to go elsewhere. We make the telephones, but it's others who use them."

Her aching abdomen today was enough of a reminder about the frustrations of being a woman. Now she had to add a condescending jackass? She glanced down at Vox, contemplating having her bite him.

"My own interests are in untethered automata, particularly of the small-form factor, luxene-powered variety, with an emphasis on research into vocal control and wireless functionality. Vox, up."

The dragon obediently fluttered into the air.

"Sit." Eden tapped the table, and Vox landed, tucking her legs beneath her.

The man's startled gaze locked on the dragon. Had the employees been told to keep an eye out for such things? He would be reporting back to Tagget, that was certain. Drat. She needed to be more careful.

"You didn't make that," he insisted.

"No." Eden scooped up Vox and tucked her underneath her arm. "My mother did. Have a nice day." She turned away, then looked back, as if she had suddenly had another thought. "Oh, and there is a woman engineer in the photo on that other pamphlet, there." She tapped the stack of papers. "I thought maybe you should know."

She strode away to the satisfying snickers of nearby students.

Once inside the AM&T building, Eden hurried up to the second floor, slipping unobtrusively into her father's classroom laboratory through the upper entrance. It was a habit cultivated during her childhood, when she hadn't been allowed among the dangerous tools and delicate inventions without close supervision.

She leaned against the rail at the top of the staircase and

peered down through the web of wires and antennae. A Tagget Industries man was engaged in conversation with her father. A second man stood some way off, examining a prototype and taking notes.

Eden's brows drew together. She liked Evan Tagget well enough as a man. He was handsome and sophisticated and said nice things to her. She didn't like him at all as a business owner. He was meddlesome, arrogant, and, she suspected, utterly ruthless.

She stretched over the rail and dangled Vox above the dilapidated old wardrobe that had been modified for use as a combination bookcase and toolchest. Miscellaneous bits of metal lay atop it. No one would notice the dragon amidst the jumble.

"Vox, down."

The dragon glided to the top of the wardrobe, landing with only a soft bump unlikely to be detected through the hum of machinery. Eden crouched in the corner. Most of her sightlines were blocked by a large fan, powered by a succession of student-made dragons. The simple creatures did nothing but run inside a metal wheel that turned the fan. The better the dragon, the better the fan worked. Today, it sat motionless. Someone would be receiving a poor grade.

With the fan blades frozen, she couldn't see what the Tagget Industries men were doing, but it did mean they wouldn't see her, either. It also made the lab unusually quiet. She spun her earring and listened.

"This joint is patented?" an unfamiliar voice asked.

"Yes," Eden's father answered. "My wife holds that particular patent. She would be happy to license the design to your company. It has been used by a number of manufacturers of dragons and other mechanical contrivances."

"Mmm." There was a long pause. "We are very interested in your research into wireless teletics. The technologies in your automata could have great commercial value. We have seen the demonstrations of the voice controls. We should like to know more of your other research."

"I'm afraid I have nothing else to share at the moment."

"You're certain? Mr. Tagget pays handsomely for quality inventions."

"I'm sure he does. However, as I have already informed him, I'm not looking to sell. All my current projects are still in the research phase, and as such, are not ready to be used in anything beyond a prototype. I appreciate your interest, but my decision is final."

"A pity. Thank you for your time, Professor. Please let us know if you change your mind."

Eden rose from her hiding place and descended the spiral staircase. She was near halfway down when the three men noticed her. She waved to her father.

"Eden, dear, how are you this afternoon? Did your mother send those plans along?"

Eden pulled a folded piece of paper from her pocket and held it aloft. "I have them right here."

At the bottom of the stairs, she passed by the wheel that should have been turning the fan. The dragon inside resembled a turtle that had been flipped onto its back, wiggling its little legs in vain. She took pity on it and its creator and righted it. It took only a few steps before it teetered, rolled, and ended up on its back once more.

With a shrug, she left it behind and took a seat on a stool at one of the long workbenches. Getting off her feet relieved some of the discomfort in her belly. The first two days of her monthly flow were awful, without fail. She'd been more hopeful than usual about the newest tonic Mother had given her; but after walking all the way to the lab, she didn't think it worked better than any other. Sometimes she thought she had tried every remedy ever known. She would need to take things easy the rest of the day, and tomorrow at the game, also. No running and jumping to celebrate touchdowns. She passed the plans along to her father, who unfolded and examined them, nodding.

"Good, good. Perfect. I will put this with the others. I love our home laboratory, but it can be such a nuisance when things are mislaid."

Eden nodded. Father mislaid something at least once a week, whether it was an item from home that needed to be here, or the other way 'round. Eden suspected him of deliberate negligence to create reasons for her or her mother to come down to the lab for a while.

"Things seem very busy today with all these visitors," she remarked, eyeing the two Tagget employees.

The man who had spoken with her father stared back, and she didn't think it was due to her bright blue corset or her cute, new hat. The second man continued with his note-taking.

"I believe the gentlemen were just leaving, were you not?"

The staring man nodded, nudged his partner, and they departed via the first-floor door. Eden waited a time before speaking.

"They're a nuisance. Are they allowed to be here? It might be disruptive to the students."

"They have the permission of the Dean. If it becomes problematic we shall have to take up the matter with him, but my hope is that they will move on in a day or two."

"I'm not so sure. They seem determined to get their hands on your inventions. Was Mr. Tagget asking to buy your ideas at the party on Saturday?"

"He was, and he did so yesterday, also, showing up in his fancy motorcar. I don't know whether he's genuinely interested in the technologies or only trying to make money."

"Both, if you ask me. Regardless, he's too curious about Vox."

Her father nodded. "Tagget asked about recognition of specific individuals, and how such a thing might be accomplished mechanically."

Eden's shoulders slumped. "That was my fault. I let slip that Vox can tell me apart from others. I've tried to speak little of her since."

"You know I will never use her as a technological demonstration piece. The recognizer technology is already in two other dragons in your mother's workshop. We had anticipated conducting full tests this semester in preparation for its announcement. Unfortunately, the voice controls have become such a big to-do that it might have to be pushed back."

"You know it's fully functional. Why wait?"

"Without proper documentation, I can't present it. And, again, I don't wish to refer to Vox as part of the research. You don't need people taking her away from you and poking her about."

"Certainly not!" She called for the dragon, caught her out of the air, and stroked her smooth, metal body. "Tagget calls her a pet."

"As does everyone, my dear."

"They don't understand."

"How could they?"

"I know," she sighed. "Plenty of people have dragons. Why does it matter that I take her everywhere? I don't mind being odd, but there are times I grow frustrated so many people look at me askance."

"Go outside and hit a few baseballs," he recommended.

Eden grinned. "I do. Often."

"Good, good. That boys' team should have let you play. You would have scored plenty of touchdowns."

"Runs, Father."

"Which one is it that has touchdowns?"

"Football."

"Ah, yes." His gaze drifted to Vox. "How is she? Any troubles? Adjustments needed?"

"She's in perfect repair. You know Mother checks her

monthly, and I've learned to do all the small adjustments myself."

"I'm still hoping to increase her transmission range."

"It's fine, Father. You can work on range increases using a different dragon. I'm happy with her as she is."

He nodded in resignation. "Very well. And there's still the matter of that blasted interference…"

Eden bit her lower lip. Two dragons like Vox could never be near one another, given the current state of the wireless transmissions. Until her parents could solve the problem, the technology couldn't be properly demonstrated or distributed. Vox would remain a one-off. A curiosity.

Her father gave a little shake of his head. "Well, let me know if you need anything."

"Only some lab time. I'd like to build one of those wind-up insect dragons, and I'm determined to make it function better than your student's silly turtle."

Her father's gaze went to the motionless fan. "Ah, yes. Poor boy isn't cut out for this field. Plans were indecipherable. What will you do with your insect?"

She shrugged. "I don't know." Her gaze drifted out the window to where the Tagget Industries men continued their zealous recruiting. "Maybe I will give it sharp claws and nasty, protruding spikes, and then build a whole colony to chase off nosy Easterners."

6

October 5

EDEN TILTED THE NOTEBOOK to get a better view. "Your handwriting is terrible."

Bruce couldn't deny it. He wrote rapidly out of habit, and there were many scribbles and additions where he had made edits. He took another sip of his excellent beer. Eden did indeed know the good saloons.

"That's the price you pay for reading the article before anyone else. If you wait for the paper you won't have to suffer through negligent penmanship and all my spelling errors."

He leaned back against the wall. She'd chosen a secluded table nestled into a corner, calling it her favorite spot. It was quiet, almost private. A tiny sanctuary where the noise and bustle of the saloon was subdued.

"The spelling isn't so bad as all that. Does it bother your editors?"

"They don't know. I rarely cover anything in Boston. I have to send the articles by telephone."

"Oh, of course. I'd thought telegraph, where the spelling would be noticed, but telephone is easier?"

"Faster. Less expensive."

"Because of the Tagget Industries technologies."

"Yes. The upgraded lines made all the difference. My first assignment, three years ago, I sent via telegraph, but I was one of the last to do that. Telephone is better, though not without its own difficulties."

Honestly, he hated submitting articles. His deadlines were tight to begin with. Having to read the article into a somewhat suspect machine, listen as it was read back to him, and then go through all the inevitable corrections was a boring, frustrating process. Perhaps a promotion would allow him to work in Boston and avoid it in the future.

A promotion you're not going to get, he reminded himself.

"I don't know much about telephones," Eden admitted. An odd statement, he thought, coming from the daughter of a teletics professor.

She adjusted the placement of the dragon in her lap and went back to his article, smiling as she read. Her beloved Wolverines had had an easy time of it against their mid-week foe. The game had been dull enough that his mind had repeatedly wandered to Eden, mesmerized by her vivacity and intense, blue-eyed gaze as they'd sat together on the sidelines, watching.

She'd been quieter today, and had only taken the wolverine mascot on a few brief trips along the sidelines, but her enthusiasm for the sport and attention to the match were unchanged. Multiple times Bruce had needed her to recap plays he had missed. She missed nothing. He owed most of the article to her. The line about "grumbling fans" when Ohio Northern had made their only first down was based solely on her half-joking comment that the defense was "falling apart."

Eden finished reading and passed the notebook back. "Why did you lie to Tagget?"

He blinked in confusion. "Pardon? Lie about what? When?"

"You told him you were here to report on engineering."

He nodded, remembering. "So I did. As to why…" He hadn't thought much about why. He'd said it almost on instinct. "I suppose he can't dismiss me out-of-hand if he thinks I might be writing about him."

"I wish he would dismiss me."

"I'm afraid, Miss Randall, you are a very difficult woman to dismiss."

"I know," she sighed. "My father is a famous inventor now. Everyone wants to study my dragon."

"Your dragon is interesting, doubtless, but *you* are more so."

She cocked her head, frowning, her gaze fixed on his mouth in a way that conjured up thoughts of kissing and further improprieties. Why did she do that?

"Me," she said, uncertainly.

"You possess intelligence and wit," Bruce explained. "You have unusual interests and habits. You have no fear of that ghastly wolverine. You're a very pretty woman, with a style all your own."

Her eyes widened at the compliment. Beautiful eyes. They matched the blue in her fancy corset, the same one she had worn during the first game of the season. She stared at him, now, with an expression that told him he was crazy.

Her brow furrowed. "Is this something men are taught on the East Coast? How to flatter a woman?"

"It's not flattery, Miss Randall. I state things the way I see them. I don't possess the slick manners that others may."

She continued to frown at him, and hugged her dragon. He'd made her nervous. Damn. What was so special about that dragon that made her so protective and suspicious? It wasn't as if he were an industrialist like Tagget, always on the prowl for unique technologies.

No, but you're a reporter. Meddlesome by profession, if not by nature.

He was also a stranger. Two football games and a drink didn't make them close. If he wanted her trust, he would have to earn it. He downed the last of his beer.

"It's growing late. May I walk you home?"

She fished a watch out of the pocket of her trousers and checked the time. "No, thank you. I don't need an escort." She rose from her seat. He pushed back his own chair and stood. He would see her to the door, at least. "Thank you for sharing your article. I'll read it again when I get the paper and see if they printed it correctly. I'll see you Saturday at the game. Have a good night." She turned toward the door.

"Eden," he called. When she didn't respond, he jogged to catch up. "Eden," he repeated, reaching to touch her shoulder.

Dammit. He shouldn't be calling her by her first name and he absolutely shouldn't be touching her.

She jumped at the contact, but stopped and looked back at him. Her expression remained wary, but he thought he detected curiosity beneath the surface. "Yes?"

"Would you, perhaps, be interested in going out to, uh…" He groped for an idea of what they might do. He didn't know the town well enough yet, but he was desperate for some way to win her over. To prove they could be friends, at least. "To the museum? Tomorrow or Friday? We could view the antiquities and you could translate the inscriptions for me. And I promise to tell my Olympics stories at last."

Her cheeks turned pink. She still clutched the dragon, but she smiled. "Friday after lunch? Meet me at the library."

"I'll be there. A very good night to you, Miss Randall."

He walked her to the door and watched her start off down the road, feeling compelled to follow. It didn't sit well with him that she was walking home alone after dark. In Boston he would never have allowed such a thing. Then again, in Boston women didn't routinely wander the streets at night with only a tiny dragon for company. Most women anywhere didn't do so, as far as he knew. But most women weren't Eden Randall of Ann Arbor.

He sighed and stepped back into the saloon, contemplating having another beer.

"The girl likes you."

Bruce turned toward the sound of the voice. The man who had spoken wore a suit the same style as any man in town, but his identity was betrayed by his New York accent. One of Tagget's men. Bruce met his gaze coldly.

"I don't see how that's any business of yours."

"It's Mr. Tagget's business. He believes that dragon possesses new and valuable technologies. He's willing to pay for any information about it. He will pay more for a chance to examine the machine himself."

"She'll never allow it, regardless of what you may offer her." Eden had an emotional attachment to the dragon. Bruce didn't want to press her about it, though the curiosity gnawed at him.

"Mr. Tagget is of the same opinion." The man wore a predatory smile. "She may, however, share information with a friend. If such information were to make its way to us, payment could be made to the accommodating individual."

"How much?"

"The exact amount will be dependent upon the quality of the information, at Mr. Tagget's discretion. I can say, however, that to a man on a reporter's salary, any compensation will be sizable."

"Tell your boss I'll give the matter some consideration."

Bruce walked past the man, ordered another beer and returned to the corner seat where he could sit alone. He sipped in silence, mulling over everything he knew of Eden Randall, her dragon, and Evan Tagget. Scraps of ideas floated through his mind, but concrete conclusions eluded him. He needed to take notes. Things made more sense when he wrote them down. The weight of his notebook in his pocket nagged at him.

The Tagget Industries man watched until Bruce finished his drink and left the saloon. Bruce didn't look over his shoulder as he walked to the hotel, but he would've been unsurprised if someone had followed him.

Locked safely in his room, he jotted some notes, considered them for a time, then jotted more. A picture began to emerge, one he thought he could confirm next time he saw Eden. It also conjured up all sorts of new questions in his mind.

Before he turned in for the night, he ripped the page from the book. He struck a match from the complimentary matchbook with the hotel name on it and watched the flames dance, burning the page to ash. He wouldn't leave any details about Eden lying around where anyone might steal them. Tagget could offer him the world. He wouldn't betray her for anything.

7

October 7

Eden paced nervously in front of the library. Vox trotted alongside, her metal claws clacking on the pavement.

It had been impossible to accomplish anything today. She'd spent half the morning in the lab, pretending to work on her wind-up insect while her thoughts wandered and she stared out the window. She'd tried to read, but had struggled to get more than a few paragraphs into the book.

Like at the party a week ago, her emotions flip-flopped between excitement and anxiety. Silly. That's what it was. Men and women went out together all the time. It was perfectly normal, and everything would be simple and straightforward. They would walk about the museum and talk and be friendly. There was nothing more to it.

If only this weren't her first experience of the sort. She didn't want to ruin it by doing something wrong. She didn't want Bruce to realize how clueless she was, or how undesirable she was to everyone else. She wanted him to like her. She wanted to be friends. And maybe, possibly, she wanted to kiss him.

He would never match the flawless features and pristine style of a man like Tagget, but Bruce was plenty handsome in his own way. Cute, perhaps, was the best word for him. He had those soft brown eyes that made her feel a little melty inside, and she itched to brush his hair back where it flopped over his brow. She'd never seen him wear a suit coat, his boots were scuffed, and he seemed to have an entire wardrobe full of newsboy caps. Not a top hat in sight, or even a derby. She could drink a beer with him at a saloon and not feel strange. He might even be willing to hit a few balls with her.

Eden had to remind herself that he was also a reporter and therefore prone to snooping. He never lacked for questions, and she knew he was curious about Vox.

She glanced down at her constant companion. Why did everyone have to be so nosy? It was odd to have a dragon with her at all times, but not wildly so. Plenty of people about town kept the mechanical creatures, some just as entertainment for children, others as companions for walks or guards for homes. Her parents had built dozens of dragons on commission. The strangest request she could recall was the man who had wanted one that was the size of a dog, resembled a cat with horns, and would keep his lawn trimmed. It made her laugh just thinking about it.

"Ah, Miss Randall! Good afternoon."

Eden's head swiveled, trying to locate Bruce. She hated it when people came up from behind her. She could never tell where they were and would inevitably turn the wrong direction, looking foolish.

This time she took the safe guess and turned away from the library, only to discover that he wasn't approaching from the outside, but was just now coming out the library door.

"Hi." She scooped up Vox. "It's this way to the museum," she said quickly, hoping to prevent his commenting on her inability to locate him.

"Lead on." He fell into step beside her, his long strides easily matching her brisk pace, despite his slight limp.

"How did you…" She stopped herself before she could ask after his injury. What if the cause was something horrible? As far as she knew, scarred war heroes never wanted to talk of their wounds, and the war with Spain had only been six years ago. He was old enough to maybe have been involved, though he didn't strike her as a soldier. "Like the library?" she finished.

A little frown of suspicion creased his brow, then he shrugged. "It was nice enough. I did a little reading. Poked through old newspapers. That sort of thing. How about you? What have you been up to today?"

"Oh, I, uh, did some work on an insect dragon I'm building." If next-to-nothing could count as "some."

"What will it do?"

"I haven't decided," she admitted. "Thus far I've only worked on the outer shell—its exoskeleton, I suppose. I haven't planned its guts."

Bruce laughed. "That's not a sentence I would ever have expected to hear."

"You obviously haven't grown up around an AM&T lab. My parents have said much stranger things than that."

"You must've had an unusual childhood."

"Yes." She wasn't ready to tell him more than that. A long pause made her fear she had killed the conversation, so she said, "It's standard practice, you know, to build the guts of a dragon after the outside."

"Is it?"

"Yes. My father teaches that to all his students. With so many working components on the inside, access to them for maintenance, repairs, and improvements is vital. When the outside is built first, you know exactly how much room you have inside and how easy it is to get parts in and out. Then you arrange the layout of your working bits to fit."

"What if the working bits are too large?"

"They shouldn't be, because you should have done an overall design as the very first step, not to mention planning your outside frame with room to spare. Usually, when creating an automaton you draw a full plan of it, including a parts list, interior and exterior views, et cetera. Once you know everything you need and how you think you want it to look, you move into the building phase, outside to in, tweaking the plan as you go. Things don't always work how you thought they would on paper."

"Sounds sensible. It seems, however, that you skipped the first step for this insect of yours."

Eden's gaze dropped to the ground. "I'm only tinkering."

"And I'm only teasing."

She quickly looked back up, not wanting to miss what he was saying.

"Whatever you build, it's bound to be better than anything I might make. I can neither weld, nor rivet, nor draw a schematic."

"Well, your parents aren't inventors."

"No. My father is a financier and my mother chairs about half-a-dozen ladies' social clubs. They think I'm crazy. Sometimes I agree."

Eden laughed. What had she been so worried about? Chatting with Bruce was easy. She had assumed there would be a vast difference between her impulsive invitation for a casual drink in a saloon and a prearranged date. It turned out they were surprisingly similar.

Like most of the buildings on campus, Eden knew the museum by heart. She enjoyed playing tour guide, leading Bruce through the collections and expounding on all she knew of them. He was suitably impressed when she gained them access to some of the storage areas, full of boxes and cabinets of items rarely on display. She even took him up to the fourth floor to show off the slapdash roof built a decade earlier when the original had been in danger of collapse.

They sat staring up at the hasty reconstruction while they talked of women's archery and the surprisingly large number of Olympic medals won by Michigan athletes. Bruce told her every detail he could remember about the mad marathon, and she told him about how she had hung around the track team until Archie Hahn had let her see his gold medals. By the time they were preparing to leave she felt a stab of disappointment that their outing was nearing its end.

They had just descended the front steps, when Bruce stopped and turned to her. "Do you mind, Miss Randall, if I ask you a personal question? You don't need to answer if it makes you uncomfortable."

Curious, but polite. His earnest expression tugged at her heart, urging her to trust him. His editors would be wise to give him all the interviews. People would talk to him. If he was working his way up to asking about Vox, she feared she might fall into the trap. Hopefully his query would be something more mundane, like why she was wearing trousers again.

"What would you like to know?"

"That jewel in your ear, is it a hearing device?"

The question surprised her. So it wasn't about Vox, at least not directly.

"What makes you think that?"

"You are unusually knowledgeable on the subject of devices related to hearing loss. You exhibit difficulty locating sources of sounds. You stare at my mouth when we converse. You never remove that jewel from your ear, though it appears it ought to obstruct your hearing. It leads me to believe it must be some sort of biomechanic."

Eden hesitated. Biomechanics were controversial—no, worse than controversial. The people opposed to them believed biomechanologists were "playing God" and likened those who used the devices to Frankenstein's monster. Many others reacted in the same negative fashion as they had to her hearing loss—she wasn't "bad," but she was "other."

Even around people who had known her since childhood, her earpiece was something that wasn't spoken of. Bruce didn't sound at all repulsed, only interested, but her habit of silence made her reluctant to explain.

"As I said, you don't need to answer. I understand if you don't want to talk about it."

Her hesitation was confession enough. It couldn't hurt to tell him part of the story. "You're correct," she replied. "It helps me to hear." There. That was all the detail she intended to give.

"Have you had it long?"

"I've had an earpiece since I was fifteen. The sounds were a bit tinny at first, but over the years it's been improved and updated. I helped design the style and it's something I'm proud to wear every day." Whatever others might think or say, Eden knew the device for what it was: a marvel of technology and a declaration that biomechanics were beautiful, too. If only everyone could understand.

"It's lovely."

Her heart thumped. Perhaps Bruce could be one of those who understood.

"I rather like the way it looks," he said, "only on the one side. Your right ear is normal, I take it?"

"No, the right ear can't hear at all. We tried devices in that ear, but it was the more badly damaged of the two. I could never hear more than low, rumbling noises. The ear is small and delicate, and even with a surgical implantation like I have our technology is limited."

Blast. She'd ruined the plan of not sharing details. He was so easy to talk to. He posed question after question with his gentle voice and his sincere eyes and more words spilled out than she ever intended.

He gaped at her. "But... that would mean, before you got the device..."

"I was entirely deaf, yes. I was almost five when I lost my hearing, and everything before is no more than a blur. But I remember after. I struggled to talk because I didn't know what sounds I was making, and learning to speak new words was next to impossible. I was angry and hurt and scared. I would scream and scream, trying to hear anything at all. My mother bought me a baseball bat and told me to go outside when I felt upset or frustrated and hit the ball as hard as I could. I became quite a good slugger."

She stopped talking because he was staring at her. Did he pity her? Did he think her strange, now? She rarely shared the full extent of her history and this was why. She hated the "you poor thing" look. She wasn't a poor thing. Her childhood had been special and wonderful. Just different.

"You truly couldn't talk until you were fifteen?" he asked. "That does explain why your pronunciation is…"

"Odd?" Eden sighed.

"Careful," Bruce replied. "As if you'd practiced."

"I did. Over and over and over. For the past eight years. And some words still come out funny."

"But that doesn't stop you talking." Eden wasn't always the best judge of tone, but she thought he sounded impressed.

"Of course not. Nothing stops me. And I may have had no voice for many years, but I could talk." She set Vox down and signed her words to show him. "I didn't go to school, but my parents brought a Deaf teacher, Miss Ames, to live with us and teach us all to sign. I am fully bilingual. They all worked so hard for me. They taught me to read and write. My parents gave me a good education."

"And, ultimately, a chance to hear again."

"Yes. They're very good to me." A flood of emotion rushed through her. She scooped up Vox and hugged her to ease it.

Bruce's staring had morphed into a smile. "You can't see it, and it certainly isn't as pretty as your device, but I'm biomechanical as well."

Her eyes widened. "You are?" The only people she had ever met with biomechanics were in Cambridge, during the summer her father had worked with the biomechanology specialists there on the creation of her earpiece.

"Here, let me show you."

He tugged his right trouser leg up past his knee, in full view of everyone on State Street. Bands of brass encircled his leg above and below the knee, attached to steel joints. It resembled a supportive brace, but upon closer inspection Eden could see this was no removable apparatus. The metal had been spliced into his flesh, a near-seamless transition between brass and skin. The knee itself had been entirely replaced, a smooth, bronze plate concealing the inner workings of the mechanical hinge. What did it look like beneath, she wondered? How did the nerves and blood vessels connect?

"You can't see much," Bruce explained, "but there are springs and gears on the inside to allow it to bend in a relatively normal manner. They're all visible and accessible when you remove the plate, but that requires a screwdriver."

A burst of excitement shot through her. "My father has tools in his laboratory."

Bruce tugged his pant leg back down to hide the contraption. "Perhaps another time." He shook his head and grimaced. "You may not be squeamish about such things, but I am. I'd need a stiff drink beforehand. I couldn't watch when they did the repairs after that dratted marathon."

"How did you stand to have it done in the first place?"

"Morphine. Lots of morphine. I was on it for pain relief after the injury." A slight tremor shook his shoulders. "It took months to wean myself off it afterward."

"I'm sorry." She signed it out of habit. Certain words and phrases she couldn't say with her voice alone. "How were you injured?"

"Football. I was on the freshman squad, hoping to make varsity the next year. Our first game I took the ball on a run around the right end. A big lug went low on me, at full speed, caved in my knee. They had to carry me off. The doctors told me if I was lucky I might walk again with a cane. I had money in the bank that was intended to pay for my education. I spent well over half of it to buy this knee. My parents were furious."

"They were afraid you would have to drop out of school and be unemployed?"

"No. I had enough funds to get my bachelors degree so long as I lived economically. But law school or business school were no longer options. I didn't realize it at the time, but my father believed I always meant to attend law school and he would have to cough up additional money to pay for it. Not that he was hurting financially, but it would have been a horrible thing for me to expect of him. We've had many misunderstandings, my family and I."

Eden frowned. It puzzled her how people could grow up in a world where communication came easily and still not be able to convey their thoughts effectively.

"But enough about me," Bruce finished.

Eden disagreed. It wasn't enough. She wanted to know more about him. More about his family, his education, his career. She was fascinated.

"Where are you off to for the remainder of the afternoon?" he asked.

Her previous disappointment returned. If only the museum were larger. "I'll be back in my father's lab. Working on my bug."

"Of course. Let me walk you there, and then, I'm afraid, I have work to do. I'm already getting questions about the stadium, the other facilities, practices, recruiting tactics… you name it, they're asking. I'll probably write fifteen articles no one will read except my editors."

"I'll read them," Eden promised.

They lapsed into silence as they walked toward the AM&T building. Eden wondered what he might be thinking. She hoped he'd enjoyed himself. She wanted to go out with him again. He knew about her deafness and her earpiece, and he didn't seem bothered, although she didn't think he understood about Vox. Perhaps she could explain eventually. After Tagget stopped pestering her father and left town.

She hopped up onto the first step of the lab building and turned around to say goodbye. The extra height gave her an excellent look into his big, brown eyes.

"I'm nearly as tall as you now."

"I can see that." He grinned. That smile was dazzling. Darn. Now she was thinking about kissing him again.

It wouldn't be so hard, really. She would only have to lean a bit closer. Her lips tingled in anticipation. She *had* been kissed before. It had been nice, and that had been with a man whom she had never thought of as more than a friend. It would be better, she expected, with someone she wanted to kiss.

Bruce was terribly close to her. His smile had faded, and he was gazing intently into her eyes. Eden leaned in.

"Oof." He took a step back and rubbed his chest.

One of Vox's antennae had poked him. Eden's cheeks flushed in embarrassment.

"I will, uh, see you at the game tomorrow, Miss Randall," he mumbled, looking flustered. "Have a pleasant evening."

"Thank you." She signed the phrase as she spoke, touching her fingertips to her lips, then tipping her hand toward him, smiling. "I had a lovely time this afternoon."

His smile returned. "So did I." He tipped his cap to her before departing.

Eden turned into the building and headed to her father's lab. She did want to work on her mechanical insect. If she could keep her mind on the work and not Bruce. That hot gaze of his. Those liquid eyes. She desperately wished to know what he tasted like.

The bug, Eden. Think about that. Maybe you can get the outside finished today.

Right.

8

October 8

THE CROWD ROARED for yet another touchdown. Bruce jotted in his notebook. Heston again, from eighty-five yards out. This was getting ridiculous. The Michigan offense was blazing fast. They wasted no time between plays, plowing down the field through the overwhelmed defenders from Kalamazoo. The Wolverines would've had even more points if it weren't for their habit of fumbling the ball. Bruce had one entire page listing only touchdowns and fumbles. He would gloss over the details in his article and focus on the final score and the speed of play.

Bruce looked down from the grandstands to where Eden walked the sidelines in her gameday outfit. She'd taken pity on the opponent after the first half-dozen touchdowns and moved her wolverine dragon to the Michigan side of the field. She strolled about like a lady on a walk in the park, a lacy maize and blue parasol tilted over her shoulder. Vox followed a step behind, more obedient than any dog.

It still puzzled him, this pet-that-was-more-than-a-pet. He didn't dare ask her about it. The less he knew, the better. It would prevent Tagget's men trying to bully it out of him. He debated whether to tell Eden they'd offered him money to steal her secrets. He didn't want her to even consider he might do such a thing. But he also didn't want her to think he had something to hide.

He could scarcely believe how close he'd come to kissing her yesterday. And on the steps of her father's building, no less. He hadn't liked a woman this much in years. His job didn't afford him much opportunity for romance. His last girlfriend had given up on him because he was never home. The one before had left him for someone who *did* go to law school. Those two had been the most serious of any of his relationships, but he hadn't been sad to lose either of them.

Because they were Mother's type, not yours.

Truth. Both women were perfect Boston marriage material: wealthy, elegant, and sophisticated. Eden was none of those things. In fact, the only thing he could think of that she had in common with his former flames was her dragon. All the fashionable women in Boston went out to be seen in their fancy clothes, walking dragons on leashes. His mother had one that looked like a weasel with butterfly wings. It was hideous and the gears made loud clanking noises when it shuffled down the street. Her friends loved it because it had real diamonds for eyes and gold filigree down its back.

Bruce decided he'd seen enough of the game from the grandstands and made his way down to the field. By the time he reached the ground, the Wolverines had scored again. He made a note of it and headed toward Eden, only to discover his opponent had beaten him there.

"...take in a concert at the Opera House this evening?" Tagget was asking. "I have secured front-row tickets."

The wolverine snarled. Tagget showed no fear of the

creature, which was certain to earn him favor with Eden. Bruce hoped it would bite him.

Eden's eyes sparkled. "I would love to! But I have to finish up here after the game and see the wolverine is properly stored."

"Not to worry. The performance doesn't begin until eight. Shall I pick you up at 7:30?"

"Oh, no, thank you. It's an easy walk from my house. I'll meet you there."

The typical Eden reply and Tagget's obvious shock almost made Bruce smile.

"Walk alone? At night?"

Eden wasn't listening. The ball carrier had broken away from the pack and she whooped in excitement, jumping up and down in celebration of yet another touchdown.

Bruce put pen to paper and walked closer. "Enjoying the game, Miss Randall? I didn't see that last play properly. Who scored this time?"

"Hammond, again," she answered. "Yes, I'm having a grand time." She grinned at him, but her smile faded momentarily. "I'm very sorry, but I won't be able to see you at the saloon tonight. I'm going to a concert." She said the word with reverence, and he had a sudden realization of how magnificent a musical performance might be to someone who had lacked the ability to hear for most of her childhood.

"You are fond of concerts, Miss Randall?"

"I love them. I can watch the movements of the musicians, feel the vibrations in my chair, hear the notes and the melodies. It's like a feast for my senses."

He did smile, then, at seeing her happiness. "I hope you have a wonderful time. You can read today's article at a later date."

"Miss Randall, about tonight…" Tagget cut in.

"Oh, yes. I'll meet you there at quarter-to. Excuse me. I need to follow the wolverine before it gets out of range. Bye!"

She scampered off, leaving Tagget scowling. He was a

man accustomed to having his own way. Eden's nonconformist habits had thrown him. Bruce couldn't hide his grin.

Tagget turned, his penetrating gaze raking Bruce from head to toe. Finding him lacking, no doubt.

"You seem rather pleased with yourself, Mr. Caldwell."

"Not with myself. I was merely thinking how very delightful Miss Randall is."

Tagget's expression shifted into a surprisingly genuine smile. "Yes, she is. A rare treasure. I'm greatly looking forward to spending the evening with her."

Bruce played nonchalant, though he seethed internally. "Enjoy the concert. But don't expect her to tell you about that dragon of hers."

"Ah, yes. But what of you? Don't tell me your handsome face and easygoing charm don't sway your interviewees to reveal more than they intend. Have you coaxed any details from our lovely friend?"

"Nothing I would consider sharing with you."

"Pity. I would have made it worth your while."

Why did that sound like an innuendo? Bruce frowned in confusion.

"I had a few hundred dollars I thought you might enjoy," Tagget continued, "but if you are determined to be reticent I suppose I shall have to take matters into my own hands."

"Good luck with that."

Tagget smirked. "Such sarcasm. I am wounded, dear boy. Cut to the quick."

Sick of the conversation, Bruce turned his attention to the game. "Excuse me, but I should be getting back to work."

"Of course. I wouldn't dream of keeping you from your perusal of these rowdy men and their... sporting endeavors. Demanding work, I'm certain."

Bruce swallowed the urge to tell him to fuck off, instead pretending to jot another note in his journal. He could almost feel that smug smile on his back.

Bastard.

Bruce glanced over his shoulder just to be certain Tagget wasn't following Eden. It was bad enough he was taking her out tonight. Damn the man for finding something so attractive to her. She didn't deserve to be interrogated simply because she loved music. Her secrets were hers alone.

The remainder of the game passed by in a blur. Afterward, Bruce killed time composing his article. He rewrote the entire thing three times, then spent the next hour on the telephone making certain it was submitted correctly. With time remaining in the evening and nothing better to do, he returned to the saloon for a drink and people to chat with. He had a mission tonight: find out all the best places to take a girl. When he sought Eden in the morning to ask her out again he, for one, wasn't going to have any ulterior motives.

· · · 🐉 · · ·

Eden twiddled her earring, adjusting the volume as the music swelled and faded, unwilling to miss even a single note. The bright call of a trumpet fanfare sliced through the pulsating murmur of cellos, reverberating off the walls of the theater. A sigh of pleasure escaped her lips.

Tagget's eyebrows twitched, his lips quirking into his smug smile. He'd been a perfect gentleman this evening, and not nearly so nosy. Eden wasn't fooled. He might be all charm and kindness tonight, but she would never trust him. Her eyes flicked up toward Vox, perched safely above on a chandelier, where no one could reach her.

When the concert ended, she called the dragon down, tucking her under her left arm, as far from Tagget as possible.

"Did you enjoy the performance, Miss Randall?" he asked, offering his arm.

Her fingers settled hesitantly on his elbow. She might balk at walking so close beside him, but he deserved politeness in return for bringing her here tonight. "It was beautiful. The music felt like floating."

"I'm pleased to hear you say so. I, too, enjoyed our outing. I hope it won't be our last. I don't know if you've heard, but I will be in town for some time to come."

She twitched. He wasn't leaving? Most of the Tagget Industries men had finished up their recruiting and left town. So much for the hope he would soon follow.

"I thought your business here was concluded?"

"The original business is. I have arranged to stay on a time, however, in order to collaborate with Professor Hart on his current teletics work. He has excellent ideas regarding telepictures. I still believe that technology to be a few years off, but my company would love to help him with the research and development."

"I see."

Eden had known Professor Hart her entire life. His inventions were often useful, but rarely groundbreaking. He wouldn't be the one to make a breakthrough in telepictures. She doubted Tagget thought so, either. It was an excuse to stay in town and attempt to steal her father's work.

After spending the evening with him, Eden was confident he too had discerned the reason for her ear cuff. She suspected he might even understand what Vox did. Tagget was an inventor himself, after all. Still, it puzzled her why he was so eager for the new technologies.

He was noted to be a shrewd businessman. He must know Vox wouldn't bring him a fortune overnight. Even if she handed over the dragon right now and told Tagget, "Go ahead, do whatever you want," he would still have to wait while prototypes were built and tests run. One dragon couldn't give him an immediate commercial product.

He would also know her father never sold his inventions to speculators, and had already submitted patent applications for everything inside of Vox. Tagget only had to wait until the designs were fully tested, written up, and presented. Then he could buy or license them for whatever purpose he liked.

Eden squeezed Vox to her side. Why did she still suspect him of wanting to steal her?

"My car will be waiting outside," Tagget said. "Please, allow me to drive you home."

He wasn't asking, merely stating politely. He expected her to nod and comply. The thought of a ride in the motorcar caused a giddy tremor in Eden's belly. All she had to do was keep silent, and he'd lead her to it and take her for a drive.

"No, thank you. I'm perfectly happy to walk." She released his arm to make certain she got her point across.

Tagget stumbled, whirling to gape at her. "In full darkness? Miss Randall, I can't allow that!"

She smothered a laugh. Her words and behavior continued to confound him. She was odd. Didn't he understand that? Everyone else seemed to catch on quickly.

"It's no trouble," she informed him. "If I can't see, I'll open the access panel on Vox's belly. The glow from the luxene provides plenty of light."

"I can't allow it," he repeated.

"Thank you for your concern, but my mind is made up."

She wouldn't take Vox into his car. Under ordinary circumstances, she could send the dragon flying up in the air in an emergency. A motorcar was too fast. If she let Vox loose they would become separated in moments. Tagget was a small man, and Eden considered herself athletic, but she was petite. In close quarters, where she couldn't improvise or escape, she was unlikely to win a physical struggle. She couldn't take the risk he might wrestle Vox from her.

Ignoring Tagget's further protests, she darted off, ducking into the crowd. Here, her small size gave her an advantage. He would never find her among the taller concert-goers and the ladies in their skirts. Still attired in her gameday outfit with its convenient trousers, she slipped easily through the throng.

Away from the theater, the darkness closed around her, protecting Vox from prying eyes and pilfering fingers. Eden hummed a tune from the concert, a lilting accompaniment to the fading noise of Tagget's motorcar.

9

October 9

"ARE YOU COMING HOME, dear, or did you have plans?" Eden's mother asked, as they filed out of the church into the sunny autumn air.

"I think I'll stop by the lab and work a bit on my bug project. I'll be home by dinner, at the latest."

Mother nodded her understanding. Sundays were Eden's favorite times in the lab. With the students and professors off for the day, campus was calm, and the buildings were quiet. The silence soothed away the stresses left by long stretches of bustle and noise. Taking these periods of quiet for herself allowed her to rest and recharge.

"Have fun," her father said. "Remember to put your tools away when you finish."

When had she ever not? Yet he reminded her every time. He was too accustomed to students who didn't always follow the proper procedures.

"I will."

They took their leave of one another, and Eden struck out in the direction of Cook's Hotel. Bruce had promised her the chance to read his article today, and she was eager to regale him with every detail of the concert. She would invite him to tour the lab and see her project, and then ask him out to lunch.

Or was that not done? She scanned her memory for any novel or account where a woman had asked a man on an outing, but came up empty. Was calling on him at his hotel even considered acceptable?

Eden shrugged. If not, it was a silly rule.

Much to her disappointment, Bruce wasn't in residence when she arrived. He'd probably gone out to church just like everyone else, and she certainly couldn't expect him to sit around waiting for her to show up. She left a note saying she would be at the lab. With any hope, he'd stop by. If not, she'd be stuck reading the article when the paper arrived, just like everyone else. For now, she had her wind-up bug to distract her.

Eden walked to the first floor door to open it with her key, a necessity when she was alone. Once inside she would flip the switch to trigger the auto-locking mechanism that opened the upper door. Not that she expected any visitors, unless Bruce called. But the auto-lock never failed to make her smile. As a child, she had loved watching the gears twisting and turning, maneuvering the lock in and out of place. In more recent times, she had learned to like the clank the heavy lock made when it settled.

A flurry of odd noises greeted her as she approached the lab. She paused just outside the door, nudging Vox closer to listen. All Eden could discern was a confusion of sounds—scratching, shuffling, clinks and clanks of moving machinery—none of it the usual consistent hum of the laboratory at work. Muscles tensing, she scooped up Vox and unlocked the door.

The lab was in chaos. The door to the closet which held student projects stood wide open, and dozens of small dragons roamed free. Eden slammed the door behind her to prevent a buzzing creature from escaping.

"Vox, up!" she commanded. The dragon flew from her arms and perched halfway up the spiral staircase. It would do for the moment.

Eden snagged the nearest dragon and flipped the toggle on its back. It went limp in her hands. She shoved it onto a shelf in the closet and grabbed for another one. This dragon was of the wind-up variety and didn't have an off switch. She hung it on her father's hatrack where it could spin helplessly until it wound down.

Something with wings flew across the room, causing her to duck. Somewhere glass shattered. Eden raced to grab more dragons. Valuable equipment and precious research could be destroyed if she didn't stop this.

Anger roiled inside of her. The lab had been sabotaged. The dragons in that cabinet couldn't have wandered out on their own. Some needed winding. Most had a simple on/off switch. Someone had set them all in motion and left them to wreak havoc.

She had corralled more than a dozen automata when a new sound joined the cacophony. A knocking sound, but not of fist on wood. Eden had no idea where it might be coming from and couldn't spare the time to look. She knelt by a table, trying to snag a particularly destructive dragon that had crawled beneath. Its long arms flailed about, waving tools and scraps of metal it had picked up. One arm struck a table leg, splintering it. Eden covered her head as the tabletop crashed down on her.

Shoving the wreckage aside, she lunged at the beast, seizing it by a leg before it could scuttle away. A wrench smashed into her arm, and she cried out but didn't let go. She dragged the horrid thing out into the open and stomped on it, pinning multiple arms. The squid-like dragon thrashed beneath her boots. A quick once-over found the off switch. Pity she didn't have the time to disable it more completely.

The banging noise hadn't ceased, and she looked around the room for the source. Outside a window, a young man peered in at her, hammering his fist on the glass. She ran to activate the switch that would open the window

"Do you need help?" he asked. "I was passing by and heard terrible noises."

Eden tossed him the building key. "Come around, quickly. Someone has let the dragons loose."

A minute later, the student joined her in the lab, ducking when the flying dragon sailed past him. The door closed in the nick of time, and the creature veered off in another direction. That particular machine wanted to escape. If only she had a butterfly net.

It took the next quarter hour for Eden and her assistant to round up the rest of the dragons, until only the flying contraption remained free. Bits of broken glass, twisted pieces of metal, and at least two former dragons she had stepped on during the chaos littered the floor of the laboratory.

Eden studied the flier, her heart sinking as she noticed the intricate wings and the methodical way it tested for exits. This was Lilah's dragon. A bat, she had called it. Like the real thing, it used echo feedback to navigate. Lilah had spoken so proudly of her work. The design was brilliant. It had the potential to win awards and make her famous.

And Eden was about to destroy it.

Steeling herself to do what was necessary, she picked up the splintered table leg, opened the door, and stood in front of it, waiting. The dragon buzzed through the room, its powerful wings stirring the air and scattering papers. Sensors blinking, it shifted, heading for the now-vulnerable exit.

Years of baseball practice served Eden well. She caught the bat-dragon with a solid hit, sending it crashing across the room into the window. It crumpled to the floor, where it lay twitching. She raced over and found the switch to shut it down.

"Sorry, Lilah," she murmured. She scooped up the broken

dragon and patted its round, metal body. "Sorry, little guy. I hope you can be repaired."

Before Eden could gather herself to stash Lilah's ruined project with the others, the student who had helped her called out, "Hey, there's one more up on the stairs!"

Eden spun around. "No, wait!"

Too late. The student grabbed for Vox, who sensed an unknown handler and bit him in self-defense. The student yelped and flung her away. For a few terrifying seconds she tumbled through the air, before righting herself and fluttering about in a panic. Eden called her down and hugged her. Thank God she was undamaged. The same couldn't be said for so many other things in the lab.

Eden stroked the dragon's back. "Poor thing."

"That monster bit me!" the young man exclaimed, stumbling down the stairs. He cradled his injured hand. "I'm bleeding!"

"I'm so sorry. She thought you were a danger. Let me find something to bandage that."

"No, forget it. I'm fine."

His growled words and pinched expression made the lie obvious, but Eden didn't push him. She understood the need to be tough. "Thank you for helping me. It made a big difference. I think we saved much of the lab."

His anger faded. "You're welcome. Will you need help cleaning up the mess?"

"My father will have to do an assessment first, I think. If you come back tomorrow morning, I'm certain we could use the help."

"I'll do that, as long as that thing is locked up." He gestured at Vox.

Eden's lips pinched in a tight frown. The thought of Vox in a cage enraged her.

"Aw, hell," the student grumbled suddenly. His gaze was fixed on the floor. He bent and picked up the remains of a dragon—the turtle that couldn't keep upright. "It's ruined. Now what am I going to do?" He dumped the broken dragon into a rubbish bin and started for the door.

Poor man. He'd helped her out and been bitten by Vox for his troubles, and his project had been a hopeless disaster, even before she stepped on it. She would tell her father he had helped, and perhaps they could find him a tutor to help him build a functioning dragon.

"I'm afraid I never got your name," she called.

He paused and turned back. "Oh, of course. Marcus Heyward."

She nodded. "A pleasure, Mr. Heyward. I'm…"

"Eden Randall, I know. The weird girl."

Her jaw dropped. She couldn't even think up a reply until he was long gone. "Well, I never!" she complained to Vox.

She locked up the lab and started for home. Her father needed to know what had happened. They would formulate a plan.

And then she would take her bat and balls and go vent some frustration.

10

ⓑRUCE HAD DEVELOPED A HABIT of wandering during his stint as a reporter. Being so often in cities where he knew no one, he routinely found himself with nothing to do and very little money to spend. So he walked—through parks, through neighborhoods, down crowded streets. Any place that looked interesting was fair game. He tried not to trespass unnecessarily, but he'd hopped a few fences here and there. The duration of his stay in Ann Arbor was proving problematic. The town wasn't large, and he'd already memorized downtown and the campus. He'd been through many of the outlying neighborhoods. Today he was following the railroad tracks, just to be different.

He walked on the rail, putting one foot in front of the other, testing his balance. His knee was decidedly better since the repair and upgrade. The right leg would never match the left again for strength and stability, but he could walk like this and he could run. There'd been a time when he'd despaired of doing either.

Bruce followed the tracks to where they ran alongside the athletic grounds on their way out of town. A good place to turn back. There wasn't much else but farmland from here all the way to Toledo. He veered off toward Ferry Field. A quick peek at it while it was empty would give him a good comparison for a later article.

The smack of a bat dashed his hopes that he would be the only one there. Who would be practicing on a Sunday? Kids, perhaps? He wandered past the bleachers, needing to sate his curiosity.

Damn. He should have known.

Eden Randall stood on the football field, a baseball bat in her hand. A variety of balls and other sporting equipment lay in the grass nearby, along with an empty canvas sack. He watched as she scooped up a baseball, tossed it in the air, and hit it across the field. It landed near several other balls.

She had her back turned to him, so he paused and waited, interested to see this side of her.

Her assertion the other day that she was "quite a slugger" proved accurate. She struck the ball well, and hit it to the same spot every time. She was much practiced, it seemed.

He walked closer, not trying to conceal his footsteps. He didn't want to startle her. She hit one more ball before she noticed his presence.

"You are a talented batter, Miss Randall."

"Oh, Bruce! I missed you earlier. I stopped at your hotel, but you'd gone."

"I've been out walking most of the day. I'm ready to head back, if you'd like to read my article, but I wouldn't wish to disrupt your practice."

"It's not practice. It's therapy. I was upset. Someone made a mess of my father's lab."

"I'm sorry to hear that. Tagget?"

Her shoulders raised and dropped in a tiny shrug. "Perhaps, though I can't see what he would gain by it." She started for the opposite end of the field. "I'm going to hit all those balls back, and then I can go with you, if you're willing to wait that long."

He jogged after her. "Certainly. You have excellent power and accuracy. Can you hit off a pitcher?"

"Absolutely. Do you want to throw me a few?"

"Why not?"

They gathered the balls and he set up a good distance away from her. Bruce tossed her an easy ball first, right down the middle. She crushed it, landing it not far from her pile of equipment.

"Too easy. Throw me a real pitch."

He pitched her a fastball. She hit it even farther.

"Are you even trying?" she taunted.

He held up his hands. "Give me a break. This was never my best sport."

Determined to at least challenge her, he hurled a slider, the pitch he'd always thrown best. She handled it with no difficulty. He threw three more, with the same result, before giving up.

"You win. I can't pitch to you."

Eden grinned, slinging the bat over her shoulder. "I've hit off the varsity pitchers here. Most of them can strike me out more often than not, but it's great practice. Regular folks don't have a chance."

"I'm impressed you can hit on them at all."

"Oh, I hit better than some of the men on the team, only not as hard. The trouble is I can't run with them. My legs are too short to keep up. I wish there was a women's team." She tossed her bat beside her bag. "Want to play football? You'll stand a better chance of beating me."

Bruce didn't see how she could have a chance at all. Artificial knee or no, he was far bigger and stronger. But he couldn't resist her offer.

"Sure. What are your rules?"

"Take the ball, try to run to the end zone. What other rules do we need?"

"No gouging?"

She put her hands on her hips. "I wouldn't do that. This is a friendly game."

Friendly wasn't how he would have classified it. The mere thought of tackling her caused a stirring in his groin. Even getting an arm around her would be a thrill.

Eden tossed him the ball. "I'll let you go first. Let's start mid-field."

They lined up, facing one another across the ball. She wore a wide grin. His own mouth curved in response. Her enthusiasm was infectious.

Bruce feared he might hurt her if he ran straight at her, or that he might trip over Vox, who hopped and fluttered a few yards behind her. Going wide was the better option. He snapped the ball and ran out to the right. Only a few steps and he would be away from her shorter stride and able to get around her.

He never had the chance. Her reactions were lightning quick, and she flung herself at him with the entire weight of her small frame. He might have remained upright had he been braced for the tackle, but he wasn't, and he went down hard.

"Ugh." He climbed to his feet and reset the ball. "You play tough."

"Of course. Second down."

"I'll be ready this time."

He wasn't. She changed tactics entirely. She didn't even attempt to tackle, instead putting her shoulder directly into the ball. It squirted free, and she scooped it up and scampered down the field and across the goal line. Vox flew after her, little mechanical wings flapping vigorously to keep up.

"Five points!" Eden cheered, doing a little dance of celebration. She wasn't the most gracious of victors.

Bruce jogged over to her side. "Okay, let's see your try at goal."

Her lips puckered into a grimace. "I'm a terrible kicker."

"Try anyhow."

"Fine," she sighed. She lined up and attempted a drop kick. The ball spun off at an angle, going no more than ten yards. "See?"

"I should make you kick off to me," he chuckled.

Eden tossed him the ball. "I'll give you the forty."

"No, no. It's your turn to be on offense. Midfield again, like before."

She shrugged. "If you like losing."

She was too cocky. It was time to step up his game. No holding back because she was small or because she was a woman.

She snapped the ball and darted left. She was quick, and made sharp cuts, but Bruce had been an athlete for most of his life, and he hadn't given up sport entirely since his injury. He caught her around the waist. Her legs didn't stop, but his size advantage was too great, and he hauled her down on top of him.

They lay on the grass, unmoving, the game in a sudden state of limbo. He held her in a wildly inappropriate manner, both arms around her waist, the length of her body crushed against his. Soft, subtle curves. Just the right fit for his arms.

Bruce inhaled deeply. Eden Randall smelled of lavender and citrus. With her honey-colored hair tumbled about her shoulders, her blue eyes bright, and cheeks pink from the exercise, she looked straight from a fairy story. Wild. Energetic. A mischievous spirit born to the outdoors.

He didn't think she realized she'd never hit the ground, and the ball wasn't yet down. A flick of his wrist to knock it away and he could score easily. Instead he kissed her.

She melted into him. Her arms wrapped around his neck, her football rolling off into the grass, forgotten.

Bruce groaned. Eden tasted divine and kissed with a reckless abandon not unlike the way she played sports. He coaxed her lips apart and explored her mouth, relishing her gasp of surprised pleasure. Her kiss was raw and hungry.

Uninhibited. Unashamed. Desire sparked along his skin, burning its way down to his tightening groin.

He pulled away abruptly. This had gone far enough. He wouldn't be the sort of jackass who would ravish an innocent girl in the middle of a football gridiron. He lifted her off of him and sat up. A dazed expression lingered in her eyes. His own brain took its time coming out of the fog. The sight of the football lying in the grass brought him down to earth.

"Back to the game, Miss Randall?"

"Huh?"

Bruce regained his feet and picked up the ball. "You were never down, I'm afraid." He jogged toward the goal. She scrambled after him, but his head-start was insurmountable. Tie game.

Eden stopped running, stalked up to him, and slapped him across the face. The blow left him reeling. She snatched her ball from his hands and stormed away.

When he came to his senses, he followed her. "Eden, I'm sorry."

She thrust her equipment into the bag, ignoring him, jaw tight and muscles clenched.

"I should never have kissed you. I apologize."

She didn't reply, only shoved her bat into the tote and cinched it closed.

"I would never have done it if I'd thought it would upset you."

Eden slung the bag over her shoulder, almost hitting him with it. "You cheated," she snarled. "Vox, come!" The dragon flew up into her arms and she strode toward the exit.

"What? Eden..." He trailed after her.

"You cheated," she repeated. "You're a cheater. You tricked me with that... that *thing* your tongue was doing. You made me forget where I was. That's not fair."

Bruce, still in a bit of a stupor himself, took several seconds to process her words.

"That isn't why I kissed you."

"I don't care."

"I'm sorry."

"Good."

"What can I do to apologize…"

"You can leave me alone."

He slowed to a stop and watched her stomp away. His cheek stung where she had slapped him. A deservedly painful reminder of his idiocy.

"Goddammit."

He couldn't let it end this way. He liked Eden. Was crazy about her, in fact. She was smart and fun and quirky. She kissed with a passion that left him breathless. Their friendship had only just begun, and he wasn't about to let one stupid mistake destroy it.

He stooped to collect a stray baseball that sat against the fence. In her hurry to pack up she had missed it. He would return it, along with an apology. A written apology. Perhaps with flowers. Did she like flowers? He had no idea. He ran through a list of things he knew she did like: sports, books, music, beer, her dragon.

He would come up with something. Bruce Caldwell was no quitter. He flexed his biomechanical knee. When things went awry, he fixed them.

11

October 11

"How could they do this to us?" Eden exclaimed.

"Who's that, dear?" her father asked, not looking up from his own paper. She had joined him for lunch in the laboratory, a brief respite before they resumed cleanup.

"Columbia!"

"The university?"

"Yes! They won't play us! Listen to this. 'The Michigan football management regretfully announces that there will be no Columbia-Michigan game on Thanksgiving day.' Morley sent a letter. He calls it 'ill-advised'! How can they do this?"

He set his paper down and blinked at her. "Who is this Morley person?"

"Their coach! He told us he was in favor of the game. More than once! The white-livered scoundrel!"

"Eden!" he gasped. "There is no call for coarse language."

"It was to be our proof," she moaned. "The whole country was going to see that we can play against anyone!"

"Eden, dear, you are taking this very hard. It's only a game, isn't it?"

She sighed. "You don't understand, Father. You don't like football."

"No, and I don't understand what you see in it. It's violent and incomprehensible."

There was no point in explaining. She'd tried before to no avail. She folded the paper and tucked it under her arm. Bruce needed to know at once. He had to report this to the Boston paper before they printed some skewed view coming out of Columbia.

A nervous shiver ran down her spine at the thought of seeing him again. She should never have slapped him. Yes, he'd cheated and flustered her with his astounding kisses, but that didn't justify her physical violence. Angry words would have been enough.

Her finger touched her lips before she realized what she was doing, and she jerked it away. The kiss had haunted her ever since, taunting her, leaving her torn between desire and fury. It had been everything she'd hoped for until he'd tossed her aside and taken advantage of her muddled mind. She'd wanted him to kiss her because he liked her, not as part of some game. Now she was unsure whether she'd give him that chance.

Today, however, she had other pressing concerns.

"Are you leaving?" her father asked. "There's work to be done yet. I want to be able to hold class as usual tomorrow."

"I won't be long. I have to find someone. I'll be back before you finish your lunch." She rushed out the door before he could protest further, leaving her own lunch uneaten on the table.

She walked briskly down the hall, mulling over the best way to find Bruce. He could be at the hotel, but it was a dull sort of place to spend time. If he were out to lunch he could be at any number of places. Prochnow's Dairy Lunch would be her first guess. The casual eatery was popular with young working men.

A door opened somewhere behind her, but she ignored it and kept walking.

"Well, if it isn't the enchanting Miss Randall."

Eden couldn't mistake that voice in the silent hall. She turned, heaving a small sigh. "Mr. Tagget. How are you?"

"In excellent spirits. Yourself?"

"Rather annoyed, in fact."

He hurried toward her, his cheerful expression morphing into a frown of concern. "I'm sorry to hear that. I heard something about a mishap in your father's lab? What can I do to help?"

"Nothing. The lab is coming along well. I'm annoyed by something else. Please excuse me."

"Of course. I won't keep you. When you have time, please stop by and see me at Professor Hart's lab, or in the evening at the American Hotel. I have a list of upcoming concerts and shows, and I would love to hear which ones interest you. I understand there is also a dance academy in town that holds evening dances, if that appeals to you. I know you love music."

"Yes, but I'm a poor dancer, I'm afraid."

"I doubt that. Your every step is full of energy and passion."

"You're very kind. Excuse me." She turned away before he could come up with something else to talk about. She wouldn't let herself get distracted with thoughts of concerts.

She reached the front door and shoved it open. Someone on the opposite side yelped.

"Oops."

Eden stepped gingerly through the doorway, prepared to receive a rebuke for her carelessness. She hoped it wasn't a professor.

"Eden!" Bruce exclaimed. He looked his usual, casual self today, with his sleeves rolled up to his elbows, a tweed cap, and green suspenders that didn't match the rest of his outfit. Like her, he held a newspaper in one hand.

They blinked at one another for several seconds.

"Have you been standing there waiting for me to arrive so you could bash me with the door in retribution for kissing you?" he asked. It sounded like a joke, but his expression was serious.

"I told you, it wasn't the kissing. It was the cheating." Color rose in her cheeks. "Did I really bash you? It was an accident."

"No, I had a narrow escape. Are you off somewhere? May I walk with you? I was on my way to find you."

"I was looking for you, as well," she confessed.

"You've heard then?"

"The game?"

"Yes."

"Isn't it just awful?"

"It's unfortunate, but don't fret. It won't reflect badly on your Michigan boys. Scores like ninety-five to nothing leave an impression. Columbia will look cowardly for declining."

"I so wanted to watch us wallop an Eastern team," she sighed. "And I was going to go to New York!" She glanced behind her, in case Tagget was still hanging around. "Without an invitation from a certain industrialist," she added quietly.

"I'm sure you can come up with some other reason to visit the city, Miss Randall. Will you be traveling down to Ohio for the game this weekend?"

She made a face. "Why would I want to go *there*?"

Bruce frowned at her in puzzlement. "You have something against Ohio?"

"They stole Toledo from us! You know all those nice glass bottles that come from Toledo? Those should be Michigan bottles!"

"Er…" He regarded her with raised eyebrows. Outsiders never understood.

"At least we have the Upper Peninsula. It has copper mines, and it's beautiful. You need to visit someday. Come inside, I didn't get to finish my lunch and I'm hungry."

He shrugged and followed her.

"You'll write an article about this Columbia fiasco, won't you?" she asked. "Tell everyone how they mistreated us?"

"I submitted one this morning."

"Oh, excellent! I apologize if the lab is rather disorganized this afternoon. We spent all day yesterday cleaning up the mess from the dragons that were set loose, and today we're finishing up repairs."

"I will keep that in mind."

She showed him to the door and waved him inside. He took only a few steps before stumbling to a halt and staring.

"Whoa."

"I know. It looks terrible. I apologize."

"No, it's not that. It's much larger than I expected. And full of so many gadgets and, um, things. My apologies, Miss Randall, but I've never been in an Automechanology and Teletics laboratory. It's astonishing. You'll have to give me the grand tour."

"Certainly." She led him first to the table where her father sat, still reading his paper. "This is the table that fell on me the other day. We've replaced the shattered leg with a steel rod. And this is my lunch, if you don't mind me eating it while we walk about." She picked up her sandwich.

His brows knitted, but then he shrugged. "Please, feel free."

Her father set his paper down for the second time that afternoon. "Eden, are you going to introduce me to your friend?"

"Oh, sorry. Father, this is Bruce Caldwell. He's a reporter. From Boston."

"Ah, so that's why you've been reading the Herald so diligently of late."

Eden's cheeks burned again.

"Is he the fellow who took you to that concert the other night?"

"No, that was Mr. Tagget. Didn't I tell you that?"

"Tagget? The businessman who wants to buy up all my ideas?"

"Yes." A strange embarrassment washed over her, and she wasn't sure why. She was old enough to go out with whomever she pleased. It was all so odd, having multiple suitors after being ignored for so long. She took Bruce by the elbow and started away from the table to avoid any further discussion of the matter. "Here, let me show you how the big fan works."

She wandered all about the room with him, explaining the machinery to the best of her ability. On several occasions she had to admit she wasn't entirely certain what some particular tool or automaton did.

Several students sat scattered about the room, making repairs to both dragons and equipment, including Mr. Heyward of the turtle dragon. Most were too busy to even acknowledge Eden. Since she now knew they referred to her as "the weird girl," her desire to talk to them had dropped near to zero anyway.

In the far corner of the room, a secluded nook where the more advanced students did individual project work, she found Lilah hunched over her dragon. At last, someone she *did* want to talk to.

"Lilah!" she exclaimed. "How did I not know you were here? Have you been hiding out in the corner all day?"

Lilah glanced up, a smile creeping over her pretty face. "I have. I'm doing repairs."

Eden let her eyes drop to Lilah's work. The broken bat-dragon lay on the table in several pieces, its outer shell caved in where Eden's improvised bat had struck him.

"Oh, Lilah, I'm so sorry. I was the one who ruined him, you know. He was trying to escape. And he had such impressive sensing technology!"

"Not to worry. I'll make him better than before."

"Good. Then everyone will have to believe you are the best in the whole department."

"People will believe what they wish. But *I* will know what I have achieved."

"As will I. And I'll proclaim it to all who will listen."

Lilah worked twice as hard as her white male classmates for a fraction of the recognition. Perhaps no one would listen to "the weird girl," but nothing would stop Eden from promoting her friend's inventions. Someday, Lilah would receive the praise she deserved.

"Of course you will. And I'll help you argue in favor of your women's sporting teams."

The two women clasped hands for a moment. Their passions may have differed—Lilah preferred quiet teas and garden parties to beer and sports—but two years of books, music, and weekend canoe trips on the river had cemented their friendship into an unbreakable bond.

"May I ask who your gentleman friend is?"

Drat. Once again Eden had forgotten introductions.

"Oh, yes. I'm sorry. Lilah, please allow me to present Bruce Caldwell, from Boston. Bruce, this is Miss Lilah St. James. Lilah is my father's most brilliant student."

Bruce tipped his hat. "A pleasure, Miss St. James. That's an interesting creature you're working on. Does it fly?"

"It did," Lilah answered.

Eden cringed. "Until I clobbered him. I cracked the window, too."

"He will fly again. The new wings will be lighter so he won't take as much power."

"Well, if you need any help or any tools, let me know. I feel awful about it. I didn't know what else to do to stop him from knocking things down and trying to escape."

"You did the right thing, Miss Randall. I'll be adding your father's voice controls this time to keep him better under control in the future."

"Still, I feel bad seeing him all dented and giving you extra work."

Lilah smiled sweetly. "You're a doll. We'll both be just fine."

Eden blushed. Again. This was happening all too often today.

"I'll leave you to your work. See you at the library tomorrow?"

"It's a date."

Bruce tipped his cap to Lilah once more before turning away. "Nice to meet you, Miss St. James. Good luck with your dragon."

"Here, let me show you the others," Eden decided. "We keep them in a big closet on the opposite end of the lab. I broke several while rounding them up, but we managed to save most."

"They were loose, you said?"

"Yes. Someone turned them all on and left them to run about the lab. It damaged a lot of things, including the dragons."

"Strange." He whispered something, but she couldn't make it out.

"I'm sorry, I couldn't hear that."

Bruce stepped closer, not understanding that it wouldn't make a difference. She shook her head.

"Here." She waved him into the storage closet. If he wanted to say something confidential, she would find them some privacy. She called to Vox, but before the dragon reached them the door banged closed, plunging the closet into total darkness.

Eden shrieked. Panicked hands groped for the door, desperate to restore her most vital sense. She collided with Bruce. Her fingers clutched his shirt and she buried her face against his chest. He was strong, warm, safe, even in the darkness. She inhaled deeply of his scent, letting her remaining senses ease some of the terror.

The door opened a few seconds later. Vox scampered inside and rubbed up against Eden's leg. Eden's clenched fingers relaxed, but she remained pressed to Bruce's chest, still reeling from the shock.

"Gracious me, I'm so sorry!" Marcus Heyward babbled. "I saw that beast heading for the closet and tried to cut it off before it did any damage. I had no notion you were inside until I heard the scream. Please forgive me."

He eyed her for a moment, his brow furrowing and his mouth curving downward. Bruce edged away from her, gently loosening her grip on his clothing.

Oh, bother. She wasn't supposed to cling to a gentleman in a public place, was she? Or be alone with one in a closet, probably, though she didn't remember that particular situation arising in any of her novels. If it was a rule in one of those books of manners, she'd never know. She'd tried to read one, once, and it had been so dry and condescending she'd hollowed it out for use as a secret storage box. And she *never* defaced books.

Eden picked up Vox and fixed Heyward with a harsh stare.

"Vox isn't a beast, Mr. Heyward, and she won't damage anything or anyone unless she's in danger. I'm sorry to have distracted you. Please, return to your turtle."

A pained expression crossed his face. "I'm not doing schoolwork today. I'm replacing dented or cracked pieces on machinery and inspecting wires for fraying or other damage. I'm hoping to receive a bit of extra credit for my efforts."

"Of course. Carry on." She was just annoyed enough not to tell him her father didn't give extra credit. "When you do build your new project, try making an individual appointment with my father, or if that doesn't suit, Miss St. James gives excellent tutorials on schematics."

"Thank you," he replied, and turned away, his posture stiff. She doubted he would heed her advice.

Eden looked up at Bruce, remembering the reason for entering the closet in the first place. Even with her sight and hearing restored, her sense of touch remained inflamed. Her skin prickled at his nearness, and his scent of cloves and cedarwood still filled her nostrils. It took all her self-control not to slide up against him once more.

"Now you can whisper." She set Vox on her shoulder and twisted her earring to make certain the volume was at its highest level.

He got straight to the point, as if the interruption had never happened. "Does anyone hold a grudge against your father, or have a reason to wish to ruin his work?"

"Not that I know of. This was more an inconvenience than anything else. All the important projects are kept at home or are locked up in my father's personal cabinet. It's extremely sturdy and only he, my mother, and I can open it. He copies all his papers for safekeeping and stores the extras at home. Too many mishaps can occur in a laboratory—fires and explosions and the like. I didn't show you the copying machine yet, did I?"

"No."

"It's spectacular. The department has a five-year goal to develop a version that can read something in one room and make a copy in another. I'm sorry, I'm wandering off topic. I haven't thought of any reason for this incident other than to be a vicious prank. It hurt the students more than anyone. If I hadn't come in on a Sunday, I suspect things would have continued until all of these were ruined." She waved her hand at the shelves of dragons around her.

"Strange. I hope the culprit can be discovered. I don't like to think that you or your family may be at risk of harm."

His words of concern caused a giddy shiver to run the length of her body. Her lips tingled. Standing there, so close to him, where no one else could see, sparked a powerful urge to kiss him. Would he welcome another kiss? A kiss for her alone, with no ulterior motives? How did one find out that sort of thing? Could she ask him outright?

Her books were terribly unhelpful in this situation. They contained very little kissing, and most of that was only alluded to.

Regardless, they were too much in public for kissing. Heyward might come wandering by again and scold them. Eden stepped toward the door, putting enough space between herself and Bruce that her body began to relax.

"Thank you. I'm sure we'll be fine. Let me show you the copying machine, and then, I'm afraid, I should get back to work."

The copying machine had sustained minor damage during the dragon fiasco, and wasn't in operation, but Bruce marveled at it, nonetheless.

"Ingenious! I can't wait to see this again, once everything is up and running. Might I come back for another visit at a later date?"

"Yes, of course. I'm here often, you know."

"Yes, I know." His crooked smile drew her attention back to his lips. Pink. Soft. Tasty. "Thank you for the tour, Miss Randall. I appreciate you introducing a poor liberal arts major to the remarkable world of science and engineering. I won't keep you from your repairs any longer."

Eden waved goodbye and watched him go, a flicker of disappointment creeping over her. Drat. She should have kissed him.

"Father," she called, "Did Sunday's copy of the Boston Herald arrive yet?"

12

October 12

SEVEN-AND-ONE-HALF MINUTES into the second half, the officials called the game on account of darkness. Eden didn't mind. It was only a mid-week game, and the Varsity had put up seventy-two points in the highly abbreviated contest. A satisfactory result. A perfect night to walk home with a smile on her face and curl up with a book until bedtime.

A half-hearted smile was all she could muster. All game long her eyes had darted about, looking for flashy suspenders and a newsboy cap. It only made sense that Bruce would watch the game from up above with other members of the press, but she missed his presence on the sideline. Even now, after the game, she saw no sign of him. Perhaps he was avoiding her.

After their amiable conversation in the laboratory yesterday, she'd thought their friendship was on the mend. Surely they had put the kissing incident behind them. Or he had. She couldn't stop thinking of it.

Eden pulled her gaze away from the crowd, back down to the mechanical wolverine at her feet. She flicked the switch to shut it down and hefted it up and into its storage crate. A flip of the lid and a few latches, and the dragon was safely packed up until the next home game. Her friend Joey, a burly blond perpetually trying to grow out his youthful whiskers, grabbed one end of the crate. One of his teammates grabbed the opposite end, and the men started off. Eden followed them, grabbing a water jug to help out.

"We'll miss you on Saturday," Joey told her.

"I'll miss you, too. Give 'em hell."

He laughed. "Eden, you'd better not let anyone else hear you talking like that. It's not ladylike."

She shrugged. "I don't care."

"You should. Don't you want to get married someday?"

Eden stopped walking and fixed her friend with a puzzled stare. She did, in fact, want to get married someday, though it wasn't something she'd been imminently hoping for. She had a fine life and a home she loved, and couldn't consider marriage unless she found a man who wouldn't try to take her away from that or think he could control her life. She'd been content to wait. The niggling thought that perhaps no such man existed made her bite her lower lip in annoyance.

"Why would someone not marry me because I said 'hell'?" she asked. "I mean, unless he wrote one of those awful manners books, but I wouldn't want to marry such a stodgy person, anyway."

"Eden, men don't like girls who swear and do unladylike things."

"*You* like me."

"Yes, but I sure as hell wouldn't marry you."

She flinched. Pain stabbed her gut. The peculiarity of her hobbies and behavior had never before struck her as anything terrible. After all, she'd grown up physically different from most people she knew, and had lived a perfectly happy life.

True, some shunned her or called her weird, but the people she cared for accepted her as she was. Or so she had believed.

Apparently, she was so odd even her friends found her undesirable. Not that she would ever have considered marrying Joey. Far from it. The very idea was repellant. He was much too brotherly. It hurt, though, to know he didn't think her worthy of romantic consideration.

"So you can say 'hell' and no one cares, but if I do, I'm unmarriageable."

"It's different."

"Unloveable."

"You're a girl."

"You're an ass. And I'll have you know I've already had a man propose to me. I rejected him. Right now I have *two* intelligent and handsome gentlemen interested in me. So excuse me if I don't believe you have any idea what men like." She slammed the water jug down on top of the wolverine's crate. "And you can carry your own damn water."

"Eden, I didn't mean…"

She twisted her earring until she couldn't hear him and stalked away.

Her furious strides carried her swiftly downtown, to her favorite saloon, where she ordered herself a beer and hunkered down in her corner, feeling sorry for herself. She watched the door as she nursed her drink. She hadn't caught Bruce at the game, but there was a chance he would seek her out here. *He* didn't think her undesirable. Maybe. If he'd been honest about the reasons for that kiss.

She swirled the glass. Sipped the beer. Stared. Men wandered in and out. Students, mostly. Young, cheerful, often handsome. Their eyes drifted past her as if she didn't even exist. By the time her glass was empty she'd given up hope.

Eden didn't often drink more than one beer at a time. Some of the local brewers made their drinks strong, and with her small size she got tipsy easily. Tonight, however, she was frustrated and lonely without a friend to talk to. She wanted to sit and drink and mope.

Leaving Vox to guard her seat, she wandered over to the bar to order another drink. She was reaching for her purse when a hand stretched past her and placed a few coins on the counter. She looked up to see Bruce standing beside her, a grin lighting his face.

Her heart leapt, and she yelped, too startled to even attempt an intelligible sound.

"You're here!" she blurted at last. Several people turned to stare at her. She couldn't hear well in the noisy saloon with Vox so far away and she'd spoken too loudly.

Bruce said something in reply, but she couldn't pick out his words among the other sounds.

"I'm sorry, I didn't catch that."

She focused on his lips for his reply. "I said, 'Good evening, Miss Randall,'" she thought he said.

"Good evening," she replied.

The bartender set two pints of beer on the counter, and Bruce picked them both up. Eden led him to the table where Vox waited. "Thank you for the drink."

"My pleasure. I was hoping to find you here." He pulled out her chair for her before taking his own seat.

"I've been here for a long time. I'd thought you must not be coming tonight."

"I had an article to submit. There wasn't much to say about the game, so I combined it with the answers to some of the questions about practices. Would you like to read my messy draft?"

"Yes, please. And the Columbia article?"

"Of course."

He passed over his notebook and she flipped through it in delight. She'd grown accustomed to his handwriting, and devoured the new articles in no time. Before returning the journal, she paused to scan the article from Saturday's game.

"I read this one in the paper yesterday. The last line is wonderful. 'Perhaps the university should consider funding the development of automatic scoreboards or returning to old technologies, as the boy cranking the current mechanical behemoth after every touchdown seemed exhausted by the end of the game.'" She laughed. "I asked my father what he thought about automatic scoreboards."

"Did you? What did he say?"

"'Why would anyone want such a thing? Can't they write the score on a slateboard?'"

"He needs to read my article."

"He did! He was so curious after you visited the lab he had to read some of your writing. He *never* reads sports articles. I'm not sure what he thought of it. He just made some grunting noises and then put down the paper and went back to his work."

"I can't please everyone, I suppose."

"You please me."

His eyebrows arched, and she got the feeling she'd said something not quite right. He didn't laugh at her, however, nor did his smile fade.

"Thank you. It's always nice to have one's work appreciated."

His low voice made her insides quiver. His brown eyes had softened to the color of liquid chocolate. Butterflies danced in her stomach, and the kissing incident began to replay in her head.

Eden shook her head. It was only the second beer making her mind fuzzy. She would have to sit here for a while before she walked home. She needed conversation to pass the time. Safe conversation that didn't make her think of his hands or his mouth.

"Tell me something about you that isn't about sports," she said. "Do you like books?"

"I love books. I believe I told you my degree is in English Literature."

"What's your favorite?"

"My favorite? I couldn't possibly say. There are so many to choose from. I could list dozens."

"Tell me a few. We can compare."

"Everything by Shakespeare. Jane Eyre. Conrad's Heart of Darkness. Robinson Crusoe. Shall I go on?"

"Yes, please."

Eden soon discovered that Bruce had read at least as many books as she had. What most fascinated her was how their tastes diverged. He enjoyed many books she thought boring, including everything by the Brontë sisters, and he didn't understand her love of monster stories and grisly war memoirs. The conversation was so engaging that by the time she checked her watch it was half-past ten.

"Goodness! How did it get to be so late? I'm sorry, but I must cut our chat short. My parents will be wondering where I am."

Bruce rose when she did. "May I walk you home, Miss Randall?"

He didn't give up, that was certain. She hesitated a moment, considering.

"Yes," she said at last. "If you answer a question, and answer it truthfully."

"Certainly."

"Why did you kiss me? Truthfully."

"Because I was having fun and you smelled nice and looked beautiful and felt so good in my arms."

Her mouth opened in a little O, but no words came.

"Truthful enough?"

She could only nod. She led the way out the door, Vox riding on her shoulder.

"My turn for a question?" Bruce inquired.

"Okay."

"Why did you slap me? Truthfully."

She sighed. She had already explained this. "Because you cheated. There's no kissing in football."

"You didn't specify that in your rules."

She had to concede the point. "Fine. Next time, any kissing results in an automatic time out until all parties have recovered sufficiently, whereupon play will resume from the location of the infraction. If such kissing should occur before the conclusion of a down, five yards will be awarded to the party kissed."

His hearty laugh echoed in the near-empty street. "You have made my evening, Miss Randall. Not only have you indicated you have forgiven me enough to consider another sporting match in our future, but your rules imply you would welcome my affections."

"I could be speaking in purely hypothetical terms. How do you know I don't have dozens of men lining up to kiss me?"

"I'm sure you do, but how many of them have a biomechanical leg and have witnessed the Olympic Games?"

Eden giggled. "Fine qualities, indeed!"

He grinned. Her whole body warmed beneath that lovely smile. Even in the dim glow of the streetlights she could see the sparkle in his deep, brown eyes. Did her eyes dance in the light when she looked at him?

"On a more serious note, Miss Randall, I should very much like to take you out again. I will be traveling with the football team this weekend, but I would love to arrange something for Monday, if you are available. I hear there's a roller rink in town."

"Yes! I would love to go."

Her eyes *were* sparkling. She just knew it. She could feel it somehow.

"Excellent. I'm available at your convenience. Let me know what time suits you and whether you prefer to meet there or have me pick you up. If you can't find me, leave a note at the hotel."

"I'll do that, thank you."

The streets grew darker as they left downtown behind

them. She led him under the railroad bridge, and down the road toward her house.

"The creek is off in that direction," she told him, waving a hand to her left. "I used to play in it often as a child. I still splash in it now and then on hot days. Up here is a school I didn't go to, though I used to hide in the bushes and watch the other children. Sometimes I played ball with them, but it was always awkward because we couldn't understand each other. My house is just up ahead."

"Nice place," Bruce commented when they reached her home. The old gaslight in the front yard was lit. Her parents always left it on when she was out at night. She paused to turn it off on her way to the porch. An interior light shone in the front hall, providing just enough illumination for anyone entering the house.

"Thank you. It's large for three people, but the entire basement and some of the ground floor are taken up by my parents' laboratories. Our library is actually upstairs with the bedrooms."

"I can't say any of that surprises me too much. I bet you like having the books so near at hand."

"I've been found more than once asleep on the library floor," she admitted.

Eden set foot on the first step. They were close enough that Vox recognized home and hopped down from her perch. She scampered over to a small door set in the wall and prodded the button with her metal head. Gears clanked and the door rolled open. She sat and waited. She wouldn't enter until Eden commanded her or opened the human-sized front door.

"Well, that's nifty," Bruce commented.

Eden turned around to look at him. He wasn't quite as close as he had been the other day on the steps of the laboratory building, but near enough to see his face in the dim light.

"Isn't it? My mother invented it so she could send a dragon out to fetch newspapers. We have so many delivered, and some inevitably are dumped on the lawn. Two years ago when Vox was updated we taught her to use the door."

"I like it." He tipped his cap to her. "Goodnight, Miss Randall. Thank you for allowing me to see you home. I had a wonderful time this evening, and I look forward to our next outing."

"Me too."

He nodded and turned away.

"Bruce?" she called.

He stopped, turned, stepped a bit closer. "Yes?"

"I know walking and talking isn't as much fun as playing football, but…" She hesitated, hoping she wouldn't sound foolish. "But I think you look beautiful and will feel wonderful in my arms."

He lifted a hand and his thumb grazed her cheek. "I had similar thoughts."

She lunged at him, wrapping her arms around his neck to keep from falling. He caught her about the waist. Their lips met. She felt his tongue slide over her lips in a slick caress. Her entire body tingled. He didn't kiss her the way Paul had kissed her. That had been pleasant. This was… sensational. Bruce was warm, wet heat and deep, fiery longing. Eden wanted to melt into him.

Each movement of his tongue sent fire racing through her body. Little whimpers of pleasure rose in her throat. When she plunged her own tongue between his lips, Bruce moaned against her mouth. No wonder her novels never went into detail. Words couldn't properly convey the dizzying excitement. The mad desire. Her body was alive with it. Her breasts felt strangely heavy beneath her corset. The junction of her thighs grew hot and moist. Bruce was hard where she was soft, he was bigger, stronger, and all she could think was, *More, more, more.*

He pulled away, his chest rising and falling in jagged breaths, his lips glistening from their kisses. His absence left a hole somewhere inside her. She shivered, the night air suddenly cold. Monday seemed years away.

"Make sure you find me and say goodbye before you leave for Ohio," she instructed. *Make sure you kiss me again.*

"I will," he promised. "Goodnight, Eden."

"Goodnight."

She watched him until he disappeared into the darkness before she entered the house. She traced her lips with one finger, finding them swollen and sensitive. The taste of him lingered on her tongue.

More.

There was more, and she wanted it. More kisses. More... him.

Eden stumbled up the stairs, her mind reeling. She would kiss him again. And then she would find the answer to the question that now plagued her.

What came next?

13

October 15

EDEN STARED AT THE TELEPHONE that hung on the wall in her father's office. Why hadn't it rung? She was sure she'd told Mr. Hughes she would be here. Even if he'd tried calling her at home, her parents would have answered and told him where she was. The silent phone could only mean one thing. The team wasn't scoring.

Eden had a long-standing agreement with Mr. Hughes from the telegraph office. When the team played out-of-town he would call her with updates as they came in over the telegraph wires. Several years earlier, she'd taken up the habit of sitting at the telegraph office with a book, waiting for scores. After observing this phenomenon throughout the season, Mr. Hughes approached her and suggested she might prefer remaining at home and having the scores telephoned in. It had been their custom ever since.

Eden looked down at her gutless insect. She had no idea

what to do with it. She didn't intend it to be anything more than a toy, but even so it needed to do something more than skitter about. Right now her mind was as hollow as the dragon. All she could think about was football, wondering what could possibly be happening.

She lifted the back shell off the dragon. It snapped off with a satisfying click. That part she had done well, at least. There was plenty of room to insert and connect the wind-up mechanism that would power the legs. She would finish that today.

Eden wandered out of the office—a curtained-off area beside the storage closet housing a desk and a bookshelf— and into the laboratory proper. She pulled open several small drawers in the spare parts chest, looking for bits to make good legs. Those would be easy. She had made a number of "spiders" as a child by attaching some number of legs—rarely the proper eight—to scrap metal bodies. As she'd grown older, she'd learned how to construct joints and to attach the legs to motors.

"Excuse… Miss Randall… past… the toolbox?"

Eden paused, trying to process the not-entirely audible words. She glanced up to find Marcus Heyward staring impatiently at her. Apparently she had heard his mumbling well enough. He had plenty of room to get by, but she took a few steps back to avoid an argument. Since he'd made a special request to be here on the weekend working on his dragon, she would be nice. Unless he made another disparaging remark about Vox.

The phone rang at last, and Eden raced over to answer it. Telephones weren't suited for her biomechanics, but in a quiet setting where she could position the receiver close to Vox's internal listening mechanism, they became usable. And Mr. Hughes was very kind if she asked for anything to be repeated.

He gave her the word from Ohio. Touchdown. The try was no good. Five to nothing.

Feeling a bit better, she returned to her work. She

picked out pieces for the legs and fetched her favorite tool: the handheld, luxene-powered welding device her father had affectionately dubbed a whatchamajigger. She had the first leg fully assembled before she began to glare at the phone again, irritated it didn't ring. She moved on to the second leg. There would be six in all, a proper insect.

The phone rang for a second time in the middle of her third leg. She dropped her work and picked up the receiver. The second half was a few minutes in, Mr. Hughes informed her, before he gave her the updated score.

"What?" she exclaimed. She adjusted the position of the receiver. She must have misheard.

"Five to six," Hughes repeated.

"Thank you." Eden hung up the phone. "Good lord," she blurted. "How did this happen?"

"Miss Randall?" Marcus called out. "Is something wrong?"

Eden pushed the curtain aside and wandered toward him, hoping for someone to commiserate with. "Yes! They've scored on us. We're losing!"

He blinked at her. "Who's losing?"

"The football team! Don't you know they're playing down at Ohio State today?"

"Oh. I don't follow football."

"Ugh!"

Eden stomped back to the office. She put her head in her hands and stared at her bug. She would never finish. What horrors were occurring down in Columbus? How could she function under this sort of stress? She forced herself to continue on with the third leg, though it took her twice as long as it ought to have.

Soon enough, the phone rang for a third time. Touchdown, try good. Eleven to six. Then a fourth time. Field goal. Fifteen to six. Whatever the trouble had been, it had been fixed. Eden's muscles relaxed and her heart rate slowed. She threw herself into her work with renewed enthusiasm as the phone continued to ring. Another field goal and two more touchdowns finished off the game, and Eden finished the legs. She bounced happily to the parts chest to get a wind-up motor. It may have been ugly, but it was a win.

"Final score, thirty-one to six," she announced to Marcus as she passed by.

"It's over, then? Thank goodness. That phone was driving me mad."

Eden suspected good manners called for an apology, but she wasn't sorry. She tried to appease him by praising his work instead.

"That looks much improved," she said. The new turtle had shorter legs which were spaced apart in a more stable arrangement. The head was smaller, and it had a tail for added balance. The shell was currently off, and the internal parts looked to be well laid out. The motor was a good size, and it had a luxene fuel tube rather than a wind-up mechanism.

"Thank you. I hope to finish it today so I can enter it in the race next week."

Eden nodded, but didn't reply. She was skeptical. The new design was functionally far better, but the dragon itself didn't look sturdy enough for heavy use. The metal casing was thin, and the welds were weak. The connection points were too few in number and spaced too far apart. It wasn't unlike her father's prototypes in that regard. He made them only as short-term demonstration pieces, then recycled the parts. If he wanted something permanent, he asked her mother to build it.

"Good luck," Eden offered, regardless. "It's nice to see how much you've progressed. Did you take a private session with my father or did you find a tutor to help you understand schematics?"

A scowl flashed across his face. "I did the design myself."

Liar. The leap from the old turtle to the new was too drastic. "My apologies. I suppose it does get easier the second time around."

"Yes."

The phone rang, startling her. What could've happened now? The game was over.

"Excuse me, I should answer that." She jogged back to the office. At least the mysterious call had broken up the awkward conversation.

Picking up the telephone, she set the receiver into a stable position on the desk and adjusted Vox's placement beside it, instructing her to stay. "Hello. This is Eden Randall," she said into the mouthpiece.

"Eden. Hi. It's Bruce."

"Bruce? You're... calling from Ohio?"

"Yeah. I need some input. There are only a few hundred Michigan fans here, and I'm having trouble getting enough interviews to get their perspective on the game. Have you gotten score updates?"

"Yes, but nothing else. You'll have to give me the details. How did they score? Was it horribly embarrassing when we were behind?"

He chuckled. "That's exactly the perspective I'm looking for. I've got my notes. Let me give you the whole story."

Eden spun her earring to an easy volume, and settled herself comfortably into her father's chair. With the game safely over, she was happy to listen to the first-half struggles and the woeful fumble return that had given the Ohio men their brief lead.

Bruce was regaling her with the tale of how the team had nearly scored once more before time expired, when she heard the curtain rustle.

"Miss Randall, I'm leav—"

She swivelled in her chair. Heyward stared at her, mouth agape.

"What are you—" His gaze went from her to the telephone receiver pressed up against Vox's belly, then repeated the cycle a second time. She watched his expression shift, understanding dawning in his eyes. "Oh, ho! So that's what your monster does."

"Eden?" She could hear Bruce's voice clearer than Mr. Heyward's. "Are you there?"

"Yes, I'm here. I'm sorry. Something has come up. I'll be just a moment."

"You hide it well, Miss Randall," Heyward continued. "I had no inkling until just now."

She shooed him away. "If you're done with your turtle, you can go. I'll clean up."

"How does it work without any wires? And what else does it do that you're hiding from everyone?"

"Vox is none of your business," she snapped.

"I think it should be everyone's business."

She glared at him. "Don't you dare touch her. She *will* bite you again."

He only smirked. "We should release information about it. What do you say? We could make a lot of money."

"Her technology belongs to my parents, and they will release it when they have determined it is out of the experimental stage. Not before."

"People would pay, Eden. We could sell to the highest bidder."

"No. She isn't for sale. Never."

He shook his head. "Think on it. It could get us out of this worthless town. I'll keep your secret for now. I think we can make a deal. I'll see you around." He nodded at her, gave Vox a significant look, and walked away.

"Bastard," Eden grumbled. He treated Vox like a thing, and called her home worthless. He thought he could buy her, and he was probably cheating on his schoolwork. Now he knew her secret. If he blabbed, she would become a sideshow freak, the girl connected to the dragon, with people begging for demonstrations. The very idea terrified her.

Being weird in the background or on the fringes of society

was fine. People might give her the occasional odd look, but they left her alone. She couldn't handle being the focus of everyone's attention, with the resultant stares and questions, the chaos, and the noise. She thought of being mobbed by reporters, pointed at by everyone on the street. Her life would no longer be her own.

Tears stung her eyes. That was what she and her parents had hoped to avoid. She wished they could just present the technologies to the world using some other dragon, but Vox was the culmination of years of tinkering and tweaking. She couldn't be replicated overnight.

"Eden?" Bruce sounded worried. "Is everything okay? What was that all about? Is someone threatening you?"

"I'm fine. It's over. I can't explain right now. I'm sorry."

She froze in the middle of signing, her hand in a fist against her chest. She would always be different. There would always be people who thought her a freak, whether for her baseball playing or her biomechanics. There would always be those like Heyward and Tagget, who saw her and Vox as a path to riches.

Would things have been better if she'd never had her hearing restored? If she'd stayed away from public scrutiny?

Impossible. She would have gone to college with or without Vox. She would be out and about no matter her circumstances.

The deaf girl. The weird girl. The girl with the dragon. It didn't matter what they called her. She was who she was, and she was proud of it.

"Are you certain you don't want to talk?" Bruce asked. "I can stay on the line. I'll pay for extra time if I need to."

"No, don't. I won't keep you. I'm well, I promise. It was only a student being obnoxious. I'll see you on Monday."

He hesitated before answering. "Until Monday, then."

"Thank you for the game summary."

"You're very welcome. Goodbye, Eden."

"Bye."

The ominous thunk of the receiver settling into the cradle echoed in the empty laboratory. She missed his voice already.

She picked up her insect and her tools and stored them safely away, then turned to the mess Marcus Heyward had left on the workbench. His schematic lay underneath the tools and the now-completed turtle dragon. She pulled it out and looked at it. Tidy and precise, drawn with clean lines and a steady hand. Not the work of a person who rushed his build and left tools lying around. She stowed it in the proper file in the schematics cabinet and put the turtle in the student closet. Heyward didn't deserve it, but she wouldn't allow her father's lab to be left in such a state.

Eden checked that all windows were closed and all doors were locked before she collected Vox and headed for home. On an ordinary day, she would have set the dragon down to walk beside her or fly around, but just now she needed Vox in her arms. Secure. Safe.

Heyward was unpredictable and selfish. Maybe he would keep her secret, but he was equally likely to go to the papers, or even try to steal Vox for himself. The threat of becoming a spectacle hovered over her like a thundercloud. She had garnered all too much attention of late. Maybe it was something she had said or done. Maybe it was only her father's recent notoriety. Whatever had caused it, she didn't like it.

"What are we going to do, Vox?" she wondered aloud. Her own voice sounded in her ear, clear as day. The voice she had lacked for so many years. Her parents had worked hard for it. She had worked hard for it. Hesitant and halting at first, it had grown strong and proud. No one and nothing would take it from her.

14

October 17

EDEN ZIPPED PAST HIM once again, her laughter ringing in his ears. Bruce swore he would track down the man who had told him about the roller rink and buy him a beer. It was the perfect place for a spunky, sporty woman.

Eden spun around backwards, sliding in front of him so they skated face-to-face. He took up her hand as if they were dancing. Several less-coordinated skaters watched them fly by, looking on in awe.

Bruce wasn't the most practiced of roller skaters, but he had ice skated every winter since childhood. It was easier on his knee than running, making it one of the sports he'd kept up since the injury. The transition from blade to wheels wasn't seamless, but he'd taken to it without too much difficulty. Part of that may have been a desire to keep up with Eden.

She was the most athletic woman he'd ever met. It likely explained her trim figure. She was in better shape than he was, to be honest. Between his career and his knee, he did less physical activity than he ought. Not that he'd ever been one of those fellows with rock-hard abdominal muscles. He drank too many beers and did too few crunches. Eden was good for him. She kept him active, and in such a way he genuinely enjoyed it.

Eden turned to skate forward, not letting go of his hand. They continued on, side-by-side, gliding across the polished wooden floor.

"Miss Randall, would you like to go out to dinner when we've finished here?"

Her feet stopped moving, and he pulled her along while she mulled it over.

"Yes, I would, but I'll have to tell my parents, or they'll expect me to come home to eat. We can stop by the laboratory and see if my father is still there. If not, we may have to go somewhere with a telephone so you can call them."

Why wouldn't she call them herself? Her dislike of the telephone was odd. He suspected it was related to her biomechanics in some way. She hadn't seemed to have any difficulty with it when he'd called on Saturday, though. He still wanted to know who had been bothering her that day, and what about.

"Let me know when you've had enough skating. We can depart whenever you're ready."

She frowned up at him. "I'm sorry, I didn't catch all that. It's very noisy in here."

He repeated his words, somewhat louder. She nodded.

"Is your knee bothering you?"

"No. It's fine. I honestly haven't had any trouble with it since the upgrade."

"Ten more minutes, then, I think."

"Sounds lovely." He turned around and reached for her other hand. "Shall we dance?"

A quarter hour later they walked out the door. Eden had Vox tucked under her arm and a grin on her face.

"You look as though you enjoyed the roller rink, Miss Randall. Am I correct in that assumption?"

"Yes, it was wonderful. It had been too long since I'd been there. Did you enjoy yourself as well?"

"Absolutely. I could easily accustom myself to such outings."

I could easily accustom myself to anything, with you.

Damn. Where had that thought come from? Maybe all the Jane Austen he'd been reading had overstimulated his romantic side. But, really, what finer example of a gentleman was there than Mr. Knightley?

"So could I," Eden agreed. "We must do it again some time."

"I hope we will. There are a number of other places in town I should like to take you first, however. I understand one can rent canoes on the river, and that there is a lovely park on an island where concerts are sometimes played."

"Yes, in the summer, though it's nice to visit at any time of year. Many people like to drive out in their carriages, and there's a nice road that runs along the river with views of town. I wish we could drive it in a motorcar."

"What, Tagget hasn't offered you a ride in his Mercedes yet?"

Hell. Why couldn't he stop being so cynical? People were often amused by the flippant remarks in his columns. It made him careless when he spoke. Unless it was the other way 'round, and his verbal impudence was creeping into his writing.

"He's offered a few times," Eden replied. "I have to turn him down. I can't ride alone with him. I still worry that he wants Vox. I had my father escort me to and from the show this weekend to prevent his asking."

"You went to another show with him? Why?"

"It was a musical comedy. It was wonderful. And he's very nice to me when we are out."

"Very nice to you except for wanting to steal your dragon."

"Well, he's never *said* he wants her, and he's never made

any sort of attempt to touch her. He doesn't even ask nosy questions anymore. I would say he's given up, except there's no other reason for him to stay in town and he doesn't strike me as the sort who ever gives up."

No, he wouldn't give up. The man hadn't become a multi-millionaire by giving up. And that meant if he wanted Eden he would seduce her with music, motorcars, or whatever else it took.

Damn, damn, damn.

Bruce was outclassed. Tagget was better looking, far wealthier, and calculated everything that came out of his mouth before he said it. There would be no accidental sarcasm or awkward misunderstandings.

Bruce had never had to compete for a woman before. More accurately, he considered, he'd never bothered. If she preferred a rival, he let her go. The world contained many women, and he had enough working in his favor to attract his share. Eden, though... Eden made him want to fight.

"Do you want me to investigate him?"

"What?" Eden gave him a puzzled look.

"I'm a reporter. I investigate things. Watch. Take notes. I can check him out for you. See if I can determine what he really wants."

There were plenty of questions to be answered. Did Tagget only want the dragon, or did he want Eden herself? What was so special about Vox that made Eden so protective and others so covetous? Why had Tagget bought out Dynalux when most of his business was in the communications industry? Why had he even come to Ann Arbor in the first place?

"I don't think that's a very good idea." The corners of her mouth angled downward in the slightest of frowns. "He doesn't like you."

"I don't care what he thinks of me. I care whether he's taking advantage of you."

"He can't. I won't give him Vox or any of my father's ideas or creations, no matter what he does."

"Yet it's acceptable to go out with him?"

"To see a show for free? Certainly. Why not?"

There was a note of genuine curiosity in her tone. Bruce tried to imagine things from her perspective. She didn't trust Tagget, so it was difficult to say he was manipulating her. She saw an opportunity to do something she loved and seized it. What worried Bruce was that she might become too accustomed to Tagget and lose her suspicion. He tried to head it off by giving her a different perspective.

"Many people would say you shouldn't be seeing two men at once."

She blinked in surprise. "Are we seeing one another? How is that sort of thing determined? Is it a certain number of pre-arranged dates?"

"Mutual agreement of the persons involved, as I understand it. But consider that from an outsider's point of view, multiple outings with the same person can look like a serious relationship."

"I see. It's all very complicated, apparently. I would prefer to go out with whomever I want whenever I want and then decide for myself if something is serious."

"Of course you would."

His understanding of her continued to grow. She was self-sufficient. She made her own decisions and did what she liked without consulting others, not out of selfishness, but because it rarely occurred to her to do otherwise. She was far from inconsiderate. Her attentiveness to her parents' needs and feelings was proof of that. She cared deeply about her friends, such as Miss St. James with the bat dragon. The rest of the world, however, she treated with a marked indifference. The biomechanics in her ear may have allowed her to communicate more easily with society, but she seldom chose to engage with it.

Her frown deepened. "Are you making fun of me?"

"No, never." He paused, then corrected himself. "Okay, not never, but never in a malicious way. If I make fun of you it will only be because something about you is silly, but adorable, such as your rabid obsession with football."

"Rabid? You think me mad, then?"

"'Fan' *is* short for 'fanatic,' Miss Randall. Would that you may someday be as great a fan of myself as you are of your Wolverines."

That threw her. She fidgeted with the decorative trim of her fancy corset and didn't reply.

Bruce shifted awkwardly. What the hell had compelled him to say that? Perhaps *he* was the one obsessed. He couldn't even keep his foolish thoughts to himself any longer. What would happen at the end of football season when he returned to Boston? And the season had been cut short without the Thanksgiving game. He wouldn't get to explore New York with her. Damn Columbia, anyhow.

The remainder of the walk to her father's laboratory passed without another word. Bruce stared at the ground as they walked. He'd made a mess of things again. He would be dining alone now. Why did he have such difficulties with her? He'd never been one to wow women with flowery speech or suave manners, but he didn't upset them, either. Most people liked him.

Eden didn't look angry, fortunately, but she remained stubbornly silent. Bruce didn't know if he ought to say something or if it would only make things worse.

They arrived to find Professor Randall in the process of locking up the laboratory. Eden waved to him, and he smiled and waited for them to approach.

"Good evening. Come to see the copying machine in action, have you?"

"Oh, no, we only stopped by to see if you were in," Eden

explained. "Bruce invited me out to dinner, so I wanted to tell you that I wouldn't be home until later."

So she did still want to go out. Bruce exhaled in relief. Next time he would think before he spoke. He would confine the conversation to sports and books.

"You're going to dinner dressed like that?" her father objected. Bruce wasn't sure whether the remark was directed at his lack of a coat or Eden's trousers.

"It doesn't have to be a fancy dinner," she argued.

He made a tutting noise. "Very well. Enjoy your evening." He turned his gaze to Bruce. "Do try to bring her home earlier this time, young man. It isn't proper to keep young ladies out until all hours of the night."

"Yes, sir."

His compliance made Eden frown. He waited until they had made their goodbyes to her father before asking, "You don't think I ought to bring you home earlier?"

"It wasn't so terribly late. I was home before eleven. I think he's being overprotective. Although I suppose I've been out late often recently, what with going to the theater and all."

Bruce bit his lip before he could make another contemptuous comment about Tagget. He didn't need to begin that conversation all over again.

He let Eden pick the restaurant. Dinner was casual, and they fell back into their usual easy rapport, chatting about roller rinks, ice skating, and bicycles. Her father was something of a bicycle aficionado, it happened, and liked to modify his rides with motors, horns, and other contraptions. The result was a surplus of bicycles at their house. She offered to let Bruce borrow one so they could go riding. He added it to his list of things to do with her.

Eden declined to go home directly after the meal—he suspected she was still annoyed about the request to bring her home early—so they wandered through town. She led him all the way out past the railroad depot to the river, where they sat with their legs dangling from a bridge, watching the water flow past beneath the stars.

They didn't talk much, but Bruce didn't feel the need. Being with her and enjoying the crisp fall evening together was enough. She made no objection when he took her hand and laced his fingers through hers.

"I had a nice evening," she said. "Thank you." She signed her words as she spoke and a sudden, fierce desire to learn this second language of hers overtook him.

He settled for replying in English. "You're very welcome. I enjoyed it, too."

"I think it's time I was getting home."

"Of course." He didn't ask to escort her home, but simply helped her to her feet and walked with her, still holding her hand. She seemed content to let him tag along.

Eden once again doused the gaslight that lit the front walk up to her house. Today several lights shone from the windows. It was early enough that her parents hadn't retired for the night.

Eden set Vox down on the porch before turning toward him. Again, she hopped up onto the first step to minimize their height difference. Tonight she didn't hesitate to wrap her arms around him.

The taste of her made his head whirl. His fingers twisted in her hair and brushed over the silky skin of her neck. She wore an underbust corset today, and he could feel her breasts, soft and round against his chest. Luscious, athletic curves. His hands slid down her back and over her shapely rear. She ought to have slapped him again for that, but she didn't. Instead, she wriggled.

Bruce groaned. She could trigger a spark of desire with no more than a look. In her arms it had become a conflagration. He kissed her and fondled her as if it could satisfy the burning hunger inside of him, knowing he only added more fuel to the flames.

Her own hands wandered over him, groping and

exploring. She was wild, eager—as sensual as any three women put together. She was the bliss of a shot of morphine, with none of the oblivion. She heightened his senses, in fact, rather than dulling them. He feared, though, that she possessed the same addictive properties as the drug. Even now, years later, he suffered periodic cravings. Would his longing for Eden continue for the remainder of his life? Would he even attempt to disentangle himself from her seduction?

He ended the kiss and staggered backward. Letting go became a greater challenge each time. He had to do it, because he didn't think she would. She seemed content to kiss him forever. He might have allowed it except he knew how dangerous a game they were playing. He didn't know whether Eden did, and he'd already taken more liberties with her than was decent.

She stared at him, and he was glad for the darkness. He didn't need to see the heat in her eyes or her flushed cheeks. Knowing the depth of her passion would be too much to withstand.

"Goodnight, Eden." His voice was hoarse. "Thank you for another lovely evening."

"Goodnight. Will I see you tomorrow? I'll be on campus all day."

"I'll look for you. I'll see you Wednesday at the game for sure."

"And drinks afterward?"

"Definitely."

"Excellent." She gave a little wave goodbye.

Tonight, he watched her disappear into the house before he started back down the road. The evening had reinforced his earlier convictions. He would fight for her, and he didn't care whether he had to take on Evan Tagget or the whole damn world.

15

October 18

"OH, DARLING, you don't need to know that sort of thing until you're married."

Penelope Randall sipped her coffee and took a dainty bite of her toast. Her manners were always dainty. To Eden her mother looked just like magazine illustrations of a "proper lady." Her necklines were high, her skirts long. She sat without slouching and never rested her elbows on the table. Despite this seeming perfection, the rest of the world considered her an oddity. Her work as a mechanist—apparently an unfeminine field to discuss, much less pursue—meant that some people shunned her.

Her style did encompass a few small quirks. She favored dark-colored gloves, often with the fingertips cut out. She needed a good grip on her parts and tools, and didn't want the grease to show. Her hair, piled up in a fashionable coiffure, tended toward wildness, and was regularly topped with one of her whimsical fascinators. Today's was a tiny red derby with a yellow flower.

Eden adored her. Mother didn't understand Eden's taste in clothes, books, or hobbies, but she never criticized them. From the first she had supported whatever studies Eden wished to pursue, and taught her never to feel she couldn't do what she wanted because of her size, her sex, or her hearing loss.

Today, however, she'd been entirely unhelpful.

"But I know there is *something*, Mother. Why won't you tell me?"

"Because it's not an appropriate topic for a young lady."

"Mechanics isn't appropriate for a young lady, but you don't object to that."

"It's different, dear. That's only men thinking women don't have brains just as good as theirs. This is a matter of manners and modesty. Young ladies don't discuss such things."

Eden sighed and stabbed at her eggs.

"Use your knife, dear, that bite is much too large."

"I'll need to know someday," she argued.

"Yes, but not now. Is this about that boy you've been seeing? Has he tried to kiss you?"

Tried and succeeded, Eden thought. *And, oh, how magnificently.* She didn't say anything, but she was certain she was blushing.

Her mother shook her head. "If he does anything to make you uncomfortable, you walk away. You don't want any man who doesn't treat you well."

"Oh, he does, Mother. He's very considerate. And he's not at all bothered about Vox."

"I'm glad to hear it. Now, how is that insect of yours coming?"

Eden gave her mother an update on her project and finished her breakfast, then set out for the day. She hurried through her shopping, leaving plenty of time to comb the library for information. Her mother might not think it was proper to discuss, but Eden wouldn't be put off. She knew there was more to romance than kisses. She'd seen her parents whisper secret things to one another and disappear into their bedroom. When she kissed Bruce her body trembled with longing for something. She was determined to learn what that something was.

To her great disappointment, she soon discovered her mother wasn't alone in her reticence to discuss the subject. Eden thought her research skills well-honed, but she could find no answers to her questions. It was a topic, it seemed, that wasn't even appropriate to write about. It made no sense. Kissing was so enjoyable. Surely whatever it led to would be equally pleasant. Why all the mystery?

"What's this?" Lilah slipped into the seat beside her, books tucked under her arm.

"I'm researching," Eden sighed. "Unsuccessfully."

"Oh?"

"I'm trying to learn what couples do after kissing, but apparently it's a big secret."

"Oh! Eden, you don't need to know that sort of thing."

"That's what my mother said. She's wrong. I've been trying to go through everything I know from novels. The closest thing I can find is married couples going away on a honeymoon, or people who run away together and are ruined or cause a scandal. It never says what they do together, though."

"Have you been kissing that reporter? Don't let him do anything else. It could have consequences."

"What sort of consequences?"

"Babies, for one thing."

"I knew there must be something about babies. I've read books with illegitimate children resulting from some scandal or failed elopement. And married couples have lots of babies. But it can't be only about babies, because my parents disappear into their room together often and I'm an only child."

Lilah cringed. "Eden, do you even know how animal babies are made?"

"Not really. Some of them hatch from eggs. Some grow inside their mothers like people do."

"Try reading up on that. It might help you understand. I'm not going to be the one to explain it, though. Good luck." She rose from her seat and turned to leave.

"Lilah, wait. How do you know about this?"

"My mother told me a few things. And my uncle owns a farm, remember? I've seen how animals mate. It's not entirely... pleasant. Don't be surprised if you're disappointed by what you learn."

"Huh. Well, on to the medical texts, I suppose."

Eden spent the next two hours devouring all sorts of interesting information. She found detailed descriptions of both male and female bodies and learned many terms she had previously never encountered. Anatomy books gave her diagrams and images of male and female reproductive parts, but nothing showing how they worked together.

She found one particularly informative book shoved into a back corner. Written by a female doctor, it was full of remedies to increase fertility and to prevent pregnancy. It also contained a chapter on easing menstruation troubles Eden intended to refer back to. It did not, however, explain the mechanics of reproduction or its connection to pleasant things like kissing while a pair of strong hands came down to squeeze your rump.

Her scholarly resources exhausted, she sat out on the library steps, elbows on her knees and chin in her hands. Bruce knew all about kissing. He must know better than she where such things led. He wasn't a "proper young lady," so people probably answered his questions.

Eden scowled. How typical that men were allowed to know such things but she wasn't. Bruce was thoughtful and objective. She could convince him such an attitude was unfair, but that would take time, and she wanted knowledge now.

Annoyed, but undaunted by her difficulties, she picked herself up and started across campus. It was time to consult her best source for information on men and the things they did: the football team.

. . . 🐿 . . .

"I have a question."

It wasn't the first time Eden had begun a conversation this way, and several of the players chuckled. She scooped up one of the practice balls and followed the men on the way to stow their equipment. Someone in this group would have an answer for her.

"Ask away, Miss Randall."

"What comes after kissing? I know men and women do something together, and I want to know what."

Several of the men stopped in their tracks. A few hurried off. Multiple voices echoed her mother's sentiments.

"Miss Randall, that's not something for a nice young lady to learn about."

"Wait until you're married, Eden."

"*I'm* not going to be the one to tell you!"

She threw up her hands in frustration. "Please?" she tried. "Joey?"

"No way, Eden."

She wouldn't be deterred. She followed him until they were alone. "Please? You must know something."

"It's not appropriate."

"What do you care about appropriate?"

"No."

"You're being unfair."

"What?" He stopped and turned to look at her. Perfect. She would appeal to his sense of sportsmanship.

"Un. Fair." She crossed her arms and stared him down, pretending she wasn't a foot shorter and less than half his weight. "You men get to know about this sort of thing. You probably talk about it all the time. But I can't even get a question answered. 'Oh, Eden, you don't need to know that. It's not ladylike.' Well, you know what? I don't care. You all sit around like you're in some kind of special secret club, hiding things from women because you think we're too stupid to handle it."

"That's not true."

"Oh, is it for our protection?" she sneered. "How sweet. Maybe you should try that tactic tomorrow at the game. You can all tell the American Medical men, 'We're only going to play with six men tonight, because we don't want anyone to get hurt.'"

"You're being ridiculous."

"I'm not. You're treating me like a child, and you know it. I'm older than you are, Joseph Bryerson!"

"But far more naive."

"I wouldn't be, if people would tell me things."

"Eden…" he pleaded.

"Just tell me."

"I can't. Really, I can't. I'm sorry."

He looked rueful. His resolve was weakening. She raised her eyebrows, giving him a look of skepticism. "What, you don't know, then?"

"Of course I know! But… Christ, Eden, it's not okay to be telling girls things like that!"

"It's not okay to curse in front of them, either, right?"

He winced. "I'm sorry."

She moved closer to him, lowering her voice. "I promise I won't tell anyone I heard it from you. If anyone asks, I'll pretend I don't know a thing, and if I let anything slip, I'll say I bribed a man at a saloon because my friends wouldn't tell me."

Joey's eyes grew round. "You wouldn't do that, would you?"

"Bribe someone? I doubt I would have to. I could just find someone drunk." This would be her new fall-back plan, but she didn't think she would need it. Joey was cracking.

"God, Eden. Okay, okay, fine. I'll tell you. I'd rather you heard it from me. But you have to swear you won't tell a soul."

She put a hand to her heart. "Promise."

His eyes darted about. "Let's go somewhere private."

"The library?" she suggested. She'd been there most of the day. No one would bat an eye if she went back. "We can find a quiet spot."

"Fine, fine. I can pretend you're helping me find books for classwork. This is crazy, you know that?"

She shrugged. As long as she got her answers, she didn't much care if anyone thought she was crazy. Most people thought so already.

Eden found the most secluded table possible in the library, and sat down across from Joey. She placed Vox up on the table and folded her hands in her lap, in what she believed to be a ladylike manner.

"Please, go ahead with your explanation, Mr. Bryerson," she told him. "You may speak softly. I can hear you."

"This isn't funny, Eden," he hissed. "You're going to get me in such damn trouble."

"Should I go to the saloon?"

"No. Stop." He leaned over the table. Eden nudged Vox closer. She would have no trouble hearing even his faintest whisper. "Okay, here's how it works."

Once she got him talking, he went on at length. His explanations were at least as interesting as the medical textbooks, and the whole picture at last became clear in Eden's mind. She tried her best not to interrupt or say anything that might alarm him, while still making certain she wasn't left with lingering questions.

Joey covered the entire process, from kissing, to removing clothing, to the act itself, which apparently involved the man inserting his penis into the woman's vagina. Joey used ridiculous words for the body parts, but Eden knew the correct terms from the medical books. When she pointed this out, it led them into a further discussion about terminology.

The sheer number of words related to it stunned her. She'd heard most of the vulgar ones, without knowing what they meant, as well as a number of euphemisms. A great many things would make more sense now.

"So you've tried it?" she asked, wanting to confirm his information was accurate.

His gaze dropped to the floor and he squirmed. "Er, yes."

She nodded, trying to keep as calm and detached a demeanor as possible. She wanted to keep him talking. Acting like a scientist collecting data seemed the best plan. "And it is enjoyable?"

"Very."

She frowned at him. "I'm confused. If men like this sexual intercourse, but they don't think women should talk about it, how do they find anyone to do it with?"

"The women who do it… they're not good sorts of girls, Eden."

"You mean the women who like it are bad people?" That made no sense. Now that Eden understood what couples did alone in their bedrooms, she was certain her mother liked it, and her mother was one of the best people she knew. "Why would you want them, then?"

"No, they're not bad people, it's just… Oh, hell, I don't know. Good girls wait until they're married, that's all."

"Why? And why don't the men wait?"

"I don't know, Eden. Lord. You've got me all flustered. I told you this wasn't a good idea."

She reached across the table and covered his hand with hers. "It was. You've been wonderful. Thank you for being honest with me. Everything makes a lot more sense, now. I promise I won't tell anyone you told me, or let anybody know about the women you've been sleeping with. Is that right? Did I use the expression correctly?"

"Yes, that's right," he sighed.

"Do you really sleep with them? All night?"

"Hell, no. I get out of there as fast as possible."

"Oh. Interesting."

"Are we done?" He wore a pained expression. Eden decided she'd gathered enough data to let him be. She nodded. "Thank God. I need a drink."

"Don't get drunk," she warned him. "Some curious woman might come along wanting you to talk about inappropriate things."

He pushed his chair back, glowering at her. "That's not funny."

She couldn't help but laugh.

"Not. Funny."

It *was* funny. He was too sensitive. She picked up Vox and rose from her seat, ready to head home. She was pleased with the results of the day's research. It was time to cook up a nice dinner, relax at home with a book, and then determine what to do with her newfound knowledge.

16

October 19

"I'VE HEARD TAGGET'S NAME linked to Lillian Russell lately."

Bruce snorted into the telephone. "That was proven untrue ages ago. Give me something better than that. And not just gossip about where he's been putting his quimstick."

"Okay, okay." Several beats of silence passed before the tinny sound of Cole Richardson's voice returned. "I scraped together some details on the Tagget Industries history."

"Let me have it."

"Founded in 1894, when he was twenty-four years old. By twenty-six he'd made his first million."

Bruce couldn't suppress a cringe. He was twenty-four and he couldn't even get a promotion. He couldn't deny that part of his dislike of Tagget was simple jealousy. The man had money enough to squander on motorcars powered with luxene. He had an enormous apartment in New York and a history of glamorous mistresses. Bruce's entire romantic life consisted of the two girlfriends who had left him, a handful of dates with others, and a pair of short-lived sexual liaisons. His football career had ended before it had even begun. Success at most anything eluded him. So far.

"The company began selling Tagget's own designs," Richardson continued, "but expanded quickly. The man has an eye for useful technologies. Buys them cheap, from inventors who never set foot outside their laboratories, then markets them under his own name and sells them for ten times the price or more. Buys out companies, too. Started with Reynolds Manufacturing in 1895. Shut the place down, sold off all the assets, kept the designs for himself and improved on them all."

"These students he's recruiting will never make names for themselves or grow rich working at his company."

"Nah. Majority of the employees maintain or upgrade the telephone and telegraph wires and facilities. There's hardly a telephone or telegraph in the country that doesn't rely in some way on a piece of Tagget Industries technology. His army of engineers works on design improvements and wireless experimentation. A few are in the dragons and small machines division. Anyone with unique ideas will have them patented under the company name. If they're lucky they'll get a small mention. Standard practice. It's all smart business. Ruthless, but smart."

"That's what my father would say. That doesn't make it any less repugnant. This is why I didn't go into finance."

Richardson laughed. "You're too soft, Caldwell. You ought to stick to sports."

"I would, except..."

Eden.

His own research and this latest talk with Richardson gave Bruce a sense of why Tagget had come to Ann Arbor. Wireless teletics were the newest development in experimental technology, and the voice controls of Professor Emerick Randall had made national news. Tagget would want control of that market from the beginning. Anything that transmitted or recognized sounds without wires would draw his notice. He would surely covet a dragon as sophisticated as Vox, who not only responded to Eden's commands but could recognize both her and her house and act accordingly.

The dragon's communications technology must be more complex than Bruce understood, but his lack of technical knowledge meant he could do no more than guess until—unless—Eden decided to confide in him. As an inventor himself, Tagget would know more.

"Except what? What's this about, anyway?"

"Nothing. It's just… Tagget's nosing around a friend of mine. That's all. I want to know what we're up against."

Richardson huffed. "You're up against a man who can either buy or charm his way to whatever he wants. Good luck."

"Thanks," Bruce muttered.

He hung up the phone and ran through the options in his head. Tagget wouldn't try to steal Vox outright except as a last resort. He'd already begun a campaign to romance the dragon from Eden. The scum. He didn't know her very well. She wouldn't give up Vox for all the concerts in the world.

Which didn't mean Bruce was going to sit on his duff. He would do all he could to protect Eden from Tagget's cutthroat schemes. And the first step was to use his own talents. He'd begun the research. Next came the other vital facet of investigative journalism: observation.

One quick question got him the AM&T lecture schedule, and a few hours later he slipped into one of Professor Hart's largest classes. He tugged at his jacket. It was hot and uncomfortable, but it blended in with the other students. He missed his cap already.

The lecture hall wasn't well lit, and no one even glanced at him when he entered. He took a seat in the back and adopted the same bored pose most of the students displayed. Two minutes into the talk, he knew the lecture content was well beyond him. His liberal arts degree had taught him little about science or engineering. The only mathematics he had studied dealt with statistical analysis. The diagrams and equations written on the blackboard were no better than nonsense. He was bored within five minutes. A quarter-hour later, he gave up.

Bruce slipped out of the room, making his best attempt to be unobtrusive, and walked one building over, to the AM&T labs. He glanced into Professor Randall's room as he passed, hoping Eden might be there. Miss St. James glanced up from her project and gave him a wave.

"Eden's not here today, Mr. Caldwell."

"Thanks. I'll catch her later. Just had a quick question." He fought off disappointment. He would see her at the game tonight, and they were going out afterward.

He continued on, across the hall and two doors down to Professor Hart's laboratory. He tried the doorknob, expecting to find it locked, and jumped when it turned in his hand. He paused and knocked, thinking someone might be inside, working. No answer came.

Bruce waited several moments more, listening, but all he could hear was the drone of machinery that pervaded the building. The hall was empty. Professor Hart's lecture wouldn't end for some time yet. He took his chances and opened the door.

Unlike Professor Randall's lab, this room was only a single story. It was darker, more crowded, and noisier. Tangles of wires crisscrossed the ceiling and ran down the walls. Bare light bulbs dangled so low Bruce had to duck beneath them. Only a few were lit, leaving large portions of the room in shadow.

He walked a slow circle about the space, weaving through the clanking machines. This room contained none of the small dragons or gadgets he'd seen in Professor Randall's lab. Hart, it seemed, specialized in large devices. Something near half the machines were running. Bruce couldn't even begin to guess what any of them did.

Hart had a small office in the back corner of the lab. Only the size of a large closet, it nonetheless felt spacious compared to the cluttered room surrounding it. Hart's desktop was clean. A chest of drawers taller than a man covered the right wall of the office. Bruce tugged at a drawer and found it locked. He poked his penknife into the keyhole and wiggled it about, but the lock was too sturdy for his amateurish burglary skills.

Damn. He was getting nowhere.

A set of schematics neatly pinned along the wall caught his eye. One appeared to be written in a different hand than the others, and he moved closer. The diagram was drawn with precision, the lines very straight and clean. The bottom right corner was marked with the loopy signature of one E. Tagget. The design appeared to be some sort of camera, but, again, Bruce's lack of scientific knowledge prevented him fully understanding what he was seeing. He wondered what the chances were of bringing Eden in here and getting her thoughts on the project.

The schematic proved Hart and Tagget were legitimately working on something, but Bruce suspected it was no more than a cover. Regardless, he wouldn't learn any more here. He started for the exit. Halfway to the door, he heard it creak.

He dove behind the nearest large machine. Footsteps announced the entry of at least two people, followed by the bang of the door closing. Lights flared. Bruce's location kept him hidden from the view of anyone near the door, but if they moved further into the room he would be easily visible. He inched back, ducking under a swinging mechanical arm.

"Have you made any progress?" Tagget's voice.

"Some, but not enough," answered a second man. There was something familiar about the voice, but Bruce couldn't place it. Whoever this man was, he sounded annoyed. "The new dragon worked well, but it wasn't very sturdy. It couldn't hold up during the race. I'll need to repair it."

"It's hardly my fault if you can't build a satisfactory

machine," Tagget answered. "That wasn't, however, what I was referring to. What do you have to report?"

"Nothing," the man grumbled. "She doesn't talk about it."

The footsteps moved closer. Bruce slid along the wall, squeezing behind the next machine over. The rough metal caught in his clothes, and sharp protrusions jabbed into his arms.

"I am well aware of her reticence." Annoyance colored Tagget's words. "You have observed nothing?"

"Nothing of import."

He was lying. His voice was too casual, lacking the emotion of all his earlier statements. Tagget didn't comment on it.

"What of other projects? Have you heard or seen anything that might be of value?"

"Only this. I used the copying machine on a paper that was already a copy, so there are a few missing lines here and there, but it should be readable."

Tagget didn't reply for a long moment. Even with the machines clacking and whirring around him, Bruce hardly dared breathe. In his cramped hiding place, he could feel the vibrations of the apparatus down to his bones. The heat from the boiler seared his skin, and the smell of oil stung his nostrils.

"This is better than nothing, I suppose," Tagget decided. "I'll take a closer look. I hope, however, that you will have a better report when next we meet. You can see yourself out."

"That's all?" the other man blurted. "You have nothing for me?"

"Perhaps you don't understand the nature of our business arrangement. You provide a service, then you receive payment in accordance with the quality of your work. If you wish additional compensation, I suggest you put a bit more effort into doing what I have asked of you."

"But…"

"Or shall I demolish that ridiculous dragon of yours permanently?"

"You can't do—"

"I can." There was a bit of rustling, then moments later a small pop. Bruce smelled the faint odor of smoke. "Do I need to make myself any clearer?"

"I'll do what I can," the man whined. A short time later, Bruce heard the door open and close once more.

Footsteps still rang through the laboratory. It was too much to hope that Tagget would leave any time soon. Bruce resigned himself to waiting. He would be able to slip out the door if Tagget went into the office to work.

Tagget seemed to have other ideas. It was difficult to tell what he was doing, but it sounded as if he were walking about the room, playing with various machines. Wherever he went, extra squeaks and clicks joined the industrial hum. Bruce extricated himself from his awkward shelter and crept closer to the door. He ducked down into a shadowy corner. From here, he thought he could get to the door in a matter of seconds.

"Well, what have we here?" Tagget murmured. "How very interesting." More squeaks and clicks followed his words. "Foolish boy," he sneered. "He has no idea who he's dealing with."

Bruce hoped Tagget would keep talking, and give some indication of what he might be doing, but he fell silent and continued his circuit of the lab. A short time later, the office door opened, then closed. Bruce breathed a sigh of relief. He started for the exit. The lab door swung open. He dove beneath a nearby workbench, wedging himself behind a toolbox for partial concealment. A pair of legs walked past.

"Tagget? Are you here?" Professor Hart called.

"In the office," came the muffled reply.

Hart moved toward the back of the lab, but before he disappeared from sight, the office door opened. Bruce was trapped once again.

Tagget and Hart struck up a conversation about the camera schematic in the office. Bruce couldn't follow all the foreign terminology. Minutes ticked by. The awkward position under the table caused his bad leg to cramp up. He tried to focus on the conversation, but his discomfort and desire to escape occupied most of his thoughts.

After what felt like an hour, the two men finished their discussion. Tagget departed, and Hart disappeared into his office. Bruce crawled out from beneath the workbench, wincing. He took care opening the door to prevent noises, and stepped into the hall, heaving a sigh of relief. Only a few minutes, and he would be back in his hotel. He needed to sit and think over all he had heard.

"One moment, sir."

Bruce turned. The hairs on his neck tingled. A uniformed police officer stood a short distance down the hall.

"Yes?"

"I think you have some explaining to do, young man."

17

Eden paced the sidelines, the wolverine dragon turning this way and that behind her. Like the last mid-week contest, this game was little more than a farce. Michigan scored at will, and the Medics bumbled about as if they had never seen a football. She cheered the touchdowns, but her heart wasn't in it. Bruce was nowhere to be found.

"Turn," she snapped at the dragon.

One of the players spun to look at her. "Something wrong, Eden?"

"No. No problem." She tried to give him a smile, and he shrugged and turned away.

Where was Bruce? He'd told her he would see her at the game. "For sure," he'd said. He had no reason to lie about it. Besides, his job required him to be here.

He might have gone up into the grandstand or hidden himself in the crowd if he didn't wish to talk to her, but she couldn't imagine what would have caused such a reaction. Their outing on Monday had been such fun.

The crowd was sparse to begin with, and grew smaller as

the score ran higher and night approached. A tall man in a cap and no jacket shouldn't have been difficult to spot. By the time the game ended—once again called early on account of darkness—she was convinced he wasn't there.

Worry crinkled her brow. What could have kept him away? Illness? An accident? Was he lying somewhere in pain, desperate for help?

The scenarios in her mind grew more fanciful. She envisioned him run over by a carriage, trampled by a steam-belching dragon. Or walking along the trolley tracks only to be crushed beneath the wheels when the conductor failed to see him. Perhaps he had slipped and fallen into the river or the creek and drowned. Maybe a bookcase had fallen on him at the library. What if his hotel had caught on fire?

She looked toward downtown, searching for smoke, but the waning light made it difficult to see anything. She sniffed the air for any smoky odor.

"Eden? Hey, are you okay?"

"Huh?" She glanced up at Joey, then over at the wolverine, who had begun to wander away, unattended. "Sorry." She called the dragon back, shut it down, and stowed it.

"Is something bothering you? You look upset. Was it that penalty? I didn't think we were offside, either."

"Yes, we were. It was a good call. The game was fine. Excuse me, I need to be going. I'm supposed to meet someone."

She began to walk away, but he jogged after her. "Eden, are you sure you're okay? It's not me, is it? I didn't freak you out with all that talk about… you know… the other day?"

"What? No, don't be silly. I'm just worried about someone. He was supposed to be here."

"Oh, that reporter friend of yours?"

His observation startled Eden. More people than she realized had noticed how much time she and Bruce were spending together.

"You're awfully sweet on him, aren't you?"

Her cheeks heated. "He's nice. He took me roller skating. But he missed the game tonight, and that's not like him."

Joey shrugged. "Maybe he's sick of these practice games. They're damned dull. I can't wait until we play Wisconsin and Chicago."

"He told me he would meet me here."

"Yeah, well, men say all sorts of things they don't mean when they're chatting with girls. You know what they want, now, Eden. If he tries anything improper, you just smack him."

"Why does everyone think he's going to mistreat me?"

"Because naive small-town girls are easy prey for boys from the big city. What does he have to lose? He'll be gone in a month."

Eden scowled, partly because Joey was being unjust, and partly because she didn't like to think about Bruce leaving town. She would miss him.

She pushed the thought away. All that mattered now was making certain nothing horrible had happened to him.

"I can take care of myself. I'm nowhere near as stupid as you seem to think." She spun on her heel and started away.

"Eden, I don't think you're stupid," Joey called after her.

She ignored him. This was neither the time nor the place for such a discussion. She needed to get to the saloon. She may have somehow failed to spot Bruce in the crowd, but she couldn't miss him inside the small barroom.

She jogged all the way to the saloon. Hot and thirsty from the exertion, she drank down half her beer in the space of a few minutes. Still no Bruce. Her hand stroked across Vox's metal body, but the smooth brass beneath her fingers offered little comfort. Eden sipped her beer and checked her watch.

Twenty-six and one half minutes after she arrived, one of the bartenders approached her.

"Miss Randall?"

Eden blinked up at him. "Yes. That's me."

"There's a telephone call for you, miss."

A telephone call? Who on earth would call her? And in so public a place? How could she answer?

"If you would like to follow me?"

She downed the last of her beer, picked up Vox and followed him. What if the call were about Bruce? Perhaps the hospital had called to say he was gravely ill, or the undertaker to say he'd died in some horrific accident. She had to know. Somehow she had to take the call.

The bartender led her behind the bar, to the back of the saloon, and handed her the telephone. Eden glanced over at the door leading to storage areas and whatever else was kept out of sight of the customers. A few steps would hide her from prying eyes. She stared down at the receiver in her hand and tried to guess at how far the wires could reach.

"Could I have a bit of privacy?" she asked, nodding at the door.

"You can try," the barkeep replied. "Excuse me." He returned to the bar to take a customer's order.

Eden stretched the phone as far as she could, which wasn't quite through the doorway. She would be obscured from view, but not hidden. The patrons of the bar wouldn't be able to see her, but anyone behind the bar would. She put her back to the wall and her left ear toward the storeroom, then hoisted Vox up onto her shoulder. It was the best she could manage.

"Hello?" she called into the mouthpiece.

"Eden! You *are* there. Thank goodness."

Her awkward position meant his voice was muffled, but the Boston accent was unmistakable. She concentrated on it, trying to shut out the noise of the bar in the background.

"Bruce, where are you?"

"The county jail."

She made him repeat himself, convinced she had misheard him. To her dismay, she hadn't.

"How? What happened?"

"It's a long story, and I don't think I have the time to explain sufficiently over the telephone."

Eden didn't wish to stand here in the saloon using a telephone in public for long, either, so she didn't argue. "Do you need help?" She pushed the phone receiver tighter against Vox.

"Do you know anyone who practices law whom I might consult? Or could you bring me some law books? I don't even know if what I did was illegal or if Tagget is simply exerting his influence."

"Tagget is involved? Oh, Bruce, I told you not to bother about him."

"Forget that, Eden. I just want to get out of here. I don't have enough money, so I need a lawyer. A law student, maybe? Someone who won't charge much?"

"You can pay your way out?"

"No. I'm told they'll drop the charge if I agree to pay restitution, but I don't have that kind of money. Not without contacting my bank in Boston."

"How much do you need?"

"It's no use, Eden. I can't come up with it on short notice."

"How much?"

"Twenty dollars." Even through the phone she could detect the wince in his voice.

"Ooh."

"Yeah." He sounded dispirited. "So, do you know anyone? Or anything that might help?"

"Don't worry. I'll be there soon."

"Eden, wait, I didn't…" She couldn't make out the rest of the sentence.

She cast a glance out into the saloon. She didn't think anyone was staring at her, but each time she adjusted the telephone a nervous tremor ran down her spine.

"I'm sorry. Could you repeat that?" She twisted her body, trying to shield Vox from the sounds of the saloon.

"I didn't have identification on me." The words were faint.

Was he whispering? "I gave them my *first* name, and that of your favorite scientist-turned-monster."

Eden grimaced. He'd given the police a false name? He was going to get himself in enormous trouble if anyone found out.

"I will be there as soon as I can," she promised once more. "Thank you."

She hung the receiver back on the telephone and carried it to the niche in the wall where it resided.

"Thanks," she called to the bartender, but he was too busy to do more than nod in her direction.

Eden contemplated the situation as she hurried for home. What had Bruce done to Tagget to get himself arrested? She'd told him not to investigate. The moment he was free she intended to give him a proper scolding.

She scurried into the house and up to her bedroom. She reached under the bed and flicked the lever that would start up her personal safe-box. The machine whirred to life.

"Open," she commanded.

The panel slid back, and the smaller inner box dropped into her hand.

The box held a few personal trinkets, most with only sentimental value, such as her very first earpiece, and the first gear ever replaced on Vox. It also held the letter wherein Paul had proposed to her. Even the sight of it made her cringe. He'd been so certain she would accept. Everyone had. She only kept the letter because she wanted the reminder that only she decided what to do with her life.

At the bottom of the safe-box were a stack of bills and a handful of silver dollars. For years she'd received a generous allowance from her parents, though she didn't purchase much besides her clothing and an occasional novel. Her current savings amounted to more than two-hundred dollars, and she had no plans to spend it. She removed two ten-dollar notes and tucked them into her bodice before closing and securing the box.

Vox had crawled into her little nest beside Eden's bed—a pile of old blankets that protected her while Eden slept. Her antennae were retracted, and she awaited the sleep command that would put her into low-power mode.

Eden picked her up. "Oh, silly. It's not bedtime. We have things to do."

Vox's antennae extended, and light flashed behind her blue crystal eyes. Eden tucked her under an arm and scampered down the stairs just in time to see her mother emerge from the laboratory.

"You're home early this evening. I thought you were going out with friends after the football match?"

"I'm heading out now. I only stopped by to fetch something."

"I see. Don't stay out too late, dear. Your father and I worry about you."

"I'm perfectly fine. If anyone bothers me, Vox will bite him."

Her mother gave a small head shake. "She's not a guard dragon, Eden."

"And I'm not a little girl who needs looking after."

"I know. That's why we worry. We can't make decisions for you any longer. We can only hope we raised you well."

"You did," Eden assured her. "Excuse me, I must be off. A friend is waiting."

They exchanged goodbyes and Eden rushed out the door. The county jail wasn't far from home, and even in the dark the walk took less than ten minutes. She must have passed it thousands of times, without ever giving it much thought. She'd never been inside.

Panic set in when she reached the building. At this time of night it might be closed to visitors. She let out a sigh of relief when the door opened.

A man at a desk greeted her with raised eyebrows and a crooked frown. "May I help you, Miss?"

"You have a Mr. Archibald Hyde in residence?" It took all her willpower not to cringe at the false name. How could he be so ridiculous?

The man consulted some sort of list. "We do, indeed, Miss."

"Good." She fished the twenty dollars from beneath her corset and waved it at the man. "Here's the money. You may release him now."

"Ah. One moment. There will be a bit of paperwork."

He disappeared further into the building and returned a short time later with what looked to be more lists. He made some notes, took the twenty dollars, and had Eden sign something. He then disappeared again while she paced about.

Her shoulders tensed and her fingers clenched. She had no guarantee that her twenty dollars wouldn't simply disappear, leaving Bruce behind bars. The man returned and sat at his desk, but there was no sign of Bruce. She continued to pace.

Several minutes later he appeared at last, half-pushed by a guard with a clanking keychain. The man at the desk glanced up.

"The young lady has paid your way out. I hope you thank her properly." He pushed a notebook, pencil, watch, and penknife in Bruce's direction. "Sign here."

Bruce looked mortified, but he scrawled something on the paper and pocketed his things.

"Thank you, Mr. Hyde, you are free to go. Behave yourself and this sort of thing won't happen again."

Eden took him by the elbow. "Come on, Archie," she urged, knowing the name would annoy him. "It's time you were getting home."

He didn't look at her, just trudged out the door. "Please don't call me that," he muttered once the door was safely shut behind them.

"It's your own fault for using that silly name."

"I know."

He looked more miserable than she had ever seen, and a bit of remorse crept over her for the thorough scolding she still intended to give him.

"Are you going to tell me what happened?"

"Not here. In private."

"This way." She led him down the street, past the opera house, and up the front steps of the courthouse, which had long since closed for the day. People might pass by, and certainly would after the performance ended at the theater, but the courthouse square was large enough they would see anyone coming well in advance. Eden sat down on the steps and tugged on Bruce's clothing until he sighed and joined her. "Now talk," she ordered.

"Dammit, Eden, what did you go and do a thing like that for?"

It wasn't what she was expecting, and she looked at him in confusion. "Excuse me?"

"I didn't want you to pay. I didn't want anyone to pay! Dammit." He put his head in his hands. "I'll pay you back, I promise."

She shrugged. "It's only money. I have more."

"That's not the point. I feel like an utter cad."

"Well, you should," she admonished. "You did something stupid and got yourself arrested, after I told you not to go spying on Tagget. It's your own fault and you ought to feel sorry."

He looked her in the eye at last, his expression now more of sorrow than shame. "You're correct. I apologize, Miss Randall, for both my behavior and the trouble it has caused you. I should have suffered the consequences on my own and never involved you."

"Never involved me? You would rather I'd been left in the

dark, going mad with worry, thinking you were lying dead in a ditch somewhere?"

He gaped at her, flabbergasted. "You thought I was dead?"

"You missed the football game."

"And your first thought was that I was dead?"

"I imagined multiple scenarios in which you had met a grisly demise." She didn't understand why this surprised him so. She didn't think any of her ideas had been that far-fetched. "Stop that."

"Stop what?"

"You're giving me the, 'Eden you're crazy,' look. I'm not crazy. You could have been trampled by a carriage dragon, run over by a trolley, drowned in the river…"

"I can swim."

"Not if you had hit your head."

He chuckled. "I don't think you're crazy. I think you're adorable and I'd love to kiss you."

"Not until you explain how you landed yourself in the county jail."

"Very well. I was sneaking about in Professor Hart's laboratory."

Bruce gave a full description of his activities that afternoon, while Eden nodded and tried her best to maintain a serious expression. The thought of him dashing from one clanking machine to the next while Tagget prowled around scowling made her want to giggle.

"I don't think Tagget actually saw me, but he discovered I was there while he was walking around the lab, checking some device. I was 'caught on camera,' the policeman said."

"Ooh, an anti-theft camera? What a good idea! My father's lab could use one. I'm still concerned someone might tamper with the dragons again. Do you think it automatically rang for the police? Tagget is a teletics man, so it's possible. But how would it know you were an intruder instead of an authorized person?" He was giving her the crazy look again. "Sorry. I didn't mean to interrupt your story."

"It was all but over. I told the police officer I had just been looking around because the door was open, but he gave me a list of offenses I was being charged with and arrested me. Aside from trespassing, the accusations were absurd, but it was enough to leave me with the choice of sitting for days before facing trial or paying a hefty fine. I thought a lawyer would help, so I called the saloon when I thought you would be there."

She nodded. "Good thinking. I don't have any lawyer friends. But I did have twenty dollars."

He grimaced. "I will pay you back."

"Don't bother. Just buy me a beer."

"A pint costs five cents!" he protested.

"Then I guess you owe me four hundred pints. Take me out twice a week and you'll have paid off your debt in under four years." She grinned. This may have been her most brilliant idea ever. She would consider it twenty dollars well spent.

"May I kiss you now?"

"Yes."

Eden began to tingle before he even touched her. The anticipation was delicious. His lips grazed her cheek, inching down to her mouth. His arm stole about her. She wrapped her arms around him, dragging herself closer.

In his embrace, the anxiety of the day melted away, leaving nothing but this sensation of pleasure and yearning. Fingers tickled her spine. His tongue slid across hers. She matched him move for move, savoring the taste of his mouth and the muscles of his broad shoulders beneath her hands.

The rational part of her mind had just enough influence to remind her that she sat on the steps of the courthouse, in full view of anyone who walked by. If she wanted the opportunity to explore further, and someday try the things Joey had told her about, they would need privacy. She pulled back.

"Should we go somewhere else?"

Bruce stared at her a moment, wide-eyed, then his lips pinched into a tight frown. "Yes. We should go home." He pushed himself to his feet and offered her a hand. "Let me walk you home."

"Oh, no, not tonight. Tonight I'm walking *you* home. After your antics this afternoon I want to see you safely in your hotel."

She took his hand and let him help her up, then tugged him in the direction of the hotel.

"Eden, you don't need to do that."

"Yes, I think I do."

"I'm perfectly capable of seeing myself home."

"As am I. And I'm not the one who was behaving foolishly and had to be sprung from jail."

He sighed. "You win. I will consider it part of my punishment."

"Thank you."

They didn't talk as they walked to the hotel. Unlike many people she knew, Bruce didn't mind these periods of silence. She was glad for it. It allowed her to spend time listening to the quieter sounds that were often overshadowed by chatter. She could even turn down the volume and shut out everything if necessary.

She walked him into the hotel lobby, where he released her hand and turned to face her, giving her a polite nod.

"Thank you for everything, Miss Randall. I apologize for your earlier worry, and I hope you have a restful night."

She frowned at him. She may not have read much of those manners books, but she didn't think it was appropriate to kiss him goodnight in front of all the people occupying the lobby.

"Shall I walk you up to your room?"

"No!" he exclaimed. Then quieter, "Eden, gentlemen don't take young women up to their hotel rooms."

"But how am I supposed to kiss you goodnight?"

He took up her hand and pressed it to his lips. "This will

have to do." He flipped her hand over and kissed the palm. "May I see you tomorrow?"

"Meet me at the lab in the morning. I'll show you my bug and the copying machine."

"I'll be there."

His fingers rubbed delicate circles over the skin of her hand. The tiny motions sent waves of desire through her veins. His warm, brown eyes locked with hers.

"I still think we should go upstairs," she whispered.

He gave her a rueful smile. "Sweetheart, if I took you to my room I might lose what little self-control I seem to have." He kissed her hand one final time, then released it. "Goodnight, Eden."

"Goodnight, Bruce."

She departed and set out for home, walking slowly while Vox trotted beside her. If she couldn't go to his hotel room, finding privacy would be difficult. He also seemed reluctant to take her anywhere alone. It was an unexpected problem, but one she was determined to solve. She had time. He owed her four hundred beers.

18

October 20

"**A**NY MESSAGES?"

The youth behind the hotel desk shook his head.

Bruce heaved a sigh, half of relief, half annoyance. While he didn't want an irate telegram from his boss asking why there had been no article about last night's game, an acknowledgement of his absence would have been nice. Everyone back home must be bored with his reports. *Michigan defeats Team by a score of Large Number to Zero.* Again. Thank God there would be no more mid-week games this season. He was sick of writing about them.

On the other hand, the lack of Wednesday games would cut down on his saloon time with Eden. He would have to arrange additional times to go out to make up for it. He believed she was serious about the four hundred pints. The ridiculous proposal made him smile. She only drank two or three beers a week. He would owe her for years. Would she charge interest, or would the probable increase in the cost of a pint over time cover that? He would ask her, because he thought it would make her laugh.

Bruce arrived at the laboratory at a busy time. A dozen students sat at the workbenches, tools and parts laid out in front of them. Professor Randall had rolled a slateboard into the center of the room. He gestured at it with his chalk, referencing the curious diagrams he had drawn. Bruce squinted at the drawings. Was there a book to make these things less bewildering to laymen? *Basic Automechanology and Teletics for the Liberal Arts Student*, or some such?

A noise by his feet drew his attention downward. Vox walked a circle around him, her wings folded back, her tail swishing across the tiled floor. He almost picked her up, before remembering she would bite anyone who wasn't Eden.

He turned around, caught sight of Eden, and waved, not wanting to interrupt the class. She motioned him over, gesturing with her head at the curtained office space. He wandered over, Vox at his heels. When he stopped, she circled him once again.

"Why is she doing that?"

"Because I told her to follow you." She picked up Vox and drew the curtain aside. "Here, sit down."

Bruce waited for Eden to sit, then took the place beside her. The pair of chairs barely fit in the tiny office. In all honesty, the space would be cramped even with one chair. It was the antithesis of Professor Hart's pristine working area. Half-formed mechanical contraptions covered the desk, cubbyholes above overflowed with rolled-up schematics, and every shelf in the bookcase was stacked two deep. Tools hung all up and down the pegboard wall to his left, including the telephone, which dangled awkwardly from a hook.

Eden had cleared a place in the center of the desk for her insect dragon. It resembled an ant, with a lightbulb for its back end. A large, steel key jutted from its abdomen. Eden cranked the key several times to wind it, then set it free to walk across the desk.

It nearly walked right off the edge, and Bruce automatically lunged to catch it. The moment it touched his hand, the lightbulb flared. Startled, he dropped it. It bounced off his lap and tumbled to the floor. Flushing with embarrassment, he retrieved it and set it back on the desk. Whenever his hand was on it, the lightbulb shone.

"Why does it do that?"

"Your hands are warm. It's heat sensitive. Watch this."

A box of matches sat on the desk. She struck one and held it near the bug. The tail lit up. When she moved the match away, the light faded.

"It's not especially useful, I don't think, but it's fun," she said. "I call it a fire ant."

He stopped it from walking off the desk again, this time without dropping it.

"It's not very smart, is it?"

"Not at all. It can only walk and sense heat. Nothing else. It's a toy."

The little legs slowed as the motor wound down. When it stopped, Eden picked it up and hung it on a free hook by the telephone.

"I'm not sure whether the sensor reacts to an absolute temperature, or relative temperature when compared to the surrounding air. If it's absolute, that could be a problem come summer," she commented. "I'll have to play with it. I think I might let it run around on the floor sometime and see if it lights up when it nears the radiators."

"I heard the buildings here are steam heated. Is that true?"

"Yes. There are tunnels underground, protecting the pipes that run to all the buildings. My father took me on a tour once, when they were new. That must have been about ten years ago, now. It was hot and dark. I didn't like it." Her shoulders twitched in the slightest of shudders.

"I suppose I won't ask you to show me, then."

"Perhaps I can find someone else," she offered. "Would you like to see the copying machine?"

"Certainly."

They emerged from the office to find the students examining the bits of machinery in front of them and drawing. One of them waved a hand at Eden and beckoned her over. She shook her head.

"Is that the same fellow who locked us in the closet?"

"Yes. Marcus Heyward." Her voice dropped. "He's become something of a pest. He thinks I should conspire with him to sell Vox to the highest bidder."

"Ah. That was the trouble last weekend."

"Yes. He was annoying me. He's been trying to talk to me all morning. He must have some new idea for a potential buyer. Honestly, if he put half as much effort into his schoolwork as he did into his ridiculous schemes, he could probably make good marks and earn a decent wage after graduation."

"The quick path to riches is seductive."

She huffed. "Some things are more important than money."

"I agree."

"Good."

"Which is why I'm accepting your offer to owe you beer for the rest of your life."

"Only four years," she corrected. "Perhaps less if we go out more often."

He almost said if he stuck around for four years he would stick around forever, but the words died in his throat. How serious was he about this? About her? He lived in a hotel. This was temporary. He had a job halfway across the country. Thoughts of the future conjured up conflicted emotions he didn't wish to dwell on.

"What are we copying?" he asked, to escape from any further discussion.

"I had considered a page from your notebook, but it would

be so scribbly it wouldn't copy well. So we're making a sign. The original goes here."

She pointed at the flat panel on one side of the machine. A handwritten sign reading, "Do not touch!" lay in the center.

"We can always use more of these around the lab." She pulled a lever, and a metallic arm dropped down. The end of it looked like a pen without a nib. "This side is the sensor. It will move across the paper. Whenever it encounters a black line, the other side will make a mark."

She showed Bruce the opposite end, where a blank paper sat beneath a second arm capped with an actual pen.

"Ready? It's rather noisy." She twisted her earring and flipped a switch.

The grinding gears and squeaking metal made Bruce wince, but none of the students even looked up from their work. Anyone here on a regular basis would quickly learn to ignore the clamor, as the copy machine moved with all the speed of an arthritic slug. He watched it for five minutes, and it had drawn no more than "Do." A remarkable contraption, he decided, but not a practical one. He could have written a new sign in seconds.

"Does it always take so long?" He looked right at Eden so she could see his lips moving, but even so he almost had to shout.

"Yes. Close to an hour for most things. I wouldn't have copied this sign except as a demonstration. We use it for schematics. When you've spent hours perfecting your drawing, it's nice to have a machine to make the copy. It frees you to start another one."

"An excellent point." He walked around the machine for a better view of the pen.

"Miss Randall, a moment, if you please."

Bruce turned toward the familiar voice. Apparently Eden's pest, Mr. Heyward, was the man colluding with Tagget. He couldn't say it surprised him.

"Oh, bother," Eden muttered. "Bruce, would you excuse me for a minute?"

"Sure. I'll just be looking around." He turned a harsh gaze on Heyward to tell him not to try anything, but the boy ignored him. Bruce thought he might have to practice his scowls in a mirror, given the way Eden collected troublesome men.

He wandered about the lab, poking through the odd things in the drawers and cabinets and watching Eden out of the corner of his eye. She was having none of whatever Heyward was offering. Her replies were curt, her expression fierce. Vox rested safely in her arms, tucked up against her body like a football. Heyward was a fool to think he could ever change her mind.

Bruce toyed with a gear with unevenly spaced teeth, wondering what possible purpose it might serve. The students were preparing to depart, and several cast questioning looks in his direction. He leaned back against the cabinet, crossing his legs at the ankle, trying to perfect an air of nonchalance. More likely he looked like a skulking ne'er-do-well.

Eventually Heyward gave up. Eden turned away, and he stalked off, grumbling. Bruce started toward her, but had gone no more than five feet when his nemesis strode through the door.

Tagget gave no indication he had ever met Heyward as the two crossed paths. A single manicured eyebrow rose when he spied Bruce. Bruce glared at him, but Tagget only smirked and continued in Eden's direction.

"Miss Randall, I'm delighted to find you here."

"Good morning, Mr. Tagget." She didn't sound eager to see him, but neither did she sound hostile.

"Allow me to be the first to invite you to the presentation Professor Hart and I will be making next week. We have an exciting new technology to announce, and I would like for you to be in the front row for the reveal."

"I will attend if at all possible. Thank you." She signed her thanks, as Bruce had seen her do before. Fingers to lips, then move your hand toward the other person. He knew that sign. She didn't smile as broadly for Tagget as she did when she thanked Bruce. Hah!

"I'm thrilled to hear it," Tagget replied. "I will send a formal invitation the moment the exact time and place have been determined." He leaned closer and lowered his voice. "I also have a more personal invitation to extend."

Bruce edged as close as he could manage without being blatantly rude. He opened a cupboard and pretended to be interested in the contents. He wasn't going to fool anyone, but they couldn't do anything about his presence, either.

"I'm very hopeful, my Elysian beauty, that you and I can continue our Saturday evening habit of attending performances at the Opera House. I will procure our usual seats."

"I'm sorry. I'm not available on Saturday. Bruce and I are going out for drinks after the game. He owes me a few beers, you know."

"Is that so?" There was a hint of annoyance in his tone. Bruce considered it a victory.

"Yep."

"You are fond of beer, Miss Randall?"

"I am."

"Do you drink wine, as well? The dining room at my hotel offers some excellent choices. I understand it to be one of the top restaurants in the city. I would love to take you to dinner. Sunday, perhaps?"

"I…" She paused, an uncertain frown puckering her lips. "I will have to think on it."

"I understand. I would never wish to pressure you into a decision. I will await your answer. I am, as always, charmed to see you." He seized Eden's hand and kissed it.

Bruce fumbled the box of parts he had picked up. Nuts and bolts bounced across the floor.

Tagget spared him a condescending look. He bowed to Eden, letting her hand slide slowly from his. "Good day, Miss Randall." He glanced down at Bruce, who had bent to clean up after himself. "I suggest you stick to writing about sports, Mr. Coldwater, lest you find yourself in trouble, once again."

"It's Caldwell, you jackass," Bruce snarled at Tagget's retreating form. He stuffed a handful of bolts back into the box.

"He knows that," Eden said. "I think he's trying to annoy you and it's working. You should ignore him."

She bent to help Bruce gather up the scattered parts. Their hands collided and they froze, faces only inches apart. The fire in her blue-eyed gaze sucked the breath from his lungs.

"I can't." His fingers closed over Eden's. "He's making moves on my girl."

A pink blush stole over her sun-kissed cheeks. "I'm your girl?"

He cleared his throat awkwardly. "Unless you object?"

"No." She drew the word out. "No, I don't object."

"Wonderful! Er…" He withdrew his hand and tried to collect himself. "I'm delighted to hear it."

Bruce scrambled to his feet and returned the box of bolts to the cabinet. "Why is that lower cabinet locked? None of the others are."

"It's where we store expensive things." Eden flipped a switch. "Open." The lock turned and the door swung wide. She waved a hand at the contents. "Experimental pieces Father doesn't want damaged, anything made of gold or silver, and our luxene supply."

Bruce knelt to examine the jug of glowing green liquid. "This powers all the dragons?"

"Many of them, yes. Some are purely clockwork."

He ran a finger over the label. "You buy this from Dynalux?"

"No. Well, we never have in the past. It wasn't worth the extra cost per gallon. This new bottle was a donation."

"From Tagget?"

"Yes. He supplied the entire department. It was a generous offer. It would have been foolish to turn it down."

"Luxene is costly, I understand?"

"That jug is probably worth about five hundred dollars."

Bruce let out a low whistle. "Lord. Why did he do it?"

She shrugged. "Bribery?"

"Probably." Bruce closed the cabinet. The mechanical lock shut tight. "Where to now?"

"The library?" Eden suggested. "I wanted to do some reading. Then maybe lunch?"

"If I buy you lunch, does it lower the beer debt?"

"No."

"Will you permit me to do so, anyhow?"

"Sure. I'm your girl, now. Maybe I'll buy *you* lunch sometime."

"Please don't. It would be enormously embarrassing."

She grinned in such a way that he feared she might do it, regardless. They walked hand-in-hand to the library, where Eden found her book and settled in a chair to read. Bruce took himself off to scour old newspapers and magazines. Tagget's involvement with Dynalux rubbed him the wrong way. He intended to find out why.

Tagget could threaten arrest all he wanted. He could keep wooing Eden with dinners and concerts. Bruce wouldn't be swayed. He was going to investigate until he figured out what the hell was going on. And he was damn well not going to let anyone steal his girlfriend.

19

October 22

Eᴅᴇɴ ᴛᴏᴏᴋ ᴘɪᴛʏ on the boy cranking the scoreboard a few minutes into the second half and took over for him. The winch that spun the numbers was heavy, but Eden was strong for her size, and it provided a pleasant distraction from what had otherwise become a boring game. Any hope West Virginia might prove a stronger opponent had long since been dashed. Now the greatest excitement stemmed from the possibility the final score might be the most lopsided victory the Wolverines had ever had.

"I wish I had a camera," Bruce mused, watching Eden add yet another touchdown. "The caption would be fantastic. 'If you think the Michigan boys are tough, you haven't met the girls.'"

The wolverine snarled at him. He no longer flinched away from the creature. Eden smiled. He had adapted to its presence better than some of the players.

The previous night's declaration of their official couplehood left a lingering warmth in her belly. She'd never been someone's girl before. Paul must have thought of her that way, she supposed, but she'd never known or approved of such a thing.

Courting had always seemed a peculiar ritual to her, full of formal visits and flowers. Bruce's way, though, where he bought her beer and took her out for activities she loved, was great fun. He may not have had the money Tagget did, but she was certain he would take her to concerts when he could afford it. Even something as simple as a walk around town was enjoyable with him. Ending their evenings with exhilarating kisses added yet one more layer to the excitement.

She had a plan for their outing tonight. Hopefully it would lead to a lot of fun and a lot of kissing. The final part remained vague, unfortunately. Her information regarding this sex business and how one worked one's way up to it remained in doubt. Joey's explanations hadn't covered how couples decided what to do and where to do it. She might have to guess and see how Bruce reacted.

Her first goal was to try some of the touching and removing of clothing. Just thinking about it made her tingly. It had occurred to her that perhaps the reason she wasn't supposed to know about any of this was the matter of displaying oneself in an unclothed state. Certain people reacted negatively when she went about with a portion of bare leg showing, or a top that didn't cover her fully to the neck. Eden had never thought any of her clothing inappropriate for public display. Surely in private it was entirely her own business how much she showed and to whom?

Another score meant she had to crank the scoreboard again. Bruce jotted the details in his notebook.

"Let me know if you get bored of that," he said.

She smiled at him. He couldn't fool her with his transparent offer. He wanted to give her a way out if she grew tired, but he understood an athlete's pride. He wouldn't tell her, "Let me help you with that," or imply weakness of any kind.

"I'm enjoying it. If we top the Buffalo score, I want to be the one who records it."

"What was the final in that game?"

"One hundred twenty-eight to nothing."

"They might just beat that," he mused. "I'll tell you this, I love watching your boys, but *I* wouldn't want to play them."

Eden just grinned.

"I've been meaning to ask you, do you ever try to read the lips of the opponents and steal their plays?"

She laughed. "I'd love to, but they're too far away and moving around too much. Lip reading is hard. I know a man who attended Gallaudet. He says the team gathers in a circular formation to discuss plays when they play other schools for the Deaf. It hides their signing. I think it could be a great idea for all teams, but it has yet to catch on. Gallaudet doesn't even bother when they play hearing teams. If they played us, I'd absolutely watch them sign and steal all their plays."

Bruce's broad smile caused a little giddy shiver inside her. "Of course you would! You're a loyal Wolverine." He chuckled, giving a slight shake of his head. "Did you know, when I arrived here I was dreading watching so many games? I'd avoided football since my injury. I was bitter I couldn't play, I suppose. I covered only one or two games per season since I took this job. But your enthusiasm is unlike any I've known. It's infectious. You've made football fun again. Thank you."

Eden's cheeks burned. "You're welcome."

He stood by her side for the remainder of the game, cheering when she did and watching her operate the massive scoreboard with undisguised admiration. When she put up the final score of one hundred thirty to nothing, he scribbled an extra note in his journal. Maybe she would get a mention in his article.

"You will need time for your work, I assume?" she asked. "Where and when should we meet after?" A new idea sprang to mind. "Or would you allow me to tag along? I'd love to see how you submit an article, and I promise not to peek over your shoulder while you're writing."

"Okay," he agreed. "But in return, you must show me what you do with that thing." He gestured at the wolverine. "Where is it stored?"

"With all the other football equipment. It has a crate. Come on, I'll show you."

She stowed the wolverine, then walked with him to the hotel, where he took a seat in the lobby and began to transform his notes into a full article. She found a newspaper someone had abandoned and read it while she waited for him. It didn't hold her interest well, and she found herself staring at Bruce.

He wrote quickly, and grinned as he worked. He possessed a naturally carefree disposition, but today he was cheerier than she had ever seen. Perhaps he, too, was excited by the alteration to the status of their relationship.

"How many Rs in embarrassed?"

"Two. And two Ss, also." Eden had always been a good speller. She'd breezed through her *McGuffey's Eclectic Spelling Book*, memorizing the look of the words long before her mouth learned to form them. The book had been invaluable, teaching her the concept of pronunciation in a visual manner. She'd known that one did not say the "p" in "pneumatic", and that "hart" and "heart" sounded the same, even when the only sound she experienced was restricted to the funny feeling she sometimes had in her ear when a train passed by.

"Nearly finished," Bruce told her. "What do you think of this line? 'Alumna Eden Randall, keeper of the mechanical wolverine, had the honor of displaying the historic score on the clockwork scoreboard for all to see.'"

"I like it. It's great fun to be in a newspaper. I shall have to clip the article out and store it in my safe-box."

"Let me read you the whole article. Sometimes it helps me edit when I read it aloud."

He read the entire column, changed several things, read it again, and made a few final tweaks before declaring it done.

Satisfied with his work, he led Eden across the street to the telephone and telegraph office.

The long-distance telephone process fascinated her. Bruce's call bounced from one operator to the next, connecting city-to-city until he could speak with the newspaper office in Boston. Despite Tagget's suspect behavior, she had to admire the work done by his company. The process took only a few minutes and the fees were a fraction of what they had once been. Coast-to-coast calls were even possible now. She might not make frequent use of the telephone, but for people like Bruce the new technology was life-changing.

He read his article again, this time in a slow, deliberate voice, then listened as it was read back and made a few corrections. He answered a question or two, and then the conversation ended, the submission complete. It hadn't taken as long as she had thought it might.

"That's all there is to it," he announced. "Shall we go have that drink now? Or would you prefer dinner first?"

"Would you mind greatly if we walked to my house? I need to pick up something, and I would like to change."

His eyebrows arched. "Are we going more or less formal?"

"Less." She started in the direction of home, and he followed without complaint. "I thought we might go out and play football later, and I don't want to ruin this top."

He nodded, his eyes scanning her fancy, brocade corset. "I know that's one of your favorites, and you will need it for the game next weekend, of course. Will you be traveling to Wisconsin?"

"I'd like to. We can't bring the wolverine, though, so I have no excuse to travel with the team. I may have to purchase a ticket and sit in the grandstands like an ordinary person."

"Do you have a camera?"

"My parents do."

"Bring it. I'll tell everyone you are my photographer and get you a press pass."

"Will I have to mispronounce all my Rs so I sound like I'm from Boston? I don't know if I can make my mouth do that." She repositioned Vox and turned up her volume. "Tell me about your schooling at 'Hahvuhd' again so I can practice."

He moved closer. "You are teasing me, Miss Randall. I must conclude that you find me silly, but adorable."

"Or perhaps just silly."

"The way you kiss me suggests otherwise."

The huskiness in his voice sent a shiver down her spine. Her plan hadn't anticipated kissing before dinner. She would improvise if necessary.

He stepped away, restoring the space between them. True, it wasn't yet dark and the streets were full of people, but a flutter of disappointment ran through her nonetheless.

The silence that fell lacked its usual tranquility. Something hummed in the air between them. Perhaps he, too, had made a plan for the evening. Perhaps he meant to be someplace private, kissing her this very minute, his fingers trailing over her skin, his hard, lean body crushed to hers...

She fanned herself with one hand, feeling suddenly overheated, and forced herself to think only of dinner for the remainder of the walk home.

Bruce shifted from foot to foot and took another survey of the Randalls' front hall. Was there anything more uncomfortable than waiting alone in the house where your girlfriend lived with her parents, trying not to think about her up in her room, removing her clothing?

Don't answer that. Stop thinking about it.

Eden acted as if it were perfectly ordinary to invite him in, but Bruce had known her long enough to know her idea of what constituted proper behavior often didn't mesh with society's.

He stared at a clockwork contraption on the wall, trying to imagine what possible purpose it could serve. A large key jutted out from the machine. His curiosity got the better of him, and he reached out to wind it. Gears spun. Two panels in the wall slid apart. A mechanical arm sprang from the opening.

Bruce yelped and jumped back, startled. The arm flexed its metal fingers, grabbing at empty air. He backed further away. Apparently fantasizing about Eden would have been the better choice.

He heard her footsteps on the stairs.

"What are you doing down there?" She appeared wearing the same trousers as earlier, but she had changed into a plain black shirt and a simple leather underbust corset.

"I, uh… sorry." He gestured at the device in the wall.

"Oh." She laughed. "It wants your hat. If my father were home, it would have offered you his hat rather than reaching for yours."

"What's wrong with a hat rack?"

She shrugged. "Too ordinary?"

"I can see where some of your eccentricity comes from."

"Much of it, I imagine. My parents are known to be unusual, but they're happy that way."

"I'm glad of it. It can be a trial for those of us who don't fit in."

"You think you don't fit in? You don't seem terribly odd to me."

"You'd be surprised."

"Hmm." She looked thoughtful for a moment, then shrugged again. "I'm hungry. Would you like some dinner? We have some eggs in the kitchen. I can scramble them up with a bit of cheese and some vegetables. And you can try some toast with my black raspberry preserves."

Bruce weighed the impropriety of remaining alone in the house with her versus the offer of a free, home cooked meal. Tempting. Both very tempting. He hesitated long enough that she took his silence as acceptance, and ushered him into the kitchen.

"The dishes are there." She pointed at a cabinet. "Glasses in the next one over. Silver in the drawer below."

She set to work prepping the food, with no further instructions. Bruce grabbed two of everything but the plates and carried them to the dining table in the next room. The plates he set on the counter near Eden. He then opened random cabinets and drawers until he found napkins.

"Could I pour something to drink? Some wine, perhaps?"

"No wine. My parents don't drink."

"Not at all?" That surprised him, given Eden's fondness for saloons.

"No, not at all. The only alcohol in the house is for the cleaning and fabrication of their inventions."

"What do you drink, then?"

"Water." She pointed at the sink, where a pump had been modified with odd bits of clockwork. "We have an auto-pump with a special filter. The water is clean and tasty."

Bruce wandered back into the dining room, retrieved the glasses, and filled them with cold, clear water. He found the auto-pump easy to use, and decided he would love to have one in his own house someday. City water was too untrustworthy.

In short order, he was leaning back in his chair, his belly full of delicious eggs and even tastier jam. His discomfort in her home had vanished along with the food. They cleaned up side-by-side, as if they did this every day.

"You'll have to show me the rest of the house someday." The foolish words were out of his mouth before he knew what he was saying.

Eden wiped her hands and hung the towel. "Of course. But first you owe me a beer."

Saved from himself. He hustled them both out of the house and back toward town before he could regret not getting a peek into her bedroom.

He soon saw her settled happily in her favorite corner, a

beer in her hand, and her football and Vox on the table. She patted the football.

"So, are you willing to play a bit when we finish here? But no cheating this time?"

"I remember your new rules," he replied. "I won't cheat. But I may not be above taking a penalty or two."

"Neither will I."

Her gaze was so hot he had to cough and adjust himself under the table. He changed the subject out of desperation.

"Tell me about yourself. When's your birthday?"

"August twenty-third. You?"

"July fifth. I missed Independence Day by an hour. The first of countless disappointments for my family."

"What, your family doesn't like you?" She sounded both shocked and appalled.

"No, I'm exaggerating. Overall I have a good relationship with my parents. They simply can't understand why I'm not suited to their lifestyle. Caldwell men have been lawyers and investors since before the family came to America. I'm the only heir and I have rejected both fields for one that pays… well, rather poorly, to be blunt. They find it scandalous. Also, my mother is certain biomechanics are the devil's work and I would've been better off hobbling about with a cane. She's always lamenting and praying for my soul. I waver between finding it irritating and hilarious."

"I've known people who think that way. It's one of the reasons I don't talk about…" She broke off and looked down at her beer. "About my earpiece."

Bruce was certain that wasn't what she'd intended to say. He studied her for a moment, sitting in silence, her finger running along Vox's tail.

Vox. Of course. The dragon was connected to her biomechanics. Some wireless technology he would never understand. It explained why she struggled with a telephone and why sometimes she had trouble hearing him when he was standing right next to her. The sound filtered through the dragon. No wonder Tagget wanted her.

Bruce itched to ask for more details, but he wouldn't pressure Eden to reveal her close-kept secrets. She would tell him in her own time.

He tried instead for an innocuous question. "Did you design Vox? Her outer form, I mean?"

"In part. Her body needed to be large enough to hold all the parts, so that limited what we could do, but I chose her tail and I asked my mother to make her fly. The football shape of her belly makes her comfortable to hold in one arm."

"She's impressive. The voice controls alone are remarkable, but I've never seen even a wired dragon respond to such an impressive array of commands."

"She was simpler to begin with. We've added commands to her over the years. Here, hold out your hand."

Puzzled, Bruce did as she asked.

"Vox, friend," Eden instructed. She pushed the dragon's nose into Bruce's open palm.

It was an odd feeling, to be nuzzled by a little brass head. The metal was cool, but not cold, and smooth as a mirror. The dragon's crystal eyes flashed. Her antennae twitched.

"What is she doing?"

"Learning you. Her sensors will recognize you now, and she will never bite you."

The display of trust warmed him inside and out. "You don't fear I might steal her?"

"If I feared that, I wouldn't have done it."

"Well, I'm honored, in any event. May I pick her up?"

"Yes, but take care with her wings."

The dragon weighed less than Bruce expected. She made no protest when he turned her all about, examining her. He set her up on his shoulder.

"Does she suit me, do you think?"

"You're cute, but she looks better with me."

"Anything would look better with you, sweetheart."

She shook her head. "Vox, come." The dragon hopped down and trotted across the table to Eden. "No matter what, only I can command her."

"As it should be. Now, about that football you brought with you..."

Half an hour later, he faced her across the ball, eager for their contest, and not caring in the slightest who won their game as long as he had a chance to kiss her at least once. Her eyes gleamed with delight and mischief.

They ran, they tackled, they fumbled and grappled for the ball, laughing and sneaking kisses. The game devolved into absurdity, both of them throwing and kicking the ball almost at random. Bruce couldn't remember the score. Eden surely would know, but he couldn't have cared less as long as they were having fun.

This was what made her so special. She shared many things in common with other women he admired. She was smart, pretty, self-possessed. Never before, though, had he spent time with a woman who was plain old fun to be with. Whether tossing back beers or running about on the ballfield, her vivaciousness enthralled him.

She took advantage of his distraction and tackled him. When she straddled him and planted a fierce kiss on his mouth, he tossed the ball aside, no longer interested. He grasped her tiny waist with both hands because it was the only way he could think to avoid touching her inappropriately.

Eden had no such reservations. Her hands roamed across his chest, her fingers delving beneath his vest for a better feel. Her lips skimmed across his, teasing their way down over his poorly-shaven jaw to his neck. The tickle of her tongue on his skin dragged a groan from deep inside his chest. His cock stiffened with every miniscule movement of her body atop his own.

Her hands wandered lower, caressing his hips and thighs. Bruce abandoned any attempt to behave and cupped her buttocks, grinding himself against her. She gave a little squeak of surprise, then slipped a tentative hand between his legs.

"Ooh." Curious fingers traced the outline of his shaft. "It does get rather hard."

"Eden," he moaned. Her bold innocence had driven him out of his head. He didn't know whether to plead for more or beg her to stop.

"Should we go somewhere private?"

"Yes."

No. No. Why did he say that? He was going to ruin her. She was too good for that, but he ached with wanting her.

"Where? Your hotel?"

"Too many people."

"My house?"

"Your parents!" A small amount of sense filtered into his brain. "We can't. We shouldn't."

She climbed off him and held out a hand to help him up. He staggered to his feet. Eden scooped up the football and called to Vox.

"I think the hotel is fine," she decided. She took hold of his hand and tugged him toward the gate.

"Eden, I can't let you do this."

"You don't want to?"

"No, I do, but..."

"So do I. I see no problem."

"What about your reputation?"

"My reputation for being weird?"

"Your reputation for being virtuous."

"They don't call me 'the virtuous girl,' they call me 'the weird girl.' I want to try what comes next. I like touching you."

God. Words like that would destroy him. "Maybe we can do a little." They would do a lot. He was a damned fool. And he was going to ruin her.

20

Eden tossed her corset on the floor beside her boots and began to unbutton her shirt. Her fingers paused two buttons in.

"Do I undress myself, or do you undress me?"

Bruce walked over to her. He had removed his vest, and his suspenders dangled in a surprisingly enticing manner. His finger caught the top of her blouse, tugging it open where the buttons were undone.

"We undress one another. Slowly."

He undid the third button, then the fourth, his fingers brushing over the skin of her chest, down to the exposed tops of her breasts. His touch made her pulse race and her skin flush.

When he popped the final button, her blouse fell open, exposing her to his heated gaze. Dark, liquid eyes caressed her, and his tongue snaked out to moisten his lips. He pushed the shirt down off her shoulders, sending it fluttering to the floor.

"God, you're gorgeous."

His hands cupped her breasts, and she gave a little gasp of pleasure. He teased the nipples with gentle flicks of his fingers, pulling them taut and erect.

"Oh," she gasped. "Oh, that's nice."

Eden tugged at his shirt, trying to open it despite the distraction. After several fumbling attempts, he paused to remove the offending garment for her.

"Let's retire to the bed, shall we?"

"Yes, please."

She clambered up onto the sheets, taking Vox so as not to miss a word he said. Bruce lay down beside her, and they came together, lips brushing, hands seeking bare flesh. She explored the warm skin of his chest, dusted with fine dark hairs. His small nipples hardened when she rubbed them.

Bruce kissed along her jaw and down her neck as his fingers continued their sensual exploration. She would have never guessed her skin could be so sensitive. Every place his lips touched burned with delight. He moved lower, his mouth replacing his hands on her breasts. His tongue traced a slow circle over one rosy nipple. Eden's head lolled back, and a low groan escaped her throat.

"Bruce," she gasped. "So... lovely."

The place between her legs was wet and throbbing. She ached for his touch there. The pleasure was everything she had hoped for, but she hadn't expected this yearning for something deeper. For some sort of satisfaction she didn't entirely understand. A satisfaction she knew he could give her.

She yanked at the fastenings on her trousers, wriggling them down her hips. Pinned beneath Bruce's body, the garments stuck fast.

He lifted his head from her bosom, and his hands settled atop hers. "Allow me, sweetheart."

Eden lifted her hips to assist him, and with one firm tug, he pulled both trousers and drawers down. She kicked her legs free and tossed the clothing aside.

Bruce stared down at her for a long, silent moment. "Eden, you are phenomenal," he murmured.

Eden had never been shy about nakedness. She had

frequently splashed unclothed in the creek as a child, and still she occasionally hiked up her skirt or slipped out of her top in private on hot days. Even so, his unabashed admiration brought a blush to her skin. She felt the strangest sensation of being vulnerable and powerful all at the same time.

"May I see the rest of you?" she asked.

Bruce quickly divested himself of his trousers, then rejoined her on the bed, allowing her to take her time studying him. She was gratified to see he blushed, too. In fact, his blush ran all the way down his neck and across his upper chest. Her fingers swept over his pink-tinged skin and down across his belly.

The pictures in the medical texts hadn't prepared her for the sight of a naked man. Her eyes drank him in, mesmerized. Everything about him intrigued her, from the union of flesh and metal in his biomechanical knee, to the strong muscles of his thighs, to the jut of his erection. She remembered the firmness of it beneath his clothing. How different would it be bare against her hand? Or inside of her? A shiver of excitement raced up her spine.

"I think you're beautiful," she murmured.

"Never had a woman say that before."

Her fingers traced the trail of hair that led from his belly to his groin. She curled her hand around his shaft. "It's true. You fascinate me."

"God, Eden," he groaned.

He reached between her legs, finding the sensitive flesh that had been longing for his touch. She gasped aloud. Everything he did made her crave him more. No longer would she be content to steal brief moments of exploration. She wanted everything. Every lovely inch of him.

Eden pushed him down onto the bed, then straddled him, bringing their hips together, squirming against him. A thrilling tension had begun to build inside of her. His finger caressed the swollen bud at the front of her sex. The proper word for it escaped her in the haze of pleasure. She needed everything. She needed him inside of her.

He was so close. She could feel him butting up against her entrance. She adjusted herself, then thrust back into him, forcing him inside of her.

Pain lanced through her. Her mouth opened in shock, but no sound came out. He didn't fit, or had gone in too far, or... what? She couldn't explain. She only knew something wasn't right.

She scrambled off of him, tears stinging her eyes. The pain lessened, but a dull ache lingered between her legs. When she moved, it smarted. A sob escaped her lips. She wasn't certain whether the discomfort or her frustration had caused it. What had she done wrong?

Bruce had gone white.

"Eden, sweetheart." His words came out in an anguished moan.

She had hurt him, too. She had ruined everything. Emotions flooded her. Anger, sadness, and above all, bitter disappointment.

"I didn't mean to..." To what? End the fun? Destroy the pleasure? Cause them both pain? "To muck it all up."

"No." Bruce started to reach for her, then jerked his hand back. "Oh, God, Eden, I'm so sorry," he choked out. "I shouldn't have let it go so far. I never wanted to hurt you." Unshed tears glistened in his eyes. What had she done to him? He blamed himself for her own stupid impatience. The shame of it twisted her gut.

She was furious with herself. She was furious with Joey. Either he had lied or he had left out crucial information. She grabbed for her clothing. Her experiment had failed, and her mind was a muddled mess. She needed to go home, think, rest, and maybe cry before she could determine what to do next.

"I'm sorry," she signed, then repeated the words out loud. "I'm sorry." It wasn't much in the way of an apology, but it was all she could give. Once she had cleared her head she would make amends. If such a thing were possible.

Bruce stumbled out of bed. His face was still white as anything, and his hands trembled. "No, Eden, it was my fault. It'll be okay. I promise. I... I'll do right by you. We can get married."

"What?"

He dropped to his knees. "I swear it, Eden. I'll take care of you. Marry me."

"No!"

Panic crushed her chest. They couldn't. She wouldn't. She was happy *here*. Her life was hers. Her future still a work in progress.

I'll take care of you.

How could he say such a thing? How could he even think it? Why would he threaten to decide her life for her? To take her away from all she loved? She had to get away. She stuffed her legs into her trousers and yanked on her blouse.

"Eden," he pleaded.

"I won't. When I said I would be your girl, that didn't mean you could make me do... whatever. I'm not *yours*."

She did up only enough of the buttons to make the shirt stay closed, then snatched up her corset. She didn't bother to button her boots.

"Eden."

Bruce's face was a mask of utter devastation. Wet trails marred his cheeks. He couldn't seem to say anything but her name any longer. Whatever pain she had done to her body and her heart, she feared she had done worse to him.

Tears clouded her vision. She grabbed Vox and clutched the dragon to her chest.

"I'm so sorry. I'm so, so sorry."

She pushed the door open and fled for home.

Bruce hadn't cried over a girl since his schoolboy days at Andover. He wiped angrily at his watery eyes. He had ruined her, caused irreparable damage to her life, and probably lost her forever. The look of absolute horror on her face when he had suggested they get married told him everything he needed to know. She despised him. He couldn't blame her. He despised himself.

Where was the relief he ought to be feeling? He'd taken leave of his senses, allowed himself to be distracted by a pretty and enthusiastic woman. He'd taken advantage of her innocence, but he'd done the honorable thing. She'd refused him. He was free of any further obligation.

He buried his face in his hands. He was free of her. Free to move on from this colossal mistake. There were other places, other women. And one massive problem. When Eden had fled, she'd ripped his heart right out of his chest.

He couldn't go on without it.

21

October 23

Eden spied Joey at church, and spent half the service looking daggers at him, which probably wasn't very Christian of her. The moment she was out the door, she rushed to catch him, calling a hasty goodbye to her parents. They frowned, but didn't try to stop her running off, thank goodness. She'd been sullen all morning, and they'd noticed. She couldn't very well explain why she was upset. Not when they didn't even want her to *know* about sex. Maybe if they'd been willing to enlighten her, she wouldn't have botched it so badly. Maybe she and Bruce would still be friends.

"Eden, hi," Joey greeted her.

"You lied," she accused.

He gave her a look of bafflement. "What?"

"You lied. You're a liar." Even after a night's sleep, her mental state fluctuated between anger and sorrow. She wasn't certain which was winning just now.

"I lied about what?"

"You know."

"No, I don't know. What are you talking about?"

Eden gritted her teeth. "The sex thing."

"Eden!" He leaned close to her and lowered his voice. "Christ, Eden, we're barely out of church. You shouldn't talk about such things."

"And you shouldn't blaspheme," she shot back. She grabbed hold of his arm, walking rapidly to keep pace with his much longer stride.

"I'm not going to talk about this now," he insisted.

"Oh, yes, you are. You lied to me and messed everything up, and I'm so furious I just want to cry!"

He slowed and looked at her, his brow crinkling in a frown of concern. "Eden, what's going on? No, wait until we get to campus. We'll find a quiet place to talk."

"Fine."

She picked up her pace even more, half-dragging him down State Street. Campus was quiet. She chose a spot near the library and stopped, spinning to face him. She hugged Vox to her chest.

"Why did you lie to me?" she demanded.

"I didn't lie to you. I don't know what you're talking about."

"You did. You told me sex was nice. Well, it wasn't. It hurt."

His eyes widened in horror. "Eden, what did you do?"

"It was all going well, and everything was wonderful, until I tried… you know." She felt a rush of embarrassment. She didn't want to discuss her ignorance and foolishness, but she had to explain or she would never learn what had gone wrong.

"And then it was awful!" she blurted. "It hurt, and I was upset, and so was he, and now I think he hates me!"

"Oh, shit," Joey moaned. "Oh, God. Eden, I'm so sorry. Hell. I never should have told you."

"No, you just shouldn't have lied about it!"

"I didn't lie."

"Then why did it hurt?"

"Because it was your first time. The first time can be bad. It hurts for lots of girls."

"And why didn't you tell me that?"

"Because I didn't think you were going to run out and try it! Christ, Eden!"

"Stop swearing."

"I think the situation calls for some profanity, if you don't mind!"

"I tried swearing last night. It didn't help." Her shoulders slumped. "So it wasn't my fault, then? I didn't do things all wrong?"

"What was wrong was that you did it at all; but that's not your fault, that's *his* fault. It was that reporter, wasn't it? Dammit, Eden, I told you to be careful with him. I'm going to go kick his ass."

"Don't you dare!"

"Eden, he took advantage of you. He stole your innocence."

"He didn't steal anything. You leave him alone. You have no idea."

"Eden…"

"If you touch him, I will kick *your* ass," she threatened. "You didn't see him. He was so upset. He looked… devastated."

"He was probably terrified you might demand he marry you."

"No."

Quite the opposite. He had asked her, and she had turned him down in the most terrible of ways—shouting, crying, running away, without any reasonable explanation. He must hate her. The books were unambiguous on this matter. Men loathed rejection.

She'd been so foolish. Had she really thought nothing would come of their dates? Had she thought at all? Courtship led to talk of marriage, and often to proposals. She knew this not only from her books, but from experience. But she couldn't marry him. Not when he would drag her away to Boston where she would be miserable and even more out-of-place than she was here.

And yet, she had welcomed and encouraged his attentions. All for her own selfish pleasures. All for roller skating and beers and a few stolen kisses. She'd done just as she pleased, as if their friendship could continue on indefinitely, and she would never have to face the future. Stupid, stupid. She whacked her forehead harder than necessary as she signed the word.

Joey grabbed at her arm. "Eden, don't hit yourself. I'm such an ass. I should never have told you those things."

She shook him off. "Oh, stop blaming yourself. It's much more my fault. I only wish you'd told me that the first time was bad. Then I would have tried it with someone else."

His jaw dropped.

"What?" she asked.

"Are you out of your mind?"

"The whole point was that it was supposed to be enjoyable. If I'd known, I could have gotten the bad part out of the way with anyone, and then it would have been good with the man I actually like."

"Eden, that's crazy talk."

"It sounds sensible to me. Is it only the first time that's painful? Will it feel better next time?"

"My first few times were awkward. I don't know for sure how it is with girls. I only know what they say: that the first time hurt and it was better after."

"Hmm. It sounds as though it takes practice." She thought for a moment, then sighed. "I don't know if it even matters. Bruce might never want to talk to me again."

"Eden, forget him. He's a stuck-up, rich city boy. You'll find yourself a nice guy from around here someday."

She shook her head. The last time a guy from around here had been interested, it had been a disaster also.

"No. I made the mess. It's my responsibility to fix it."

The thought of Bruce miserable and hating her made her chest ache. She owed him an apology and an explanation. He owed her three hundred ninety-nine beers. Also, she had left her football in his hotel room in her haste. They needed to reconcile. Did the library have books on how to repair ruined friendships? It was worth looking into.

She would research. She would learn. And then she would win him back.

22

THE WHOOPS AND CHEERS of the little boys brought a smile to Bruce's face for the first time that day. He had stumbled upon their play while out for his walk and it had been the balm his wounded soul needed. When they'd seen Eden's football and begged for a game, he'd leapt at the chance to redeem himself in some small way.

"Michigan wins again!" the oldest boy shouted.

"Harvard is crushed!" called another. "Can you play another game, Mister?"

Bruce tucked Eden's football under his arm and shook his head. "I'm afraid you three will have to find a tougher opponent. I do have a job, and I need to return this football to its owner."

Liar. He was badly neglecting his job, and wasn't at all ready to face Eden. He had other work in mind. Work he wouldn't be paid for and would be wiser to abandon. An echo of his father's condemnation of his career choice played in his head.

You're damned stubborn, boy, and none too bright.

Probably true.

He bid the boys goodbye and left the fairgrounds behind. The exercise had done him good, and brought some morning fun to the local children. He remained Bruce Caldwell, Colossal Fool and Seducer of Innocent Women, but he wasn't a complete reprobate. He followed the trolley tracks back into town, the long walk leaving him plenty of time to contemplate his life and set himself several new goals.

A few hours later, he ducked into a private phone booth for the last telephone call of the day, armed with stacks of notes and very little money. He would be eating lean for the remainder of his time here, and there would be no more beer. When he reconciled with Eden, he would have to take her on outings that cost nothing.

If. *If* he reconciled. More likely she never wanted to see him again.

"So, Dynalux, eh?" Richardson asked. "You're gonna love what I found."

"Spill."

"So, they were founded about a decade ago as one of many new luxene suppliers…"

"The good stuff, you ass. I know the whole history."

Bruce had lived through it. Ten years ago the glowing fuel had just taken hold as an important source of power for small machines. Its scarcity and corresponding high price made it uneconomical for use with larger devices, which continued to be powered with combinations of steam engines and clockwork. His father had raved about luxene while deciding which supplier to invest in. He'd picked Dynalux because they'd been the most aggressive in their attempts to increase the longevity and efficiency of the fuel.

"Okay, okay," Richardson said. "You told me there had been prior offers to buy the company."

"Yes."

"I found records of four offers between January of '03 and

March of '04. All turned down. No one thought the owners would sell. Then, in mid-June, Tagget Industries swooped in and acquired them. But, get this. Tagget paid half of what the others had offered, and the deal went through in a week. Someone at Dynalux was desperate."

Bruce shuffled his papers. "I was right, then. They were hiding something. It was in April they stopped reporting on their experiments in the trade journals. Their ads changed, too. Instead of praising their special additives, they focused on how long they'd been in business."

"And this is where you thank me for spending an hour searching for one article based on your rumors and oblique references. Dated twelve June. From a New York rag magazine. Entitled *Luxene Power Failure?* I won't read the whole thing, but it quotes a company rep as saying they had unforeseen difficulties with an experiment. Then it talks of explosions, catastrophic breakdowns, malfunctioning machinery. All unsubstantiated, but likely true given what happened with the sale. The article even goes so far as to imply that all Dynalux fuel was tainted."

"Damn."

"Yes."

Bruce chewed on the end of his pen, frowning. "Why would Tagget want an ailing luxene supplier?"

"Most sources suggest it was a vanity purchase to supply fuel for his fancy car."

"Bullshit."

"He's done several interviews and has stated clearly he desires to make Dynalux the fuel of all automobiles."

"There's more to it than that. Thanks for your help. Mail me that article, would you? I've got to go. I can't afford to talk longer, and I have some fieldwork to do tonight."

"Fieldwork?"

"I'm going to go take a look at this legendary Mercedes."

Several seconds passed before Richardson responded. "Be careful. Tagget's not a guy to mess around with."

"Right. Thanks."

Bruce had dressed nicely for church that morning, and he only had to throw his jacket back on to look respectable before walking the few blocks to Tagget's hotel. The car was parked out front, where it resided whenever Tagget wasn't driving it. His personal driver stood beside it, polishing the brasswork.

Bruce paused near the vehicle, admiring it as he had seen many others do, when he heard a painfully familiar voice behind him.

"I'm fond of champagne," Eden said, "but I have little experience with red wine. What do you recommend?"

He forced himself not to turn around, and hoped she wouldn't recognize him. The jacket and derby hat would help disguise him, especially from behind.

"There are many wonderful choices," Tagget responded.

Bruce couldn't say he was surprised Eden had accepted the invitation to dinner. Which didn't stop his fists from clenching in anger. Some of the fury was directed at Tagget, but much of it was self-focused. If he hadn't been so irresponsible, perhaps Eden would be with him tonight.

"Perhaps I shall order us one bottle from Italy and one from France. Then you can compare."

"That would be ridiculous," Eden argued, in her usual, blunt manner. "We can't possibly drink so much with a single dinner. As you can see, I'm not a large woman, and I have no intention of getting drunk. One glass will suffice."

Tagget chuckled. "I do admire your candor, Miss Randall."

Bruce risked a glance over his shoulder in time to see them disappear through the door. He had to trust Eden knew how to take care of herself. He turned back to the car.

"She's a beautiful machine," he said to the driver, adopting his best upper-class bearing. "A Mercedes-Simplex, new model this year, correct?"

The driver looked up, pausing his polishing. "Yes, indeed, sir. You have familiarity with automobiles?"

"I do," Bruce lied. He'd ridden in a few cars, and admired many, but he'd never driven one himself. His parents preferred their dragon-pulled carriage. "I understand this particular vehicle is adapted to run on luxene, and I couldn't resist coming by to see for myself."

"Oh, she is, sir. Mr. Tagget had her specially altered. She's lighter than a standard automobile and has just as much power."

"Intriguing. Would it be too forward if I requested a look under her hood? I should love to see the modifications."

The driver grinned. Bruce guessed he was pleased to have someone to talk to. When his entire day consisted of keeping the car clean and chasing away curious children, a real conversation must be a relief.

"Let me show you." He opened the hood and began to describe the innards.

Bruce nodded and pretended he understood. All he cared about was the tank of green liquid from Dynalux. Made of steel, it looked large enough to hold a full quart, a vast difference from the tiny glass tubes that held the fuel inside dragons like Vox.

"Impressive. What is her top speed using a fuel of this sort?"

"Upwards of fifty miles per hour," the driver stated with pride. "She has everything—speed, comfort, beautiful looks—as fine a piece of machinery as you will ever see, I dare say."

Bruce thought the man to be over-enthusiastic in his praise, but it was a lovely automobile.

"Mr. Tagget said he runs experiments with different fuel samples to aid in the Dynalux research. Is that true? I know he's very involved in his company's work, but I would be concerned experimental fuels could be dangerous."

"They may be. I couldn't say. He's been driving for years,

as have I. We know how to handle a car should a malfunction occur, and so far that has never happened."

"I'm glad to hear it. I would love to have such a system to power my own car back in Boston. Do you know, has his research made any progress in increasing efficiency?"

"I don't know, I'm afraid. You will have to ask Mr. Tagget, if you are acquainted."

"I will do that. This evening, however, he looks to be occupied with a young lady."

"Yes, though I don't understand his interest in the girl. He usually keeps company with much prettier women. I suppose around here one can't be too choosy, can one?"

The slight to Eden made Bruce want to hit something. He turned away to hide his scowl, swallowing a furious retort.

"Ah, well," he sighed, forcing an air of nonchalance into his voice, "I shall have to call upon him at another time and learn all about it. I dearly wish him success in his experiments. His work may mean we all will drive vehicles like this someday. It must be nice, owning a company and having access to all the free fuel one could want."

"Oh, Mr. Tagget pays for all his fuel."

"Does he? That's generous of him."

"It's for the experiments. He buys ordinary, unaltered luxene, then tests additives on an individual basis. It's very scientific, I understand."

"It sounds that way. Thank you for your time. She is a most fascinating vehicle, and I can see you take great care with her."

"Thank you, young man."

Bruce nodded to him and started down the road. He needed something to occupy himself, lest he decide to pace in front of the hotel until Eden finished dinner. The new information on Tagget's motorcar would help.

Tagget didn't use his own company's product in his vehicle. Why not? It had to be connected to the problems Dynalux had experienced just before the sale. What was wrong with their luxene? What Bruce needed was a scientific comparison of the Dynalux product with luxene from another source.

And why not do just that? The university had a chemistry department. The AM&T department was filled with Dynalux fuel. He would just need to dredge up a sample of unaltered fuel.

What did Eden use in Vox? Plain luxene, or something special? Could he bring himself to face her and involve her in this discussion?

A rough hand on his arm interrupted his musings. He jerked and tried to turn toward the offending man, but another hand seized him from the opposite side. The two men hauled him down the sidewalk and shoved him into an alley.

Bruce stumbled forward, fighting to regain his balance. A boot to the rear sent him crashing to the ground. Pain shot down his arm. He prayed the tearing sound was his jacket, and not a body part.

He used his other arm to help him stand, but only made it as far as his knees. A heavy-soled boot caught him in the ribs, driving the air from his lungs.

"You just can't keep your nose out of other people's business, can you, boy?"

Lying on the ground, gasping for breath, Bruce finally got a look at his assailants. At five-foot-eleven, Bruce was a tall man, but both these fellows dwarfed him. They stood well over six feet, and must have weighed half-again what he did. The fabric of their expensive suits hugged bulging biceps and torsos of solid muscle. The two men wore identical scowls on their near-identical faces.

The Bafford brothers. Bruce had skimmed over any references to Tagget's bodyguards, but he had seen enough to tell him he now faced the fiercely loyal ex-wrestlers who protected one of America's richest men. In a surprise to no one, they also did his dirty work.

"The boss warned you."

Bruce twisted away from another kick, sparing himself the worst of the damage.

"The girl warned you."

Anticipating the next attack, Bruce curled into a ball. He covered his head just as one of the men stomped on him. The cushion of his arm saved his skull from smashing into the pavement. It still hurt like hell.

The second brother spoke for the first time. "Some people just don't learn."

Bruce expected another kick, but instead a pair of hands hoisted him off the ground. He saw the fist coming too late to do anything but turn his head. Blood spurted from his nose.

He lashed out with his own fists. He wasn't much of a fighter, but he feared these men might not stop until he was dead. He caught the brother pummeling him in the ear and followed the blow with a kick to the shins. The brute answered with a punch to the gut.

The brother holding him let go to deliver another jab to the head, but Bruce ducked and took only a glancing hit. He was faster than the brothers. That speed might be his only salvation.

The pain no longer registered. His heart pounded and all he could think was that he needed to escape at any cost. He would fight dirty. He didn't care. He whirled around and took a swing at brother number two. His fist connected with hard muscle, likely doing more damage to him than his assailant. It didn't matter. The move was only a distraction. The smirk creeping across the man's face contorted into agony when Bruce's metal knee came up into his groin. He crumpled. Bruce kicked him in the kidneys for good measure.

Brother number one jumped him from behind. It had been years since Bruce had played real football, but his muscles hadn't forgotten how to be tackled. He tumbled to the ground unharmed, Bafford's momentum carrying him up and over Bruce's head. The thug rolled, sprang to his feet, and grabbed for Bruce's legs before he could scamper away.

Wrestling on the ground seemed a sure path to defeat, and Bafford Two looked to be recovering. Bruce called upon all the dirtiest things he'd ever seen a footballer do while fighting for a fumbled ball. He clawed at Bafford's face, drawing blood and jabbing him in the eye. The bigger man howled in pain and his grip broke long enough for Bruce to scramble free. His brother had gained his feet, but Bruce had a step on him, and he tore down the alley.

He burst out onto Liberty Street, missing a collision with a carriage by no more than a foot. He shouted an apology to the driver and whirled to his left, not risking a glance back at his pursuers. He veered left again at Fourth Avenue. His hotel was only two blocks away.

By the time he reached it, the pain had exerted itself once more. He staggered up the stairs, his breath coming in gasps and wheezes. Somehow he got the door locked behind him before he collapsed. He was certain he had broken ribs. His left eye was swollen shut, and blood trickled from his nose. His elbow still smarted, as did a number of other areas, but he didn't think those were more than bruises. He didn't have the energy to do a more thorough assessment of his injuries.

Bruce closed his eyes and tried to breathe easy. He was glad to be alive. He would lay low and heal for a few days, but he wouldn't quit investigating. Tagget had made a serious error in judgement. Now it was personal.

And if he hurts Eden, Bruce vowed, *I'll kill him.*

23

"Mm-hmm."

Eden nodded and smiled as she finished the last of her dessert. She didn't even know what Tagget was talking about anymore. Some drink he'd tried in some city he'd been to, or something equally boring. By this point he'd probably mentioned every single place he'd ever visited, telling her how much she would like it, as if he intended to take her vacationing.

Maybe he did. Between his excessive babbling about himself and his over-the-top compliments of her, she had begun to think him a little... well, odd.

"I trust you enjoyed your dinner?" His question was casual enough, but his expression betrayed the feelings beneath. He wanted her approval. Fascinating.

"Yes, it was quite good," she replied.

He beamed.

Oh. Oh, dear. Perhaps she ought to have paid more attention to his chatter. She did that babbling thing, too, because she wasn't good at making conversation with people she didn't know well. Tagget was genuinely trying to befriend her. He was simply... bad at it.

And, of course, his motives were still suspect. He'd hardly glanced at Vox the entire dinner. A calculated move, no doubt, meant to put her at ease. Which she was, after a glass and a half of wine. But at ease didn't equal careless. She was confident he posed no danger to *her*. She couldn't say the same for Vox.

A waiter whisked away the last of the dishes, and Tagget walked around to help her from her seat, a custom which Eden didn't understand in the slightest. Even in the long skirt she'd worn today, she had no trouble getting herself in and out of chairs.

"Do you find that fancy ladies in the fanciest dresses need help to sit and stand?"

He chuckled. "Not in my experience. I help them nonetheless." His voice dropped. "I enjoy being of service to lovely ladies."

Eden's eyes widened. That was an innuendo. Only days ago she wouldn't have recognized it.

"I'm sure you do."

His brow furrowed. "Er, quite." He slipped back into his customary facade of composure. "Thank you for a lovely evening, Miss Randall. May I drive you home? Or would you prefer I walk you there?"

"I can go home on my own," she answered. "If you have something you'd like to talk about in private, we can go up to your hotel room."

He cocked an eyebrow. "You feel we have something private to discuss?"

You want my dragon. I want to know why.

"This is a nice hotel, and I imagine you have the nicest room, but it's no place for a millionaire. I want to know what you want so badly you'd rather stay here instead of returning to your fancy home in New York."

Tagget took his time before answering. "Very well. We

shall have a talk. This way, if you please, Miss Randall." He offered his arm and escorted her to the nearest staircase.

His room was large, with a wide bed, a generous sitting area, and a sturdy desk for conducting business matters. In all, she guessed it to be about three times the size of Bruce's hotel room. She set Vox by the door, instructing her to stay.

A gold-colored dragon with a serpentine body sat on its haunches in one corner of the desk. Eden wandered over to examine it.

"You have your own dragon?"

"A novelty item, given to me by an admirer. I have modified it." He touched the creature's head. It opened its mouth and breathed out a jet of flame. Tagget withdrew a slim metal case from his pocket. "Care for a cigarette, Miss Randall?"

"No, thank you." Eden had never smoked. It would only make her cough.

Tagget used the dragon to light a cigarette, took a single draw, and blew out a steady stream of smoke. "Not a ladylike habit, smoking."

She shrugged—a rather unladylike habit, itself. "I do plenty of things that are unladylike."

"Such as visiting a gentleman's hotel room alone," he observed.

"I'm not afraid of being alone with you."

"Aren't you?" He set the cigarette in an ashtray and walked around the desk toward her. "Perhaps you aren't familiar with the things that can happen to a beautiful woman left unsupervised." He didn't stop until he was mere inches away. "She might fall prey to a terrible seduction." He ran a finger down her cheek. Eden shivered. He may have been bad at friendship, but he understood this flirting business. She ought to take notes. "Sometimes all it takes is a single kiss."

"I know all about that."

"Do you? Let's find out, shall we?"

He cupped her chin in his hand and kissed her, slow and

deliberate. It wasn't as thrilling as Bruce's kisses. No greedy hands twining in her hair or gasping breaths. Still, it was pleasant enough. Eden parted her lips and used her tongue, the way she had learned.

It was some time before Tagget pulled away. "You are, indeed, a most enthusiastic kisser, my lovely garden of Eden. Have you lain with a man before?"

"Yes." No need to tell him it had only been once and she'd done a terrible job of it.

Tagget was perfect. He was attractive, and her body responded well to him. He was obviously interested. This is what she ought to have done in the first place, and would have if Joey hadn't omitted crucial information. She would learn how to have sexual intercourse the correct way, and then maybe she could convince Bruce to try it again. Assuming he would ever speak to her.

"I'm pleased to hear that," Tagget purred.

His fingers popped the clips of her corset, one by one. The shirt she wore beneath was nearly transparent. He leered at her exposed breasts, then covered them with his hands.

"A paradise, indeed," he murmured. "I will enjoy sampling your forbidden fruit."

He bent to kiss her neck, the hair of his short goatee tickling her skin. She put her hands to his chest and began to unbutton his vest, but he brushed her away. Didn't he want to be undressed?

Eden wrapped her arms around his waist instead, not forcing the issue. She'd already proven she didn't know what she was doing. Follow and learn. There would be time enough for taking charge at a later date.

Tagget paused in his massaging of her breasts and unfastened her skirt. It fell in a pool at her feet, leaving her in only the see-through shirt and her lacy drawers. He stepped back to admire her.

"I've been looking forward to the day when I would lay

between your thighs." His green eyes gleamed with desire. "I hadn't anticipated it would be so soon. You are full of surprises, darling Eden."

He scooped her up and carried her to the bed, where he peeled the shirt and drawers from her body. His hands and lips traveled across her skin, exploring her body, sending pleasurable sensations coursing through her. She let him lead, vowing to be patient, though passivity didn't come naturally to her. No need to repeat her painful first experience.

His hand slipped between her legs, doing the same extraordinary things Bruce had done. The urgent longing was growing again, and she twisted to get more of his touch. He whispered things to her, but with Vox across the room she couldn't hear them. Probably the same silly sorts of things he always said. She didn't give a damn. All she wanted was a release from the incredible feelings torturing her.

It came in a rush. Her back arched. She cried out. Her entire body contorted in ecstasy. This was how it was supposed to be. How she wanted it to be.

Sometime during his fondling, Tagget had managed to unfasten his trousers. He pulled her toward him and entered her. Any soreness from the night before seemed nothing in the haze of pleasure. She lifted her hips to match his thrusting, taking him deeper, drawing the tension inside of her to heights she hadn't imagined. The climax was delicious. Long, powerful, lingering. He thrust hard and fast, and it wasn't long before he, too, was shuddering and gasping.

He rolled off and lay beside her, silent and unmoving. Eden stared up at the ceiling, her body relaxed, her mind in a blissful peace. Joey had been right, after all. Sex was excellent. She only wished he had warned her about the first time being terrible. If she'd known, she could have done it with Tagget first, and not tried anything with Bruce until she'd known it would bring pleasure to the both of them.

A melancholy sigh intruded on her repose. It was too late.

She'd messed up, rejected him, and now he hated her. She didn't even know where to begin to fix that, though she was determined to try. In the meantime, she could get plenty of practice sex from Tagget. As long as he wanted Vox, he would keep wooing her.

She flipped up onto her side and looked down at him. "That was lovely, Mr. Tagget. Can we do it again sometime?"

"Evan," he corrected her. With Vox still across the room his voice sounded distant. "There is no formality in bed. And, yes, I would be delighted to do it again whenever you wish."

"Excellent." She fought off a yawn. The excitement had made her tired, but she didn't dare sleep here and leave Vox unguarded.

Tagget curled an arm around her to draw her closer, but she slipped from his grasp and hopped out of bed, reaching for her clothes.

"Leaving so soon, my flower?" Of all possible emotions, disappointment was not one she had ever thought to see in Evan Tagget's eyes. Did he really want to cuddle? Or had he been hoping she'd fall asleep so he could grab Vox?

"I have to get home. But I will see you again tomorrow."

He rose from the bed, straightening his clothing. Before she left, he took hold of her hand and kissed it. "Until tomorrow. Thank you for a lovely evening. It was my extreme pleasure."

"Mine, too. Good night."

"Good night, Miss Randall."

His smirk had returned. He probably thought he had won her over, and soon she would give him anything he wanted. Well, the more fool he. She would take his concerts and dinners and sex, but she would never give up her secrets or her dragon. She picked up Vox and headed for home.

24

October 27

AFTER LYING ON THE FLOOR in pain all night, Bruce swallowed his pride and summoned a doctor. Considerable poking and prodding verified that two ribs were cracked. The doctor wrapped them tightly to promote healing, applied cold compresses to his battered face, and prescribed regular doses of alcohol to dull the pain. When he offered a shot of morphine, Bruce stupidly accepted.

He spent all of Monday in a drug-induced haze. Tuesday and Wednesday he spent drunk on bourbon, wishing he had enough money left for more morphine. Now on Thursday, he had finally begun to come to his senses, drinking only enough to combat the hangover. The morphine cravings had dropped to an endurable level.

Moderately endurable. He still couldn't do ordinary things such as sneezing or yawning without suffering spasms of agony. Dressing himself in clean clothing hurt enough to start his eyes darting around for the hypodermic.

Bruce considered taking a swig from the bourbon bottle, but stopped when he saw how little he had left. He couldn't afford more alcohol or drugs, and he wouldn't send a wire to his bank in Boston to withdraw money until he was certain he wouldn't waste it on either, even if it meant starving this weekend.

A quick walk along the river cleared his head and stretched out muscles too long unused. His ribs were a constant bother, but not so much that he would delay resuming his ordinary activities. Most of his superficial injuries had been reduced to dull aches, or an occasional stab of pain if he bumped the wrong spot. The bruise around his eye, though, had turned a vivid purple that was impossible to hide.

He dropped in for a shave without thinking about it, only to receive a shocked stare and a, "Yikes!"

"Big guy hit me," he muttered.

"Yes, well, you can't be too careful these days. Kids are out of control."

Bruce winced. "Uh-huh." He shouldn't have bothered tidying himself up. His stomach was rumbling, and that dime could have bought him a decent dinner.

Clean, but unfed, Bruce ducked into the lecture hall for Tagget and Hart's new technology reveal. Faculty, students, and curious locals swarmed the room, eager to be the first to hear potentially groundbreaking news.

Bruce slipped into one of the few remaining seats in the back, hoping to blend in with the students. He pulled his cap down low to hide the black eye as much as possible.

Several comments from curious young men suggested his efforts were futile. After the third such remark, he growled, "You should see the other guy."

Unfortunately, he *could* see the other guys, sitting in a corner near the front of the lecture hall, looking in perfect health. He hadn't won, he had escaped.

Eden sat front and center, uncomfortably close to the

Bafford thugs, Vox in her lap. The sight of her banished any fear he'd had about speaking to her. In fact, he wanted nothing more than to throw himself at her feet and apologize for every stupid thing he'd ever done. To her or to anyone. He would tell her again he'd never meant to hurt her or scare her. He would say he wanted to start over and beg her not to hate him.

Not that she would want to hear any of it. She would take one look at his eye and demand to know what had happened. Then she would scold him and tell him once again to stop investigating Tagget.

"The girl warned you."

A shiver ran through him. How had Bafford—and presumably Tagget—known that? He tried to think when she had said anything about it. The day they had gone rollerskating. That had been when he'd decided to begin researching Tagget's history and business. They'd been walking and talking. Someone might have overheard. At the time their conversation had seemed private, but he hadn't been checking for anyone possibly spying upon them.

When else had she made similar remarks? The courthouse steps, after she sprung him from jail. He was certain no one had heard that. Had she said it earlier, as well? When they were on the phone?

His breath quickened. Either someone had been at the saloon watching Eden while she was alone, or Tagget had the capability to listen in on a telephone call.

His eyes darted back to Eden, who had risen to talk to Tagget. Her smile stung worse than the black eye. He would prefer she hate the man as much as he did. But Eden being Eden, she continued to be content with Tagget's company.

Bruce shifted in his seat. Would she think differently if she knew what had happened to him?

He told himself not to expect too much. She had probably rescinded Vox's friendship already. He was willing to let the dragon bite him if it would give him the chance to renew their courtship. It couldn't hurt more than the broken ribs.

Professor Hart took the stage, waving Tagget up to join him. "Good evening, everyone. Thank you all for coming for our presentation of this exciting new research. As most of you know, I am Professor Ruben Hart, of the Automechanology and Teletics department. I would like to introduce my collaborator on this project, Mr. Evan Tagget, renowned inventor and owner of Tagget Industries."

"Thank you," Tagget said after the polite applause died down. "I am honored to be here today, and delighted to participate in the development of this innovative new product."

The genuine tone of the reply surprised Bruce. Either this project would be highly profitable, or Tagget was an excellent liar. Probably the latter.

The lecture began in earnest, with Hart doing most of the talking. He hung several large schematic drawings on the wall and reviewed them in detail. For once, Bruce wasn't left gawking like an idiot. This presentation had been designed with the layman in mind. Those with teletics knowledge were certainly getting more out of it, but the overall concept was easy to understand.

The design was for an echo machine. The two sections of the machine were like a telephone. One emitted a sound, while the other section listened. If the device picked up the echo of the sound it emitted, it knew something was in front of it, and could respond accordingly.

"The practical applications of this device are numerous," Hart explained. "For example, it could be mounted on the front of a vehicle. This could prevent motorcars from crashing into one another, or prevent boats from crashing into land in the dark. While the current design only triggers a light as an alert measure, it has the potential to be wired to more complex mechanisms. Our long-term goal is to use this technology to develop a motorcar that can brake on its own."

Bruce had to alter his earlier assessment. Tagget was likely a very good liar, but he would be well-pleased to be involved in this project. It could bring him a great deal of money. The crowd seemed impressed. They applauded the presentation and asked a number of questions, many of which were too technical for Bruce's liking.

Eden, he noticed, didn't appear enthusiastic about the design. When the questions finally ended, she spent several minutes talking alone with Tagget, her face pinched in an irritable frown. Whatever he had to say didn't appease her. She threw up her hands and stomped up the aisle toward the rear door. Tagget rushed after her.

Her sharp eyes caught Bruce before he even reached the aisle. He waited for her beside the door. He couldn't make his apologies here in public, but he would say hello, if nothing else.

"Bruce, what happened to your eye?" she exclaimed.

"Ask him." Bruce gestured at Tagget.

Her eyes widened. "Evan hit you?"

Dammit, she was using his first name. Bruce had to do something. He couldn't lose her to that self-centered, unethical bastard.

Eden's expression changed into an odd, almost hopeful look. "Were you fighting over me?"

"No!" Her face fell. Had she wanted him to get into a fistfight? "I mean, I don't fight like that. I try to avoid violence."

"Yes, that's good," she agreed. "But why did he hit you?"

"I didn't hit anyone," Tagget said. He snaked an arm around Eden's waist. "I'm a lover, not a fighter, you know that, my sweet paradise."

It was a very good thing Bruce was almost out of bourbon. If he'd been even the slightest bit tipsy, he would have given Evan Tagget a shiner to match his own.

Eden twisted from Tagget's grasp. "I'm going out for a beer."

"I'll see you later?" Tagget asked. His hand remained hanging in the air, reaching for her.

She shrugged. "Maybe."

Tagget's arm dropped, his jaw tightening. Eden strode from the room, the two men watching her.

The moment she was out of sight, Tagget resumed his customary smirk. "She'll come. I know how to give her what she likes. She's a very passionate girl, did you know that, Mr. Caldwell?" He gave a nod in a mockery of civility and departed.

For a long moment Bruce could do nothing but stare after him, shaking in outrage. He was lying. He had to be lying. She would never sleep with a man like that.

Bruce sank into the nearest chair and put his head in his hands. Who was he kidding? Of course she would. What did she have to lose? She *was* passionate. She lived her life the way she liked. She hadn't turned down any of Tagget's other offers. Why should she turn down this one?

And it's all my fault.

For an instant, Bruce thought he might simply lay down and die from humiliation and heartbreak. Then he took a deep breath to calm himself and his broken ribs screamed in protest. The pain snapped him out of his stupor.

"You can't have her, do you hear me?" he shouted into the near-empty hall. The few people remaining turned to stare at him. He continued on, expounding on his feelings in the manner of an orator addressing a crowd. "It doesn't matter. It doesn't matter how much money he has, or how many motorcars. It doesn't matter how many inventions he's stamped his name on. It doesn't matter how many thugs he sends after me. I can't compete with any of that, and I don't care. I won't even try. I might be a broke, nosy, one-time morphine addict with a shit job and a metal knee, but I love her, dammit!"

He had said the words—as he so often did—without thinking them through, but now that they were out nothing in the world could make him take them back. They were God's honest truth.

"I love her," he repeated. He thought he might say it over and over, a sort of magical incantation.

One of the men lingering in the hall approached him. "I'm a medical student," he said. "I can get you some morphine on the cheap."

This was perhaps the least helpful "help" anyone had ever offered. "I don't want your morphine. I want Eden."

"Eden? Eden Randall? That weird girl?"

"Yes, Eden the 'weird girl,'" Bruce snapped. "Is there something in the air out here that addles men's brains? Why can none of you see her for the treasure she is?"

"It's your foul big-city air, if you ask me. She's not normal."

"No one is normal! We're all different, and we all deserve love, damn you!"

The medical student shrugged. "To each his own."

Bruce stomped off before the man could irritate him any further. He contemplated walking to the saloon to see if Eden were, indeed, having a beer, but quickly thought better of it. He had no more than a quarter to his name, and he needed to eat *something* this weekend. And he had to consider the possibility she simply had no interest in him any longer.

Tomorrow he would spend all day on a train to Wisconsin. That would give him plenty of time to sort through his various predicaments. At the beginning of this week he had set himself three life goals: expose Tagget, reconcile with Eden, and get a promotion. Due in part to his mistreatment at the hands of the Bafford brothers, he had made progress on only one of them, and suffered a serious setback in another. Now those goals had shifted.

New list: send Tagget to jail, marry Eden, quit my job for something better.

He was setting himself up for failure. He'd be damned if he wouldn't try anyway.

25

October 28

EDEN BORROWED HER FATHER'S CAMERA. She wasn't certain she knew how to use it, and she couldn't find any film, but it would give her a chance to watch the game from the sideline. Assuming Bruce was willing to carry through with the plan. She had so hoped he would stop by the saloon last night. He hadn't, and she'd sat at her table alone, missing him dreadfully.

Tagget—rather snobbishly, in her opinion—didn't drink beer and preferred restaurants to saloons. He wasn't entirely dull, but he wasn't fun, either. He didn't like any of the same things she did. They'd been to one concert this week, which was nice, but nothing else interested her. The only other good thing was the sex, and she suspected the other night was going to be the end of that, because she was almost certain he had done something unforgivable. Two things, actually, if he was responsible for Bruce's black eye, but she didn't know how to determine that without talking to Bruce. And he didn't seem to want anything to do with her.

Time was short this morning, because she had a train to catch, but Eden couldn't leave town without first stopping by the lab. If her hunch was correct, she needed to act immediately.

She found the door unlocked.

Her fingers clenched on the doorknob. Only one person would be here so early in the morning. One student her father trusted with a key. One woman who had more invested in this matter than Eden did.

She pushed the door open.

"Lilah?"

Eden rushed across the laboratory to the corner nook where her friend liked to work. Lilah sat in her usual chair, cradling the bat dragon, her eyes red from crying. Eden needed only a quick glance at the schematic on the workbench to confirm her fears had been well-founded. The echo-machine was a duplicate of the inner workings of Lilah's bat.

"That son of a bitch!" she exclaimed. "It's true! He stole your design!"

Lilah looked up. Anger and heartbreak marred her beautiful face. "I've been working on this since the day I came to this school. It's all but perfect. I have poured my heart and soul into it!"

"He won't get away with this," Eden vowed.

Lilah sniffed. "Oh, yes, he will. He's a white man, with money enough for a million lawyers. How do I fight that?"

"But you're a genius!" Eden declared. "Go to my father. He will help."

"I know he will, but it won't be enough."

"I'll help," Eden declared. An idea sprang to mind. "Bruce will help. He can write an article for the newspapers."

"Papers can be silenced with money. Reporters can be silenced as well."

With fists? Eden shuddered.

"Don't tell me you're giving up, Lilah. You don't give up. You wouldn't be here if you gave up."

She took a deep breath and dabbed at her eyes with a pristine, white handkerchief. Eden didn't understand how everything about Lilah was always so neat when she worked in such a messy field.

"You're right, Eden, I'm not giving up. I don't ever give up. I promise, I didn't intend to let my grief consume me, but…"

"But sometimes you need a good cry?"

"Exactly." She reached for Eden's hand and gave it a squeeze. "Thank you for coming by. For caring."

"Of course I care! You're my friend. Should we run another copy of your schematic on the copying machine? We don't want to risk losing it."

The slightest smile touched Lilah's lips. "Already done. I have one copy at home and there is another in your father's safe." She pursed her lips. "I think I'll run two more. One I will mail to my parents, and one to the patent office. I don't have an application ready, but I can write something up."

"That's where my father can help. He knows all about patenting inventions."

Lilah drummed her fingers, thinking. "I will need to send it as an express. I doubt it will be long before Tagget's people submit his stolen version."

"Do he and Professor Hart have a contract, do you think?" Eden wondered. "They must have some agreement, because Hart wouldn't let Tagget take all the money. He's spent years hoping for some invention of his to draw national attention, but noisy, hulking machines just aren't the fashion any longer."

Lilah nodded. "They've been losing their appeal ever since luxene became a viable fuel."

"Oh!" Eden exclaimed. "Our new luxene—it's all from Dynalux. Don't put it in your dragon, just in case any of those 'special additives' are harmful."

Lilah's brows rose. "You think he would risk tainting the supply of the entire department?"

"I think he must have *some* reason for giving us the fuel. A reason that benefits himself."

"True. Though if he were caught at such a thing… no, he would place the blame on someone at Dynalux. Good thinking. I'll dig up an older bottle if I need to refuel."

"Good. I need to leave now, to catch my train. If you want to contact me, send a telegram to my hotel in Madison. My parents will have the name and address. Good luck. You can do this. It is *your* design, and you deserve the credit."

Lilah smiled a true smile at last. "I'm going to spend all day imagining the look on Tagget's face when he realizes I'm not backing down."

Eden frowned at that. "He might be kind of impressed."

"Right. Have a wonderful weekend. I'll let you know how it all works out."

The two women embraced, and Eden started off, pausing only to pick up Vox and the traveling bag she had left by the entrance. She checked her watch. She had enough time to walk to the train station, but she couldn't delay longer.

She reached the station to find the train had already arrived. The entire football team and coaching staff waited to board, along with a crowd of fans who were traveling aboard the same train to see the game. Locals who had come to see the team off pressed in behind them, waving and cheering. Eden squeezed past them, smiling up at the children who had climbed to the platform roof to watch. She'd been one of them in her younger days.

A tweed cap caught her eye. Bruce stood near the train, talking with some of the players and taking notes. She inched toward him, mulling over what she might say.

"Goodness sakes, Miss Randall, where have you been? I was near ready to telephone your father."

Her chaperone.

Eden sighed.

Eden's parents, of course, had no interest in spending an

entire day traveling in order to watch football, only to then turn around and spend another entire day coming home. Which hadn't bothered Eden. She'd fully intended to go on her own. Until two days ago, when they had informed her widow Holtzmann was delighted to share a train compartment and a hotel room. Since they were paying for the trip, Eden could do nothing but agree.

Now she was stuck being supervised.

Ordinarily, Eden was very fond of Frau Holtzmann, if for no other reason than she was a fellow female sports fan. Today, however, she was a nuisance.

"Whatever are you wearing, dear?" Mrs. Holtzmann asked. "And you can't mean to bring that dragon along, can you? A train is no place for a pet."

Eden sighed. She'd chosen to wear a pair of soft brown trousers and one of her father's shirts. She wanted to be comfortable on her journey. As for Vox...

"She goes where I do," Eden replied. "She won't be trouble. She doesn't wander unless I say so."

"It's most irregular, but I suppose we don't have time to do anything about it now. Come along, boarding is about to begin."

Eden followed her companion onto the train and into a compartment already occupied by four other women. Eyebrows raised and mouths turned down at the sight of Eden's outfit. She ignored the snub and took her seat, Vox in her lap and a book in her hand.

Eden had always loved trains. She enjoyed the sway of the cars, and the countryside rolling by outside the window. The tickle of the vibrations through her body and the rumbling in her ears had delighted her in the years before Vox. These days, a few books and occasional food and drink from the dining car were all she needed to keep her mind occupied.

Today, it seemed, was doomed to be an exception.

She struggled with her book, rereading paragraphs

multiple times over without comprehension. Lilah's stolen design and Tagget's treachery nagged at her. As much as she looked forward to the game, she feared some new trouble might crop up during the three days she was away.

Bruce's presence, so near and so far, also contributed to her distraction. Was he uncomfortable in the hard, cramped second class seats? Was his eye bothering him? Who had hit him, if not Tagget?

She tried once again to read.

"I wish I'd never set eyes on your infernal island. What the devil—want beasts for on an island like that? Then, that man of yours—understood he was a man. He's a lunatic; and he hadn't no business aft. Do you think the whole damned ship belongs to you?"

Wells' novel ought to have kept her riveted. She wanted to lose herself in the adventure, the grotesque experiments, and the words like "damned" she had only recently realized weren't considered suitable for a young lady to read.

"Miss Randall loves books, as you can see. Tell the ladies what you are reading, dear."

Eden glanced up at her companions. *"The Island of Doctor Moreau.* It's a scientific adventure/horror story."

"Oh, my," gasped one of her fellow passengers, about whom Eden now knew more than she wished, thanks to Frau Holtzmann's chatty nature. Unfortunately, part of the role of chaperone was introducing one's charge to whomever happened to be around. Instead of talking about herself, Frau Holtzmann talked about Eden.

The entire compartment knew who her parents were and what they did, why she was traveling, and various odd tidbits. And now they knew what kind of books she liked to read. Books as shocking as her clothing, apparently.

"What of your pet, Miss Randall?" another woman asked. "Do you take it everywhere with you?"

"Everywhere."

"Fascinating. I suppose it is quiet and well-behaved, but I can't quite understand why one would choose it over a cat or a dog. No one would ever wish to cuddle with a cold jumble of metal."

Eden pulled Vox tighter against her belly. The dragon nuzzled her. "She's special."

"Ah."

Enough was enough. Eden closed her book. "I'm going to find the dining car for a bite to eat. I might stop to say hello to some of my friends, so don't fret if I'm gone for some time."

"I'll come with you, dear," Mrs. Holtzmann replied. "I didn't have time for a large breakfast this morning."

Oh, hell.

At least getting out of the compartment with a companion was better than not getting out at all. Eden led the way, carrying Vox because the corridors were too narrow to let her walk or fly. The two women sat down with food and tea, and had a far more pleasant chat about expectations for the game the next day.

Eden tried to excuse herself again once they finished, but Mrs. Holtzmann attended fervently to her job as chaperone and insisted on following Eden on her quest to locate her friends.

"You won't want to walk alone, dear. There are strangers about, and you're such a tiny little thing."

Eden's fingers curled into fists. "I'm stronger than most people think," she declared, and strode off without waiting for a reply. If only her parents had come along. They didn't fear things like strangers attacking her on a train.

The football team had commandeered an entire car. Some of the men were sleeping, some playing cards. Several were eating and playing cards at the same time, grateful heirs to the legacy of the Earl of Sandwich.

They greeted Eden with a chorus of hellos. Joey set down his cards and hopped up to talk to her.

"Miss Randall!" he exclaimed, giving a little bow in deference to Frau Holtzmann standing behind her. "I saw you gave Mr. 'I'm from Hahvuhd' a black eye," he whispered. "Good on you!"

"I did not! And don't mock him." Her defense of Bruce was a bit hypocritical, perhaps, but she never intended to be mean when she teased him.

"You didn't? Then who did?"

"I don't know. That's among the many questions I need to ask him. Do you know where he is?"

Joey waved an indifferent hand. "Thataways. In the cheap seats."

"Thank you." She squeezed past him.

"Wait, Eden, why don't you come play cards for a while?"

She twisted to look at him. "I will later, but I need to talk to Bruce. I won't be able to concentrate on anything until my questions are answered."

"Eden, just forget him. He's not worth your time."

She started down the hall, unwilling to block the corridor to argue with him. "This isn't about what you think. I'll explain everything another day."

"But..."

She didn't look back. She really needed to stop ending their conversations this way.

"Miss Randall, is there some trouble?" Mrs. Holtzmann called, scampering after her.

"No trouble. I simply need to talk to my friend." She paused, leaning with her hand on the door out of the car. "Please, feel free to return to our compartment."

"I'm a bit concerned..."

"Oh!" Eden teetered and nearly fell through the suddenly opened door. A hand caught her arm. She looked up into Bruce's pretty, dark eyes. He smiled at her.

"Miss Randall, we must stop meeting like this."

A moment later, his smile faded, and he released her arm. Eden gave him her best smile.

Please like me again.

"Yes," she said. "We seem to have door troubles."

She looked him over. Some of the purple around his eye had faded to green since last night. Other than the ghastly bruise he looked very well today—tidy, but casual. His black trousers and light gray vest were clean and unrumpled. He'd either skipped a tie or removed it, leaving the top button of his shirt unfastened. Today's cap was a gray tweed with subtle brown stripes. Eden didn't think she'd seen it before. She'd never met a man who owned so many different caps. How many more did he have at home in Boston?

Her gaze settled on his suspenders. "Why are you wearing red?"

"These are my favorite suspenders. I like the way they stand out against the neutral colors."

"Don't wear them tomorrow. Red is Wisconsin's color."

He chuckled. "Superstitious, are we?"

Mrs. Holtzmann tugged at Eden's sleeve. "Miss Randall, surely this isn't the friend you spoke of?" she hissed. Oh, bother. Eden had forgotten others saw Bruce's lack of a coat and tie much the same way they saw her trousers. And the black eye wouldn't do him any favors.

"I'm sorry," she said. "I forgot introductions. Bruce, this is Mrs. Ursula Holtzmann. Mrs. Holtzmann is also traveling to watch the football game."

He bowed as well as he could, still standing in the doorway. "A pleasure, Madam. I'm Bruce Caldwell, reporter with the Boston Herald. I have been following the team this year and writing articles for readers back East."

"Pleased to meet you, Mr. Caldwell," Mrs. Holtzmann replied. Her tone was polite, but Eden thought she detected a bit of suspicion. "You are a friend of Miss Randall?"

"I am."

Eden felt a rush of relief. He did still consider her a friend.

"Perhaps we should move our conversation out of the corridor?" he suggested. "I don't wish to impede the other passengers."

"I agree," Eden said. "Our compartment is full. Is there room by your seat?"

"You don't want to sit there, Miss Randall. The seats are dam—darned uncomfortable, and it's noisy. I don't recall any empty seats, in any event."

"We could go to the dining car," she suggested. "I've already eaten, but I wouldn't mind returning. Have you had lunch?"

He shifted uncomfortably. "I'm not particularly hungry."

It was an odd statement from someone who had a hearty appetite most days. She hoped he wasn't feeling ill. She knew some people didn't like the motion of the train.

"Is there a lounge car on this train, do you think? We could sit there."

"That's only for first class passengers, dear," Mrs. Holtzmann pointed out. Eden couldn't have cared less, but others like her chaperone would. She didn't want Bruce to be embarrassed if he were kicked out for having the wrong sort of ticket.

"This is all very vexing," she exclaimed. "How is one supposed to have a private conversation?" She shook her head. "We'll simply have to talk as we walk about. I'd like to see the entire train and get some exercise."

"An excellent notion," Frau Holtzmann declared. "A brisk walk after lunch is good for the constitution. Mr. Caldwell, would you be so good as to escort us to the rear of the train?"

He tipped his hat. "Certainly, madam." He opened the door and held it. "After you, Miss Randall, Mrs. Holtzmann."

Eden gave him a pained look as she walked by. She wanted privacy. She wanted him to call her Eden again. She picked up her step, setting a rapid pace for their walk. She didn't think she was going to get any of the other things she wanted today, but at least she would get the exercise.

26

October 29

Eden didn't make a very convincing photographer. No one had questioned Bruce when he'd said she would be taking pictures for his articles, but since entering the Randall Field gates, she had yet to even lift the camera. It dangled from a frayed strap, banging against her hip as she paced the sidelines beneath the shade of her maize and blue parasol.

Bruce could have done with a parasol of his own. He'd rolled up his sleeves to his elbows, but he continued to sweat under the relentless sun. Late October wasn't supposed to be so hot.

Eden seemed agitated. She didn't talk, she didn't smile, and she fidgeted with her earring. Bruce suspected her of blocking out the cheers of the eleven thousand Wisconsin supporters in attendance. He wasn't certain the game was the source of her anxiety. Wisconsin was tough, and Michigan hadn't helped itself with a fumble and penalties, but they had taken a six-nothing lead twenty minutes in. This game wasn't expected to be a high-scoring affair. He thought it was going well so far.

She'd been out-of-sorts on the train yesterday. Burdened, no doubt, by her chaperone, though the three of them had held an excellent conversation on sports and the women who liked to watch and play them. It had led to a mention of the women's archery events at the Olympic Games, and then to further retellings of all he had seen during his time in St. Louis. He'd even mentioned a few things Eden hadn't yet heard about, but she remained unmoved. Her remarks had been polite, and she'd made many good observations, but there had been little life in her voice or expression. She had been, and continued to be, unhappy.

Bruce made a few more notes in his journal. At least the game was interesting, because it helped distract him from Eden. It made for an odd turnaround from the usual situation, in which Eden distracted him from the game.

"Oh!" she exclaimed. "Oh, no!"

Bruce jogged to her side. He didn't even need to ask what was wrong. She pointed at Coach Yost, who had walked onto the field. Coaching during games was strictly prohibited. The officials noted the infraction and signaled for a penalty.

"Oh, another penalty!" Eden moaned. "That ruins our chance to score again this half. This game is so frustrating!"

"I think the boys are doing fine," Bruce argued. "Talk was, we're only expected to win by a few touchdowns."

Eden shook her head. "We're not playing as a team." Her head snapped around to look at him. "Wait, you said, 'we.' Have you become a fan?"

He reflected on his words. "Yes, I suppose I have."

A smile touched her lips for the first time that day. "Good. Thank you for not wearing the red suspenders."

He grinned and hooked a thumb under a black suspender strap. "I'll have to buy a blue pair to match you." The smile dissolved as quickly as it had begun. He was getting far ahead of himself. Matching was the sort of thing couples did. He wasn't even certain whether she wanted to talk to him. One step at a time.

Eden's smiled faded with his own. "When this game is over, I want to find a private place to talk. I want an explanation for what happened to your eye."

He wasn't going to argue with that. Anything that made Tagget look bad made Bruce happy. He had a serious jealousy problem, he reflected. Fortunately, Tagget was a legitimate ass, which lessened the guilt considerably.

"I'll give you the full story," he promised. "For now, give me your thoughts on the game. How are we not playing as a team, and how can we fix that?"

"Well..." she began. Bruce readied his pen.

Eden talked the entirety of halftime. Her knowledge of the game continued to astound him. It was better than his own, because she had a stronger grasp of the rules and strategies that had changed since he'd played. He would have wagered money she had read the entire rulebook, probably more than once.

"You would make a good referee," he joked. "You know every rule, you have sharp eyes, and you have the stamina to run up and down the field. Plus, you wouldn't back down if a player tried to argue a call."

Her eyes lit up. Oh, dear. He'd given her an idea. No one would ever hire a female official. If she tried it, she would only have her dreams crushed, and he would be at fault again. He was going to change the way he introduced himself.

Pleased to meet you. I'm Bruce Caldwell, Crusher of Dreams.

"Or maybe you could start a girls' team? You'd be a good coach, too." That was probably just as unrealistic. He told himself to keep his damned mouth shut from now on.

"I'll have to make a sling and wear Vox on my back," Eden mused. "She would use up all her fuel flying back and forth to keep up with me."

"You couldn't just let her sit on the sidelines?"

"You saw how she ran after us when we played football. Her range is exactly ten yards."

He couldn't help but chuckle. "Tested on the gridiron, I assume?"

"Naturally."

"And you can't allow her out of range for any period of time?"

"No."

He nodded. "I understand. You want to be able to hear the game."

She flinched. "So, you know, too."

"I've suspected for a while she had some connection to the device in your ear. I should have seen it immediately, but I can be... dense."

"Don't tell anyone," she ordered and spun away to watch the second half.

Bruce Caldwell, Exposer of Secrets.

It was hard not to be. It was his job, after all. He really needed to stop probing into other people's business and just stick to football.

The Wolverines took the ball down the field for a touchdown on the opening drive of the half. It gave him something to write about and improved Eden's mood. He didn't dare spoil it by saying anything to her that wasn't about the game.

Her halftime analysis was first rate. The team looked more of a unit now, and the result was a lopsided second half. Michigan added three further touchdowns, finishing with twenty-eight points in all. Wisconsin had only one chance to score, on a drop-kick, but the try failed. It was a solid victory over a stingy team. The fans back home would be pleased.

No. Not back home. In Ann Arbor. Home was Boston. Was the oppressive heat melting his brains? He needed a cool drink. He should suggest to Eden they find a saloon in the area. They could find a quiet table, maybe in a corner. If she put Vox up on the table, he could whisper.

He didn't get the opportunity to propose the outing, because Eden snapped her parasol closed, grabbed him by the arm, and dragged him under the bleachers. She called to Vox, who flittered up into her arms.

"Mrs. Holtzmann is certain to come get me within minutes, and I haven't yet thought of a good location for a private talk, so tell me quickly now, how did you get that black eye?"

"I was asking about Tagget's car. He must not have liked that, because his two thugs dragged me into an alley and pummeled me until I was able to escape." His matter-of-fact tone offered only a thin veneer for the seething anger inside.

Eden glowered. "Why does he hate you?"

"Because he's the pestiferous son of a syphilitic whore." The veneer was crumbling.

"Insults aren't helpful. Do you know something dangerous to him? What have you learned about him?"

"Sweetheart, I've learned all there is to know about the man except the size of his John Thomas," Bruce snarled. "Seems he shared that bit of information with you, though."

Oh, shit. That sounded like an insult. He hadn't meant it to be, but that couldn't change how it sounded. His stupid mouth. His stupid, too-quick, over-cynical mouth.

She ought to have slapped him. He wished she would slap him, or even punch him. He had one perfectly good eye available. But she just stood there, staring at him in stunned silence.

"Eden…" he began—far too late.

"Are you… calling me a bad girl? Because I had sex with him? You think I'm…" Her brow creased as she groped for a word. "A whore?"

The slur on her lips sent a knife of pain straight through his heart. His disgust was aimed fully at Tagget, not at her, but she couldn't know that. And he couldn't unsay the words.

"No, Eden…"

"My chaperone is here." She turned and walked away,

not running, not stomping, just leaving him. He stared at her retreating back, deserving the stabbing pain that came with each step she took out of his life.

When she disappeared from sight, he turned in the opposite direction. He needed to distract himself with some post game interviews. Anything to take his mind off Eden.

Lady Luck despised him today. As the football team headed out, Eden's friend Joey came straight at him, an empty water jug in each hand.

"Where'd Eden go?" he asked.

"I am the stupidest man in all of recorded history," was all Bruce could say. He wondered if a biomechanologist could repair a broken connection between one's brain and one's mouth.

Joey's brows knit together. "Yeah. Yeah, you are." He shrugged and walked on.

"If you see her, tell her I'm sorry."

"No fucking way."

I don't deserve it anyway.

Bruce abandoned any thought of interviews and headed to the hotel to write his article. He didn't expect it to be very good. Maybe he'd get fired. He probably deserved that, too.

27

October 30

EDEN DIDN'T EVEN PRETEND to read, nor did she participate in any conversation. She stared out the window of the train, wallowing in her misery. She had feigned illness after the game, saying it was brought on by the heat. She had neither left the hotel room nor eaten dinner. Frau Holtzmann was a dear, fetching tea and toast, offering blankets and tonics. Eden turned down everything but the drinks and a bit of food. None of it made her feel better.

Eden rarely wallowed this long. She was a woman of action. When there was trouble, she did something about it. Now here she was, with a complete lack of ideas for what to do. Her world was a disaster. Not long ago, she had lived a simple and happy life. Why had stupid, handsome men had to wander in from out-of-state to mess it all up? It had all started well, and she'd had great fun. Now she had gone from two suitors to none, and she was devastated.

Evan Tagget was evil and had stolen Lilah's invention. Eden didn't know how to prove it or stop him from doing it again. She feared Vox would be next.

Bruce was too nosy, which put him in danger, and he hated her. Enough to insult her. Not that she understood what was so bad about being a whore, anyway. For all that society wouldn't talk about sex, it seemed awfully concerned with who was doing it.

She'd been up half the night, mulling over their last conversation. He'd been so angry. But at halftime, when he'd asked about the game and suggested she try officiating or coaching, he'd been his usual self. He hadn't avoided her. He'd even smiled.

Bringing up Tagget had caused it. Bruce got irritable whenever he was around or when Eden mentioned him. The two men snapped at one another like dogs fighting over a bone.

Her back stiffened. She was the bone.

"Oh, blast."

Bruce was jealous. And hurt. He probably believed she'd picked Tagget over him. And she hadn't had any chance to explain because they never could find a time and place for a proper private conversation. When they did talk, one or the other of them always said something wrong.

"Miss Randall?" Frau Holtzmann asked. "Are you unwell?"

"No, no. I just realized I need to make a note of something. Do you have pen and paper?"

"Only a pencil, but nothing to write on."

"That will do." Eden plucked her bookmark—a receipt from a purchase she had made at the Main Street corset factory—from her book. She didn't remember most of what she had read, so it wasn't a great loss.

She composed a brief, pointed explanation, writing small to ensure it fit, then stuffed the finished letter back into the book at a random page.

Done. Bruce would read the letter, which would at least

make him willing to speak to her. She hoped. Then she could explain about Lilah and ask him for any information on Tagget that could help solve the crisis.

Delivery would be the next obstacle. She needed to get him the letter today. An entire weekend had already passed since the reveal of the echo machine. She turned to stare out the window once more, pondering now, rather than moping.

· · · 🐿 · · ·

They changed trains in Chicago. Eden dawdled on the platform until Bruce passed by on the way to the second class section, then slipped close enough to thrust the letter at him.

"Read this, please," she whispered.

Step one completed. Now she needed to get him alone.

Her new compartment was nicer than on the train from Madison. The upholstery was soft, and the seats comfortable, with more room to stretch out. Their only companion was a man of middle years with thick, graying muttonchops.

Frau Holtzmann and Mr. Whiskers got on splendidly. Eden pretended to read again, eavesdropping on their chatter. Whiskers lived in Ypsilanti. He owned a saloon down near the Normal School. He was a great football fan and rode the interurban into Ann Arbor for every home game. He was, "so pleased to find a charming young woman who shared his interest." He didn't mean Eden. Mrs. Holtzmann blushed and tittered.

As the conversation went on, the two of them moved closer together, and their voices grew softer. With her own recent experiences in flirtation, Eden noticed things in the tone of their voices and their expressions that would have gone right over her head in the past. Her two compartment-mates were deeply attracted to one another. Perhaps she ought to give them some privacy. They certainly wanted to kiss, and maybe even have sex.

Or did one not do such things on a train, even in private?

Huge gaps remained in her knowledge. She had begun to think Joey didn't really know all that much about it.

"Mrs. Holtzmann," Whiskers said, "I am hungry for dinner, but fear my appetite will suffer for lack of pleasant companionship. Would you do me the great honor of saving me from such a fate?"

The older woman's eyes lit up for an instant, then her smile faded and she looked at Eden.

"I can't neglect Miss Randall, of course. She has been ill of late, and needs looking after."

Eden faked a yawn, seizing on her opportunity. "Oh, I'm quite recovered, Mrs. Holtzmann. Don't I look much better to you? I feel I have my color back."

Mrs. Holtzmann blinked at her. "Oh. Oh, yes. You're looking far better this morning."

"I think a nap is all I need any longer. A quiet compartment would be a blessing. I could draw the drapes and get quality rest before anyone else comes to these seats."

Whiskers consulted his watch. "We have a full forty-five minutes before we reach the next station. It would be sufficient time for the young lady to get her rest, I think."

Frau Holtzmann hopped up from her seat. "I agree. We must leave her be. Miss Randall, I will see to it you are not disturbed."

Eden smiled up at her. "Thank you. You are most kind and helpful."

"Think nothing of it, dear. Would you like me to bring you back a sandwich or other bit of food?"

Eden hoped her rumbling stomach wasn't loud enough to be overheard. "Yes, please, but don't hurry yourself. I will be asleep for some time."

The infatuated couple didn't need further encouragement. They scampered out the door with a last, "Rest well!" on their way to their private dinner.

Eden counted to thirty before rising and peeking out into

the hall. They were out of sight. She hurried down the corridor in the opposite direction, headed for the basic accommodations Bruce's newspaper had paid for. She found him crushed up against the window, shying away from a loud-mouthed man taking up more than his fair share of the seat. Bruce didn't notice her at first. His gaze was fixed on something far away, his expression unreadable. Her letter was clenched in his fingers.

"Bruce!"

He jumped. "Eden!"

"Quickly, come with me. We haven't much time."

He looked bewildered, but he squeezed past the annoying man, who now declaimed how rude some people were.

"We have maybe as many as forty minutes," Eden explained, leading the way back to her compartment, "but I wouldn't depend on more than half an hour. I'm sorry to be so rushed, but it's been impossible to get any time alone."

"Yes."

She pushed open the door, and ushered him into the compartment, checking the door was securely latched, and the curtains drawn. "Did you read my letter?"

He still held the paper. He lifted it to the light. "Indeed. One underbust corset—unboned leather, black. Paid in full."

Her heart leapt with joy. Teasing meant he liked her.

"Or did you mean the other side where it starts, 'Dear Bruce, I'm not evil'?"

"I'm not."

"I never thought you were. I'm so sorry if I made you feel that way." A look of pain flashed in his eyes. "Any anger you saw was directed wholly at myself or at Tagget. I thought he was using you."

"He's not."

"So I gather." He pocketed the letter. "Now, why this secret tête-à-tête?"

"Tagget stole Lilah's design. That echo machine he showed off is no more than a modification of the guts of her bat dragon.

I don't know how to prove it or how to expose him, or anything. I hoped you might have dug up some useful information."

"Heyward," Bruce answered immediately. "Heyward stole the design. I overheard him giving something to Tagget. He called it a 'copy of a copy.'"

"That little brat," she huffed. "He must have copied Lilah's schematic. Maybe we can find it in Hart's office?"

"No. Tagget is too smart. He would have destroyed the evidence the moment his design was done. We will have only the dates on the schematics and the words of Miss St. James and your father."

"What about Heyward? He's a pushover. We could get a confession out of him. He'll be facing expulsion. His new designs must have come from Tagget. I thought they were too nicely drawn."

"I've seen Tagget's work. He has a camera design hanging in Hart's office. If you show me Heyward's new schematics, I can confirm if they look the same."

"That's a start. We'll have to be careful. Heyward knows about Vox. I don't know whether he's vindictive enough to make the knowledge public if we expose him." She shivered. "If he did..."

"You'd be hounded by curious scientists and dogged by the press. I pray it won't come to that, but if it should, I'll chase them away for you. I know a thing or two about nosy reporters."

He favored her with a sheepish grin. He looked adorable, even with the bruise—now a sickly yellow—marring his face.

She answered with a blush. "Thank you." She set Vox on the seat and paced as best she could in the tiny compartment. "Good. We have the beginnings of a plan. We can confront Heyward and gather proof of the theft. I should confront Tagget about it, too, perhaps after we know more."

"Whoa. No way. That's too dangerous."

"He won't hurt me. He likes me. It's you he hates. He's jealous that I like you better."

"Sweetheart, I think you're ascribing human emotions to him that he doesn't actually possess."

"You say that because *you* are jealous." She punctuated her words with a jab to the ribs. He yelped in pain. She sprang back, alarmed. "What did I do?"

"Not you," he winced. "Broken ribs."

"What? Show me." She grasped both his arms and pushed him down onto the seat. She hiked up her skirt to straddle his thighs and tugged his shirt free from his waistband.

"Eden…"

She couldn't lift the shirt to inspect his injuries until she got his vest unbuttoned. Fortunately, this particular vest had a deep v-cut, and only three buttons.

"Eden, you're undressing me on a train. If someone should walk in…"

She pulled the watch from his vest pocket.

"We have plenty of time. No one will disturb us." She pried the vest open and yanked up the shirt to reveal a bandage wound around his torso. Her fingers trailed across the white cloth. "Here?"

His hand covered hers, guiding it. "Here. And here. But the whole area is sore. The doctor said several weeks for a full recovery."

"I'm sorry." She caressed him, letting her fingertips slide past the edge of the bandage to feel his skin. "Tagget's men?"

"Yes."

"I'm going to punch him." She slid her other hand up underneath his shirt to stroke his chest.

His hand closed over her wrist. "No, don't."

She stilled. "Don't touch you?"

"Don't punch him. You can touch me all you want."

Eden grinned and resumed her caresses. Bruce's hands slid down to cup her buttocks, and he pulled her closer, bringing their hips together.

"You're hard already," she breathed.

His lips brushed across her forehead. "Can't resist you."

"Good."

Eden nuzzled his neck, reveling in the scent of him and the salty taste of his skin. Her fingers splayed across his warm skin. In his arms her other senses were so heightened she could close her eyes and silence her earpiece and never feel lost.

His lips brushed her right ear. A finger flicked at her earring.

"Does this one do anything?"

"It looks pretty."

He unhooked it and dropped it onto the seat. A shiver ran clear down to her toes when he sucked on her now-bare earlobe. The multitude of sensitive places on her body astounded her. His fingers had wormed their way beneath her loose top and now ran in ticklish little strokes along her spine.

"Eden, we're on a train," he mumbled. She didn't think she would've heard him were Vox not right beside him.

She tilted her head to kiss his lips. "Yes." She wasn't going to waste her time with extra words. He was delicious. Her mouth had better things to do.

"...shouldn't..." he continued. She couldn't catch all the words while he was kissing her. "...get caught..."

Despite his protestations, he didn't appear inclined to end their amorous grappling. One of his hands was beneath her skirt now, tugging at her drawers.

"...stop?"

Ah. He was asking for her thoughts. She wasn't worried. Mrs. Holtzmann and her hairy companion believed she was napping. They wouldn't return for some time yet.

"Don't stop," she said. "I want you."

She squirmed off him and pulled down her drawers. A bit of wiggling got them off without removing her boots. Bruce yanked down his trousers and underthings, stopping just shy of exposing his mechanical knee. Did he keep it covered out of habit? Had other women been repulsed by it? She hoped he didn't think it had contributed to their previous difficulties.

She perched on his left leg and tugged his trousers lower. Her hand settled on his opposite thigh, caressing slowly down to his knee. She lingered there, intrigued by the contrast of warm flesh abutting cool metal. Someday, she would convince him to let her unscrew the bronze kneecap and inspect the inner workings.

"I like you just as you are," she said. "Your biomechanics are beautiful."

A fingertip grazed her left ear. "So are yours."

She let her hand slide back up his thigh and curled her fingers around his erection.

"You have such a lovely, hard cock," she murmured. It was her new favorite word. Gritty. Biting. Arousing.

Bruce groaned her name and pulled her close again, his hand burrowing beneath her skirts.

Eden sighed at his touch and kissed his lips, chin, neck, anything she could reach. Excitement and hunger suffused her. Every stroke of his hand twisted her insides until she was coiled tight as an overwound clock. She ground her hips against him, begging him to spring her loose. He caught her waist and repositioned her, entering her in one smooth thrust.

"Bruce," she moaned. He felt so good. Better than she had imagined. She rocked with him, thinking she might go mad from the pleasure of his body. It would be worth it.

She cried aloud when the orgasm shook her. Her fingers clutched at his shirt, her head lolled back. Blissful shudders ran the length of her.

She was still reeling when he lifted her off of him, snagged a handkerchief, and spent himself into it. In her haze she couldn't think of a good reason for it.

"Why did you do that?"

"Huh?" He sounded dazed, too.

She pointed at the soiled cloth.

"Oh, that. So you won't get pregnant."

"Oh. Evan doesn't do that."

Bruce scowled. "That's because he doesn't care if he saddles you with his bastard."

She shrugged. "I won't get pregnant. I drink a tisane made from wild carrot every day and eat a teaspoon of the seeds after each time."

His scowl faded into a look of bewilderment. "Does that work?"

"The book of remedies says it does. It's said to be 'very effective' at preventing babies."

He looked skeptical. "I'll buy some condoms."

"Some what?"

He shook his head. "I'll show you next time."

Joy rushed through her. He anticipated a next time. She might have proposed they do it again immediately were time not a consideration. She had no idea how long it had been since they started.

She retrieved her drawers and straightened her clothes as best she could. She couldn't suppress a yawn. It had been a long weekend, and the sex had left her sleepy. Bruce adjusted his own clothing, wincing as he did so. Eden laid a comforting hand on his arm. She had forgotten to be gentle.

"I'm sorry about your ribs."

"Eh, it was worth it," he replied. He gave her a grin, a touch of pink coloring his cheeks. He handed her earring back to her and took the seat by the window. It pleased her that he didn't feel the need to run back to his own car.

She snuggled up beside him, yawning again. His arm wrapped around her shoulders.

"It's okay, sweetheart, you can sleep if you want."

She did want. She rested her head on his shoulder and called Vox to her. She placed the dragon in Bruce's lap. "Sleep," she commanded.

Vox folded her wings, retracted her antennae, and curled

up into her sleeping position. The sounds of the train faded away as she went into low-power mode.

Eden closed her eyes. She could feel the gentle sway of the train car and the warmth of Bruce's body. He would keep Vox safe. Sleep came swiftly.

Bruce wasn't certain what to think. Had all of that really just happened? He almost couldn't believe he'd gone from certainty she despised him to making love to her in a train compartment, of all places. Her letter had turned everything upside down. He didn't need to look at it. He'd read it so many times he had memorized it.

> *Dear Bruce,*
>
> *I'm not evil. I wasn't with Tagget because I love him or agree with him. He has done some terrible things, and I won't be seeing him anymore. I never preferred him to you. He gave me an easy and pleasant way to learn the things that go on between a man and a woman. If I'd known better, I would have done it with him first and then it wouldn't have been awful with us and ruined everything. I promise it will be good next time. Please tell me you don't hate me. I miss you and want things to be the way they were when I was your girl.*
>
> *Your friend,*
> *Eden*

He thought perhaps it was the most absurd thing ever written, though also quite logical, in its own way. Well-raised girls, so far as he could tell, were kept entirely in the dark on matters of sexual relations. Eden, who eschewed society and obtained most of her knowledge through novels, had come to it even more clueless than most.

She was also insatiably curious. Her response to a

statement such as, "You should never let a man touch you," would be, "Why not?" If no one gave her a satisfactory answer, she would draw her own conclusions on the matter. He loved her indefatigable spirit.

Peculiar though her explanation may have been, he loved it because it was quintessentially Eden. It also cleared up all the troubles between them. They had both been blaming themselves. Perhaps neither was truly to blame.

We still need to talk things over, he reminded himself.

But at least they were headed in the right direction. He wouldn't lose her to Evan Tagget.

He shivered, even with Eden's warm body pressed against his. Tagget wouldn't react well to rejection. The ache in his ribs was testament to Tagget's ruthlessness. Whatever happened, Bruce vowed to guard Eden with his life.

He ran his fingers over Vox's smooth, metal back. The trust Eden had placed in him made his heart soar. Someday, perhaps, she might come to love him the way he loved her. A man could hope.

He flinched when the compartment door opened. Eden stirred and snuggled closer, but didn't wake. An unfamiliar man and woman entered, stowing their things and taking the seats across from Bruce and Eden.

"Good evening," the man greeted them. His gaze fell to Eden and he lowered his voice. "My apologies, young man. I wouldn't wish to disturb your wife. Long day of travel?"

Bruce nodded. He felt no need to explain they could shout at the top of their lungs and she would hear nothing. Quiet would be welcome. He was also happy to play at being her husband. It would be good practice for the future. The *possible* future. He couldn't go assuming things. That path led to heartbreak.

He was now well and truly stuck in Eden's compartment. He hoped that jackass who had been next to him wasn't rifling through his possessions and stealing things. Bruce had no money or valuables, fortunately.

He passed the time by playing with Eden's hair and watching out the window. His stomach gurgled. He'd spent his last nickel on a sandwich at noon, and he hadn't had much to eat the entire weekend. He blamed his hunger on Tagget. With Eden securely in his arms, Bruce found heaping a multitude of sins upon his rival to be rather enjoyable.

Soon the compartment door opened once more, this time to admit Eden's chaperone and an otherwise distinguished gentleman with unfortunate sideburns. Mrs. Holtzmann's cheeks were rosy, and she wore a broad grin. She waltzed through the door, only to freeze in shock the moment she spied Bruce and Eden. She gaped for a long moment, then closed her mouth and took a seat, saying nothing.

"I say!" exclaimed Mr. Muttonchops. He held a tray of food Bruce guessed to be for Eden. He plopped himself in the last available seat and also fell silent.

Bruce tried not to squirm. In the presence of strangers, Eden's chaperone couldn't say anything to him. Revealing he didn't belong would cause a scandal, which would be far worse than letting things remain as they were. He did stop winding her hair around his fingers, in a futile attempt to make their situation appear more platonic.

The uncomfortable silence lingered until Eden woke from her nap. She yawned and stretched, making a little squeak of surprise when she noticed how many people were now in the compartment. She tapped Vox on the head, and the dragon roused herself.

"Did you sleep well?" Bruce asked. It seemed an appropriately husbandly question.

"I did, thank y—"

At that moment, his stomach made a horrible rumbling noise loud enough for anyone nearby to hear. He could only guess at what it must have sounded like to Eden, with Vox only inches away.

"Gracious, Bruce, is that your stomach? You must be starving." She looked across the compartment, at the man with the overabundant facial hair. "Is that my dinner?"

"Er, yes." Still looking flummoxed, he handed it over without another word.

Eden inspected the tray. The large sandwich was cut neatly in half, and was accompanied by a generous pile of fried potato wedges. "Excellent, thank you." She picked up half the sandwich and held it out to Bruce. "Here you go."

"Oh, no, Eden, I…"

"Eat it."

He took the sandwich from her hand and adopted what he thought was a proper dutiful husband tone. "Yes, dear."

She gave him a puzzled look, then shrugged and picked up her own half-sandwich. Soon, she was foisting potatoes on him as well, and he accepted them without complaint.

His father had said a good marriage was all about compromise and choosing one's battles. Bruce preferred to avoid battles, physical or otherwise. He anticipated many "yes, dears" in his future. Still, he would try to ensure she lost now and then. She would never love him if he weren't a worthy competitor. No one could win all the time.

Except maybe Yost's football team.

28

October 31

"YOU WILL LOVE IT." Eden entered the lab hanging on Bruce's arm, smiling and chatting happily. "Joey convinced me to go for the first time last year. I get nervous about parties, because they can be overstimulating. With so many people talking at once, I don't always know what to listen to. But at the same time, I love things that are new and interesting. So I went last year, and had great fun. There will be a big bonfire and games. Apples, nuts, hot drinks. Also, you can dress up as something scary—a witch or a ghost, or one of those dead creatures that come out at midnight when the barrier between life and death is at its weakest. I will be dressed as a fairy."

Bruce frowned at her. "A fairy is hardly a creature of the night."

"No, but I like fairies."

He chuckled. "Okay, then. I'm afraid I don't have anything that might pass as a costume. I'll have to come as myself."

230 CATHERINE STEIN

"But you'll come?"

"Yes."

Eden grinned and allowed herself a small hop of excitement. "I'm so glad." She steered Bruce to the schematics cabinet. "Now that everyone thinks we are discussing frivolous things, we can investigate."

"I hope you don't mean to indicate either your invitation or my acceptance thereof wasn't genuine."

"Of course it was genuine! Did you think I faked my pleasure?"

"No, I was teasing. You veritably abound with sincerity."

Eden began to flip through the drawers. "You should've gone to law school, with all your big Latinate words."

"I would've hated it. Legal matters bore me to no end. I do love books, though."

"A not-insignificant mark in your favor," she replied. "Here, look at this." She pulled a schematic from the cabinet and held it up for him to see. It was smaller than a standard design, and done all in pencil—a rough draft. "I believe this was his original sketch, done the first week of classes."

"I know nothing about this field, but it looks messy," Bruce observed. "Not scribbly like my handwriting, but hard to follow."

"Your penmanship would be neater if you slowed down."

"And then I would miss my deadlines."

She had to concede his point. She replaced the paper and continued flipping until she located the new turtle dragon schematic.

Bruce looked it over. "That's far better. It almost makes sense."

"It does make sense," Eden assured him. "Does it look like Tagget's work?"

"Yes. The lines are clean and precise, and it has the large overview with details clarified in these smaller boxes. But I'm no expert. I see nothing that would constitute definitive proof."

Eden nodded, moving on to another drawer. She wanted to show him Lilah's bat while they were here. "I don't know if we need proof to confront Heyward. We only need enough that he *thinks* we can prove it."

"We can imply he's in danger not just of expulsion, but of going to jail."

"Which may be true. He's a thief, after all."

"He is that. I'd hoped he would be here this morning."

"No, this is a different class. More advanced. Not up to Lilah's level, though. Here, take a look at her design."

"Oh. Wow." Bruce pointed at the belly of the bat. "This section here is what you mean, I assume? It looks just like the echo machine. I understand none of this, and I can see the resemblance at a glance."

She nodded. "That's because Lilah's schematics and Tagget's schematics are of professional quality. They're clear and concise. They can be followed by anyone with mechanical training. Even a layman like you can grasp much of it."

"We need to get our hands on a copy of the design Tagget and Hart presented. It will be unmistakable proof."

"It shouldn't be difficult. It was a public presentation. All the records should be in Hart's office. They can't discard them or they will no longer have an invention. The trouble comes from proving Lilah invented it first. How many would corroborate her story, save for my father?"

"I see your point. A date is easy to fake, and Tagget has the advantage of a name and money." He chewed on his lip as he thought. "You go after Heyward. Use all this and intimidate him. He'll never admit it, but he's scared of you. I'll hit the library, look up industrial theft cases, and see what evidence has been used in the past. That should give us an idea of how to use what we have and what else we might need to look for."

"What was that about law being boring?" she teased.

Bruce shrugged, that slightly bashful grin of his lighting

his face. "Maybe I misspoke. Regardless, I think I'm more cut out to be a detective than a lawyer."

"That's because you're nosy. Let me know what you find, and be careful. No more broken bones. We have a date tonight at the Halloween party."

"I wouldn't miss it for the world. Shall I pick you up, or meet you there?"

"Meet me there. You can walk me home after."

"Will do. Until this evening, then."

He stepped closer, but looked past her at the class working in the lab behind her. Eden glanced over her shoulder. She didn't see anyone looking. She stood on her toes to give him a quick kiss.

"More later," she promised. She walked him to the door and waved goodbye.

Eden ducked into her father's office to check the class schedule. Heyward wouldn't be here until this afternoon unless he decided to come in for personal work time. She had no idea where else to find him, so she had nothing to do but wait.

For the next half hour she tinkered in the lab, but with no particular project in mind she found it difficult to focus, and soon decided her time would be better spent at the library. She would help Bruce if she saw him, otherwise she would just get some reading done.

She was cleaning up her tools when an unwelcome voice spoke from somewhere behind her.

"I thought I might find you here, my flower of paradise."

She almost said a very naughty word. Catching herself, she turned slowly, trying to keep her demeanor calm. "You can save your poetical compliments, Mr. Tagget. I've had enough of them. Vox, come." The dragon flew up into her arms, and she moved toward the door.

Tagget's brows knit together in a frown of concern, and he rushed after her. "Eden, is something wrong?"

"Several things are wrong, as a matter of fact. I'm

attempting to remedy them. Excuse me, I have things to do today."

She swept past him and out into the hall. He followed. She shook him off when he tried to take her arm.

"Eden, let me help you."

She turned to face him. She hadn't wanted to confront him yet, but it seemed she had no choice. "You? Help me? Ha."

"Have I done something to upset you? Did something happen over the weekend?" He glowered. "Is this about your reporter friend?" Before she could answer, he composed himself, and his customary arrogant smile returned. "I assure you, my forbidden fruit, I can keep you every bit as satisfied as he can."

She scowled. If he thought he could make her happy with nothing more than his bedroom skills, he was delusional.

"Oh, really?" she challenged. "What's my favorite football team?"

He smirked. "Michigan, of course."

"Who is my favorite player?" He met her stare with a blank look. "Which do I prefer deep down: good offense or good defense? What sport have I played since childhood? What style of beer do I prefer? What is my favorite sandwich? When is my birthday? What sorts of novels do I like to read? In what field did I earn my degree? Where do I shop for my fancy corsets? What do I do on very hot days? What's my address? What command would I use if I wanted to tell Vox not to bite someone?"

His expression turned cool, calculating. He might have finally realized he'd underestimated her.

"You know next to nothing about me, Mr. Tagget. Don't expect me to enlighten you."

She spun on her heel and headed for the door. He jogged to catch up.

"I promise you, darling, I will learn all those things and

more. Anything you feel I should know, tell me. I will listen. What do you want of me? I will fight for you, Eden."

The sincerity in his voice roused her pity, but it could never make up for the things he'd done. She rounded on him. "You mean you'll send your thugs to beat on my friends?"

"Ah. So it is about him. I sent my men to keep him away from my car. If he was foolish enough to let things become violent, that is hardly my fault."

"You're a terrible liar."

"Forget Caldwell. He has nothing to offer you that I cannot match or outdo." His voice rang with certainty. Eden admired his self-confidence, misplaced though it was.

"This isn't about that," she snapped. "Even if we ignore what you did to Bruce, you still have to answer for what you did to Lilah."

"To whom?" He sounded genuinely confused.

"Lilah St. James. She studies with my father. You stole her design and turned it into your echo machine."

"I stole nothing, Miss Randall."

She sighed and rolled her eyes to the ceiling. "I'm not stupid, Mr. Tagget. Stop defending yourself with absurd technicalities. Marcus Heyward stole the schematic and brought it to you. The designs are nearly identical. It's theft, plain and simple. You think you can use your money and your unethical lawyers to silence any complaints. You'll step on anyone if it gets you more money. You're a heartless, immoral bastard, and I don't want anything to do with you."

She turned away, and this time she swore not to stop again, whatever he might say.

"I never meant to hurt you," he asserted. "I had no idea the paper came from your friend."

Eden kept walking. "You knew it was stolen. That's enough." She pushed the door open and slammed it behind her. She hoped it had hit him.

29

THE DANCING FLAMES emanating from the hearth in the center of the empty warehouse kept the space nice and warm, but Bruce couldn't help but think of it as a fire hazard. With the fire station so close to his hotel, he'd been awakened too many times by clanging bells and galloping horses. He made note of all the exits, just in case.

He walked a circuit of the room while he waited for Eden to arrive, surveying the selection of games and the young men and women playing them. The ages of the guests looked to range from late teens to mid-twenties. College students, most of them, he guessed. Many of the men were showing off at games of skill such as apple bobbing and snapdragon, though a majority of the women appeared focused on the fortune telling rather than on any demonstrations of male prowess.

Bruce headed for the refreshment table. He didn't know anyone here, and was uncertain what the protocol was for introductions at such an affair. Informal, he guessed. He preferred to wait for Eden, regardless.

He had just paused to get a drink when she entered, hanging her cloak by the door, near a dozen similar ones. They could make a game out of guessing how many people would leave with the wrong outerwear this evening.

Eden looked around the room, and Bruce waved to catch her attention. She adjusted a metal contraption strapped to her back and waltzed over to him. He handed her a hot toddy.

"Strong, but delicious."

She took a careful sip. "I like it. Last year we had only beer and warm cider."

Bruce nodded absently, distracted by her fairy costume. The thing on her back had unfolded into a pair of metal wings that resembled Vox's, and a coronet of brass leaves sat atop her golden hair. Today's corset was sleek black satin, laced tightly over a bright blue shirt with short, puffed sleeves. Her skirt, also black, hit only mid-thigh. Black silk stockings with a vine pattern in the same blue as the shirt covered her legs. He could just see the edge of her blue garters peeping from beneath her hem when she moved.

It would have been scandalous in any other context. At a fancy dress Halloween party, it was only one of many such costumes. Short skirts and low necklines abounded. One woman had arrived wearing a skintight silver suit. The outfit puzzled Bruce until she walked close enough to reveal the eight small legs jutting from her black hat. The lady was spider silk.

Lacking anything but ordinary clothes, he had improvised and dressed all in black, from his tie to the shiny shoes he usually wore only on Sundays. He'd pinned the trousers to make them look snug, and cinched his vest tighter than was comfortable.

Eden looked him over, her brow furrowed in a thoughtful frown. "What are you? Night? A shadow?"

He took hold of her free hand and lifted it to his lips. Doing his best to look haughty, he said, in a terrible approximation of a New York accent, "Evan Tagget, at your service, my dulcet darling."

She erupted into a near-hysterical fit of the giggles.

Bruce stayed in character. "I am pleased to have amused you so, my diaphanous fairy queen. Let me tell you about the comedy troupe I saw in Paris when I flew there in my diamond-encrusted dirigible."

Eden almost doubled over. "Oh, Lord." She wiped tears of mirth from her eyes. "Oh, Bruce, that's terrible! And terribly funny." He handed her a handkerchief, and she straightened up, patting at her eyes. "Don't ever do anything like that where he might find out. He'd kill you."

Bruce shrugged. "He wants to kill me already, so I doubt it matters."

"I encountered him this morning. I told him we knew Heyward stole Lilah's design. Then I slammed a door in his face."

"That's my girl. Always attacking men with doors."

"This is going to be a thing with us forever, isn't it?"

Forever. Was there any more beautiful word on her lips?

"I sincerely hope so." He offered his arm, and she took hold of it. "Show me around. I wandered through a minute ago, but I'm not familiar with all the games. I've only attended one other Halloween party, and all we did was force one another to bob for apples in icy water and light things on fire. It was outdoors, and that's what teenage boys do when it's freezing cold and snowing."

"We can roast nuts and apples at the fire if we get hungry," Eden said. Her eyes lingered on the food. She had an impressive appetite for such a small woman.

"We can bob for apples over there," she continued, "but I would prefer to save that for later. I'm not feeling inclined to get wet just now. And I think there are raisins for snatching from the flames, too."

"What are the ladies doing over there?" he asked, pointing at a huddle of young women around a candle and a bowl of water. "It looked like they were melting lead."

"Ooh, molybdomancy! They're divining the future. The

shapes made by the molten lead when it cools in the water predict things. I'd like to try it."

"Sounds a bit dangerous."

She shrugged. "It's much better than reading entrails, you know."

"Ugh. Why would anyone do that?"

"Haruspicy. Animal sacrifice for the purpose of divination was common practice in Roman times. They would read the organs—livers, chiefly—to find omens. It's how Caesar was warned of the Ides of March."

"Which warning he famously failed to heed."

"He probably thought entrails were icky, too. Perhaps he should've tried lead." She pulled Bruce toward the fortune-telling crowd.

"Oh, a doctor!" one young woman exclaimed. "I knew it!"

"What?" said another. "How do you figure that?"

"It's clearly a caduceus. See how the snakes wind around the rod?"

"I see no snakes. It's a hammer. You're going to marry a carpenter."

"Perhaps a professor at the medical school," the first woman continued, ignoring her friend. "Now we'll have to play another game to see how soon it will happen. Come along, Mabel."

"It's a hammer," Mabel muttered, but she followed the other girl to a new game.

Eden peeked into the bowl. "Definitely a hammer."

Bruce saw nothing but a lump of metal. The woman running the game scooped it out with a spoon and dropped it into a pile of other lumps.

"Would you like to try?" she inquired of Eden, handing her the spoon and a lead ingot.

Eden held the spoon over the flame, watching, wide-eyed, as the metal liquified.

"When it's molten, pour it through the hole of this key into the water. The shape it takes will give you an indication of your future husband's profession."

Bruce had an insane hope the lead would resemble a pen or a book or something equally journalistic. He scolded himself for playing along with something so obviously nonsensical.

Eden appeared quite serious about the entire endeavor. She was patient during the melting process, and she poured the lead with care. The metal solidified into yet another blob that resembled nothing.

"What is it?" she asked.

"Look carefully," the fortune teller prompted. "What do you see?"

"Um… the number four?"

Bruce could almost see it, if he squinted and was looking at it upside down.

"The sign of four," the fortune teller agreed. "It is a merchant's mark."

Eden's nose scrunched up, and her lips pinched together. "A merchant?"

The woman nodded.

"Oh." Her shoulders slumped. "I'll probably never get married, anyway."

"Let me see your hand, child."

Eden held out her hand. The woman took hold of it and turned it palm up. Her other hand rose from behind the table. Metal rods ran through the back of her hand from her wrists to fingertips, with several knuckles replaced by biomechanical joints. Her pointer finger was entirely metal. Eden didn't flinch when the steel finger ran across the lines of her palm.

"Strong love lines. Not just for romance. You will have choices to make. What do you love the most?" She tapped a particular spot. "Here is your merchant. He is but one of your options."

Eden withdrew her hand. "Because that's just what I need.

More suitors making life difficult. I'm hungry. I'm going to go roast some nuts."

She hurried off. Bruce moved to follow, but was stopped when the fortune teller laid her biomechanical hand on his arm.

"You love her. Let me see your palm."

"I don't believe in any of this stuff," he said, but allowed her to examine his hand.

"You wish to be her husband." The metal finger traced a line across the center of his palm. His flesh tingled. "You have asked her once and been refused."

He shivered. He had no idea how she had guessed that. "That was under distressing circumstances. When she's ready I will properly ask her to marry me."

The fortune teller smiled. "You will never speak those words to her."

"What?" He reminded himself this was all nonsense. "I will. I promise you."

She shook her head, but the smile remained. She closed his hand into a fist, then released it. "Do not forget, 'there is divinity in odd numbers.'"

"Shakespeare. *The Merry Wives of Windsor*." She couldn't fool him with quotations. He had an English degree.

"Indeed. That does not make it less true. A Happy Hallows' Eve to you, young man." She turned away to assist another group of women who had come to try her divination.

Bruce rushed off to catch up with Eden, needing a distraction. Not wanting to admit how much the fortune teller had unnerved him.

He found her at the fire, talking with Joey Bryerson. Joey was dressed as some sort of living dead creature, wearing multiple shades of gray, with streaks of charcoal smeared across his face and through his blond hair.

"...always vague," Joey was saying. "Could be anyone. Maybe he sweeps the floors in a shop. Or drives a delivery carriage. You'll be poor and have fifteen children dressed in rags."

Eden glared at him. "That's not funny."

He chuckled and popped a nut into his mouth.

"Eden is much too savvy for such a fate," Bruce predicted. "Either she would have only as many children as she could afford, or she would find a way to earn more money."

Eden smiled at him. "Thank you. Besides, I won't be marrying a janitor or cart driver."

"Who knows," Joey disagreed. "Maybe you'll fall in love with someone wildly inappropriate." He glanced at Bruce. "What are you supposed to be? A shadow?"

"I'm evil incarnate," he replied, eliciting a new round of giggling from Eden. Joey looked confused, then shrugged it off.

They filled their bellies with nuts and apples, and warmed their insides with the hot drinks. Vox wove her way between Eden's and Bruce's legs, rubbing against them like a cat. He was growing fond of the little dragon who was both her own creature and a part of Eden. Eden scooped her up and thrust her into Bruce's arms.

"Hold her while I dance." She dove into the crowd of revelers twirling in time to the music.

"She friended you?" Joey asked in surprise. He gave Bruce a sideways look, appraising him. "Do you know how rare that is?"

"No."

He pointed at Vox. "I can't do that. She would bite me."

Bruce's jaw dropped, but no words came out.

"Don't hurt her," Joey warned.

"Never."

"Good. I'm going to bob for apples. Interested?"

He nodded. "I'll try. As soon as Eden finishes her dancing."

When Eden and Bruce finally joined Joey, they found a large crowd surrounding the tub of water. A red-headed man dunked himself and came up with an apple clenched in his teeth. Several young ladies cheered him, including Mabel and her friend who wanted to marry a doctor. When the redhead bowed in their direction, she blushed and giggled.

Eden nudged Bruce with her elbow. "He's a carpenter," she whispered. "Told you it was a hammer." She stepped into line behind a dozen or more men, the only woman who appeared interested in participating. Bruce followed her.

He'd always had a knack for apple bobbing, but several years had passed since he'd last played, and he suspected his skills might be rusty. He watched the others ahead of him, analyzing their techniques.

Everyone stared at Eden when her turn came up. She removed her crown and adjusted her ponytail. Bruce could hear the whispers of others wondering if she would really try it. He gave a little head shake, a smile touching his lips. They didn't know Eden.

She performed admirably, catching an apple on only her third try. The crowd gave her an enthusiastic round of applause.

Eden grinned at Bruce, wiping water from her face. "Three times. Beat that!" she challenged.

"I'll do my best," he said, refusing to let her cocky attitude fluster him. He thought he could match her.

He did even better, coming up with an apple on his first try. A new round of cheers rose from the crowd. Eden stared at him in shock for a moment, then offered a half-hearted congratulations. She really did hate losing. It was too bad there weren't varsity sports for women. With her drive to win and solid work ethic, Eden could've been a multiple letter-winner.

They dried off by the fire, and she perked up within a few minutes, though a hint of irritability persisted in her blue-eyed gaze. The music and more dancing soothed her, and by the time the party began to wind down she was her usual self again.

Somehow she located her cloak from among all the others, and folded down her fairy wings to fit beneath it. Bruce offered his arm, and they started off to her house, chatting as they walked.

"I had a lovely time this evening, Bruce."

"Despite my victory at apple bobbing?"

She turned up her nose at him. "Yes, even despite that. Thank you for coming."

"It was my pleasure. It was an excellent party."

"Yes, it was. Did you like the fortune telling? I'm a little skeptical."

She didn't sound skeptical. She sounded annoyed. "Don't like merchants?" he teased.

"I must have misinterpreted it. Probably entrails would've worked better."

Bruce chuckled, and let her ramble on about historical augury practices. At some point the conversation took a turn into an animated comparison of historical events as portrayed in Shakespeare's plays versus current scholarly understandings.

They reached the Randall home far too quickly. God, but he hated to leave her for the night. Fantasies played in his mind of walking her instead to a home they shared, continuing their conversation snuggled on a sofa by the fireplace, or even wrapped together under a blanket in bed. A deep longing stirred inside him for those little intimacies he could only achieve through marriage. His body stirred as well, eager for another taste of the physical intimacy they had already shared.

Eden's thoughts, he suspected, also trended in that direction. She'd drawn closer to him, and she didn't pause or release his arm on her way up the front stairs. Bruce took a reluctant step back when she reached the door.

"Sleep well, sweetheart. I'll see you tomorrow."

She frowned at him. "Come inside with me." She wrapped her arms around his waist. "I have a comfortable bed. We can take our time tonight. The train was exciting, but frantic, don't you think?"

"Eden…" He planted a kiss in her hair. "Sweetheart, it was

magnificent, but we can't enjoy any horizontal refreshments at your house. Your parents would be in the next room over. That is beyond inappropriate, and I can't even fathom what they might do to me if they found out."

"I'm certain they're asleep by now. They'll never even know you're here."

He shook his head. "You underestimate their concern for you."

"There's no need for anyone to be concerned. If you were the sort of person to treat me badly, you would've done so by now, and I would've promptly refused to see you."

"I used to think that was exactly what happened that first night we were intimate."

"What?" she gasped. "No, it was my fault! My research was inadequate, and I was too hasty. I tried to convey that in my letter the other day, but I didn't have much room to elaborate. I thought you were upset I had ruined things."

"No. I was upset I had ruined *you*."

"I'm not ruined," she huffed. "I'm perfectly fine."

"I know." He kissed her then, letting himself get lost in the taste of her for much longer than was prudent. Every sweep of her tongue lit a fire in his veins. The crush of her warm, sweet mouth sparked the most primal of urges inside him. He wanted to grab her, hold her, claim every inch of her as his own. *Mine*, his body screamed, and for those few moments he allowed himself to believe the lie. He pulled away just in time to maintain his resolve not to ravish her in her parents' house. "I'm sorry I can't give you more than a kiss tonight. I'm available at any time tomorrow. Come to my hotel and we can do whatever you like."

"But I'm feeling amorous *now*," she protested.

"So am I, believe me, but I won't risk bringing worlds of trouble upon you to satisfy my lust. I'll have to suffer and dream of you." He brushed his lips to hers for one instant more. "Goodnight, sweetheart."

He backed down the stairs, unable to look away from her disappointed face. His heart ached with wanting fully as much as his body did. The truth smarted. She would never be his unless she chose to be, and each time he upset her he felt the odds grew longer. Now she had lost to him twice in one evening. He stood at the edge of a cliff, with the ground crumbling beneath his feet. Only Eden could save him. Somehow he needed to prove himself worth the risk.

"Goodnight, Bruce," she sighed at last. "I will see you tomorrow."

Not a rejection. He let out a breath he hadn't realized he was holding. He waited to leave until she had closed and locked the door, then he turned and walked slowly toward town, already missing her.

30

November 2

THE HOT WATER BOTTLE was now more accurately a tepid water bottle. Eden set it aside. There was no point in refilling it. She couldn't sit around at home any longer. She had too many things to do. Her belly protested as she moved around. It twisted and tightened, telling her to sit down and rest. She gritted her teeth and ignored it.

Her monthly flow had started yesterday morning. She'd tried a revised version of last month's tonic, but it had only made her feel worse. She'd been forced to telephone Bruce's hotel to tell him she didn't feel well and wouldn't be able to see him that day. The remainder of the day had been spent sitting in bed or on the sofa with the hot water bottle on her aching abdomen and a book in her hands.

Today she'd skipped the tonic, but it still should've been another day of light work—mainly at home, perhaps riding her father's motorized bicycle downtown if she needed to visit a shop or preferred to sit at the library.

She couldn't do it. Staying home and taking things easy was out of the question. She had yet to find Marcus Heyward, and she was worried about Lilah. Bruce might go poking around without her and have another run-in with Tagget's men. She packed up a few snacks for the day and went down to the basement to tell her mother she was leaving.

"Are you feeling better, dear?"

"Not really," Eden admitted. "But I'm frustrated with staying at home."

"We'll try something new next month." She said the same thing every time. Eden knew exactly what she would say next. "We live in a time of great scientific progress. Medical discoveries are made every day."

"Women have always had these problems, without the benefits of our modern medicines. I can be tough."

Her mother ruffled her hair. It made Eden feel like a little girl, but she never complained, choosing instead to cherish the expression of love. "You're always tough, my darling. Don't worry about dinner tonight. Your father has plans."

"Oh, dear." Her father's dinner plans usually involved newfangled machines that either made the cooking process slower than usual or failed to work entirely.

"Yes, well, he needs to have his fun, too." She smiled fondly. Penelope Randall adored her husband and wasn't ashamed to let everyone know it. Eden was in awe of their love and happiness. She would settle for nothing less in her own marriage. Sadly, that was part of why she feared it might never happen.

She ended up eating all her snacks on her walk from home to campus. Lunch had been inadequate, it appeared. Or maybe eating was no more than a way to distract from her cramps.

She arrived at the laboratory between classes, finding her father with his feet propped up on a workbench, reading the newspaper. He passed her Sunday's Boston Herald.

"Your friend quoted you again. He praised your analysis of the gameplay."

Eden squirmed a little. Why was her father reading all Bruce's articles now? He didn't follow or enjoy sports. Was he spying on her, via Bruce's writing? She scanned the article. Bruce had portrayed her as an expert in a lengthy segment on the halftime adjustments. The compliment to her knowledge brought a bashful smile to her lips.

"He writes well," her father said. "It's too bad he covers such pedestrian topics."

"Uh-huh." There was no use in arguing the merits of her passion. Father would never understand.

"Oh, Miss St. James asked after you this morning. Said she had something to show you. Seemed nervous. I think that patent application is stressful for her. It's her first one, you know. The first of many, I've no doubt. Girl's a genius. She'll grow accustomed to it. I told her you were resting at home, but promised to pass on her message if you did venture out today, and here you are. She's at the library until two o'clock, when she has a class in the engineering building."

"Thank you, Father. I'll go see her." She folded up the paper and placed it in the stack with the others. "Have you seen Marcus Heyward at all? I had a question for him about his recent schematic."

"The one he copied from someone?" He shook his head. "He owes me an explanation for it, and I'm certain he doesn't have one. He hasn't been here all week. It's near time to file a formal complaint. He'll be expelled for cheating, of course. Pity. Seemed a nice enough boy at first, but he got in over his head."

"He thought he could get everything he wanted without working for it," Eden opined. "Well, if he ever comes to class, tell him I'm looking for him."

That'll probably scare him all by itself. He knows we know or he wouldn't be hiding.

She bid goodbye to her father and headed to the library. Lilah sat in her usual place, with her nose in a book, but she didn't look to be concentrating as intently as Eden would have expected. She hoped the situation with Tagget and the echo machine hadn't gotten worse.

Lilah smiled when she spied Eden, and beckoned to her to pull up a chair.

"You won't believe what has happened!" Her voice was almost too loud for a library. "I've received the most astonishing communication this morning. I don't even know what to make of it. I want to be happy, but part of me insists it must be a lie. Here, see for yourself."

She handed Eden a letter.

The first thing that jumped out was the Tagget Industries letterhead printed at the top of the page. Evan Tagget's loopy signature had been written at the bottom, in blue ink. Eden scanned the body of the document, her eyes widening in amazement. She had to read the beginning aloud to convince herself she wasn't seeing things.

"We at Tagget Industries would like to contract with you for a license of your echo production and detection device."

"It all looks so legitimate. Can it possibly be real? The second page is a contract I am to approve and sign, and the third a draft of a press release to be sent to papers nationwide, and even scientific journals! And then there is this."

Lilah pushed a smaller paper across the table.

Eden read the handwritten note.

Your design is flawless and your timely patent application shows determination and wit. If you ever desire employment, a place awaits you among our elite engineers. The number below will reach my personal office in New York.

"Goodness."

Eden set the note aside and turned back to the letter,

rereading it slowly. She'd seen letters of this type before, when her parents had drawn up licensing contracts for some of their inventions. She could see nothing to indicate this one wasn't genuine. She flipped to the contract. That, too, looked like what she had seen before. The financial particulars were generous for a first-time inventor, but within the normal range for the industry. One thousand up front, and a percentage thereafter.

"I can't believe this."

Lilah's face fell. "It's a forgery, then? That's a cruel joke."

"No, it's real enough," Eden assured her. "That's Tagget's signature, and this is exactly what I would expect from such an offer."

What she couldn't understand was why the offer had been made at all. Tagget had the money and the connections to ensure no one ever heard of Lilah or suspected the design was anything other than his own. The only reason she could think for him to do this was to assuage her anger. She shivered.

"I'll pass on the good news to your father, then," Lilah decided. "I haven't yet attempted to explain my haste to file for a patent, though I'm certain he must have some suspicion. I also have a friend at the law school who can review the contract for me."

Eden's eyebrows twitched. "A gentleman friend?"

A hint of a shine appeared on Lilah's dark skin. "Mr. Willingham is a gentleman and a friend, if that's what you mean."

"Is he the tall black man with the perfect smile and the stylish moustache I saw you talking with the other day? Especially handsome? Smartly dressed?"

"That sounds very like him, yes," Lilah replied, her prim tone unable to mask her feelings.

"Well, I won't tease you further, but I wish you would tell me more. Have you kissed him? Is he good at it?" Eden shook her head and turned the topic back to the important matter. "Never mind that for now. Getting his opinion is a good idea.

If something is amiss he can tell you, but I expect you'll find everything to be correct."

Lilah nodded. "I don't know what you said to Mr. Tagget to make him repent of his original behavior, but I know you must be responsible for this."

"For bringing you to his attention, perhaps." Eden's fingers skimmed the handwritten job offer. "But this is all you. Congratulations. You will be a famed scientist. As you deserve."

"I suppose I'd better get working on my next project, if that's to be the case." She pulled a weighty book across the table and opened it to a marked page. Eden gave her a little nod and a wave before departing.

She scampered out of the library and headed for Cook's Hotel, her mind reeling. The size and scope of the offer made it clear Tagget respected Lilah and her work. Even so, Eden was sure he'd never considered seeking out the true inventor of the echo machine until she'd railed at him. Why share the profits when one quick payment to a shady lawyer could silence any troubles?

What was his true purpose? Did he think he could coax her back into his bed? Was he trying to win her affection? It had to come back to Vox. For some reason she was so valuable to him the loss on the echo machine was worthwhile.

Eden slowed to a halt. "Vox, up." The dragon flew into her arms. "Why does he want you? The recognizer? The sound transmission?" Her range was only ten yards. She couldn't be duplicated until the interference issue was resolved. Tagget couldn't make a telephone replacement out of her. Not without extensive research. And many people were already involved in other wireless teletics studies. Tagget's company was an industry leader. Was Vox so far ahead of them? It was possible, she supposed. She didn't keep up with the scientific journals.

Eden raced into the hotel, past the raised eyebrows of the lobby denizens, and up the stairs to Bruce's room. She rapped on the door, praying he would be there. She needed his research.

The door opened moments later. Bruce stared at her, open-mouthed. His fingers were stained with ink, and he held a pen in his right hand.

"Eden? What are you doing here?"

She hurried inside and closed the door behind her, setting Vox on the floor. Bruce had been working. All day, she suspected, and perhaps yesterday, too. The small desk was covered with papers written fully from top to bottom. More papers were spread about the room in what appeared to be an organized fashion. She had to step carefully not to kick any of them.

"Eden, you look distressed. Are you still unwell? Here, sit down." He seized her arm and helped her through the maze of papers to the desk chair.

She was grateful for the seat. She'd been on her feet since leaving home, and her belly was displeased. She let out an audible sigh of relief. Bruce shifted to and fro in an agitated fashion, gazing down at her with wide, worried eyes.

"Why have you come? Is there some trouble? You shouldn't have left home if you're ill."

"I'm not ill," she assured him. "Only tired, and flustered. The craziest thing has happened."

He dropped to his knees beside her and took her hand in both of his. "Tell me."

Eden ran her fingers through his hair. "You needn't worry so much. It's good news, though strange. Lilah has received an offer from Tagget Industries. They wish to license her invention to produce their echo machines."

Bruce dropped her hand and rocked back on his heels. "You must be joking."

"I'm not. I saw the letter and the contract. I'm convinced it's genuine. The signature looked like what I know of Tagget's writing."

"Round letters, very fluid, easily readable?"

"Yes."

"That's how it looks on his schematics." His jaw tightened. "He didn't care a whit who created that machine. Probably still doesn't. What's his game?"

"I think he must be trying to please me. He was apologetic when I yelled at him for stealing Lilah's design."

"I don't know what he wants, but I won't let him use you," Bruce vowed.

"Is that what this is about?" She waved her hand at the array of papers.

"Yes. This is the result of all my research. Every scrap of information I could discover about him."

Eden frowned a moment, then held her hands about six inches apart. "It's about this long."

It took Bruce a moment to comprehend her statement. He grimaced. "I did *not* want to know that."

"Well, you said it was the only thing you didn't know about him. So, now you do. Where does that go in your notes?"

"Nowhere. It makes me boil with rage to think of him touching you."

"Why? I was just trying to learn and have some fun. It wasn't anything special."

The statement didn't placate him as she had hoped. He only looked away, dejected. "Yeah. I know."

Eden shrugged and changed the subject. "Tell me about your research. Have you discovered anything of import? What can I do to help?"

"I'm working to put what I've learned into a cohesive series of articles, but there are whole sections I can't write until I understand what he's doing here. The papers to your left contain all my theories on that. I also think the Dynalux luxene is tainted, but I have no proof. Everything I know on that topic is here on this side." He gestured in the opposite direction. "Behind you is the personal information, which gives insight into his character, but is of no other use. Closer to the bed are the business files. On the desk are my drafts, giant holes and all."

"What are those letters?" she asked, pointing at the stack in the corner of the desk.

"Interviews with disgruntled former employees. To a man they refused to discuss the matter over the telephone."

Eden's brows rose. "That's suspicious."

"I agree. It tells me they fear he can eavesdrop on telephone calls. I would love to find proof of that."

Eden shuddered. "Perhaps I will change my mind about using the telephone more often."

"How *do* you manage the telephone?"

"I have to put the receiver to Vox's belly. It looks crazy to anyone else, which is why I avoid the device except while at home or very occasionally in my father's office."

"I understand your reluctance to explain Vox's purpose to strangers, but why do you care if they think you're crazy? You're so beautiful the way you are. If others can't see it, they're fools."

The sincerity in his words tugged at her heart. She was in terrible danger of letting her affection get out of hand. She pushed the thought away. A niggling fear that she had passed that point long ago lingered.

"I don't care if they think I'm crazy. I care that they call me names and don't treat me like everyone else."

Bruce took hold of her hand once again and kissed it. "They shouldn't treat you like everyone else. You deserve better than anyone else." He rose to his feet, pulling her along with him and embracing her. "I missed you yesterday."

He kissed her with an abandon that brought heat to her cheeks and goosebumps to her skin. She thought by now she ought to be accustomed to his kisses, but somehow they continued to take her breath away. The depth of his passion threatened to make her forget a world existed outside the two of them, emptying her mind of all but his musk and spice scent and the feel of his muscles beneath her fingers. Only the cramping low in her abdomen kept her grounded. When he moved toward the bed she stepped away.

"I can't today."

His worried frown returned. "What's wrong?"

Eden placed a hand on her belly. She blushed, embarrassed to have to explain this to him. "Woman's troubles. I'm uncomfortable."

Bruce's cheeks flushed far worse than hers. "I'm sorry. I had no idea. Do you need to sit back down? Can I get you anything?"

"A hot water bottle, perhaps?"

"I can do that. Rest here. I'll return shortly. There's a swallow or two of bourbon left in the bottle there if you need to ease your pain."

"How did you get alcohol in the Temperance hotel?"

He gave her a lopsided grin. "From the doctor who treated my injuries. For medicinal purposes."

"Hmmm."

Eden settled herself on the bed while she waited. She sniffed at the bourbon and decided it was worth trying. It burned going down, but it had an interesting smoky flavor and left a pleasant sensation of warmth in her stomach. She wondered if she could convince her parents to keep a bottle "for medicinal purposes."

Bruce was good to his word and returned before long with a hot water bottle and a pot of tea. Eden added some honey and the last of the bourbon to her tea and sipped it with relish, feeling happy and as comfortable as she had all day.

They spent most of the afternoon sitting together in Bruce's bed, going through the papers. She read through his drafts, teased him about his bad handwriting—which she could decipher with little difficulty these days—and asked questions. He covered several more pages with revisions.

"I'm done for the day," he sighed hours later, dropping the pen and massaging his hand. "Shall we go get some dinner?"

"Come to my house. My father is cooking."

His eyebrows rose. "This I have to see."

. . . 🦋 . . .

The kitchen was a disaster. Her father's experimental dumpling maker had dripped dough on the floor and splattered filling onto the wall. He proudly informed them that after adjustments the third batch had come out perfectly. Bruce, not in the least flustered by the mess, cleaned his plate, complimented the food, and asked questions about the machine while helping with the cleanup. Eden watched it all with a heart full of admiration. He may well have been the nicest man she'd ever met.

Much to her chagrin, she didn't get a proper kiss goodnight. Her parents walked with her to see him to the door, where he kissed her cheek and promised to see her again the next day. She had a momentary hope her parents would disappear into the house before he left, but they were too eager with their goodbyes and their invitations for him to join them again someday. She had to content herself with watching them smile and wave as he walked away. At least they liked him.

"You should marry that boy," her father declared. "He's a good sort."

"He seems exceptionally fond of you," her mother added.

Eden headed for her room, heart sinking, pretending she hadn't heard. She couldn't marry him, and she didn't want to talk about it. She didn't want to even think about it. She needed to deal with the matter, however, and she needed to do it soon. Otherwise it was going to be Paul all over again. Except this time the rejection might break more hearts than one.

31

November 4

EDEN LAY ON HER BELLY on Bruce's bed, reading through tedious articles on wireless teletics experiments. She tossed the latest one aside, having discovered nothing of import. This was hopeless. If only blasted Marcus Heyward hadn't skipped town. He'd been their best link to Tagget's schemes.

She propped herself up on her elbows, watching Bruce at his desk, scribbling and shuffling papers. He was stripped to his shirtsleeves, his hair was mussed, and his fingers stained with ink. He hadn't shaved in several days, either, leaving a coarse stubble across his jaw. She liked him this way. She liked him any way, really.

She crossed her ankles and swung her legs up into the air, causing her skirts to pool at her knees. If he turned around, he would have a nice view of her striped stockings. If he joined her in bed he could have more than a view.

What should she say? *Come to me, darling.* No, that sounded like a lady in an opera about to sing an aria. "Darling" wasn't right for him. Nor were silly phrases like "my pet" or "my angel" or anything at all like the flamboyant endearments Tagget used. Bruce called her "sweetheart." It might do for him, as well. *Come here, sweetheart.* Perhaps. *Come to bed, love.*

No. Not that word. Too strong. Too dangerous. She wouldn't go down that path.

Before she could say anything at all, Bruce twisted in his seat, leaning over the back of the chair. A grin lit his face.

"I wish my bed always looked like that."

"Tidy?" she teased, smoothing the bedding with one hand in what she hoped looked like an inviting gesture. She had made a point of straightening his tangled sheets before lying down.

He chuckled. She admired his ability to laugh at himself. She was nowhere near as good at it.

"Occupied by a lovely lady," he corrected.

"I prefer double-occupancy," Eden replied. "Do you want to join me?" Forget subtlety. Coy flirtations would never suit her.

"I do. And will. But first, can we go to the laboratory?"

"What?"

"We should go this afternoon, while the building is still open. Can we do that now? Are classes over for the day?"

"I, uh…" It took her several seconds to process the questions. "I think my father's final class ends at two."

He tucked his journal and a few folded papers into a pocket of his vest, then crossed the room to sit beside her. His hand caressed her silk-clad calf.

"It will be past two by the time we walk there. Do you know any chemistry professors?"

"What?" she asked again. How could he expect her to hold a conversation while he touched her so? His fingers tickled the back of her knee and crept up her thigh. "I can't get out of bed while you're doing that."

"I know. I'm having trouble myself. You're exceedingly tempting." He took a deep breath and released her. He pushed himself up off the bed and held out his hand to help her to her feet. "Let's go. The sooner we can drive Evan Tagget out of town, the sooner I can stop worrying for you."

Ah. That was his problem. Eden could empathize. She worried about him, too. She stepped into her boots, lifting one foot at a time for him to do up her laces.

"What I want is to compare the Dynalux fuel with ordinary luxene. See if we can get some proof it's tainted. Do you know any chemists? Could we get someone to run an analysis of the two specimens? With a microscope or whatever chemists use?"

Eden frowned at him. "Did you ever take any science classes at Harvard? At all?"

"No."

An inferior education. The poor man. "Well, I don't personally know any chemists, but my father does. We'll tell him it's an academic research question."

They found her father cleaning after his final class and preparing to leave. He preferred to close up early on Fridays and work from his home laboratory. He and her mother did some of their best collaborating on Friday afternoons.

Without giving a reason, Eden explained what they wanted to do with the luxene samples. He nodded thoughtfully at the request, peering at her from behind today's red-tinted spectacles. She would make certain he wore the blue or the yellow pair during the game tomorrow.

"Bottle up a few samples while I finish here. I'll drop them off with Stokes on my way home. He loves this sort of thing. You'll have results early next week, I imagine, though I doubt you'll find anything amiss. The latest news from Miss St. James has eased my mind considerably. Apparently Mr. Tagget is more open to compromise than our initial acquaintance led me to believe."

Eden answered with a harrumph.

"You disagree, daughter?" He cast a glance at Bruce. "Has he given up his attempts to woo you?"

"He only wants Vox." She patted the dragon and set her up on her shoulder. "Also, he's silly and tedious and only talks about himself."

Bruce stepped up just behind her. "I'll never say a word about myself ever again," he murmured.

She turned to look at him. Mischief sparkled in his coppery eyes. He was such a tease. It was one of the things she loved best about him.

She shied away. *No, no, no.* Not that word again. She shouldn't even think it. She would *not* love him. Not when she couldn't marry him. She refused to move away to Boston where there were too many people, a propensity for banning books, and dull, unimaginative football. This was her home and this was where she would make her career.

She had a meeting scheduled on Monday with Director Baird, to discuss athletic opportunities for female students. The university had a women's basketball team, and physical fitness classes were held at the women's gym, but Eden had plans to organize sports of all kinds, with the ultimate goal of seeing Michigan women competing with—and defeating—similar teams from other universities. She would start by arranging contests with local clubs and the Normal School in Ypsilanti. State Agricultural College in East Lansing and the Toledo Manual Training School were also in her list of potential nearby foes.

Eden doubted anyone would pay her for this sort of work, but she believed she could get permission to do it as a volunteer. The idea grew bigger and more important to her by the day. She wasn't going to let it go.

If she needed money, she could make a bit officiating for local schools in baseball and football. They were always in need of people. The testimony of the U of M athletes and demonstrations of her skills could get her over the hurdle caused by her gender. Someday, perhaps, she could officiate a college game. Not at Michigan, though. She would be too biased.

She could never thank Bruce enough for planting the seed of the idea in her brain. He'd turned a vague grumpiness over the lack of sports for women into a confidence *she* could do something about it—that she had the skills and knowledge to organize a game, officiate, or coach.

An unseen hand clenched around her heart. She owed everything to him, and when the football season ended in just over a week she was going to lose him forever.

"Eden? Are you okay?"

She tried to snap herself out of her dour thoughts. "Sorry. I was, er, thinking."

His eyebrows arched, but he didn't press her for further explanation. Another thing she loved about him: his patience and willingness to suppress his curiosity until she revealed things in her own time. She was in such terrible trouble.

She filled the luxene samples and saw her father out the door, but the distraction didn't last long enough. *That word* still floated around her head. In desperation, she looked around for something else to do. A radiator along the wall caught her eye.

"While no one else is here, I think I ought to test my fire ant. It's chilly enough today the radiators should be nice and warm." She ducked into the office to retrieve it before Bruce could question her.

She wound up the small mechanical insect and set it down on the floor. She had to admit it wasn't especially interesting. It would make a good toy for a child, if she knew any children to give it to.

She followed it around, observing. It walked right into a radiator, getting itself wedged underneath, its little tail shining. She pulled it out and repositioned it, trying to make it walk near enough to light up without touching the radiator.

It scuttled in an unexpected direction and under the copying machine.

"Oh, blast. One of the legs must have bent."

She crawled as far under the machine as she could manage, sliding her arm between gears and pistons toward the wiggling fire ant. It lay several inches beyond her reach. She squirmed and stretched. The tip of her finger brushed metal. She grunted and tried once more, but couldn't get a grip on the automaton.

"Bruce, could you help? My arms are too short." She scooted backward, twisting around to look at him. "I think there's enough room under here for..."

She froze.

"Eden?" Bruce called. "Are you okay down there?"

She couldn't speak. Her eyes were glued to the bottom of the machine, where a strange device ticked away, making notches in a coiled strip of paper with every spoken word.

32

Eden plunked another device on the table "That's four."

Bruce picked up the wrench and popped the cover off the eavesdropping machine the way Eden had instructed. He pulled out the fuel cell and set it beside the three identical tubes from the other machines.

"How many more do you think are in here?" she wondered.

He shrugged. "Who knows? These have been spread out, but it's hard to tell if they covered the entire lab."

"Pop that fuel tube back in. We'll test the range."

Her investigation was methodical. She mapped out an arc some ten feet from the machine, then paced the lab to see what area the four known devices could cover.

"There must be one in or around your father's office," Bruce opined.

"I agree. The layout is very logical and efficient."

"Tagget."

"His plan, I'd guess, yes. One last device should be off in that corner. There's nothing over there to put it under, so I bet it's on top of the cabinet. I can climb up there. You check the office."

The device in the office was easy to find. He simply pulled

the desk out from the wall and checked behind it. The small machine had been attached to the back of the largest drawer. He was about to pry it off with the wrench when a thought hit. He dashed out into the lab.

"Eden, leave that one where it is," he called.

"What? Why?"

She was atop the cabinet, her legs dangling over the edge, her skirts hiked up to mid-thigh. He was tempted to walk right over and ask her to drop down into his arms.

"I want to take photos. As proof. Wait right there."

He ducked back into the office and grabbed a camera dangling from a hook on the wall—the same one Eden had brought to Wisconsin. It was empty of film, but a quick search through the drawers found a roll. He popped it in and jogged back to Eden.

She couldn't hold on and take snapshots at the same time, so Bruce had the pleasure of steadying her by gripping her shapely calves. He had quite the eyeful of her nicely rounded posterior. A bit more work and they could head back to his hotel. Bedding his extraordinary girlfriend would be the perfect end to what had become a fine day. He supposed he oughtn't be pleased spy devices had been placed around the lab, but the evidence of Tagget's wrongdoing had him bursting with excitement. They might have to track down Heyward—who Bruce assumed had placed the devices—but he had a real story at last. He wasn't an attorney or a judge. He didn't need enough proof to put Tagget behind bars, only enough that the news was worth publishing. The police could take care of the rest.

Finished with her photographs, Eden unscrewed the device and slid to the floor. Bruce caught a flash of her lacy drawers. His trousers were uncomfortably tight. The brilliant smile she bestowed on him didn't help matters.

He tried to focus on work while they photographed the office device in situ. They removed it to the workbench, where Eden dismantled it entirely, taking several pictures during the process. Bruce wrote down every detail he could think of in his journal.

"Can your father get the information off these paper rolls?" he wondered. "I'm certain they are recording us, but I'd like to hear it for myself and learn how far back the recordings go."

"No more than a few days, I would guess. They aren't long enough for more. My guess is Marcus Heyward was sneaking in and swapping out the rolls. I'm sure he installed these devices. He was much too helpful when we cleaned the lab after the dragon rampage—which he must have set off in the first place. Oh, but to answer your question, my mother can come up with something. She excels at that sort of thing. We can take these things home. Do you want to come for dinner again?"

"I would enjoy that, thank you. Shall we adjourn to my hotel in the meantime?"

She twirled a screwdriver around her fingers. "I have a better idea." Her gaze dropped to his knee.

He took a step backwards. "Oh, no. No way. I told you I would need to be drunk for that."

"Nonsense. I'm handy with a screwdriver. You'll hardly feel a thing. Besides…" She arched her eyebrows. "You will have to remove your trousers."

If he had ever needed proof he was crazy, he now had it because he simply watched her gather old blankets from a cabinet and spread them on the floor of the back nook. He didn't protest when she brought out a set of a dozen different sized screwdrivers. He didn't even say anything when she took his hand and led him to her improvised bed/examination table.

She sat cross-legged, facing him, holding both his hands. "I'll show you mine if you show me yours."

"Huh?"

She reached up and unhooked something behind her left ear. She slipped the cuff and attached dangle from her ear and handed it to him for examination. He glanced at it, but he was more interested in the ear itself. Besides the hole in her lobe, she had two others higher up where the cuff attached. A bit of metal protruded from her ear canal. She turned toward the light to give him a better look.

"There's more inside the ear beyond what you can see. With my earpiece attached, it becomes a receptor for the signals Vox emits."

The dragon trotted over at the sound of her name and rubbed against Eden's leg.

"It's fascinating." He took a closer look at the earpiece. He could see how the copper filament jutting from the back of the central crystal would plug into her ear. He handed it back and watched her clip it into place, impressed at the speed with which she could don the apparatus.

"What did you say?" she asked. "I couldn't hear."

"Right. Sorry. I said it's fascinating. Your biomechanics, I mean."

"Thank you. Now may I see yours?"

He chewed his bottom lip, hesitating. "Okay," he said at last. "But I can't look." He removed his trousers and lay back on the blankets, pulling his hat down over his face.

Eden ran a hand across his bare leg. "I'll be gentle."

He hardly noticed what her screwdriver was doing, because her other hand moved in languid strokes up and down his naked thigh. He neither knew nor cared whether it was a deliberate distraction or simply a way to keep her hand occupied. He closed his eyes, reveling in each lazy movement of her delicate fingertips. Perhaps he wasn't so crazy as all that.

"Wow." Her hand paused in its stroking and he risked a glance.

It was the wrong decision. The false kneecap lay off to one side, leaving a gaping hole where a human knee ought to have been. He could see the strange metal workings inside and his leg tingled with an uncomfortable awareness of where they were spliced into his flesh. Delicate copper wires disappeared into his skin, merging with his natural nerves, and blood flowed through glass tubes between the upper and lower sections of his leg. He was a living machine. His skin crawled. The pleasurable feelings Eden had roused faded to a distant memory.

"This is incredible," she breathed. "You're so intricate."

She put a hand to either side of his knee and flexed it slowly, watching the mechanics at work. Her soft fingers glided over him, heedless of the transition from skin to metal. No one else had ever touched him this way. The biomechanists poked at the knee with their tools to make it function, but everyone else avoided it. He didn't even like to touch it himself. When he didn't see it and didn't feel it, he could forget he was broken.

Eden didn't treat him like he was broken. She touched his biomechanics as eagerly as she touched any other part of him. He remembered her words on the train. She thought him beautiful.

He sat up and reached for her, grazing her cheek on the way to her glittering left ear. His thumb caressed her—skin and gold and sparkling crystal nestled against her inner biomechanics.

"Just as you are," he breathed.

She dropped the screwdriver and lunged at him. He caught her in his arms and pulled her down on top of him. Lips smashed together. Limbs tangled. Hands tore at clothing.

They were even more frantic than on the train. Bruce vowed someday he would get her into a real bed and make a thorough exploration of all her luscious curves. Today, though, he wanted no more than to sate his ravenous hunger for her.

She straddled him, pressing her thighs against his hips, yanking her skirts up and out of the way. He delved for the opening in her drawers, while she clawed at his, freeing his cock and wrapping her fingers around it. Guiding him to where she wanted him.

Their union drew low moans from her throat. She was so eager, so full of energy. She packed more passion into her petite frame than he'd ever thought possible, and it drove him wild. She was tight, wet, unquenchable heat. Every thrust was torturous bliss.

She rocked down hard onto him, writhing in pleasure, jarring his tender ribs. The pain was no more than a distant curiosity.

"Bruce," she gasped.

"Eden."

She shuddered. He groaned. They clung to one another until the waves of ecstasy subsided, leaving them spent and breathless.

Bruce stared up at the wires criss-crossing the laboratory ceiling. A dull ache throbbed in his left side. The rest of him was in a state of drowsy relaxation.

Eden rolled off and curled up against him. A satisfied flush colored her skin, and her lips curved in a sleepy smile. He knew women who were more conventionally beautiful, but none had ever looked lovelier to him than she did at that moment. He pressed a kiss to her brow and wove his fingers through her golden hair.

"I love you," he sighed.

She flinched. It was a tiny little twitch, over in an instant, but that fraction of time was more than long enough to break his heart.

Eden eased herself into a seated position, twiddling her earring as if she hadn't heard him. "We can't sleep here. Let me fix your knee and then we can clean up."

He looked down at his exposed biomechanics. His usual revulsion was lost in the pain. She didn't think him broken. But it didn't matter. She didn't love him.

He stared dumbly into the distance while she worked. She used a tiny bellows to blow away any dust, then sprayed the workings with a protective oil. Her nimble fingers screwed the knee plate into place with no discomfort. He couldn't appreciate the care she took. A numbness had stolen over him.

He cleaned himself up, straightened his clothes, and helped Eden tidy the lab without speaking a single word.

Eden made no attempt at conversation. She avoided touching him. They hardly looked at one another until she gathered up the eavesdropping machines and reiterated her invitation to dinner.

He declined, claiming a headache, and hurried out of the lab. For the first time in weeks he wanted his job to be over. He wanted to be back in Boston, hundreds of miles from Eden. The end of football season couldn't come soon enough. If he never saw her again, maybe someday he could learn to forget her.

33

November 5

"WHERE'S HESTON?"

Eden jumped, nearly tripping over the mechanical wolverine as it stalked down the sideline. She turned around—the wrong direction, as usual—to locate Bruce. He'd spoken to her. Perhaps he wasn't avoiding her, after all.

One quick look at his face quashed any hopes of a reconciliation. He wasn't pleased to see her. His expression was neutral, almost bored, but there was pain behind his soft, dark eyes. He held his notebook open, pen poised. Business, nothing more.

"Heston?" she echoed.

"Yes. The captain of your football team? He isn't here and the game is about to start."

"He's in Chicago."

The bored look faded, replaced with something far more familiar: eager curiosity. "Chicago? Why?"

"He and Coach Yost have gone to scout the Maroons."

"You're kidding."

"I'm not. They're our biggest rival, and Coach wanted a look at Stagg's men in action."

"But to just skip today's game? That's insane."

Eden shrugged. "We can beat Drake without Heston. I'm not worried."

Bruce scribbled furiously. "This story will be a sensation. It'll leave everyone clamoring for next week's article. I have to get the word out before anyone hears about it from the Chicago folks. What more can you tell me?"

Eden gave him a rundown on the history of the rivalry, all she knew about the current Chicago men, and the talk of Stagg's manic desire to defeat Yost. Bruce copied down every word she said. He paid no attention to the game happening behind him. It would be no more than a side-note to his story.

Eden tried to pretend he was enthralled by her and not the story, but the lie couldn't sustain itself. He stood too far away, didn't smile, and rarely looked her in the eye.

Why did he have to love her? She'd suspected he might, but hearing him confess it had caused her to panic. Again. She'd fled from the conversation she'd known was coming and now they were both hurting. It was up to her to remedy the situation.

"Thank you, Miss Randall. I think I have all I need."

The formal address pained her. "Won't you call me Eden?"

"I don't think that's wise. Excuse me." He turned to leave. She couldn't let him walk away. She grabbed his arm.

"Bruce, wait. We need to talk."

He shrugged away from her grip. "We don't have anything to talk about."

"But…"

"You want to be friends. I don't. End of story."

"No. Please, let me explain."

The wolverine snarled at him. "Oh, shut up," he growled

at it. It sat back on its haunches and gave a little whimper, like a chastized dog. Eden didn't think it had ever obeyed anyone aside from herself or her parents before.

"There's a story I need to tell you," she said, reaching for him once again. "So you can understand."

Bruce stepped back out of arm's reach. "Eden, I'm working."

"Give me five minutes." She would have to talk fast.

He tucked his notebook into a pocket and crossed his arms. "Fine."

"When I was a child, I had a friend, a boy named Paul. Deaf, like I was. He lived in Ypsilanti, close enough that I could see him relatively often. His parents had a large house, and would host gatherings of deaf children from neighboring towns so we could learn and play and talk with others who would understand our signing. Paul was always very social and chatty, whether with deaf children or hearing children. He had three hearing brothers and was a fantastic lip reader. He got along well with everyone. I was the girl who sat in the corner with a book, or who played ball but didn't talk about anything but the game. You've met my parents. You know they're odd."

"They are kind and generous people."

"Yes. But they're bad at social things. I can tell, in the rare cases we go to parties, they don't know what to say. They can talk for hours about their inventions, but ordinary topics leave them tongue-tied. I'm the same. I'm sure you've seen it. I forget introductions. I babble crazily instead of chatting politely. Remember when we met? I was just rambling on about the Olympic Games. Spewing wild questions. Even all the books I've read don't help much. I love talking when I'm with my friends, but I hardly have any of those. Lilah. Joey. You."

He looked away. Eden rushed on, desperate to keep his attention.

"So, Paul was a friend—my best friend—but we were opposites, and he was three years older. He was always telling me how he thought I should do things. I don't think he noticed.

It was a thing boys did. Do. Tell girls they're wrong. I ignored all the advice I didn't like."

"You are a woman who knows her mind." His voice had the oddest tone, thick with emotion, but constrained, almost choked. He still didn't look her in the eye.

"I should've told him I didn't like the advice. He didn't know how I felt. I didn't know he didn't know.

"He went to study at Gallaudet, a college for the Deaf in Washington, D.C., at about the same time I got my hearing device. He loved it there. Went on and on about it in his letters. I was delighted when he returned to town after graduation, but he wasn't the same. Or maybe I wasn't. I don't know. By then I'd had Vox for years and I was in college.

"We didn't seem to have anything in common anymore, but he was still a friend, so I continued to spend time with him, letting him talk about what he liked because he'd listen if I talked about what I liked. One day, he kissed me. It wasn't at all like the way you kiss, with that impulsive, chaotic intensity. He was calm, deliberate, quiet, but I enjoyed it, and I didn't think anything of it when the kisses grew longer and more frequent.

"He received word from Gallaudet one day, saying they wanted him to return as a teacher. It was his dream job. I'd never seen him so excited. I congratulated him and told him I would miss him. It was true.

"The next day, my parents and I were invited to his family's house to celebrate. He handed me a letter in front of everyone— my parents, his parents, his brothers—and asked me to read it."

"A marriage proposal."

"Is it so obvious?" Eden sighed.

"Yes." Bruce spoke with conviction.

"Naturally, I was the only person who hadn't seen it coming. It was a long letter, full of the same excitement he'd shown about his new job. He told me how wonderful it would be. How much he loved Washington. He even told me I wouldn't need to bother with Vox and 'unnecessary biomechanics.' He would 'take care of me,' he said.

"I actually screamed, 'No!' He couldn't hear me, so he didn't know until he saw my face. I had to reject him in front of everyone, and I wasn't nice about it. I was so angry at how he thought he could decide my life for me, assuming I would be happy with it. I shouted that nothing in the world could ever compel me to move to Washington and I called him stupid for his comments about my biomechanics."

Eden blinked away a tear, wanting to hug herself. Or even better, have Bruce hug her. "It was awful. He was wrong, but I was, too. Neither of us had ever truly paid attention to what the other wanted. It took a long time for me to understand that. His choices were right for him, just like mine were right for me. I regret losing a friend, but I don't regret turning him down. Only the way I did it. I think he's happy in Washington without me. I never meant to break his heart. It still hurts sometimes to think I did."

Bruce's hand had clenched into fists. His shoulders rose and fell as he took a deep breath. "Eden, what's your point?" He looked her in the eye finally, his eyes dark and cold. "That you're going to do the same thing to me?" His bark of laughter was the most desolate sound she had ever heard. "Perhaps he and I can form a gentlemen's society—Eden Randall's Broken Hearts Club. I may even invite Evan Tagget."

She stepped toward him.

"No, you don't understand. I don't want the same thing to happen to you—to us. I want you to know about me and where I come from and what I want. I'm happy here. I've made a life for myself. I have a grand new idea for a career, thanks to you. That's why I panicked when you said maybe we should marry."

There had been no "maybe" about it.

"I can't go away to Boston any more than I could let Tagget take me away to New York or Paris, or wherever is fashionable. I *can't* be more than friends. But I don't want to lose you. I don't want this to end. I want to find some way around it. I like to travel. I can visit you in Boston, or meet you somewhere where you have an assignment. You can come visit me here."

Her voice sounded in her left ear, ringing false and unfamiliar. She couldn't even fool herself. She knew her suggestion for what it was. Cowardly.

Bruce shook his head. "I'm sorry, Eden. That's not what *I* want for *my* life."

"Please. There must be some way."

Their eyes met, hers wide and wet, his distant and brokenhearted. Somewhere behind her, men grappled for an inflated spheroid while a crowd of onlookers cheered them on, but in that long moment she could swear everything had gone still save for the terrible beating of her heart.

"Not any I can see. I'm sorry." He turned away. In desperation, she chased him.

"Can we talk about it tonight? At the saloon? You still owe me three hundred ninety-nine beers."

He pulled a wallet from his pocket and handed her two ten-dollar bills. "Keep the change." He walked away and didn't look back.

Eden stared after him, the money crumpled in her fist. A finger tapped her shoulder.

"Excuse me, miss, your wolverine is wandering away. People are afraid."

"What? Oh, I'm sorry." She jogged after the stupid machine and shut it off. There was no joy in her job today. No joy in her beloved sport. She plunked down on the ground beside the silent dragon and watched the remainder of the game through unquenchable tears.

34

November 9

WHAT A WEEK. Bruce stared down at the pair of letters that had awaited him this morning, curious what he'd find inside. Bad news, probably, if his recent luck was any indication. All week he'd stomped angrily around town—which, to be honest, didn't suit him at all—visiting Eden's saloon every night, drinking for two. Wondering if she would drop in. Hating that he wanted her to. Haunted dreams of her had plagued his nights. He'd slept better last night, but he didn't know if that was because he was recovering or because he'd merely exhausted himself.

He settled into a chair in the lounge and opened the first letter. He rocked back in surprise. Good news. He'd tracked down Marcus Heyward at last. The brief note gave an address in Ypsilanti. It would take only a quick interurban train ride to interrogate him.

Folding and pocketing the paper, Bruce turned his attention to the second, much longer letter. He opened it and froze. Impossible. This had to be a dream.

He read the lines again and a zing of elation shot through him, a brief burst of happiness cutting through the pain of his broken heart.

He'd gotten his promotion. Fulton's signature was there at the bottom of the page, clear as day. Persistence, it seemed, paid off.

The editors expressed delight with his recent work. He would have a say now in what assignments to take on, and his salary was going up. Significantly up. He was to go into the office promptly upon his return next week to finalize the details, sign the new contract, et cetera.

He wiped his sweaty palms on his trousers. This was true. It was real. The beginning of a new and better life. Far from this place and its bittersweet memories. He deserved it. He'd worked hard for it.

Honestly, though, this assignment had never felt hard. It had been fun and rewarding.

Thanks to Eden.

Bruce folded his letter, turning it over in his hands as he watched the flames dance in the nearby hearth. He would pitch the offer straight into the fire for her. He would throw his whole life away and take a job sweeping floors or mucking stables just to hear her say she loved him. He would do anything.

The one thing he couldn't do was give her what she wanted. His feelings had moved too far beyond friendship and he'd never be able to undo that. Spending time with her, knowing she'd never feel the same, would tear him apart. Better to end it all. Let her have the life she desired and deserved. He'd focus on the promotion. Try to move on.

He'd seen her a few times this week, always keeping his distance. He'd nearly lost his resolve yesterday, when he'd spied her talking to Tagget outside the laboratory building. It was only too easy to imagine him showering her with jewels, private concerts, and rides in his damned Mercedes on his way to making love to her in a swanky hotel room.

Bruce didn't expect she would welcome Tagget's advances after all the proof of his wrongdoing, but neither could he rule out the possibility. She was looking for fun, not for romance.

He shoved his job offer into his pocket. He needed to stop brooding over her, dammit. A few more days. A few more days and he'd be on the way back to Boston, never to return. Maybe with enough miles between them he could learn how to stop wanting her.

In the meantime, there was work to be done. He would see this investigation through to the end. He would protect her from Tagget's meddling, even if he had no right to do so. It was time for a trip to Ypsilanti.

It took him some time to locate the boarding house, tucked away on a little street outside of town, near neither downtown nor the Normal School. Heyward had somehow found himself a nice place to hide where no one would bother him.

The door opened to reveal a woman of indeterminate age, with kohl-darkened eyes and bright red lips. A tight, low-necked dress flaunted her fine figure. Her eyes raked him from head to toe, nodding in approval. He didn't think she was a prostitute, but he wouldn't have been surprised to find she availed herself of the charms of the young men who roomed there.

"Are you Mrs. Langford?" he inquired.

"I am. Are you looking for a room, dearie? I'm full up just now, but I should have an opening in a few days, if you can wait." Her mouth curved in a sensuous smile. "We'd love to have a tall, strong thing like you about."

"Er, thank you, but I'm not looking for a room." He willed himself not to look down at her prominent breasts. Her well-displayed assets conjured up a multitude of impure thoughts, all of which led to memories of Eden. "I'm looking for one of your boarders, a Mr. Heyward. Is he in residence today?"

"He is, dearie, he is. Think that boy would sleep 'til noon

every day if he could." A frown pinched her painted lips. "I'll fetch him for you. You make yourself comfortable."

She waved him inside and pointed at a worn sofa. Bruce sat and fidgeted, thinking through what he would say to Heyward. He ought to have swallowed his pride and brought Eden. Heyward was terrified of her.

Mrs. Langford returned within a few minutes, a rumpled, surly Marcus Heyward in tow. The young man had dark circles under his eyes and a sallow complexion. Carousing? Or guilty, sleepless nights? The moment Heyward saw Bruce, he flinched and his eyes went wide with horror. Eden's presence, it seemed, wouldn't be necessary.

Bruce stood, offering his hand in a cordial gesture. "Heyward. How good to see you. We've missed you in Ann Arbor these past weeks."

Heyward shied away. "What do you want?"

Bruce gave him an honest answer. "Ultimately, a confession. You've gotten yourself into quite a bit of trouble of late. I'm willing to make a deal. You tell me everything you know about Tagget, and I'll cite you as an anonymous source. Otherwise, we may have to get the police involved."

"You don't know anything," Heyward grumbled with a complete lack of conviction.

The landlady followed the conversation with undisguised enthusiasm. News of a possible scandal involving a tenant she didn't care for must have been a rare sort of excitement.

"I know far more than you might expect, Mr. Heyward," Bruce continued, keeping his tone formal and even. "It seems you have fallen behind in your work for Mr. Tagget. Not only have you failed to provide him with any additional innovations, but you haven't changed out the tapes in the eavesdropping devices. The machine near where Professor Randall gives his lectures had run out of paper entirely."

"I don't know what you're talking about," Heyward squeaked.

"There's no point in denying it." Bruce ticked off Heyward's sins on his fingers. "You set the dragons loose in the lab. Did you steal a key yourself or did you need Tagget to do that for you, too?"

Heyward fidgeted, but said nothing.

"You installed spy devices while you pretended to clean up the damage," Bruce continued. "You stole a schematic from an advanced student. All to get Tagget to create a simple design for you so you wouldn't fail a class. I expect it took him all of five minutes. Tagget has been playing this game for years. I'm not sure what made you think you could get the best of him."

Bruce felt a sudden queasiness in his stomach. *What makes me think I can get the best of him?*

"You don't know anything," Heyward insisted, his voice rising in panic. "You have no proof. You... you..." His eyes darted to and fro, but he would find nothing and no one to help him. "That girlfriend of yours, her dragon uses wireless teletics," he blurted in desperation. "And I'm going to sell it to the highest bidder."

He shoved Bruce with both hands and ran for the door. Unprepared for a physical attack, Bruce toppled onto the sofa. By the time he regained his feet, the front door had banged closed. He tore off after Heyward, with a hasty, "Excuse me," to Mrs. Langford.

"Come back any time, dearie!" she called. "That was the most excitement we've had here in years."

Heyward raced toward town, quickly losing ground to Bruce's longer stride. The moment they reached a more populated area, however, Bruce lost his advantage. He didn't know the city. Heyward did. He darted around corners and ducked into alleys, zig-zagging through the streets until he was out of sight. Bruce took a gamble and headed for the interurban station. He reached it just in time to see the train pulling away.

"Damn."

35

"*O*H, BLAST. *One of the legs must have bent.*"

Her voice sounded tinny coming from the machine. Eden kept cranking, listening to her own words played back at her.

"*Eden? Are you okay down there?*"

Her hand froze. Hearing his voice, so full of concern, sent a jolt of pain through her. She pulled the tape from the machine.

"It works well, then?"

Eden turned to her mother. "It does, thank you."

"Was that your friend Mr. Caldwell's voice? When are you going to bring him to dinner again?"

Eden shrugged, not trusting her voice.

"You should extend an invitation. He's a sweet boy, and I can tell you are taken with him."

"We're just friends." She couldn't keep the hitch from her voice. She didn't think they were even that anymore.

Her mother gave her a skeptical look. "Uh-huh."

Eden turned back to the machine, threading the roll of paper much further in, far past any words she and Bruce might have spoken.

For several minutes she cranked and listened, hearing scattered bits of conversation from students as they had walked through the lab or used the copying machine. It was frightfully dull. Tagget would have to employ people to sit and listen to hours of boring recordings in the hopes of picking up something useful. She tried to think if she had said anything significant about Vox in the days since this had begun. Probably. She talked to her father in his office often, and Heyward had caught her using the telephone that one day.

She noted with some satisfaction Heyward hadn't yet come to her claiming to have found buyers for Vox's technology. She honestly doubted anyone would take him at his word if he went about claiming to know of breakthroughs in wireless teletics. He had no prototype and he couldn't even draw a proper schematic.

A few more minutes and she gave up on listening. It didn't make much difference if she knew what was on the tapes. It only mattered that the devices were proven to be unauthorized recording machines. She packed up the tapes and the playback machine. She would have to share them with Bruce. Whether he wanted to see her or not, they were inextricably entwined in this business with Tagget and his industrial espionage.

The sound of the front door marked her father's arrival. He swept into the room, green-tinted glasses glinting under the electric lights.

"Ah, Eden, my girl, I have your results." He waved a paper at her. His other hand held the luxene samples she had sent to the chemistry department. "Plain luxene is just that—plain. Dynalux sample contains a whole host of other ingredients. Most look to be entirely useless. Here, see for yourself."

He passed her the samples and the paper for perusal. The additives to the Dynalux fuel were more numerous than she expected. She didn't recognize the names of many of the chemicals off-hand, but she could look them up at the library.

Many of them were already marked with words such as "inert" and "inactive."

"Looks to me all their work to make the luxene more efficient is bound to result in the opposite," her father continued. "The more nonsense they put in, the less fuel you get in every spoonful."

The phone rang, and he excused himself to answer it. Eden continued her scan of the list, hoping something suspicious would jump out at her.

A moment later her father reappeared in the doorway. "Eden, dear, a phone call for you."

"Me?" she squeaked. She didn't get unsolicited phone calls. "Oh, dear."

Please do not be Evan Tagget.

The man had been a terrible pest these last few days. He seemed to think she ought to be flinging herself at him merely because he'd done right by Lilah and her invention. He'd sought out Eden every night this week. He'd given her flowers (dead, because she'd forgotten to put them in water), chocolates (stashed away in her room for secret nibbling), and a necklace to match her ear jewels (promptly returned for being too personal, then delivered to her front porch the next day). He was nothing if not persistent.

Eden was sick of his gifts, his poetic flatteries involving gardens and paradises, and his inability to comprehend her lack of interest. She had, however, begun to feel a certain pity for him. He acted more desperate by the day. She thought perhaps he'd realized he might not be able to get what he wanted, and didn't know how to handle it.

The telephone sat in a special niche in the dining room wall, and Eden had to stretch the wire all the way to the table to use it. She set Vox on the tabletop and snugged the receiver up to her belly.

"Hello?" she said into the mouthpiece, her voice heavy with suspicion.

"Eden, it's Bruce."

She started, shocked he had phoned her. Whatever the reason, he sounded anxious.

"Bruce? What's wrong?"

"I need you to come down to the lab, and I need you to bring a key. Marcus Heyward has gone inside, and I'm afraid he may be wreaking havoc."

"I'll be there in ten minutes."

She hung up the phone and raced back into the living room. She stuffed the luxene analysis into the bag that held all the eavesdropping tapes. She could deliver it all to Bruce tonight. She would have to go by bicycle to be there when she'd promised, but the short skirt she wore today wouldn't be a hindrance.

"I'm going out," she informed her parents on her way to the front hall.

"Now?" her mother asked. "But dinner is in the oven and it's already dark. This is hardly the time to be rushing off alone to meet a gentleman."

"I'm sorry, it can't be helped. Excuse me."

She snatched her coat and ran outside, stuffing her arms into the sleeves as she went. She grabbed her favorite bicycle from the half-dozen in the shed, plopped Vox and her bag of evidence into the basket and pedaled downhill toward town at breakneck speed.

She fretted the entire ride. They would handle Heyward together. Afterward, she would present Bruce with the playback machine and the luxene analysis. Perhaps it could lead to some amount of reconciliation. She hated to think of him angry with her, deserved though it might be. She'd known what was coming and had put off discussing it, as if pretending it didn't exist would make it go away. Childish. Stupid. She yearned to make amends.

And if she did? Then what? She would still lose him in under a week. The reality of the situation stabbed at her gut.

The idea of never seeing him again devastated her. How could she bear never to laugh together over pints at the saloon or run crazily about on the gridiron? How could she stand never to feel his strong arms around her, to taste his wild, sweet kisses? His casual, good-natured charm put her at ease. His chaotic intensity, as she had termed it, made her ache with desire. He was tenderness and passion mashed up into one tall, pretty-eyed package. He was everything she wanted in a friend and a lover. He loved *her*, not some idealized facsimile of herself. And she loved him too, dammit, much as she had pretended she never would.

How could they be so perfect and yet so incompatible? She could see no way forward. She couldn't marry him. Even if she gave up everything and moved to Boston, it would be a disaster. She wasn't a suitable Boston wife. She would be "the weird girl" wherever she went. Which was fine with her, and fine with him, but not okay to others. It made no sense to sacrifice her own career only to jeopardize his.

She had to let him go. All she could do was attempt to make it as easy as possible for him. It would hurt. And she would miss him. Lord, she would miss him more than she had ever missed anything in her life.

She wheeled onto campus, willing herself not to sniffle, forcing herself to focus on meddlesome Marcus Heyward and the business at hand. Her muddled-up romantic life would have to wait.

When she reached the laboratory building, she found Bruce with his face pressed up against the window, squinting in an attempt to see into her father's room.

"What's going on?"

She startled him. He jumped and spun to face her. "That was fast." He shook his head. "I haven't been able to see much. A flicker of light now and again. He must have a lantern, but he's keeping mostly out of sight."

Eden propped her bicycle against the wall of the building

and brandished her key. "Let's go see what he's up to, shall we? Vox, come."

She hurried to the front door, Bruce and the dragon close on her heels. She had no sooner closed the door behind herself than Marcus Heyward came trotting down the hall, a smug smile plastered across his features. He flinched when he saw them, but recovered quickly.

"Ha! You're too late. The apparatus has been deployed. No one will be able to prove anything." He grinned. "He'll probably reward me for this."

Eden wanted to grab the brat by his lapels, fling him up against the wall and demand to know exactly what he had done. Bruce was several steps ahead of her due to his long legs, however, and he took a different approach. He walked calmly toward Heyward and asked, in a scolding tone, "Were you authorized to deploy this apparatus?"

Heyward took two stumbling steps backward. "N-no, but... It was in Hart's office, just waiting... It will be a successful demonstration. He will be pleased."

He was convincing no one, not even himself.

"Confess, Heyward. Tell me everything you know and I'll never breathe your name to anyone. Otherwise, you'll face not only Tagget's wrath, but mine, Miss Randall's, and ultimately, that of the United States legal system."

Heyward fled. There was no point in following him. Getting to the lab and stopping whatever he had done was first priority.

Eden unlocked the door and fumbled for the lightswitch. The clanging and banging told her the dragons had been loosed once again. This time, she hoped, they hadn't had sufficient time to do great damage. She vowed when she finished here she would take that stupid turtle dragon and pummel it with her baseball bat.

She'd walked no more than five feet into the room when a strange new noise gave her pause.

"What is that?"

"What is what?" Bruce already had two rogue dragons in his hands, and he swatted at another buzzing about his head.

"That noise. Low. Rumbly." She tugged at her right earlobe. This was the only type of sound she could hear on that side— the only sort of sound she had ever heard for so many years. The rare experience still affected her, even now.

Bruce dumped the two now-disabled dragons on the floor and snagged another one. "I don't hear anything like that."

Eden strained to make out the odd noise through the turmoil of scuttling automata. She blocked the path of a rat-like creature, catching it by its twisted wire tail. Could the noise be the apparatus Heyward had spoken of? Where was it coming from?

A loud pop made her jump. Alarmed by the new sound, she spun toward Bruce. He would know better than she where it had come from. A second pop followed, and he yelped and flung the dragon he was holding to the floor. Blood, red and bright, welled from a long gash on his cheek.

Eden gasped, her eyes darting from his injury to the dragon on the floor. One end of it was charred and broken, a wisp of smoke curling up from inside.

A bigger explosion shook the room. The squid dragon had detonated, spraying broken tentacles across the lab. Eden reeled at the realization of what was happening. She cried out and threw the rat-dragon across the room before it could explode in her hands. A tool chest blew open, tossing screwdrivers and wrenches in the air. Her father's whatchamajigger smoldered in the bottom of the mangled box.

The apparatus. There would be no proof, because there would be nothing left. She clamped her hands over both her ears. The strange noise had become a terror.

Bruce grabbed her and propelled her toward the door. "The luxene! I told you it was tainted!"

Luxene. Oh, Lord, the safe. She squirmed from his arms and ran for the locked cabinet, jerking the switch.

"Open!" she cried above the din.

Powerful fingers clamped on her shoulders. "Eden, what are you doing? We have to get out!"

Something exploded overhead. Shards of metal rained down on her, and she couldn't contain a little half-scream. She grabbed for the jug of luxene. If it blew, it would destroy all the most valuable work and half the lab.

The glass jug was hot to the touch. She gasped and jerked back involuntarily. Bruce shoved her toward the door.

"Get out, Eden! Get out *now*!"

"But the safe!"

He pushed her again. "Go!"

She stumbled, arms flailing as she fought to keep her balance. Her foot caught on Vox, and she fell. Vox scrambled out of the way, coming to a stop beside a large student dragon. A dragon that had begun to smoke.

"Vox, no! Bruce, grab her!"

Eden looked to him in desperation as she scrambled across the floor, terrified she wouldn't reach Vox in time. Bruce had his hands full, dragging the heavy luxene jug from the safe. The green liquid boiled inside. He winced in pain as he hefted it. Eden's chest constricted in fear.

"Bruce!" she gasped. "Get rid of it!"

With a grunt he heaved the bottle at the window. It smashed through a windowpane, sending shards of glass flying, before shattering on the ground below. Green liquid splashed across the window, some of the droplets smoking, others bursting into flame.

Eden reached Vox at the same time Bruce reached her. He hauled her to her feet, and this time she didn't protest when he pulled her toward the door. They dove into the hall, slamming the heavy door behind them. Muffled explosions continued unabated. Eden could still hear the strange, low thrumming in her right ear.

"Outside," Bruce urged.

She nodded, and they hurried from the building. Eden circled around to the laboratory window. Burning Dynalux ran across the walkway where the jug had burst. She retrieved her bicycle and wheeled it out of harm's way. Plunging her hand into the bag she had brought, she rummaged around for the luxene samples. The Dynalux tube was warm, but not hot. This "apparatus," or whatever caused the explosions, had a limited range. She moved well beyond what she guessed to be a safe distance, then sank to the ground, her legs shaky, her breathing only beginning to slow. Bruce sat beside her.

"Are you okay?" he asked.

She nodded. "What about you?"

"Fine."

She took hold of his hand, turning it over to examine his reddened palm. It looked sore, but not too badly burned. He pulled it from her grasp. She looked up into his face. Blood still dribbled from the wound on his cheek. She plucked the handkerchief from his vest pocket and dabbed at the injury. His hand clamped over her wrist, halting her ministrations.

"Stop."

"You're hurt."

He pulled the cloth from her fingers and backed out of her reach. "I can't do this."

"Bruce, please."

"I'm not going to torture myself." He lurched to his feet. "I'll fetch the fire department. If you think you're in any danger, get on that bike and get the hell away from here."

She watched him run off, once again feeling the sting of losing him.

· · · 🐷 · · ·

An hour later, the lab was declared safe and she was admitted back in. The damage was extensive. Tables and benches had collapsed. Shelves had toppled and cabinets had blown open, their contents strewn and ruined. Twisted and charred bits of metal littered the floor. In the flickering light of the few remaining bulbs, Eden could see a single survivor: Lilah's bat, hanging from a wire on the high ceiling, out of harm's way.

The door to the safe was dented, but it still responded to her command. The contents looked unharmed, from what she could tell. Her father could do a full assessment. She would thank Bruce for disposing of the contaminated jug.

The low rumbling hadn't stopped. She turned down her volume, listening with both ears. She turned in a slow circle, trying to discern where the noise was loudest. After several minutes she located a small device in the center of the room, beneath the copying machine. It wasn't fancy. A small, cubic box, vibrating as it projected the low sound in all directions. One flip of a switch and the noise ceased. There was no more to be done here.

Outside, Bruce was giving a statement to the police. Her father, looking heartsick, was in conversation with a pair of firefighters. Eden stood by her bicycle and waited.

Her father finished first. She told him about the safe and Lilah's bat. The news heartened him somewhat, and he headed inside to salvage all he could.

Bruce remained busy. It seemed the police wanted a full physical description of Marcus Heyward, along with a thorough explanation of why he ought to be presumed the culprit. By the time he was finished, Bruce looked exhausted.

Eden handed him the bag with the tapes, the playback machine, and the luxene analysis. "Here's all your proof. You should have plenty to write about." She held out the device that had made the strange noise. "I think this is what caused all the luxene to explode. You can test it on our sample, if you need to."

He nodded. "Thank you. I may even photograph my tests."

"Let me know if you need anything else."

"I will."

They stood for a long moment, staring at one another. Eden fought the urge to throw her arms around his neck and kiss him. She had to respect the distance. She had to let him go. If she had to take on more pain to lessen his, so be it.

"Good night, Miss Randall," he said at last. He gave her a little bow and turned away.

"Bruce!" She raced after him, stopping just shy of touching his arm.

"Yes?"

"Please be careful," she whispered. "If Tagget should realize how much you know..." *If anything should happen to you...*

"I promise." He stared into her eyes, and for a moment she thought he might be the one to initiate a kiss. He spun and hurried off. She sighed and watched his retreating back once again.

Her father emerged from the building a short time later. "The most valuable of the research has survived, fortunately," he told her, "but the rest..." He shook his head. "My poor students. They've lost all their hard work. This will cost the University time and money. It's a terrible blow to the department."

"Sue Evan Tagget," she suggested.

"What?"

"The fuel he donated was unstable. This is his fault. Make him pay for it."

"Our legal team will look into that, I'm certain."

The legal team would spend years tussling with Tagget's own attorneys. It might be more effective if she simply walked up to him and demanded he fix everything—for her sake. Would he pay up, she wondered, or would he disavow all knowledge and let Heyward take the fall? Both. He would graciously pay damages while lamenting how a misguided student had tampered with his merchandise and used it for evil. He would look generous and repentant. The scoundrel.

Her father held out a cap to her. "I believe your friend dropped this in the laboratory. It's a little dirty, but I think it can be salvaged."

Eden brought the hat to her chest, rubbing the wool between her fingers. "I'll return it to him."

Or maybe she'd take it into her bed and clutch it while she cried over him. It was hard to be certain. Her novels weren't wrong. Love made people do stupid things.

36

November 11

BRUCE RAPPED ON THE DOOR to the Randall family home, then took a step back, steeling himself for another painful meeting. He didn't want to be here. He didn't want to see her. Each time he did, his resolve weakened. He couldn't convince himself she didn't care when her worried blue eyes bored into his own. The other night, when she'd tried to tend to his injuries, he'd nearly sunk back into his old delusions.

It had been no more than a reaction to a scare, he told himself. Eden was a devoted friend. It was natural for her to be concerned for him. It didn't mean anything beyond that. His courtship had been doomed from the start. He needed to accept it and move on.

Mrs. Randall answered the door. She greeted him with a broad smile. There was a strong resemblance between mother and daughter. That smile was so familiar Bruce almost had to look away.

"Mr. Caldwell, so good to see you. Please, come in."

He stepped into the hall and removed his cap, but didn't continue further into the house. He meant this to be a brief visit.

"Eden is upstairs in the library. Can I interest you in staying for dinner?"

"Thank you, but no. I'm afraid I have a great deal of work to do. Is Miss Randall available for a time this afternoon? I promise to do my best not to keep her overlong."

"I don't think she is busy with anything today but her reading. I'll let her know you are here."

"Thank you."

Mrs. Randall disappeared into the house, and not a minute later Eden bounded into the hall, an eager expression on her face.

"Is your article finished? May I read it?"

God, that enthusiasm. It would be the death of him. This was precisely why he didn't want to be here.

"It is, and you may," he replied, forcing his voice into a semblance of neutrality.

It was difficult not to get excited, himself. He had worked non-stop for the past day and a half, writing, developing photos, and playing with the machines Eden had left him. He'd spent an all-important hour at the telephone and telegraph office. The article was going out today. He lacked only one thing. He hated to ask for it, but this was bigger than his pride.

"I'm headed to the telegraph office now. I have a copy written out in full, including photographs, that I have already sent by express to my paper in Boston. I'll do the rest by telegraph. I want this news to reach as many papers in as many cities as possible. Do you have any money?"

Being Eden, she wasn't at all perturbed by his question. "I have almost two hundred dollars."

He gaped.

"How much do you have?" she asked.

"I, uh…" He swallowed his embarrassment. "About ten dollars."

She fished something from her corset and pressed it into his hand. "No, you have thirty. I'll run upstairs and grab mine, and then we can leave."

"Grab a toolkit, also."

"Of course."

"Thank you. I couldn't have done this without you."

She gave him a smile much like the one her mother had given him earlier and scampered off.

He looked down at the bills in his hand. The same twenty dollars he had given her the other day. Had she been carrying it around, tucked into her clothing, all this time? He didn't want to spend too much time contemplating her reasons for that.

She read the article while they walked into town. She had that avid-reader talent of walking at full speed with her nose in a text. He fended off her questions until they reached their destination. She would see soon enough.

Mr. Hughes gave them a cheerful greeting when they walked through the door. He had been a great help to Bruce throughout his time here in town, and particularly during his visit yesterday. Bruce shook his hand.

"Do you think you could show Miss Randall what you showed me yesterday?"

"Of course, of course. This way." He waved them through the office. "We had our lines inspected and upgraded in early October, when the Tagget Industries men were in town. They did good work. Service has been excellent since. One of the things they did—what Mr. Caldwell wishes me to show you—was to install quality monitoring devices. We change the papers daily and send them in for evaluation at the end of every week. I understand if they ever find something amiss they will return and fix the problem at no cost to us."

Eden crouched to examine the devices, one each spliced

into the main telegraph and main telephone lines. Having already read his article, she didn't react in surprise.

"Recognize those?" Bruce asked.

"Indeed. They aren't identical to the machines from the lab, but they are very similar. I think I can remove them."

"Remove them?" Mr. Hughes echoed.

Eden stood up. "I'm afraid these are spy machines attached to the lines. Tagget is recording everything." She turned to Bruce. "I can disable these, so he can't record what we send out here, but we can't do anything about the receiving and retransmitting offices. They might have similar problems."

"Problems they will all be looking for once this news goes out. By the time he hears anything, it will be too late."

Eden nodded. "Okay. Let's do this. I'm curious how many different newspapers we can contact for two hundred thirty dollars." She paused and frowned at him. "In return for my help, I would like you to come to dinner and stay the night with my family."

Bruce understood. She was afraid for him. As much as he hated the thought of spending the entire night under the same roof, he couldn't argue. They were safer together. It was one night. Tomorrow was the last football game. He could get through this.

37

November 12

ⒷRUCE WOKE TO THE MOUTH-WATERING SMELL of frying bacon and promptly decided it was worth a night spent on the sofa. He stretched out his stiff back, smoothed the wrinkles from his clothes as best he could, and wandered into the kitchen to see if he could offer any help.

Eden had full command of the situation. She bustled about cracking eggs, frying heaps of bacon, and making toast, gliding from one task to another without pause or misstep. He watched in silence, afraid to speak, lest he disturb her concentration.

A hand settled on his shoulder. "Best stay out of her way," Professor Randall suggested. He steered Bruce toward the dining room. "The queen of the kitchen tends well to the health and happiness of her subjects, but her wrath is great and her justice swift when her territory is invaded. Sit down with me and have some coffee." He lowered his voice to a whisper. "She didn't make the coffee. Fantastic cook, but she brews terrible coffee. You might want to keep that in mind for the future."

"Um…"

Eden's father pressed a cup of coffee into his hands. "Here, sit down, my boy. Would you like a newspaper? We have several."

Bruce sat, flustered. He took a newspaper, but didn't read it, which was fortuitous, because Eden's father didn't stop talking.

"So, young man, tell me about your plans for the future."

"Er…" Bruce blinked dumbly, feeling not quite awake.

"Career hopes? Where you intend to settle?" Randall prompted.

Lord, he was being interrogated as a suitable husband for Eden. Of all the horrible, painful, embarrassing topics…

"You must have some thoughts. You seem an intelligent lad."

"I haven't contemplated anything beyond Monday morning, when my train leaves," Bruce blurted. He sounded petulant, even to his own ears. Goddammit. "But I, uh, was just offered a promotion," he added. Pointless though it might have been, he wanted Eden's parents to approve of him.

"Ah." Professor Randall picked up his newspaper and pretended to read. Bruce stared into his coffee.

Eden saved him from further embarrassment by appearing with toast and jam. As he slathered the sweet spread across a crispy piece, he came to a decision. He was going to have fun today. He was going to squeeze every last drop of enjoyment out of his time here, and sate himself on pleasant memories. His heart would be broken regardless of what happened. He may as well finish his time here in a positive manner.

He returned to his hotel after breakfast to change and prepare for the football game. The showdown for the Western Conference championship would be the culmination of all his articles. Everyone was waiting for it. He hoped the game didn't disappoint. He hoped, too, that he could do it justice.

Eden insisted on accompanying him to the hotel, but

didn't try to follow him to his room. She took a seat in the lobby and informed him she would wait. He told himself that was exactly how he wanted it.

Alone in his room, he realized how mistaken he was. He missed her flirtations. He craved that spark between them that had driven them past friendship and had at one time provided him with such great hope. A tiny ember of that hope still smoldered deep within him. He fanned it each time he saw her, and he was going to suffer its burns until he left her behind.

Today it burned altogether too brightly.

Bruce dressed slowly, anticipating a brazen knock at his door. None came, and when he returned to the lobby, he found her reading, apparently unmoved. The disappointment was keen. She was done with him. Enjoying the day might be harder than he had thought. He forced his mind back to football.

"The weather is gorgeous today," he said. "What would you say to walking to the field now and watching the crowd roll in?"

A slight smile touched her lips and his heart skipped a beat. "I would like that."

And roll in the crowd did. People poured into town, swarming campus and filling every inch of the temporary bleachers that had been erected around the field. Thirteen and a half thousand people, the university rep told him. His own estimations gave him a similar number.

Photographers took up stations all around the field. A crew with a motion picture camera arrived to record football in action. Overhead, a small dirigible contained more photographic equipment. This would be the most thoroughly documented game in history. Bruce scrawled note after note and worried he might run out of room in his journal.

Eden hummed with nervous excitement. She set her wolverine moving faster today, running behind it up and down the sidelines. Only when Michigan scored on two back-to-back drives to go up ten-to-nothing did she relax somewhat and slow to a walk.

Chicago, though, was no pushover. They soon cut the lead to four, and Eden began to jog again.

Bruce had fallen back into his old habit of watching her. He would forever remember her like this, her eyes riveted on the field, shouting encouragement to the team. No wonder things had gone awry. He'd fallen in love with her while she clapped and cheered for other men. Had she ever shown so much passion for him? When they'd played football together, he'd thought so. It seemed he had misconstrued her love of sport and in doing so had sealed his own fate.

"Touchdown!"

She did a happy dance, seizing his arm and whirling him around. It startled him enough that he stumbled. She jumped back, her cheeks flushing.

"Oh, sorry. I got a bit excited." Her smile was bashful, and it remained transfixed on him for longer than was appropriate. That spark refused to die.

Would that you may someday be as great a fan of myself…

"Need any commentary?" she asked, recovering herself. "For your article?"

"Always."

He took down her analysis because he liked listening to her talk. The sixteen to six lead had her in good spirits, and she gave him plenty to write about. Though he spent half-time interviewing other fans, his eyes never left Eden for long.

People were eager to talk today, and the article was coming together well in his head. He walked back toward Eden with a smile on his face. Somehow, he had achieved his goal. He'd wrung some enjoyment out of their last time together.

This was a better way to end things than angry and hurt. He didn't want to leave her worrying about him. Let her think he was recovering, that maybe he didn't love her and the words had been only an aftereffect of passion.

She let out a cry of alarm before he reached her side. The opponent's sideline erupted in cheers. Chicago's Eckersall had scooped up the fumbled ball. He flew down the field for a touchdown, past thousands of groaning Michigan supporters. The score was within four points once again, and the Maroons had new momentum.

The game ground on. Penalties and additional fumbles hampered the Wolverines' offense. Each time Chicago possessed the ball Eden's shoulders tensed up. Bruce had never seen her this anxious at a game, even the contest at Wisconsin. He almost whispered to her, "Sweetheart, it's only a game," before thinking better of it. Words like that might earn him a slap in the face. Instead, he scribbled a line about the unusual atmosphere of tension that permeated the enraptured crowd.

Chicago's punting had been excellent all game, and midway through the half, Michigan found itself on its own twenty, another dauntingly long field ahead of them. They hadn't subbed out any players, though Chicago had replaced several. Bruce found himself leaning in to watch and calling out encouragement.

"Come on, boys! This is where we show them how real men play ball," he shouted.

Eden rounded on him. "You *are* a real fan!" She took hold of his arm, clasping both her hands around his biceps. "Will you comfort me if we lose?"

"Yes." He tried to envision what that might entail. Food. Beer. Cuddles in front of the fireplace. All the same things she liked when the team won, but subdued. "But we won't lose." He hoped not. He wasn't certain he could make good on his promise.

The team had his back. Bit-by-bit they marched down the field, carrying the ball over the goal line for a two-score lead. For the remainder of the game, Bruce and Eden cheered together, followed the growling wolverine together, and for that short time were again a couple enjoying an outing as one.

Bruce toyed with the idea of asking her to marry him. He wasn't that Paul fellow. He wasn't going to force her to move to D.C., or even Boston. He wouldn't be the Crusher of Dreams. They could work together to make her happy.

More likely, he would just get the sort of sound rejection he apparently needed to stop fantasizing.

As the jubilant crowd trickled from the stadium following the twenty-two to twelve victory, Bruce and Eden separated, Eden taking her dragon away to be stored until next fall, and Bruce doing post-game interviews with several of the players. It was a strange feeling, to realize his work here was so close to done. The months had flown by, and yet Boston seemed a lifetime away. He felt a sense of belonging here he didn't think entirely due to Eden. He would miss it.

He would not, however, miss his hotel room.

Eden finished before he did, and hung nearby, waiting. The victory had left her bouncy and smiley, her cheeks rosy and her eyes shining. He was going to wipe the smile off her face. He would try to make it as quick as possible, for both their sakes.

"That was a good way to end the season, wasn't it?"

She grinned and nodded. "I'm going to celebrate with a beer. Are you going to the saloon after you submit your article?"

"No. I think I'd better not. I... I think it's time we said goodbye."

Her smile dissolved. "You mean forever."

"Yes. I'm sorry, Eden."

"Why are *you* sorry?" She sounded disdainful, but she looked hurt. "You're the one with the broken heart."

"I had a lovely time today. I think that has to be enough. This is hard as it is."

She nodded her agreement. Her aloofness had returned. "You're right, of course. But what about Tagget?"

Tagget. Bruce had nearly forgotten about him, lost in his own romantic concerns. Had he heard yet? Would he seek revenge? Bruce had no idea how his articles had been received. For all he knew, the whole world thought him crazy.

"I'll be fine. I promise." He bowed over Eden's hand and pressed a kiss to the soft skin there. The taste of her lingered on his lips. She smelled of lavender-scented soap. He yearned to hold her forever. "Goodbye, my sweetheart," he murmured.

He dropped her hand as abruptly as he had seized it and whirled away. He would keep his composure. He would. He had an article to finish.

He worked longer than usual on the writing. He wanted to get this right. The last thing he needed was for Fulton to rescind his promotion offer. He quoted Eden, but not by name. He didn't need his biases showing. She would recognize her statement.

With the article submitted, he wandered up to his room. There would be no beer for him tonight, however much he would have liked one. Instead, he would read and he would pack. Once he was back in Boston, this entire thing would fade like a dream, and he could move on.

His room was unlocked. He froze with his hand on the doorknob, thinking back to that morning. He'd locked up, hadn't he? He hadn't been that distracted over Eden.

He let the door swing open, but didn't step inside. He half expected to find his possessions scattered and any valuables missing.

One of the Bafford brothers sat on his bed.

"Mr. Tagget wants a word with you," the man drawled. His grin was malevolent.

Bruce bolted.

38

For once, Eden wasn't pleased to be right. She'd been
about to follow Bruce upstairs and make certain he was safely
in his room, when he came thundering down the stairs, one
of Tagget's giant hangers-on right behind. They flew past her
without noticing. No one expected her to be sitting in the
lobby, hiding behind a newspaper. She pulled up the hood
of her cloak, checked Vox was securely hidden beneath, and
followed them outside.

The second bodyguard waited out in the street. Bruce
almost crashed into him. He tried to dodge, but his pursuer
had caught up. A big hand clamped down on his arm.

"What's the hurry? No time for a chat?"

Eden took a few steps backward, unwilling to take her
eyes off the scene. At the first sign of violence, she was going
for the police.

"How're the ribs?" the second man chuckled. He jabbed
his finger into Bruce's side.

Bruce didn't even flinch, and he met the man's mocking
smile with a harsh stare. "You can't hurt me. The story is out

all across the country. If anything happens to me, everyone will know who did it and why."

"Who said we're going to hurt anyone? Boss wants to talk. That's all we said, right, Bobby?"

"Right," agreed the man restraining Bruce. "Maybe we should go get the girl. Boss always likes having her around, and I bet then he'd come willingly."

"If you hurt her, I will kill you," Bruce vowed.

And if you hurt him, I *will kill you,* Eden added silently, running through all the possible ways someone of her stature might fight these men.

"Let's go," Bobby ordered. He forced Bruce down the street, twisting his arm until he gasped in pain. Eden trailed after, just close enough to hear. With people everywhere and the sun going down, she was simply another body.

Bruce wrenched himself free. "I know how to walk," he snarled.

The second man shoved him. "Just makin' sure you don't run off."

"I'd watch myself, if I were you," Bruce retorted. "This town is packed full of people from the football game. Some roughhousing and a few angry words might be ignored, but get too carried away and you'll get noticed. Townies will be looking for strangers to blame trouble on."

"You're a stranger, too, idiot," Bafford growled, missing the point. "Keep walking. Boss is at the saloon."

Eden couldn't picture Evan Tagget in a saloon, and when she entered, she could see why. She'd never seen a man look more out-of-place when out for a drink.

Tagget was dressed in his customary black, except for the silver brocade of his vest. Like all his clothing, it was perfectly fitted and pristine. The suit itself didn't belong in a saloon. Tagget's stiff posture made it stand out all the more. He sat alone at a table, holding a tumbler containing some measure of spirits. He glared down at the drink as if he thought it might be poison.

"Caldwell. Sit down." His voice was unnervingly calm for someone she feared to be in a murderous rage.

Bruce sat. The bodyguards stood behind him. Eden used their large bodies to shield herself and walked right past their table. She set Vox on the floor and nudged her beneath Tagget's chair, then walked to the far end of the room, out of Tagget's line of sight, hidden from the others by several tables of tall men. She could see both Bruce and Tagget if she leaned down and peered between people. She turned her volume all the way up and leaned forward, concentrating intensely.

"Sit down." Tagget snapped his fingers at his goons and pointed at an empty seat. "You look like imbeciles standing there."

"Just making sure he won't leave."

"He won't leave," Tagget laughed. "He's a reporter for a reason. He wants to hear me out. Sit. Drink a beer. Isn't that what one does in this sort of establishment?"

The bodyguards shrugged and sat.

"That's not beer," Bruce pointed out, gesturing at Tagget's glass. "What are you drinking?"

Tagget waved his drink about. He still hadn't taken a sip. "I'm told it's Cognac. I suspect it might be turpentine."

Bruce laughed, took the glass from Tagget's hand, and took a sip. "It's brandy all right." He thunked it back on the table. "Probably not from France, but it won't kill you. Unfortunately."

Tagget reclaimed the glass and tasted it. "Terrible. I should demand a refund."

"Try the beer instead. It's excellent."

"I loathe beer. This is preferable, swill though it may be."

"You are the most pretentious jackass I've ever met."

Eden winced. Bruce was so impulsive. She wondered if he ever thought before he spoke.

Fortunately, Tagget only chuckled. "Thank you, Mr. Caldwell. That is a compliment, I'm certain, coming from you, with your sanctimonious charade of poverty. You are heir to quite a fortune, as I understand it."

"I get nothing until my father is dead, and I don't wish ill health or misfortune on my own family."

"I worked for my money, you know," Tagget sneered. "Earned every penny."

"So did I. Legally, in fact."

"Drop the superior attitude, boy. You've never needed to work a day in your life. If you found yourself in the street, your mother would dust you off and buy you a new suit you would then wrinkle and tear because it means nothing to you. You're a spoiled brat, Caldwell."

"*I'm* spoiled? Says the man with bodyguards and a car that runs on luxene?"

Tagget thrust a hand nearly into Bruce's face. "These scars are not from a pampered childhood. You have no idea where I come from or how hard I have worked to get here, and I will not let a smart-ass, selfish, prep-school brat ruin it."

"What do you want, Tagget?" Bruce snapped.

"A full retraction. Immediately."

"Never."

"I thought you might say as much. I'm prepared to negotiate."

"I don't negotiate with thieves and spies."

"I'm a respectable businessman, Mr. Caldwell. I have experience defending myself from enemies. I assure you, I can make certain no one will believe the jealous ramblings of a little boy who wants attention. Especially when said boy is afflicted with a terrible morphine addiction."

"What?"

"How long was it, before your hands stopped shaking? Or does it still happen, now and again? Are you craving it as we speak? Perhaps it will dull the pain of leaving Miss Randall behind."

"I don't need your drugs, thank you. You'll have to do better than that with your threats."

"Will I? All it would take is a single accident. A bit of pain and a doctor who doesn't know any better. A shot or two to get you started, then easy access to more. You would be ruined before you ever woke from the haze."

Bruce shoved his chair back from the table. "We're done here."

"I think not. If you walk away, you'll find yourself in a world of hurt. I have defeated far more powerful men than you. Since I'm a generous man, however, I will give you one more option. Give me what I want, and you can keep your silly article. Tour around the world telling them what a scoundrel I am. Enjoy it. I won't bother you."

"Eden's dragon."

Tagget laughed. "Well, that would be nice, but that's another issue altogether. One I can resolve fully on my own. No, Mr. Caldwell. I want Eden. Just her. Nothing more. Give me the girl and you and I are even."

Eden rocked back in her seat, stunned. They were negotiating over her? Like she was some sort of... of *thing*? She sprang to her feet, ready to punch Tagget for his arrogance, but Bruce's voice pushed her back into her seat.

"Only Eden can give you that, and I think she's made it clear she's not interested. Please excuse me."

Bruce started to rise, but Tagget lunged across the table and grabbed his arm. His eyes were wide and panicked. "Then tell me how to win her. How did you do it? What does she like? I give her everything I can think of, but she only wants you. Why? What's so special about you?"

Bruce extricated himself from Tagget's grip and rose to his feet. "I like beer," he replied. He tipped his hat, spun, and walked out.

Eden's heart swelled with pride. Bruce had handled the threats and insults like a true gentleman. He refused to back down in the face of danger. Maybe Tagget would discredit his articles. Maybe he would even jab Bruce with a needle full of morphine in an attempt to ruin his life. Perhaps Bruce could never truly win against someone like that. It didn't matter. He would always be her champion.

Tagget snapped his fingers at his guards again. The two men jumped to attention.

"Please see to it Mr. Caldwell is escorted somewhere where he can't cause any trouble for the next few days."

"The bottom of the river?" chuckled one of the men.

"Do I look like a murderer, Mr. Bafford?"

"No, Boss."

Eden didn't feel the relief she thought she might have at that statement. Murder was tricky. It wasn't the sort of crime one could talk one's way out of. Tagget would avoid it. That didn't mean he wouldn't consider it an option in the future.

"Oi!" One of the Baffords looked down at his feet. "What have we here?"

Eden gasped. The man bent and picked up Vox. She bit him, and he grunted but didn't let go.

"Nasty little piece of work, isn't it?" he mused, dangling her by the tail and holding her away from his body to avoid her teeth. Vox twisted and flapped her wings, trying to free herself.

Eden ran across the room and grabbed her dragon, trying to tug her from the large man's grip. "Let her go!"

"Miss Randall, have you been spying on us?" Tagget asked, a grin splitting his handsome face. "How terribly devious. Are you *trying* to inflame my passions? Release the dragon, Bafford."

The bodyguard released Vox and he and his brother tromped from the saloon in pursuit of Bruce. Eden pulled Vox to her chest and hurried toward the exit. Tagget followed.

He grasped her wrist to pull her to a halt. "Miss Randall,

you and I need to sit down and have a frank discussion about that dragon of yours. Where would you like to go? I will take you anywhere. Detroit, Chicago, New York, Paris, Cairo. Name your location."

"I wouldn't go with you next door," she snapped. She pulled away and ran out of the saloon, hoping she could find Bruce and warn him Tagget's goons were coming for him. Hoping she could get away before they came for *her*.

39

"**B**RUCE!"

Bruce spun around at Eden's terrified shout.

"Run!"

It was too late. The Bafford brothers were bearing down on him. Perhaps if he hadn't turned he could have fled, but now he would have to fight his way out. He should've stuck to more populated areas, but he'd been reluctant to return to his hotel. He'd thought perhaps the library would be open, for those overzealous students who worked through nights and weekends. Now he stood on an empty campus, bracing himself for the inevitable impact.

This Bafford brother had learned from the mistakes of the previous tussle. He wrapped both arms around Bruce as he tackled, leaving no chance to slip away. Bruce hit the ground hard, the air driven from his lungs. He gasped for a few seconds before drawing a precious full breath. He squirmed beneath the larger man, trying to get in a position to poke at an eye, ear, or other soft part.

A rag smashed against his face. He reached to rip it away,

but his hand never arrived. The world spun around him. Chloroform. Damn.

They were in a darkened room. Bruce blinked and tried to get his bearings. He was dizzy, unsteady, and sick, but at least they had stopped shoving vile-smelling wet rags in his face. He wasn't certain he'd ever been fully unconscious—they'd made him walk here, wherever here was—but he was so disoriented, he may as well have been. His hands were bound behind him, and the floor seemed to tilt upward at an alarming angle.

No. That wasn't the drug. The ground had given way beneath him. He was falling. He heard a scream, then realized it came from his own throat.

The impact with the ground sent shooting pains through him. He lay stunned, afraid he may have shattered every bone in his body. Somewhere above him someone was shrieking.

"No!" Eden cried. "Stop! Let her go!"

Eden. Vox. He had to help. He had to move. He tried to fight through the pain and confusion. Each movement seemed to take an eternity. *Turn over. Try to sit.*

"Vox, no!" Eden wailed.

She came crashing down atop him and he screamed again. The pain from moments ago hadn't been so bad, really. Not compared to this. She had landed full-force on his side, damaging the ribs that had only recently been feeling normal again. The rest of him hurt less, so that, at least, was a relief.

The opening overhead slammed closed, plunging them into complete darkness. Banging and scraping suggested heavy objects being moved about. Whatever hatch they had fallen through, they wouldn't be climbing out of it.

Free from noxious fumes, Bruce's head finally began to clear. He couldn't see a thing, but his other senses were functioning again, and his muscles cooperated when he tried to move. Not so broken, after all. He twisted around and smashed his head on a wall.

"Fuck!"

Where the hell were they? He was up against a wall, and when he stretched his legs out, he easily touched the opposite side. He turned himself ninety degrees, kicking out to feel for more walls. Nothing. A long, narrow passageway. The floor beneath him felt like brick. The air was moist, the heat stifling.

"The steam tunnels," he concluded. Not hopeless, then. They were safe enough here, if uncomfortable. The heating pipes ran all over campus. There would be other exits, assuming they could untie themselves and find their way in the dark.

Eden didn't answer him. She couldn't hear him. By now, Tagget's thugs would've taken Vox out of range.

Bruce could hear her, though. She'd rolled off of him and lay a short distance away, whimpering. She'd panicked in the dark before, he remembered, when Heyward had shut them in the closet. He could only imagine how she must feel now, trussed up and deprived of her most vital senses. He squirmed to her side. She jerked away. Her foot lashed out, leaving a nice bruise on his shin. She was terrified.

How could he help? Tell her he was there? Reassure her she was safe? Or as safe as one could be, given the circumstances.

First things first. He needed to show her he wasn't an enemy.

He scraped across the rough floor, repositioning himself. She kicked again when he bumped her, but he inched around until he could press his knee into her bound hands. She would know the feel of the steel braces and the smooth, bronze kneecap, even beneath the cloth of his trousers. She had touched him as no one had.

She recoiled when his knee met her hand, but he didn't pull away. A moment later, her fingers began to explore him.

"Bruce?" Her voice was small and shaky. Tremors shook

her slim body. He pressed himself against her, finding the top of her head, then her ear, then her cheek.

"Eden," he murmured. He knew she couldn't hear him, but he let her feel his breath, his lips against her skin. "I'm here."

Something tickled his hand and he cried aloud. Oh, God, oh God. It was one of those centipedes that lurked in dark places. The four-inch ones with ten thousand legs. The carnivorous ones. The kind his cousin had dumped down his shirt when he was four years old, leaving him screaming like a madman. There were probably hundreds down here. Millions, even. He burrowed against Eden, trying to soothe his own phobia. Some pair they made.

"Bruce? Are you okay?"

He took a deep breath, pressed his cheek to hers, and nodded. He wasn't okay. He was hurt, he was scared, and he was trapped in a dark, sweltering tunnel. But he wasn't alone. They could do this together.

He rolled over, let his hands brush hers, then tugged at her bindings. Eden understood immediately. He felt her fingers run over his wrists, studying the ropes that held him.

"Turn around," she instructed. "Upside-down. It will be easier to reach that way. No, wait, I'll do it. There isn't much room in here."

He listened to her shuffling, felt her body rotate next to his. When she was settled, she squeezed his hand, then moved her fingers to the rope.

Bruce fumbled for the knot that held her wrists. With the way his hands were crossed, he could only pull at it with one hand at a time. His fingernails weren't long enough to dig into the rope, and getting even a feeble grip on the knot was difficult.

His fingers slipped. He swore. Something grazed his arm, sending a tremor down his spine. Damned bugs. He grabbed at the knot again, twisting his wrist to get a better hold on it.

The rope tore into his skin, stripping away a new layer of flesh with each movement.

The pattern continued. He fumbled, tugged, swore. His skin crawled. In his mind, many-legged creatures were all over him, worming their way beneath his clothing. He used words that would have made his father blush and his mother faint.

The knot was loosening, but in such small increments the wait was excruciating. His wrists cramped and stung. Something wet trickled into his palm, but he couldn't tell whether it was blood or sweat.

The oppressive heat sapped his strength. Sweat ran into his eyes and down his neck. Each little tingle against his skin conjured up more images of wriggling vermin.

A new pain shot up from his wrist, and it took a second to realize it was from the rope shifting.

"Haha!" Eden cried in triumph.

The rope shifted again, then fell away completely. Her nimble fingers had freed him.

Bruce shook off the bindings and leapt to his feet, bashing his head on the low, curved ceiling. This time he cursed Evan Tagget for putting him here.

"Damnable, odoriferous hornswoggler!"

He ran his hands over his arms and legs, shaking and swearing, trying to dislodge any critters.

"Bruce? Where are you?"

"Eden, I'm so sorry." He dropped to his knees beside her, groping for her bindings. He was glad she couldn't hear or see him. She would've thought him the world's greatest ninny.

Not true.

She understood no one was perfect. She was a loyal teammate with a strong sense of fairness. She would support him through his weaknesses and thank him for supporting her through hers.

He found the knot, which came undone easily now he could work it with both hands. He pulled the ropes off and helped her to her feet. She flung her arms around his neck and kissed him.

In her embrace, the centipedes were all but forgotten. Her kiss was sweet but fierce, no holding back. In the press of her lips and the sweep of her tongue, he could taste everything he loved about her: her indomitable spirit, her zest for life, her wit, her quirkiness.

She shouldn't even be here. Tagget wouldn't have wanted her thrown into a dark tunnel. She'd risked herself in an attempt to warn him. She hadn't given up on him.

He crushed her against his chest, and heard her gasp in surprise at the collision. He kissed her with everything he had, telling her without words how deeply she had entrenched herself in his heart. Only the heat and the darkness kept him sensible of his surroundings.

He drew back with reluctance, then took hold of her hand. He poked her pointer finger into his chest, laid her palm flat over his heart, then pressed her finger to her own chest. I. Love. You.

He repeated the gesture, to ensure she understood. She responded with a squeeze of her fingers and a soft brush of her lips. No flinching this time.

What had he been thinking, trying to walk away from her? This love was too new, too intense. He'd been unprepared, and he'd stumbled, blinded by the pain of thinking he might never win her. But he'd be damned if he wouldn't keep trying. He wouldn't leave this town until he'd asked her to marry him. Returning to Boston was a necessity, but it needn't be permanent. Even if she turned him down, he would find his way back here as soon as possible, to continue wooing her until he felt comfortable enough to try again. As long as she kissed him the way she had moments before, he wasn't giving up.

First, to get her out of here. He turned her hand palm up and traced out letters with one finger. W-H-E-R-E…

"Where are we?" she asked. Unable to hear herself, her

words were spoken too loudly. Bruce delighted in the way they echoed in the darkness. He gave her a squeeze as a yes. "The steam tunnels, under the laboratory."

O-U-T

"I don't know." Some of the tremor was back in her voice. "There should be connections to all of the buildings on campus, but they may be locked up, and I don't know the way. I told you I didn't like it down here."

L-O-V-E-Y-O-U

It was the most reassuring thing he could think to spell out. How else could he tell her he wouldn't leave her? They would get out of this together.

"So I've heard."

There was a note of sadness beneath her teasing response. Did she feel bad she couldn't love him? Or did she love him, but feel they couldn't be together?

No. He was reading too much into her words. She was trapped and scared, making jokes about hearing, when she had just lost hers. How could she be anything but sad? She put up an admirable fight.

L-E-T-S…

Something brushed against his leg, and he shrieked and jumped, smacking his head on a pipe. He let out a new string of curses, hopping about to shake off anything that may have climbed on him.

"Bruce, what's wrong?"

He steadied himself and took up her hand again.

B-U-G-S

"Oh. Probably," she said matter-of-factly. "Could be rats, too."

He shuddered. She gave him a reassuring pat on the arm.

"A rat got into the laboratory once. It made a terrible mess. It chewed up several schematics and made a nest in one of the machines." She led him down the corridor as she talked.

"Everyone was frantic, thinking someone had stolen things, but then we began to find piles of rat droppings all over!"

The delight in her voice over such a discovery caused yet another involuntary shudder. She laughed.

"It was exciting for a bored twelve-year-old! I tracked it down, and then we had to chase it all over the lab. My father tried to sic a half-finished cat dragon on it, but the poor thing just kept getting all turned about and gnawing on our shoes." She was shaking again, but from laughter. "Eventually I chased the rat into a corner and my mother dropped a bucket over it. Then we spent nearly a half-hour discussing how to get the bucket outside without letting the rat out!"

Bruce laced his fingers through hers. Her silly tale had put him at ease. With his other hand, he traced a heart on the inside of her wrist. She was ticklish there, and made an adorable "ooh" noise.

T-E-L-L-M-E-M-O-R-E

"More? More stories? Do you want me to talk while we search for an exit?"

Y-E-S

They continued down the tunnel, hand-in-hand. They would search. They would escape. They would survive together.

"Uh, well, once I broke a window playing baseball and tried to replace the ball with a rock so my parents would think it was a hooligan who did it."

"You *are* the hooligan," he laughed, wishing she could hear him. He began to spell it out on her arm.

My hooligan. My love. My everything.

He'd suffer centipedes for her any day.

40

Vox was confused. She flew about, her sensors flaring.
Not-Eden. Not-Eden.

Eden was out-of-range. Vox couldn't find her way back.
A Not-Eden touched her, and she snapped and clawed. The
Not-Eden made a noise and moved away.

"Vox!"

Her antennae perked up at the familiar voice. It was
distorted, but it registered as Eden's. Vox took in the Eden
noise, awaiting a command. She tried to transmit, but Eden
remained out-of-range.

"Sleep."

A command. Vox curled up in her sleep position and
turned down her power. An alarm wakened her. All her sensors
flared. A tool touched her belly.

Unauthorized!

A Not-Eden held her. She bit it, and it made a big noise
and dropped her.

She righted herself and unfolded her wings to fly away.
Something stopped her. She nudged it with her head. It

registered as a wall. She turned all around, but the wall was everywhere.

Wall. Wall. Wall. No Eden.

Emergency Mode triggered for the first time. Vox sat. Her legs and wings went to sleep. All transmissions ceased. All noise storage ceased. All listening ceased. Her shell electrified, preventing anything from touching her.

Only a single sensor continued to operate.

Out-of-range. Out-of-range.

Vox waited.

41

Eden shivered in the cool night air. Her eyes drifted over the buildings and the trees, drinking them in, relieved at the restoration of her sight. More than relieved.

"A little light makes all the difference in the world," she sighed. "What time is it?"

Bruce checked his watch and spoke, then remembered himself and tilted the watch for her to see. Quarter to twelve.

Lord. Hours. They'd been in that tunnel for hours.

She took his hand and jogged away from the law building, her skin prickling at the memory of the darkness and the despair of finding one exit after another locked tight. She raced across campus, the freedom of the open air pounding in her veins, her hair flying out behind her. Bruce clutched her fingers, loping alongside. They didn't stop until she spied a familiar object on the ground near the library.

She stooped to retrieve the cap, dusted it off, offered it to him. "I'd hate for you to lose this. I know you don't have many."

A dimple formed in his cheek. Her knees went weak. She could see his smile again. She'd known it was there, in the tunnels. She had felt it in the grip of his fingers and the letters he had traced upon her skin. The sight of it pierced her heart.

"Oh, Bruce, I…"

She stopped. She couldn't say she loved him. Not when he'd become so adamant in his own affections. Not when she had sworn to let him go. She could not, *would not*, add that burden to the inevitable hurt.

She accepted his embrace, dropping her head onto his warm, inviting chest, clinging to some faint hope that tomorrow would never come.

He was burned into her memory: the scent of his clove and spice aftershave, the near-painful tug on her scalp when he played with her hair, the way his pen and journal poked into her whenever she hugged him.

He stepped back and withdrew said objects from his pocket. He scrawled on an empty page, then handed it to her. She angled it to get as much light as possible.

That was just awful, wasn't it?

"Almost as bad as your handwriting. It's hard to read in the dark."

Ha ha ha.

His grin had broadened. His lips were so kissable. Her heart couldn't take much more of this.

"We should…" What? Go home? Go to the police? They were free, but Tagget's men were out there, ready to do them harm, and they had Vox.

The journal appeared in her face once more. *Go get Vox back. I have an idea.*

She seized a fistful of his shirt. "Is it dangerous?" She would give up Vox and choose never to hear again before she let any harm come to him.

Yes. It can go up to fifty miles an hour.

"No!"

You said you wanted a ride in the Mercedes.

A bubble of laughter welled inside her. She fought it, but

she could feel the amusement seeping into her voice. "We can't steal his motorcar!"

He stole your dragon. Fair is fair.

"Okay. Show me your plan. But you must promise to be careful. I couldn't bear it if anything were to happen to you."

He made a cross over his heart, then lay his hand flat atop it. Eden tensed, willing her muscles not to fling herself at him. Her hand inched toward him. One foot shuffled forward. Her disobedient body ached to kiss him again. Distance was imperative. She had to spare his heart. She forced herself to turn toward Tagget's hotel.

He followed. Too close. A warm breath made the hairs on the back of her neck stand on end. A hand settled on the small of her back. She couldn't hear the sigh escaping her lips, but she felt it. The journal rose in front of her face.

I will not stop until you have Vox and Tagget is gone for good. I swear it. I love you more than life and I will see this done!

The hand on her back slid around to settle on her belly, drawing her into his strong arms. She was done for. She whirled to kiss him. A kiss for eternity. A kiss that she could relive when she was old and gray and thought back on how once she had loved a man more than anyone had reason to.

He ended it. She couldn't. His lips slipped away, a tender whisper, leaving her at once starving for him and drunkenly sated on his love. She lost herself in the depths of his eyes, drowned in their warmth. Something had changed in him, down in the tunnels. He held nothing back. He had handed her his heart, and a knife to stab it with, yet he wasn't afraid.

"Oh, Bruce, I love you." Dammit. She was a fool.

"I thought you might."

She blinked. Trying to read his lips in such low light was difficult. Had he really said that? His beatific smile sliced into her. Even the dark couldn't hide it. It conveyed his meaning more than any words ever would.

Damn her heart. Damn the knife that would slay them

both. Damn Boston and Ann Arbor and the hundreds of miles between them.

She took his hand and they walked. Tomorrow, she promised herself. Tomorrow they would tackle their pending separation and their stupid, foolish hearts.

Tonight they would get her dragon back. Together.

42

November 13, midnight

BRUCE FLINCHED WHEN the engine caught. In the quiet streets, the rumble of the engine pounded like a roar in his head. He was out of his mind. How could he steal a car? He'd never even driven one. His heart thumped. He wiped a bead of sweat from his brow.

He would do this. He couldn't beat Tagget without taking a risk. And he was going to give Eden the time of her life.

He hopped into the driver's seat. His knuckles clenched on the wheel. "Here goes nothing."

The first few yards were an exercise in terror. The motorcar slewed to the left, then swung back right, scraped the curb, bounced, then settled. Bruce let out a breath. He could do this. Gentle on the wheel, light on the throttle.

Eden giggled beside him. He tore his gaze from her shining eyes. He would crash if he didn't stop watching her.

He reached the corner and swung the vehicle in a wide, leisurely turn. At the next corner, he did the same. Easy. A smile touched his lips and he picked up speed.

The rush of wind tore the cap from his head, and only Eden's lightning reflexes saved him from losing it once more. The thrill of the speed couldn't outshine that of their shared laughter. This was an intoxicating mixture: the crime, the sense of freedom, and Eden's declaration of love.

He roared down Washtenaw Avenue, past too-large houses with too-rich inhabitants. His parents owned a house like these. He never would. He belonged elsewhere. He belonged in a world of roller rinks and pick-up football. Of a small kitchen where his wife did the cooking and made bad coffee. In a house where none of the doors hung correctly due to his inept carpentry skills, but one could always snuggle in front of the fire. They might never own a motorcar, but he would feel this sensation of joy in a million other ways for a lifetime.

"Why are we stopping? You're not regretting this, are you?"

He dared a glance at her as he brought the car to a halt. He pointed at her chest. "Your turn." He vacated his seat, offering it with a sweep of his hand and a bow.

She drove like a maniac. He desired no less. He held on for dear life and feasted on her smiles and exclamations of glee. If she killed him, he would go out a happy man.

When the thrill ebbed and she'd had her fill of driving, she handed control back to him. "What now?"

He looked her right in the eye. "We go fetch Vox."

Downtown remained quiet. Saloon lights spoke of drinkers inside, but few ventured out. Bruce meant to change all that.

The moment he spied Tagget's hotel, he laid on the horn. The high-pitched shriek reverberated through the street and pierced his skull. No turning back now. He circled the block, honked again. Around and around.

Windows flew open. He breathed deeply, willing himself calm before the sea of angry faces.

"Evan Tagget!" Bruce pounded the horn. "Evan Tagget, give back the dragon!"

Eden's nails dug into his arm. "Bruce this is crazy. He's going to kill you."

The pain only spurred him on. He turned right. Another right. Three, four.

"Tagget! You gutless bastard! Eden wants her dragon back!" Another circuit. "Evan Tagget!" The horn wailed.

"Ow!" Eden's hand flew to her ear. "Vox!" She leapt from the moving car.

Eden ran for the hotel door, skittering to a stop when it opened. Tagget loomed in the doorway, a thunderous expression on his face. She staggered, shying away from the raw fury in his eyes. She could hear the motorcar stop behind her. She wanted to scream to Bruce to run, but she knew he wouldn't.

Tagget's anger faded the moment he realized who stood before him.

"Eden, darling." He held out a box to her. "Forgive me for keeping her. When my men brought her to me, I knew it would in turn bring you to me."

Eden yanked the box from his hands and freed Vox. She pressed her cheek against the dragon's cold, metal head and glowered up at Tagget.

"How was I supposed to come to you when I was tied up and thrown into a sweltering hellhole?"

A new fury flashed in his eyes. "They will be dismissed immediately. I would *never* give such an order. That was reserved for *him*." He glared over her shoulder at Bruce. "I hope you have a good explanation for the police, Mr. Caldwell."

Eden took a step backwards and linked arms with Bruce. "You mean, you hope *we* have a good explanation."

"No. I will not hold you responsible for his stupidity. I'll press no charges."

"Then I'll confess," Eden declared. "I admit my crime freely."

"No!" He lunged toward her. "My blossom, you can't. I won't let you be trundled off to jail."

Eden pressed herself tight to Bruce's side. "Where he goes, I go."

"My love, be reasonable. Why can't you see it? I can give you everything he can and more."

"Fuck off, Tagget," Bruce snarled.

"You, boy, are going to wish you had stayed in that rat-infested tunnel. I will see to it that you never see the light of day for the remainder of your long, painful life."

The clop of hooves made Eden turn.

"Ah, here comes an officer of the law now."

Bruce pulled Eden toward the car. "No one will ever catch us."

Tagget laughed and pulled a device from his pocket. A small box, similar to the one that had triggered the luxene explosions. A low rumble sounded in Eden's right ear. The motorcar's engine coughed, sputtered, died. "You run that fast?"

"So that's what you've been doing with Dynalux," Bruce said. "Impressive. You've tweaked the recipe so you can disable a car remotely without destroying it."

"I isolated the component in the fuel that reacts to sound waves and separated it out from the chemicals that made it volatile. Terribly useful, isn't it? I intend to control all aspects of motorcars in the future."

"You intend to control everything," Bruce retorted. "That's what this is all about, isn't it? Control. That's why you're obsessed with wireless teletics. You can't let them replace your wired network until you can find a way to spy on the transmissions. You'd hate to give up all that power, wouldn't you? You don't want to sell Randall's technology. You want to suppress it. You were even prepared to destroy his research as a last resort."

Eden clutched Vox.

Tagget only chuckled. "You're cleverer than you look, Caldwell. Which you must be, I suppose, for my beloved Eden to be so fond of you. Pity your mind will waste away in prison from now on. Excuse me, I believe the police have arrived."

Eden leapt to bar his path. "Tagget, no, please."

"It's for the best, my garden of delight."

She shoved him hard enough that he stumbled. "I am not a paradise!"

"What seems to be the trouble here?" The police officer's voice rang with authority.

A malicious smile crossed Tagget's face. He lifted a finger to point. "That man…"

Eden grabbed his hand. "No. Stop. I'll do anything. Don't do this. Don't hurt him."

"He brought this on himself."

"No! You brought it on. You stole Vox! You threw us in the steam tunnels! You're a thief and a liar and a horrible person, and I hate you!"

"Miss, do you think you might be able to tell me what the trouble is?" the officer asked.

"Him," Eden hissed, pointing an accusatory finger at Tagget.

Tagget seized her hand. "Eden, my floweret, what has he done to you? Officer, that man has harmed my…" He froze, eyes on her wounded wrist. "My God, you're injured!" He raised her hand toward his lips. "I'm so sorry, my sweetheart."

The endearment infuriated her. That word belonged to Bruce and no one else. It held a special place in her heart, and Tagget was making a mockery of it. She jerked her hand from his grip and hammered on his chest with her fist.

"I am not your sweetheart! I will *never* be your sweetheart."

Tagget remained calm. "Officer, that man stole my car. There are plenty of witnesses. He was riding around with Miss Randall here, and I'm frightened to think of what he may have done to her. You see how distraught she is. There was talk of rats and a tunnel. She may be drugged. I would like to press charges of theft, kidnapping, attempted murder…"

"No." Panic seized Eden's heart. It didn't matter the absurdity of the charges. Tagget had the power to make good on his threats. "No." She thrust Vox at him. "Vox, friend."

"What?" Tagget stared down at the dragon nuzzling him.

"Take her. You can have her. You can have anything. Please, just leave us alone." A tear dribbled down her cheek. She ran to Bruce and clutched his shirt with both hands. "Do whatever you want," she continued. "Study her, take her apart. I'll tell you everything I know. I'll give you the schematics, and the new research."

Tagget's bewildered gaze was fixated on Vox. "You would… but, why?"

"You should be flattered Tagget." Bruce's words were calm, but he trembled with rage. "She doesn't do that for many people."

Eden crumpled against his chest. "For you. Only for you."

"Damned kids and your romantic troubles," the policeman muttered. "I ought to arrest all three of you."

"Eden," Tagget pleaded. "You don't need to do this. Come with me. Let me give you the world. You can have your dragon. I'll keep it safe from everyone. I don't want it. I don't want your father's research. I only want you."

Eden turned her watery eyes on him. "Vox is the only part of me I can give. The rest is taken."

"No." His eyes took on a crazed look. "No. Eden, please. Eden, I will give you everything. We will attend the symphony in Vienna, take in an opera at La Scala! I will buy you private concerts from the finest musicians in the world. You like my Mercedes? It's yours. I'll purchase a fleet of them, if you so desire. A train. Your own airship. Name it. Ask anything of me."

The desperation in his voice softened Eden's anger. She

spoke gently. "The only thing I want is for you to leave me and Bruce in peace."

"Jewels, gowns!" Tagget was raving now, flinging his hands in the air. He had Vox by the tail, dangling. "You can have your fancy corsets designed by the House of Worth! What else? God, what else? Beer! I'll take you to Germany. Buy you a damned brewery! I'll... I'll buy you the New York Giants!"

Her gaze locked with his. She could find no trace of his usual haughtiness. His eyes were wild, his face creased with worry. His shoulders slumped. His youthful features, ordinarily so attractive, now made him seem a scared little boy.

"I'm so sorry, Evan."

Something broke in him. A last spark of hope died in his eyes.

"You were mine," he gasped. "You were mine, and he stole you! You stole her from me! I had something precious and beautiful and you took it away from me and now I have nothing! Nothing! All I have left is a stupid, worthless dragon!"

He swung Vox with all his might. Eden's eyes widened in terror. Her heart leapt into her throat. A primal scream tore from her lungs. Metal and brick collided in a screeching, twisting wail of horror.

The world went silent.

43

THE SHOCK HAD PARALYZED HIM. His jaw hung open. His feet remained cemented in place. Bruce willed himself to do something—do anything but stand there, dumbfounded and heartsick.

Eden sat on the ground, cradling the crumpled body of her dragon, keening in abject misery. The sound tore at his heart.

God, to take that pain from her. He would break all his ribs, destroy his other knee, suffer any agony for her, if it could mend what had been broken.

A tear dripped from his nose. He sniffed, wiped at it, shaking off the stupor.

Tagget had collapsed nearby, and sat weeping into his hands, intoning, "What have I done?" in an unending mantra of well-deserved torment. Bruce's fury had settled into a dispassionate anger, tempered by the thought that Tagget might be genuinely out of his mind.

He hauled the smaller man to his feet. Tagget met his gaze without cowering or sneering. Bruce could find nothing but sorrow in his expression.

"I should kill you."

Tagget nodded. "Indeed. It would be less painful, I imagine, than this. But you won't. She wouldn't want you to bear such a burden."

"You should go. Far, far away from here. Fly to Europe in your dirigible."

A thoughtful frown brought back some of Tagget's usual self. "I don't own a dirigible. Perhaps I shall buy one."

"Go ahead. Just leave."

He inclined his head, the first sincerely polite gesture he had ever made in Bruce's direction. "Take care of her, Caldwell."

"To the very best of my ability."

The police officer stopped Tagget before he could turn and enter the hotel. "You gonna press charges?"

"No."

He turned to Bruce. "You?"

"No."

"The young lady?"

"I will see her home. If she has any accusations, she can make them in the morning."

"I ought to cite you all for disturbance of the peace."

Tagget withdrew a wad of bills from his vest pocket. What the hell was the man doing so properly dressed and carrying cash at this time of night, anyway?

"This should be sufficient to pay any fine for all three of us. Thank you for your prompt attention this evening." He spun on his heel and disappeared into the hotel.

Bruce knelt beside Eden. Her weeping had diminished, but she continued to rock back and forth, Vox's broken body clutched to her breast. He caught a wisp of hair, brushed it from her cheek and tucked it behind her ear.

"I love you," he said. He thought she would understand, but he covered his heart to make the meaning clear.

She set Vox in her lap. "Watch me. I love you." She signed it for him.

He copied her gestures, and she nodded, a sad smile touching her lips. "Good."

He reached for his journal, words coalescing in his mind. He wrote furiously. She could read his scrawl well enough. He handed her the book, watched her eyes scan each line.

> *If they take your hearing, I will show you works of fine art and the most stunning of vistas. If they take your sight, I will cover your skin with the sleekest silks and the softest furs. If they take your touch, I will bring you the finest of perfumes and the most delicate of flowers. If they take your sense of smell, I will feed you the sourest lemon, the bitterest coffee, and the sweetest honey. And if they take your taste, I will still be here. I will hold you. And I will love you.*

A lone tear ran down her cheek and fell with a plop onto the paper. As she handed it back, her eyes rose to meet his, soft and sad.

"Take me home?"

He responded with a press of his fingers. He hoisted her to her feet and settled his arm around her shoulders. Her head fell against him.

"Stay with me tonight?"

He nodded. "I would stay with you until the end of time. You need only ask."

Eden shook her head to indicate she didn't understand, so he brushed his lips across hers and steered her toward home. He would show her.

44

November 13th, 5:21 am

$\mathcal{A}$ TRAIL OF SOFT KISSES along her inner thigh dragged Eden from the depths of slumber. Ooh. So nice. Lovely dream. The slick caress of a tongue jolted her. Bruce's mouth inched higher, creeping closer to the junction of her legs. No. Definitely not a dream.

Her eyes flew open. If he intended to do *that* again, she wanted to be fully awake.

He turned up the bedside lamp, illuminating her bedroom with a warm glow. He looked gorgeous splayed naked across her sheets. His journal sat open on the end table where she could see it. Lovely man.

He jotted in the journal.

Have to go. Make love 1st?

"Mmm," she agreed. She wove her fingers through his thick hair. He needed a cut. It was getting shaggy. "Don't stop."

His kisses were merciless. His mouth tortured her until

her back arched and her fingers clenched in the sheets. Only when he pressed a finger to her lips to quiet her did she realize she was moaning.

She didn't need the lamp, after all. Her eyes were closed. She had fully succumbed to her sense of touch. She savored every stroke of his fingers, each intricate flick of his tongue against her sensitive flesh. The climax lifted her, shook her, sent her tumbling. She clutched at him, dragged him atop her, pulling him inside, begging him to ride the wave of pleasure with her. She hit a second peak, toppled, crashed.

They rolled apart, spent and satisfied, no longer touching, but close enough to share warmth. This was bliss. *He* was bliss.

Bruce sat up a few minutes later. "I love you," he said, signing as he spoke. He reached for the journal.

Have to go. Back this afternoon. Come to the hotel if you need me sooner.

"I'll be okay."

He kissed her cheek. She watched him dress and slip from the room. Casting her blankets aside, she went to the window to watch him walk away. In the predawn darkness he disappeared all too soon.

She padded back to the bed, her feet cold from the floor. She huddled under the covers, chilled now without him. She stared at the ceiling, unable to rest, her mind awhirl with thoughts. She wouldn't lose him. She would give anything for him. She could live in Boston, if she had to.

But only if she had to. She played through possible scenarios in her mind. She would find the best way for them both.

· · · 🦋 · · ·

Hours later, she had come up with no good solution. Every possibility involved one of them giving up everything for the other. The only idea resembling compromise was the mad thought of them both giving up everything and running away to someplace entirely new. It seemed the worst idea of all.

She had broken down once more that morning, when she had explained to her parents what had happened. They tucked her back into bed and told her not to worry about skipping church. She lay awake and cried and brooded.

Eden forced herself to rise and dress. She'd neglected to return the cap Bruce had dropped in the lab, and she put it on now, adopting it as her own. It soothed her to have this small part of him with her. She made herself some lunch, but food helped less than she had hoped. Too soon she abandoned the half-eaten meal in favor of pacing the room.

As things stood, she had no choice. She would have to move to Boston. She'd heard Bruce tell her father he'd gotten a promotion. She couldn't destroy his career by asking him to live elsewhere. She also couldn't go as she was, unprepared for the city, unable to communicate. She couldn't expect everyone to write in a notebook to talk to her, and years with Vox meant her lip reading wasn't as strong as it might have been. She could fix that, but it would take practice. Her only other choice was waiting until Vox could be repaired or replaced.

A shudder ran through her. Replaced. The word made her cringe. A replacement could never be the same. Vox had grown and changed with her through the years. She was both a part of Eden and her beloved companion. Her father always had ideas for improvements. He might make her a new model, sleeker, smaller, with double the range and a filter for background noise. It would restore her hearing. It would allow her to better hear the music she adored. It would be no more than a *thing* to her.

A flash of red caught her eye. Someone was at the door. Her mother had installed the alert lights years ago, before Eden could hear. They had never been removed.

She raced to the front hall, heart pounding. Had Bruce

come back? What would she say to him? She had so much to confess and so much yet uncertain.

A grubby boy stood on the porch. He thrust a letter at her and said something.

"Thank you." She dug in her pockets and produced the only coin she had. He bounded away with shining eyes and the quarter tight in his fist.

Eden looked down at the letter, addressed to her from Evan Tagget. She returned to the dining room and sat, staring at her food, once again fighting tears. She gave some consideration to chucking the letter into the fire, unread. As it usually did, her curiosity won. With fingers trembling, she broke the seal on the letter and unfolded it. A pile of large bills spilled onto the table. Ignoring the money, she read the short note.

My Dearest Miss Randall,

Please allow me to express my deepest apologies for my behavior last night. I cannot begin to atone for the hurt I have caused you, but I must at least make some attempt to ease the troubles I have heaped at your door. I have enclosed five hundred dollars toward the repair or replacement of your dragon. If you cannot or will not accept it, please send it on to the charity of your choice.

By the time this letter reaches you, I will have left town, with no intention of returning. I neither deserve nor expect your forgiveness. Nonetheless, I must beg it of you and tell you again how unutterably sorry I am for the grievous wrong I have done. If you ever have need of anything, the address on the outside of this letter will forward to me anywhere in the world. I will not await your reply, but I will hope for it, and until that time I will remain…

Yours in despair,
Evan Tagget

She took the money to her room and stashed it in her safe box. The letter she kept in her pocket for further contemplation. She stoked the fire and settled herself on the sofa, hugging her knees to her chest.

Her parents found her there a half-hour later, in the same place, in the same position, still without a solution to her troubles.

"Your Mr. Caldwell is waiting in the front hall," her mother signed.

Eden's hand went to her hat.

"Should I invite him in, or send him away?"

"Invite him in, please," Eden signed back.

"I will do that. Do you need anything? Tea? Food? Your baseball bat?"

Eden managed a small smile. "No, thank you."

"We ran into Miss St. James downtown. She will be joining us for dinner and bringing her mother's pie."

"That will help."

"We've asked her to consult with us on the repairs for Vox."

Eden blinked away a tear. "I love you all."

"We love you, too, darling."

Her parents each kissed her cheek before departing. A moment later, Bruce entered, a slateboard in his hand. He perched on the opposite end of the sofa and turned the board toward her.

Nice hat.

She blushed and reached to take it off, but he held out a hand to stop her.

Keep it. It looks cute on you.

He wiped, then wrote.

How are you feeling?

"Sad. But improving."

Vox?

"Mother can't say yet. The damage was significant." She

sniffed and had to brush away a tear. "I miss her. She... she gave me my voice."

Your voice is magnificent. Strong, proud, full of life.

"Thank you."

No one can take it away. <u>No one.</u>

"Thank you." This time she only signed. Bruce beamed at her. Some might find her soundless voice inferior, but he never would. She loved him more than anything.

You're welcome.

"At least now I can say whatever I want," she said aloud. "If anyone complains, I'll never know."

Good point!

He drew a smiley face next to the words, and she laughed. It was a short laugh, possessed of a touch of sorrow, but it was her first real laugh since the madness of last night.

Tagget is gone.

"I know. He sent a message."

She passed the letter to Bruce for perusal. He scowled at it for several seconds before handing it back.

He's insane.

"No. He's lonely."

Bruce's eyebrows arched.

"I don't think he has any friends. I doubt he's *ever* had a friend."

He doesn't deserve one.

"That's unkind. Everyone deserves a friend."

Bruce sighed, nodding. *Then you've forgiven him already?*

"Well..." She had to think about it a moment. "No. But I think I will, someday."

Maybe <u>you're</u> insane.

She could see a grin tugging at the corners of his mouth, the tease. It banished another chunk of her sorrow.

She narrowed her eyes at him and folded her arms across her chest. "Oh, really?"

Or maybe you're an angel. He drew a heart. *I love you.*

"I love you, too."

Will you marry me?

Her heart skipped a beat. Uncertainty flooded her. All day she had longed for that question, and dreaded it. She had never formulated an answer. Options raced through her mind. Yes? No? Yes with qualifications? Perhaps a lengthy explanation of how every idea seemed doomed to bring someone unhappiness? She had to say something. He looked so expectant, his eyes wide and glittering with hope.

Her hesitation crushed it. The spark died. His posture stiffened.

"Oh, Bruce, I want to!" she blurted, desperate to spare his heart. "But… but…" Words escaped her.

You can't. I understand.

"You don't understand! I can't… I can't live like this! I can't decide anything at all until I know if I'm ever going to be able to hear again. Can I stand to replace Vox? If I can't hear, how will that affect my ability to coach or officiate a game? I have so many questions, and I just don't know *anything*."

He slid across the sofa to embrace her. She crawled into his lap, wrapped both arms around his neck and pillowed her head on his shoulder. She blinked away tears. God, she was so *sick* of crying!

"I'm scared to go to Boston. I'm afraid I'll be so unhappy I'll make you unhappy. I certainly can't go until I have Vox back, or… or have adjusted to life without her. And I can't ask you to stay here and give up your career."

He grabbed for the slate. *It's not such a great job.*

"You'd give it up?" Hope flared briefly, then faded. "But how will we live? My new career will be almost entirely volunteer."

Working on it.

"Will you really be rich when your father dies?"

Yes. Hope not 'til my own kids are grown. He cleared the slate and wrote more. *Some $ from Grandfather, too.*

"I'd rather we work for our money, anyway."

Agreed.

Eden straightened her spine and forced a smile. "Ask me again, once you think of a good idea. If I come up with one, you'll be the first to know."

You marry Tagget, kill him in his sleep, inherit his $.

Eden punched Bruce in the shoulder. His mouth opened in a yelp, then he grimaced and rubbed the affected area.

"Sorry!" she signed.

He kissed her cheek.

That's my girl.

"You know it."

His hands were warm on her backside. Her fingers wove into his hair, pulling his head down to hers, her lips seeking his.

Her mother walked into the room.

Eden had no time to spring from his lap or to do anything but turn terribly red.

"Eden Randall, this is most inappropriate," her mother signed. "Even a married woman doesn't sit in her husband's lap when others are about."

Eden clambered to her feet and tidied her skirt. "Why not?"

"It's just not done."

"But it's nice. People are so weird."

Her mother turned to Bruce with a shake of her head. They conversed for a time, Bruce looking as embarrassed and apologetic as Eden had ever seen. Her mother looked cross. Her father entered and joined in, leaving Eden to kick at the floor in annoyance while they yelled at Bruce for touching her. If that was what they were doing. It looked calmer than most arguments. Her parents deliberately stood so she couldn't even attempt to see what they might be saying.

I have to leave, Bruce wrote.

"Why?"

He glanced at her parents. *I need to pack. Train to Boston tomorrow.*

Boston. He hadn't said "home." He would come back to her. She nodded.

He bid goodbye to her parents, then bowed to her and pressed his lips to her hand. That was to be her goodbye kiss? All she could think was how much better it had been that morning when he had kissed her in so many other places.

"I love you," he signed.

She echoed his words with her own hands. He handed her the slateboard.

I will be back. Wait for me. ♥ *4ever*

Enough was enough. She defied her parents, flung herself at him, and gave him a good, hard kiss on the mouth.

"I'll be right here," she vowed.

Once he had disappeared from sight, her mother guided her back inside. "I think you're right, dear. I think it's time we talked about the things that go on between a husband and wife."

"Don't bother," Eden signed back. "I already learned about it."

"What? How?"

She shrugged. "Research."

45

November 20

*D*EAR *B*RUCE,

How is Boston? I miss you terribly already. Vox is in bad shape, but Mother and Lilah have a plan. Father is designing a prototype for presenting her technology to the world. This way I need no longer fear becoming a showpiece if when! she is repaired.

Lilah has received another offer requesting to license her echo machine, from a Tagget Industries competitor, starting a bidding war for exclusive rights. Tagget has already countered with an even more lucrative offer, including extra incentives. Lilah says his latest letter suggests he is actually more eager to have her join his team of engineers than he is to produce the echo machine.

The lab repairs are happening at a furious pace. Tagget sent swarms of men to fix everything, at his own expense. He also hauled away all the remaining Dynalux fuel and replaced it with pure fuel. Father's chemist friend

is running tests on it all, but I don't think he will find

*anything wrong. I don't think we'll ever have to worry
about spy machines in the laboratory, either. Evan might
be unethical, but he's not stupid.*

*Marcus Heyward has pleaded guilty to trespassing
and criminal mischief. He won't spend any more time in
jail, but he has a long sentence of restitution. He has also
been expelled. I don't expect to ever see him again.*

*I had the most vivid dream about you last night. I
didn't want to wake from it, it was so delightful. We were
in my bed, entirely naked, and I was trailing kisses down
your chest, with a very clear goal in mind, while your
hands were doing quite remarkable things to my…*

December 26

Dearest Eden,

*Thank you for the handsome cap. I will wear it often
and think of you. And scandalize my mother, who can't
believe a young woman would send her sweetheart a
Christmas gift when they are not (yet?) engaged to be
married.*

*Did you hear Tagget has left the country? He bought
a dirigible and flew to Paris. I don't know if he'll ever
come back. I'm not sure what people are angrier about,
that he could listen in on their phone calls or that he hid
the fact that the Dynalux fuel was unstable. The scandal
is massive. He won't ever go to jail, though. His lawyers
must be the shadiest men in America. The contracts for
his teletics installations are so vague it's near impossible
to claim damages or press charges for the use of those spy
devices. And he's already promoting some "pure" and
"filtered" fuel alternative to Dynalux and offering refunds
to customers. He's getting away with everything, but I
find I care less than I probably should. He's gone and not
harassing you. That's what matters.*

On an entirely different note, you might give some

thought to your continued detailing of your (utterly rapturous and deliciously arousing) dreams and fantasies in your letters. I have to hide them from my family. In retaliation, please allow me to tell you just what I am imagining doing to you at this precise moment...

46

February 2, 1905

THE SNOW CRUNCHED beneath Eden's boots as she trudged toward campus. The wind whipped at her hood, and she tugged it back into place. Up ahead a ladder barred her way. A man stood halfway up, reaching to hang a sign above the shop door.

Curious as always, she stopped to look. "Are we getting a new store at last?"

The man answered with a grunt. "More books. Some kid from out-of-town."

"Books?" Eden pressed her face against the glass. Up front, a number of tables had been pushed into a corner, chairs stacked beside them. On the opposite wall, she spied a food-service counter. It didn't resemble any bookstore she'd ever seen. She cupped her hands around her eyes for a better look.

There. In the back, beyond the tables, were a series of half-empty shelves and dozens of boxes. In the midst of the clutter, a man in a cap hammered upon a lopsided bookcase.

Eden let out a squeal so loud the ladder trembled. "Sorry, didn't mean to startle you!" she called. She wasn't certain if the worker heard her, because halfway through her sentence she was already inside the shop.

"Bruce!"

He spun. His hammer clattered to the floor. Eden couldn't draw a breath. She'd never seen anyone, anywhere, look so handsome. His unadorned white shirt stretched across his broad chest, sleeves rolled up past his elbows. He lacked a vest, but wore blue suspenders and the maize and blue plaid cap she had sent him at Christmas. When his surprise morphed into joy, it sent a shockwave of pleasure through her body.

He vaulted over boxes toward her. She shoved past a stack of chairs, not caring when they clattered to the floor. Their bodies collided, lips and tongues tangling in a frenzy only months of separation could incite. She came up gasping, chest heaving. She thought her heart might pound its way right through her ribs.

"What are you doing here?"

"Opening a bookstore." He took two steps back, pursed his lips in concentration, then signed at her, "Opening a bookstore. I wanted to surprise you."

"I'm surprised!" she laughed. "And you learned to sign!"

"A little bit. I'm not good."

"I think you are wonderful," she signed back.

He blushed. "How is Vox?"

Eden fished the dragon out of the pouch hanging at her hip. "Improving. I can hear clearly again. We've focused on her internals, so she still limps and can't fly. She will be better in time. The good news is that the repairs allowed Father to isolate and fix the interference problem. He can replicate the technology now and present and share it. She'll never have to be an exhibit."

"Wonderful!" Bruce reached to give Vox a pat.

"Be careful. I don't know how much she remembers. We had to retrain her for some of the commands."

His finger touched the top of her metal head, and she nuzzled his palm.

"See? She knew I'd be back."

Eden burst into tears.

"Oh, sweetheart." Bruce pulled her into his arms, Vox squeezed between them. "Don't cry."

"I didn't mean to!" she huffed. "I'm just..." She wiped at her eyes. "Happy."

Bruce had to blink a few times, himself. "So am I. It's good to be back."

"How long have you been here?"

"Two days. I hoped to have it all set up before I brought you in, but it's taking longer than I thought. Some of the shelves need repair, and I'm a poor carpenter."

"Why a bookstore? We have many here already."

"I love books. And if any town can sustain another bookstore, this is it. But it's more than a bookstore. We'll have tables up front where customers can have coffee or tea and a snack while they relax with a book. Behind me, that raised area will double as a stage for book talks and poetry readings. We'll host events, book clubs, signings by local authors. It will be a literary salon. And I have a great name, with your permission, of course."

"Oh?"

"Vox Paradisi."

"*The Voice of Paradise*? Who do you think you are, Evan Tagget?"

"I..."

He turned red, and she lifted up on her toes to kiss his cheek. "I love it. And Vox approves." She looked around the room. "I meant to go to the library, but may I help you instead?"

"Absolutely. Then I might finish before my family arrives this weekend. They want to meet you."

Eden's cheeks heated. "Do they know I'm weird?"

"You? They think *I'm* the weird one. Only my grandfather considers me sane. I asked him for a loan to get this started, and he signed over my entire inheritance. Said he'd rather see what I do with it before he dies. He's more excited to meet you than anyone. He wants to hear your ideas for a better ear trumpet."

"I'll introduce him to my parents."

Bruce took a step back. "Ah, and on the topic of bringing families together, I have a very important question to ask you."

"Yes!"

Eden reached for him, but he backed further away, stumbling over a box of books. "Wait. I've been practicing."

Eden slipped Vox into the pouch and crossed her arms. "Okay. I'm waiting." She bounced in place, every nerve afire.

"My beautiful Eden," he signed at her, his fingers spelling her name so rapidly she knew he must have done it thousands of times. "I love you more than anything. I can't imagine life without you. Will you marry me?"

She tackled him, toppling boxes and scattering books. "Yes, yes, yes!"

She smothered him with kisses, tears of joy dripping down her cheeks. She had his shirt half unbuttoned before she realized people outside could see through the windows.

"Maybe upstairs?" he offered.

"What's upstairs?"

"My apartment."

"Oh, excellent. Does it have a bed?"

"No. No furniture yet. Just a pile of blankets on the floor."

Eden sprang to her feet, yanking him behind her. "Good enough."

A short time later, she reconsidered her statement. The mess of bedding in an empty apartment was well beyond, "good enough." Tangled in his arms, her body awash with pleasure and love, it was perfection.

EPILOGUE

April 6, 1905

My UNEQUALLED ELYSIUM,

    Many thanks for the invitation to your upcoming nuptials. I regret that as I am currently seeing to my overseas ventures (due to certain circumstances necessitating a prolonged absence from the country), I will be unable to attend in person. Please accept the forthcoming gift as a token of my esteem and my best wishes for your future happiness.

    Please also convey my regards to your fiancé, and let him know I harbor no hard feelings as a result of our prior disagreements. I ask only that he give you the love and respect that are your due. In all honesty, I believe this to be a foregone conclusion. The man seemed quite besotted, and I know something of that sentiment.

    Paris is beautiful as always, but I continue to feel it lacks that special spark you alone could provide. If you should ever change your mind, I would be more than happy to welcome you here. I am certain you would be an excellent mother to the future Evan Junior.

In closing, I offer my congratulations and profess I take genuine pleasure in your joy.

Yours truly,
Evan Tagget

April 21, 1905

Dear Evan,

Thank you for your generous offer to join you in Paris and bear your children. I'm afraid, however, I must decline. I'm extremely happy with my husband, and, to be frank, I don't think you and I suit as romantic partners. Don't despair. I'm certain there is someone out there for you.

If you are interested in a platonic visit at any point, we would love to spend time abroad wherever you might be. Likewise, if you should ever return to Michigan, we would be happy to have you visit us. Let me amend that. I would be happy to have you visit. Bruce would grumble about it. (Don't tell him, but I have noticed his attitude toward you continues to soften as he reads our correspondence). Our apartment isn't large, and is still lacking some furniture, but you can always stay in a hotel, if necessary.

I also wish to thank you (so, so much!) for the Mercedes (and the accompanying vat of fuel). Bruce and I drove it on our honeymoon, and had a splendid time. I do not, however, recommend making love in the backseat. It was terribly awkward.

I wish you all the best in Europe and with your future endeavors. Feel free to write any time. I enjoy your letters.

Your friend,
Eden Caldwell

THE END

*A*UTHOR'S *N*OTE

The idea for this book began with tiny mechanical dragons and the desire to set it in my hometown around the turn of the twentieth century. When I discovered an interactive map of the city from 1904—the height of Fielding Yost's point-a-minute days—I knew I had my story.

The names and locations of the buildings around town and campus are historically accurate, with the exception of a few invented places, such as Eden's house and the AM&T laboratory. Those I based on similar real places. Eden's saloon is generic, as Ann Arbor boasted dozens of such establishments. The college kids have always needed their places to drink.

The scores of the football games and any specific plays mentioned are also true to history, as written up in University publications from the time. While some of the rules may seem odd to modern fans, they are all accurate to the 1904 rulebook. Like Eden, I read the whole thing. Yost and Heston really did travel to Chicago to scout the Maroons, and Columbia really did renege on the Thanksgiving game (leading to angry articles in the Michigan newspapers).

The invention of the football huddle is credited to Paul D. Hubbard of Gallaudet University, where he played during the mid-1890s. Though a few mentions of the huddle pop up during the following decades, it wasn't until the 1920s that it caught on throughout college football.

The 1904 Olympic games in St. Louis were held in conjunction with the World's Fair and nearly all the athletes were American. It was only the second Olympics to have events for women, including women's archery for the first time. The marathon was absolutely as insane as I said. Even mechanical dragons couldn't make it stranger.

Many thanks to the University of Michigan Bentley Historical Library and the Ann Arbor District Library for all of the books, information, and incredible historic photos that brought the 1904 version of my city to life.

And if you are ever in Ann Arbor and want the Eden's Voice Historical Walking Tour, just find me on social media and drop me a note. I'd love to show off the real places that inspired this story.

ABOUT THE AUTHOR

AWARD-WINNING AUTHOR CATHERINE STEIN believes that everyone deserves love and that Happily Ever After has the power to help, to heal, and to comfort. She writes sassy, sexy romance set during the Victorian and Edwardian eras and full of action, adventure, magic, and fantastic technologies.

Catherine lives in Michigan with her husband and three rambunctious girls. She loves steampunk and oxford commas, and can often be found dressed in clothing that was purchased at a Renaissance Festival, drinking copious amounts of tea.

Visit Catherine online at
www.catsteinbooks.com
and join her VIP mailing list.

Follow her on Twitter @catsteinbooks,
or like her page on Facebook @catsteinbooks.

Also by Catherine Stein

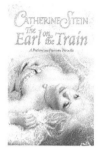

The Earl on the Train

An earl with a problem.
A woman with a plan.
The journey of a lifetime.

How to Seduce a Spy

A barmaid with a rare talent.
A spy on a mission.
A love neither can resist.

Not a Mourning Person

A determined widow.
An ancient curse.
Crime and passion.

Available at your favorite online retailer.

www.catsteinbooks.com

· · · 🌸 · · ·

Thank you so much for reading.
If you enjoyed the book and are so inclined, I would love for
you to leave a review. Happy readers make an author's day!

I love hearing from readers,
so feel free to contact me on social media, or email:

catherine@catsteinbooks.com

CPSIA information can be obtained
at www.ICGtesting.com
Printed in the USA
FSHW010515061019
62681FS